Talking
After Midnight

D0029311

Also available from Dakota Cassidy
and Harlequin MIRA

Something to Talk About
Talk Dirty to Me
Talk This Way (ebook novella)

Dakota Cassidy

Talking
After Midnight

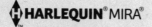
HARLEQUIN® MIRA®

ISBN-13: 978-0-7783-1631-2

TALKING AFTER MIDNIGHT

Copyright © 2014 by Dakota Cassidy

The publisher acknowledges the copyright holder of the individual works as follows:

TALKING AFTER MIDNIGHT
Copyright © 2014 by Dakota Cassidy

TALK THIS WAY
Copyright © 2014 by Dakota Cassidy

Recycling programs
for this product may
not exist in your area.

For questions and comments about the quality of this book, please contact us at CustomerService@Harlequin.com.

Printed in U.S.A.

www.Harlequin.com

First, to my editor, Leonore Waldrip, for my repetitive overuse of so many thighs and eyes, this one's for you! Also, for suggesting a very unusual heroine, and the challenge creating her presented.

And to my BFF, Renee George, who always knows when I'm on the brink. She listens. She hears. She nurtures. I love you much.

Last, but never least, my husband, Rob— you're the best decision I foolishly almost didn't make. Thank you for some of the best years of my life!

One

"Heaven and a ring o' fire…"

Under normal circumstances, Marybell Lyman would have laughed at her employer and friend Dixie Davis's shocked words when she pushed her way into her small basement apartment, stopped dead in her tracks and tipped her head to the side as if she'd just witnessed the second coming.

But this circumstance wasn't normal.

Dixie stood poised in her doorway for a moment, the cold draft from the late-winter evening ruffling her knee-length burgundy sweater. Dixie, never without words, stared at her, speechless. She tucked a strand of her long auburn hair behind her ear and hummed something else Marybell couldn't quite hear because of her clogged ears.

Marybell scurried back to her couch without a word, plunking herself down on the new sofa she'd just had delivered. She huddled into her bathrobe, keeping her head down as far as she could without making her nose begin running again.

When her friends from work had all shown up to

coddle her with chicken soup and some good ol' Southern love, she'd panicked. Her heart racing, her head full
of cotton, throbbing an endless, crushing beat, she'd
battled with whether to answer the door.

No one saw her this way—unmasked—ever, and definitely not Dixie, the owner of the phone sex company
where she worked as a phone sex operator.

But it wasn't as though there was any hiding from
the three pretty faces full of concern, pressed against
the glass of her front door like a trio of suction-cupped
Garfields in the back of a car window.

She couldn't simply shoo them away or make up
some excuse to keep them from barging in even if she
truly wanted to. As a whole, Team Call Girls was un-
stoppable. If you told them no, they yelled, "Bless your
heart," and trampled all over you and your nos with
their cute heels.

Why, oh, why hadn't she thought to pull the shade
down over the glass before she'd taken those cold meds
and fallen asleep?

Breathe, Marybell. Act natural.

Ha! Easy for the voice inside her head to say. It didn't
have to fend off three gawking mother hens, as well
meaning as they were, and remain calm while its insides twisted into a knot fit for a Boy Scout.

LaDawn Jenkins, coworker, friend, best phone
sex operator in the universe, stood next to Dixie, a
woven basket with a red-checkered napkin covering
what Marybell suspected were freshly baked rolls,
and cocked her platinum-blond head. "I have rolls,"
she mumbled, dropping them on the end table next to
her box of tissues. "With butter," she added, her brow
furrowing.

Marybell hunkered farther down in her bathrobe, fighting another violent shudder of chills, almost too feverish to care about her friends seeing her for the first time devoid of what she'd secretly dubbed her "people shield."

Almost.

She should be in the process of making a break for it. Or at the very least, putting a paper bag over her head. But she'd spent herself simply finding her gel eye mask and answering the door. Her legs were so weak, her chest so congested and tight, it would take everything she had left in her to move again.

Instead, she cast her eyes toward her feet, covered in fuzzy black calf-length socks with the slipper-grippers on the soles.

There's nowhere to hide but in plain sight now, Marybell Lyman. You're stewed. Try not to look obvious.

Emmaline Amos, soon to be Emmaline Hawthorne if the way things were shaping up between her and Jax was any indication, almost fell smack into Dixie and LaDawn when she rushed in the front door. The skid of her conservative black pumps screeched to a halt against the wood floor.

She gasped in her "clutch your pearls" way but covered by quickly clamping her lips shut. Naturally, she didn't mean for her mouth to open before her brain properly filtered her shock. Em was nothing if she wasn't the epitome of Southern decorum.

That Southern diplomacy was why Dixie had given her the position of general manager at Call Girls Inc. She was tactful, kind and able to appease even the crankiest of customers.

And she always did what was right and decorous—

even if it killed her. Though, mostly this behavior was due to her incredibly kind heart. She'd earned Marybell's deepest respect since coming to Call Girls, newly single after her ex-husband had all but abandoned her and her boys to live his life as a cross-dresser.

Em was down-home tough. Soft and pliable like Play-Doh on the outside, but made of steel parts of resolve on the inside. There wasn't a coon dog's chance in purgatory she'd acknowledge just how astonished she was.

Instead, she carried in a large Crock-Pot bowl with two heart-covered oven mitts over her hands to protect them from the heat. Em assessed Marybell for a moment, brief and fleeting, before her eyes flickered, and proper Em was firmly back in place. "We brought you…" She almost stuttered the words, gazing down at Marybell. But then she caught herself reacting and forced her shoulders to square and her spine to straighten. Em cleared her throat. "Soup," she finished with a warm smile full of perfect white teeth and ruby-red lipstick. "Chicken soup—for your poor, flu-riddled soul, you sweet, phlegmy angel." Em set the Crock-Pot on the old chest Marybell used as a coffee table, dropping the mitts next to it.

Marybell murmured a thank-you into the collar of her bathrobe.

Em flapped her hands in the way she always did, signifying that her kind gesture was much ado about nothing. "Did you really expect we'd let you suffer all alone? Not on my watch, miss. Mercy, we've been worried to death about you ever since you called in sick earlier today, sugarplum. Dixie said you sounded like a congested bullfrog, and weak as a kitten to boot. You hafta feed that cold. Which is why we all cooked up something and forced our way in here like the interfering henpeckers we are."

"Rolls," LaDawn repeated again stiffly, clearly still experiencing aftershocks of the "holy Hannah in a wet suit" variety. "I brought rolls. *With butter.*" She pointedly tapped the basket.

Marybell smiled in an abstract, afraid-to-meet-their-eyes way, too cold to pull her hands from the confines of her bathrobe to take a roll, too rattled to move. "Yum, butter. How kind. Thanks, girls." She dabbed at her eyes, red-rimmed and drippy under the mask.

Now that formalities and justifications were made, she waited, quietly, if not inquisitively, for an answer to the unspoken question.

Why haven't we ever seen who the real Marybell Lyman is?

They all waited.

For an explanation about her appearance, with plenty of side-eye and questions in the form of an entire conversation played out with only the expressions on their faces.

Em folded her fists at her waist, resting them on her slender hips, her teeth working the corner of her lower lip.

Dixie placed her forearm over her chest, resting her other arm in the crook of it, and cupped her chin with her hand, blatantly stumped.

LaDawn just left the opportunity for flies to congregate in her mouth, which was now, unabashedly, wide-open.

Marybell waited, too. Her fuzzy, medicated brain was searching for a way to handle this without turning it into a topic of long discussion wherein she explained why no one ever saw her freshly scrubbed face.

Under any other circumstances, mentally guessing who'd crack first under the pressure of etiquette would have been as much fun as watching Nanette Pruitt bluster when Marybell sat next to her in church and sang "Onward, Christian Soldier," loud and entirely off-key.

The stunning difference between this MB—sans red-and-green-spiked Mohawk, heavy eye makeup, nose ring and facial piercings—and the one sitting before them had to be killing them.

This was the Marybell Lyman not a solitary soul had seen in at least four years, except her bathroom mirror just before she spent an hour applying the "people shield."

If she were a bettin' kind, she'd lay bets on LaDawn, the most vocal of their group, and while Southern to her last breath, she was also unashamedly opinionated and outspoken. There was no subtext to LaDawn, and it was probably one of the things Marybell loved most about her. She was an ex-lady of the evening, or as she jokingly called her former profession, a "companionator." Words weren't something LaDawn struggled with.

Yet nothing. The old clock on her coffee-with-cream-painted wall ticked away the seconds while each woman internally struggled with her appearance and fought not to visibly squirm.

Marybell's sudden sneeze into a crumpled tissue made all of them jump, forcing her to address the issue. If she made light of it, they would, too and she needed them to make light. She prayed they'd follow her lead.

"My nose ring is at the cleaners," she teased, breaking the ice with a honking snort into a brand-new tissue.

Dixie finally spoke, her voice just above a whisper, as though if someone heard her, she'd be tagged responsible for letting the cat out of the bag. "If I didn't know this was your apartment, I'd never have—"

"Known you from a hole in the wall!" LaDawn crowed, her voice now located. She planted her hands on her hips, encased in her usual skintight jeans, and pushed her hair over her shoulder with daggerlike-tipped fingers of glittery purple. "Dang, girl." She pulled the words from her lips as if she were pulling a thick milk shake from a straw. "You'd better hurry up and get better so you can do up that hair before the town fair starts next week. I'll never be able to find my way to the cotton candy stand if that Mohawk o' yours isn't stickin' out in every direction, pointin' me to the land of sugary pink heaven." She chuckled, leaning forward to tweak a wet strand of Marybell's hair with affectionate fingers.

Marybell sniffled, wincing at the sharp tug to her sinuses, afraid to let loose a sigh of relief. Keeping her chin tucked inside her bathrobe, she forced a chuckle. "Oh, you hush, LaDawn. You don't need me to do that. You have Doc Johnson to light your way."

LaDawn chuffed, popping her dark-purple-lined lips. "Don't you talk to me about Doc Johnson. That man hasn't come callin' in three solid days."

Em, obviously unable to stand it anymore, plopped down on the couch next to her, directing LaDawn to bring her a bowl and ladle from the kitchen. She smoothed the fan of her skirt over her knees. "First off, Cat sends her love. She didn't want to, but we made her stay home. Wouldn't be good for her to catch somethin' from you with the baby on the way."

Marybell loved Cat Butler. A free spirit, a hugger, one of her first real friends, and now madly in love with Flynn McGrady and well on her way to beginning their family. "Tell her I said thank you, and keep that bun in the oven safe."

Em popped her lips. "So, how is it that we've been friends for all this time now, and we've never seen the true Marybell?" She plucked at the eye mask, making Marybell swat at her hands. "Well, almost the true Marybell. You've seen us in all sorts of manner, miss. Drunk, seminaked, riding a mechanical bull, for heaven's sake. Fair is fair." She asked the question as though it were some slight for Marybell never to have revealed herself without her makeup and gel-spiked hair.

She really wanted to ask why they'd surprise-attacked her with food and hospitality when she'd expressly told Dixie she'd be fine and back at work within the week. All she needed was some rest and cold medication. She'd done that with the fervent hope they wouldn't catch her exactly as they'd done.

But leave it to Em and Dixie to have to see for themselves she wasn't going to do something as dramatic as die of the latest illness they'd hunted down on WebMD.

Still, her friends made her smile. They were a reason to get up these days when for so long, there wasn't any reason at all.

They were loving, nurturing machines, the lot of them. Give them an ailment, and they were fixing it with age-old home remedies and more smothering love than you could shake a stick at. How could she be angry with them for caring about her?

But she hadn't been prepared for their insistent knock on her door. It left her more than uneasy without her cloak of heavy makeup and piercings in place. There was always the chance, even in small-town Plum Orchard, Georgia, she'd be recognized. The people here had been ever so slow to come to terms with how different her appearance was from the likes of them.

Yet she'd sucked up the strange looks and whispers behind hands at Madge's Kitchen where she had dinner almost every night before her shift for a reason. It beat the livin' daylights out of the alternative.

Rather than answer Em, Marybell deflected, looking her friend square in the eye. She was the master of deflection. "Do I ever see the true Emmaline?" she asked with mock innocence, glad for the cloak of her congestion concealing her weak attempt at subterfuge.

"Bah! You most certainly do see the true Emmaline. You see her with lipstick." Em pursed her lips, dragging a throw from the back of Marybell's couch to cover her with it. She tucked the edges under her chin with gentle fingers, pressing the back of her hand to Marybell's forehead with a wince.

Marybell coughed, turning her head and using her arm to shield Em from her germs. "Exactly." She smiled.

"Gravy," Dixie murmured, patting her on the back while setting a cup of steaming lemon tea laced with honey on the end table, her eyes perusing Marybell's freshly scrubbed face. "Even stricken with the flu and a gel eye mask, you're beautiful. I don't like this turn of events Ms. MB," she joked with her infamous flirty smile. "I'm glad Caine didn't see you without your goo or I'd be a goner. Plus, you're younger than me by six years. I simply won't have you, or anyone in this town, bein' prettier than me."

Em clucked her tongue, shooting Dixie a chiding finger. "Are you sayin' Caine wouldn't fall for her with her makeup and the pointy green-and-red things all over her head? Are you sayin' he doesn't love you for what's on your insides, Dixie Davis? That he's nothing more than a shallow shell of a man with a heartbeat and a chiseled jaw?"

Marybell giggled, letting a little of her tension ease. Conversation successfully deflected. "I don't think you have to say anything, Dixie. Caine can't see anyone but you, whether you have insides or not. Now, I thought I told y'all to stay away so you don't catch this nasty bug. Surely you don't want to leave me to answer everyone's calls because you're all too sick to do your jobs, do you? Especially if I have to answer LaDawn's calls. I'm not nearly the Jedi master with the flyswatter she is. I always miss and end up swatting myself."

The joke at the Call Girls office, situated in the guesthouse of dearly departed multimillionaire Landon Wells, a man who'd given Marybell everything when she'd had nothing, was LaDawn's skill with her beloved flyswatter.

She was like Bruce Lee with a pair of nunchakus. Daryl from *The Walking Dead* with a bow and arrow. Phone sex operators throughout the land should all cower in fear when LaDawn broke out the flyswatter.

It was really just an audio prop for her BDSM clients to hear over the phone, but she fooled them into believing it was a flogger every time. For her birthday, they'd collectively had a real flyswatter bronzed with her name on it, which she proudly displayed in her office on her desk.

Dixie rolled her eyes at Em. "First off, not a chance

we'd let you go this alone. There's nothing like some love and coddlin' when you're so sick. Second, you hush, Em. I'm not saying that at all, and you know it. I love our Marybell—even today, nose redder than a tube of crimson lipstick and eyes drippin' from behind that mask like a leaky faucet."

Marybell took the tea with a grateful sigh, still keeping her eyes semiaverted over the rim of the china. "I think what Dixie's saying is, I'm not Caine's type."

That was okay, too. She was no one's type, and that was just as well. Buried in small-town Georgia, she'd never have to worry about the temptation of finding someone whose *type* she was.

There were few available men in town, anyway, but the men here liked women who wore pretty dresses, the proper-height heel for the appropriate time of day and subtle makeup. Their hair was always long and flowing, or up and smooth. It wasn't riding a colored line along the tops of their heads, and they certainly weren't wearing clunky black work boots and leopard-skin leggings slashed as if a knife had been taken to them.

LaDawn sat down on the chest, scooting the Crock-Pot to the side, tilting Marybell's chin upward to look her in the eye. Well, as much as her cooling gel eye mask allowed, anyway.

Her heart stopped cold for a moment, her fingers trembling on the handle of the teacup. Caught. She was caught. They knew who she was and her safe, quiet, if not terribly exciting life would be over.

That clawing anxiety, usually reserved for late-night insomnia and mentally backtracking every move she made, pushed its way to lodge in her raw throat.

LaDawn's lips, the color purple meant to match her

nails, turned into a smile. She plucked at a strand of Marybell's now drying, shoulder-length hair "As I live and breathe. You're a natural blonde, aren't you? How do you get all that red-and-green gunk in your hair every day? You know, I'd hate you if it wasn't for Brugsby's Drugstore and Miss Clairol."

Marybell gulped before she forced a smile, praying she could stare LaDawn down without looking away. "It's a spray. It washes out easy. And you'd love me any ol' way, LaDawn. Who'd bring you those frosty pink doughnuts and coffee from Madge's on the night shift, if not for me? Not even Doc Johnson does that. I'm forever your girl."

LaDawn's eye grew critical, though it still twinkled beneath her purple eye shadow and glittery gold eyeliner. "And when did you stop shavin' half your eyebrow off? Next thing you know, you'll be pluckin' 'em into a fine arch like the rest of us ninnies. Why, if this keeps up, you might even wear a dress. Now, wouldn't that be somethin'? Our Marybell in anything other than ripped-up or spotted with some kind of animal-print britches?" She chuckled deep and rich.

Conformity. Blessed be.

Em rubbed Marybell's arm and smiled before pulling her frozen fingers into her hand and warming them. "Never you mind LaDawn and her teasin'. I think you're hair's pretty as a picture. All that natural curl leaves me with ugly envy in my heart. I don't know why you hide it behind black eye shadow and all those colors and hair gel. It looks like it takes an awful lot of work to get it to stand up straight like someone scared the life outta you, but I don't give a fig either way. I like the way you stare society and all its preconceived notions right down, look 'em square in the eye, and dare 'em to say anything. I like it especially when you do it to Louella Palmer. It always makes me giggle till I swear I'm gonna wet myself when her eyes are forced to give you the look of disdain and you growl and snap your teeth at her."

Rage against the machine.

Marybell squeezed Em's hand. Her snarling at Louella Palmer, the most hateful woman she'd ever encountered, was all part of the act to keep everyone she didn't allow into her circle at bay.

Marybell lifted her shoulders in a shrug. "I have a gift. Some people paint. I snarl. If I didn't have my hair gelled up like I'd been scared half to death, she wouldn't be afraid of me. Louella fears what she doesn't understand. Besides, you just like when I growl at her because it keeps her too busy tanglin' with me to hatch another plot against you and Dixie," she quipped, accepting the dose of thick emerald-green cold medicine LaDawn handed her, chugging it down like a shot of tequila.

"You're a wingman for the ages, MB. No doubt," Dixie assured with her familiar warmth, rubbing her arms and shivering. "So explain to me why it's so cold in here? Surely this isn't on purpose, is it?" Dixie's brow creased, her pretty face lining with concern. "Are you conserving heat for budgetary reasons? I won't have it with it being so cold out and you ragin' with flu, Marybell. A raise—I'll give you a raise," she offered, pushing through her purse to find her phone and make a note of it. "Em, turn up that heat while I let Nella know, would you?"

Dixie in a nutshell. Generous, funny, gorgeous and

loyal to the core. Plum Orchard legend had it back in high school she was once feared for her horrible pranks.

Yet she'd come home just a few months ago, emotionally broken and cash poor only to turn around and win, in what the folks of Plum Orchard called the "phone sex games," the entirety of the company Marybell worked for.

Since then, Dixie'd redeemed herself for the most part with nearly everyone who'd once held a grudge against her—well, everyone except the snotty Magnolias, the group of women who considered themselves the backbone of fine Southern breeding and ran Plum Orchard as if they were the mob.

Though, the people of Plum Orchard still didn't love that not only did she own a phone sex company, but she consorted with her employees on a regular basis. Some of them still made no bones about sayin' so.

Oddly, those same people who frowned upon her and the wicked women of Call Girls sure didn't mind Dixie and her fiancé, Caine Donovan, funneling their alleged ill-gotten gains into town functions and fundraisers for the elementary school.

Either way, Marybell didn't give a hoot about the things Dixie had once done when she was just a teenager. Not a one of these set-in-their-ways folk were above making mistakes. Small towns had a way of holding a grudge the likes of which she'd never seen.

But Marybell had liked Dixie from the moment she'd been assigned by Cat as her guide to the world of the phone sex industry. Dixie had risen above ridicule and cruel attacks, and she'd defended the women of Call Girls right in front of God and man. Now, several months later, Marybell liked her even more.

And she didn't want to lose Dixie, or any of them,

on the chance they might recognize her. Knowing who she really was would create an invasion the likes of which Plum Orchard had never seen. But it wouldn't just invade her life; it would invade the women's lives. Women she'd come to care a great deal for, and she'd die before she let that happen.

Her gut tightened with the fear of loss in that way it always did—uncomfortable, choking her from the inside out. The fear that almost never entirely went away—even after all this time.

Always. It was always with her. Sometimes the panic muted, became a dull roar, but it never truly left. It hovered around the fringes of her life, poking at her like an animal in a cage, reminding her.

Em's voice interrupted her private misery. She stood over the thermostat, studying it. "It says it's eighty-five degrees in here, Dixie, but that can't be right." Em had a gift for most things DIY. Except anything electrical, as evidenced by the enormous hole Jax Hawthorne had in his backyard gazebo when she'd decided it would be pretty to put in a paddle fan with a light.

"It's broken," Marybell croaked, her nose itchy and raw. "And put your bags of money away, Dixie Davis," she teased on a cough. "I don't need a raise. You pay me just fine, thank you. I just forgot to ask Miss Carter to fix it with the warm spell we had not long ago. Leave it be, Dixie. I'll have it taken care of when I'm better."

She loved the basement apartment she'd rented from Blanche Carter. This apartment was the first place she'd called home in four years. It harbored all the things she'd lovingly collected when she finally decided it was safe to stay in Landon's, and then Dixie's, employ. But it was mighty cold in the winter.

Dixie planted her hands on her hips. "I can't, in good conscience, leave you here to freeze to death. Blanche is in Atlanta till Tuesday and the weatherman said it's going to be down in the thirties this weekend. With you so sick, it'll just make it worse. I won't have it."

The cold medicine was beginning to work its magic, leaving her too exhausted to fend Dixie's mothering off.

Suddenly Em was digging in her purse, too, pulling out her phone, her beautiful blue eyes lit up by the face of her phone. "Oh, I know! I'll call Jax's brother—he's a licensed electrician. He'll come take a look. If he can't do it today, then you're comin' home with me until he can, MB. Hear me? Or maybe with Dixie. Sanjeev'll take fine care of you."

The cold meds LaDawn had given her began to affect her train of thought. Was it irony she could pound down a half bottle of vodka shots with the best of them and not feel a thing, but give her a cold remedy meant to help you sleep, and she was a goner?

Words became hazy, her fear of exposure growing dull. She realized her head was falling back to the couch, yet she had no energy to stop it. Hands comforted her, moved over her to lift her feet up on the couch. Dishes clanged in faraway tones and then someone with warm fingers brushed her hair from her face, pressing a heating pad to her chest and dropping a kiss on her burning forehead just before she succumbed to the quiet of her stuffy head.

Though she did remember to do one thing before she allowed her drug-induced haze to take over. It was as important to her as her "people shield" and had become almost a superstition of sorts. Or maybe it was just a stinkin' crutch.

That's probably what a therapist would say. Be it crutch, superstition, good-luck charm, whatever, no matter where Marybell Lyman was, who she was with, before she laid her head on a pillow and closed her eyes, she said a quick prayer just in case the universe really was one big ball of positive thinking. It was the prayer she said every night before she went to sleep.

Thank you for all these wonderful blessings, for food to eat, for my friends and for my job.

But please, please don't take them away.

Two

More banging on her door. Loud. Obnoxious. Heavy-handed.

Gravy sakes, could a sick woman just be left to die in splotchy, ugly red runny-nosed peace?

Not if Emmaline Amos and Dixie Davis are your friends, Marybell. With friendship came a certain amount of invasion of privacy, she'd learned. Still, she was going to kill them for waking her again, and just when she'd found a bit of sleep without the threat of coughing her left lung to implosion.

Muddled and fuzzy, Marybell sat upright, her head pulsing its angry protest, making her reach for another tissue. The last time she'd looked at the clock while the girls were still here, it was five in the afternoon. She'd slept for three solid hours.

Pulling herself to a standing position, she shivered as she left behind the warmth of the heating pad and made her way to the front door, jamming her hands into the deep pockets of her favorite, albeit ratty, flannel bathrobe.

She began to open it with a moment's hesitation,

warding off another coughing spell. Then she caught hold of her runaway fears, forcing herself to rationalize through the thick haze of cold meds. Clearly, her friends hadn't made the connection to her past, and they'd already seen her. So seeing her twice without her makeup and hair gel wouldn't change anything. What was done was done.

Still, Marybell kept her eyes averted—in hindsight, she'd wish her tongue had done the same. She yanked open the door, her eyelids at half-mast. "You know, you three are like havin' really annoying sisters. Maybe akin to the stepsisters in Cinderella, only nicer and with smaller feet," she grumbled, sneezing into her tissue. "How will I ever nab the prince if you pair of mother hens won't let me rest? Would you have me search for my Prince Charming lookin' like *this?*"

A delicious man with hair the color of a dark, exotic wood, worn just long enough to brush the collar of his black sweatshirt, partially covered by the navy-blue knit hat he wore, smiled a smile surely carved with the tool of a god. "Wow. Prince Charming's a lot of pressure, don't you think?"

Her breathing stalled while her heart crashed against her ribs and her eyes swiftly hit the floor.

"Are you Marybell Lyman?" he prompted, rough and chocolaty rich, cocking his head in question.

Oh, no. Heaven, no.

She knew that voice. That voice had been in the Call Girls office on more than one occasion as of late. The voice that was always looking for his brother, Jax, who'd created some security software for Dixie and Caine, specifically designed for Call Girls. The voice that belonged to this man—an unconventionally delicious man.

One who made her tremble in her zebra-striped leggings and work boots. One she'd avoided purposely for several months now—even with her Mohawk and trimmings in place.

A man from her past she'd only vaguely known socially, but who would most certainly know her sans her "people shield."

And hate her for the knowing.

But she had her eye mask. Everything was okay. Her hands self-consciously flew to her face to find her eye mask was no longer there.

Oh, gravy.

Think fast, Marybell Lyman, or all your carefully built walls, all your beloved friends, job and possessions will come crashin' around your ears.

As the woman who answered the door made a stumbling, wobbly break for another room, Taggart Hawthorne stood awkwardly at her door, tool belt in hand, remembering only that Em had told him this Marybell Lyman's protests weren't an option. She was sick, it was cold out and her heat was broken. *Take no prisoners*— Em's exact words.

Which, if you considered her current relationship with his brother, Jax, didn't surprise him. Em was a warrior disguised in pretty dresses and flowery perfume. Her lipstick was really a magic wand that made you do things you wouldn't normally do, and her sweet nature bent you to her will without ever realizing you'd been manipulated by flirty eyelashes and pretty words.

Yet she'd become a part of not just his brother's and

his niece Maizy's world, but his universe, too. And when Em demanded, he listened, largely because he respected the hell out of her.

Tag leaned against the door frame, savoring the smell of chicken soup, tea and Vicks as he assessed the view of this woman's small but nicely decorated living room.

A thickly cushioned couch in soft ivory, littered from one end to the other with overstuffed pillows in gold and a light turquoise, sat in disarray. What was it with a woman and some fancy pillows?

It was as if the damn things made everything okay. That must be it, because every woman he'd encountered so far always had a mess o' pillows—little Maizy included.

Though he had to admire her choice in the chest she'd chosen to use as a coffee table. The surface was scarred, battered from years of use, holding a simple, darkly stained bowl of colored balls. It was sturdy, the lines of it clean and squarely crisp, the color a deep walnut, streaked with hints of red and antique white.

If he had a place of his own, and he wasn't sponging off his brother, Jax, till he got back on his feet, he'd definitely put his feet up on something like that—every night with a plate of hot wings and a football game.

Perusing the walls, where abstract rectangles of ivory, red and that same turquoise she seemed so fond of, streaked the canvases, reminding him of somewhere warm. Somewhere the sun shone all the time and you sat in the sand with a bottle of Corona while salty waves rolled over your toes and buttery-rayed days turned to purple-hued nights.

There was a big square rug in the center of the

bleached white barn-wood floor, woven in the same willowy color of her couch.

So this was the apartment of a phone sex operator? Huh. Truth time. He'd been expecting all manner of paraphernalia. In fact, he'd been damn curious when he thought about running into her tools of the trade.

Yet not a hint of a shelf with hooks where rows of worn floggers and masks in black and red might hang. No fuzzy handcuffs tossed carelessly over a doorknob, and there certainly weren't any leather catsuits.

Obviously, the job did not define the lady.

It didn't bother him in the least that Em ran a phone sex company. True, when Em had hired him to fix some faulty wiring at Call Girls, it had made him a little uncomfortable to hear the women talking to their clients through the walls of one office or another. Especially LaDawn. Damn, that woman could make somethin' out of nothing.

But the discomfort had nothing to do with disapproval and everything to do with the fact that even he had to admit, their breathy sighs and softly moaned words turned him on a little.

Still, he just couldn't connect with the notion. It was a false connection. Once the operator hung up the phone, she was creating another relationship just like the one she'd had with the caller before. He couldn't submerse himself enough—or maybe his imagination just wasn't vivid enough to get past the idea. Of course, Em didn't do the dirty-talkin', either. This woman, according to Em, did.

Either way, he'd stick with one-on-one, messy, down-in-the-mud, flaws-and-all, human connections.

Speaking of messy, when Marybell finally reappeared, it was with the floppiest-brimmed hat he'd ever seen cover a woman of no more than five foot two. It was white with black polka dots, sporting a big, shiny pink bow around it. The brim was so big it fell over her eyes, masking almost every feature of her face but the tip of her cold-infested nose and her full, chapped lips. It would have swallowed her whole if she didn't hold it in place.

"Fancy date?" he asked, unable to stop himself from noting how comical she looked in a moth-eaten bathrobe and summer hat, still trying to figure how she fit into the sparse but colorful landscape of her apartment.

She rocked back on her fuzzy black feet. Not amused, said her posture. "Not unless he wants the black plague."

"So you kiss on the first date?" he asked, almost looking around to see whose mouth those suggestive words had come out of—and more important, why they had come out at all.

She clucked her tongue, her lips never changing their pursed disapproval. "Only if my date doesn't mind some snot."

Unfriendly fire, Captain. Man your battleships. "I'm Tag Hawthorne." He offered his hand, noting it was cracked and calloused from working outside in Jax's unheated barn.

She backed away, covering one foot with the other in the process. "I'm dying of the flu."

"Is dying your first name or your last?" Beneath that wide brim of her ridiculous hat, he'd swear he saw her almost smirk. What was with the hat to begin with? Sure, she was sick, but no one could be that vain, could they?

"Why are you here?"

Tag paused. If he was reading her right, there was a whole lot of territorial in her. *This is mine. Keep out.* So he smiled, opting to reassure her. "Zombie outbreak."

Her sigh crackled, wheezing from her chest as her fingers pulled a tissue from her bathrobe pocket and pressed it to her nose. "You're no Daryl," she replied, her voice, even congested and tight, so sweet it almost hurt his teeth. Fascinating.

"Really, who is?" he joked, still trying to figure out what it was about this woman that made him want not only to get a rise out of her, but to have her treat him with something more than an upturned nose of total disregard. He was all but pulling her pigtails for no reason other than to pull.

Maybe it was the hat. He damn well wanted to see what was under the hat.

Marybell tapped an impatient fingernail on the door she held on to as if it were the armor that helped her protect her castle. "So, you're here why?"

She wasn't biting. Not even a nibble. So he slapped on his serious face and played the Emmaline card while still trying to figure out how, in all the trips he'd made to Call Girls over the past few months, he'd missed seeing her. "Em sent me to fix your heat."

She flapped a hand at him. A ringless hand. Interesting. There were plenty of unattached women in Plum Orchard, a thirsty crew, if you asked him. They'd shown up at Jax's on more than several occasions with all sorts of casseroles and pies, but he'd never seen Marybell in the mix. "Not necessary. I can take care of it when I'm better." She began to close the dungeon door on him.

Tag stuck his hand in it, shaking his head. "Uh, no.

I mean, wait. That came out wrong. What I mean is, you do know Em, don't you? I mean, you work with her, right?"

Still nothing but cool disdain and the scent of Vicks. "I do."

"Well, try living with her. Or almost living with her. She doesn't like the word *no.* If I don't at least look at the problem, she'll have my head. You don't want carnage on your hands, do you?"

Her sigh was full of phlegm, making him wince in regret. He was teasing her while she was standing at the door with the raw wind nipping at her. Em wouldn't like that, either. "Listen, you need to get inside out of the draft. If you get sicker, Em'll have my head. Just let me take a look, okay? You can trust no one will read a story about you and your hacked-off limbs hanging in a smokehouse in the *Plum Orchard Herald.* I'm safe. Call Em and check, if you need to."

Her chin lifted a little, still standoffish. "No, thank you. I'm fine."

Patience. She just needed patience. He had time for that. "It's going to be down in the thirties tonight, Marybell, and if I remember right, this apartment has concrete floors. Great in a hot Georgia summer, not so great in the winter with this recent cold snap. One quick look and then I'm out of your hair. Deal?" He smiled wide, hoping to sway her with his winning grin.

Yet as he held that grin for as long as his mouth would allow, Marybell clearly wasn't affected in quite the way he'd hoped. In other words, letting him in had nothing to do with the magic of the Hawthorne charm.

While his teeth stuck to his cold lips from smiling so hard, she finally rolled her hand toward the thermostat, keeping the hat pulled down over her eyes. "Fine." She turned on her fuzzy foot without another word, leaving him to wipe his feet on the small mat outside her door and enter the enemy's castle.

Oddly, as she made her way back to the couch, clinging firmly to her hat, he couldn't help admiring her petite frame, even in a rumpled bathrobe. Compact and curvy.

Then guilt stung his gut. *Jesus, Hawthorne. She's full up with snot, and her nose, what you can see of it, anyway, is redder than a poker fresh from the fire, sick as a dog and still, you gawk.*

Jackass.

Like before when the girls sneak-attacked you, remain calm. Walk to the couch. Sit your backside down. Hang on to your hat and say as little as possible.

When Tag sauntered past the couch, he stooped at her feet, making her freeze and stiffen. "Dropped this," he offered casually, picking her throw blanket up and placing it on her lap before scanning the room and locating her thermostat.

As Tag popped the face of the digital thermostat off, Marybell let her fingers drift to the arm of her couch and gripped it hard. Every cell in her body ordered her to run and hide. Yet her aching muscles refused to unclench.

Watching him from beneath the brim of the ridiculous hat Dixie had given her as a gift when they'd all watched the Kentucky Derby together was like watching the numbers grow smaller on a ticking bomb.

They were sexy numbers, no doubt. Tight, muscled, encased in a pair of jeans that set her heart to flutter-

ing and skipping as if she were jumpin' double Dutch.
He wasn't classically handsome like his brother, Jax.

On the contrary, he was rough, unkempt, his large
hands spotted with a dark-wood stain that had set into
the rough calluses on his fingers. His skin was ruddy,
hard-weather worn and kissed by the sun. His eyes were
an odd combination of brown and gold, as rich and deep
as his voice, making her wonder what lay behind them.

As Tag tinkered with the dial, emitting a sound from
deep within the strong column of his throat, Marybell
fought a sigh of girlish admiration. He was strong and
rock-solid, all hard edges and craggy surfaces.

If she wasn't already flush with fever, she'd swear
she was on fire while watching him bend over and scoop
up his tool belt.

When he lifted his head, Marybell tugged the brim
of the hat down again, leaving only his lower torso for
her eyes to feast upon.

If she didn't stop gawking, at any moment he'd realize who she was and her whole life in Plum Orchard,
so carefully crafted these past months, would explode.
She'd lose everything. Admiration turned to panic,
clawing her gut, making her blood run cold in her veins.

Tag turned to her, not as smiley as he was a few moments ago. "Where's your water heater?"

Instead of being gracious, or even just a little grateful Em had insisted out of the goodness of her heart that
Tag come fix her heat, she pointed to the back of her
small kitchen where a door led to the garage.

In fact, she all but grunted the directions like some
cave dweller.

As Tag strode past her, his muscled thighs working
beneath his jeans like well-oiled machines, he looked

as though he was going to stop and say something, then thought better of it because he liked his head attached to his neck, and wandered out to her kitchen.

When Marybell heard the door leading to the garage shut, she attempted a sigh of relief, only to end up thwarted by the crackle of her chest. Hopping up off the couch and grabbing her phone from the end table, she ignored the unbelievable ache of her muscles and the wheeze in her lungs and headed straight for the bathroom, where she took one look at her image and almost fainted dead.

Closing the door, she gripped the edge of the sink until her knuckles were white. She was in no condition to apply her "people shield" tonight, so the ridiculous hat stayed. Pulling it from her head, she wet a cloth and pressed it to her flaming cheeks, bright with fever, her body still warring with chills and the sweats.

You're being incredibly rude, Marybell Lyman.

Mercy, she was indeed. Yet better rude than revealed.

A brisk rap of knuckles on the door made her jump, almost tripping on her work boots, carelessly discarded beside the bathtub when she'd come home last night.

"Marybell?"

Yes, Prince Gruff And Hot? She shivered, at war with his affect on her as much as her wish to remain hidden behind the door until he went away. "Yes?" she managed to croak. *Think, think, think, Marybell!*

"I just need to grab a few things from my truck. I'll be right back."

Her lips trembled, but she managed to force the words out. "Okay…and thank you," she remembered to add.

Tag's footsteps rang in her ears just as she sank to

the edge of her tub. What to do, what to do? Clearly, she had to leave the bathroom. She couldn't hide in here the entire time he was fixing her heat. How ungrateful and rude would that appear?

Lost in misery, she jumped when her phone rang, screeching out a Marilyn Manson tune. With shaky fingers, she rode her finger across the surface without even bothering to look and see the identity of the caller. "Hello?"

"Oh, my poor, sweet angel! You sound just dreadful. If this keeps up, I'm calling Doc Johnson," Em crooned into her ear. "Are you okay? Is Tag there with you?"

She nodded as though Em could see her. Oh, yes. He was here. So very here.

"MB, honey?"

Marybell gnawed on the inside of her lip, perusing the shelves above her toilet, looking... "Yes! Yes, he's here. Thank you, Em. I told y'all I'd be fine. You didn't have to bother."

"Oh, hush. Friends are never a bother. So, has he figured out the problem?"

Not yet, but when he does... She frowned. "Problem?"

"Yes, dumplin'. The problem with your heat," Em insisted.

Oh, he has no problem with my heat. He's got me plenty heated. Marybell cringed. Finding this man attractive was absolutely a no-no. "Um, not yet. He's in..."

"Are you all right, MB? What's goin' on over there?"

Realizing she was distracted, Marybell pressed the heel of her hand to her head, massaging the incessant throb. "Everything's fine, Em. I'm sorry. The cold meds are making me fuzzy, is all."

Em giggled into the phone, light and sweet. "Or is it Tag makin' you fuzzy? He's pretty cute, you know, respectin' the fact that he's the love of my life's relative, of course."

Of course. Boundaries and such. "I didn't really notice," she muttered just as her eyes landed on a way to solve her problem, hoping to hide the fact that her pants would be on fire right now if her denial wasn't for such a good cause.

"Oh, you did, too. Why, surely you're not blind from the ragin' flu, are you, MB?" Em teased her, sliding into a thinly disguised, nosy inquiry. She was forever trying to set Marybell up with someone, declaring she just wanted everyone to be as happy as she and Jax were.

"He's been very nice." There. No more discussion. She reached up, pushing her endless bottles of conditioner out of the way. The Lord was good. Eureka!

"Nice? Is that how one describes men like the Hawthorne boys? *Nice?*" she prodded.

Marybell fished out the large container, filled with green goo. "Em?"

"Marybell?"

Her sigh was ragged as she tucked the phone under her chin and tried to screw the lid off the jar, putting it between her knees and giving it what little she had left. "I look horrible. I smell like I've been swimmin' in a mentholated pool, my eyes are swollen and goopy and my nose is red as your mama's roses. What difference does it make how I describe this man? I can promise you this, as crazy bag lady as I look right now, he'll just be glad to get out of here visually unscarred. He won't give a hoot how I describe him."

Em sighed into the phone, the happy noises of her

household full of children and assorted pets in the background. "Sorry. I was doin' your dreamin' for you, wasn't I?"

Because every girl dreamed of falling for a man who, if he knew her true identity, would rather spit on her than acknowledge her existence. End of dream. "I have to go now, Em. I don't want to be rude to the very *nice* Tag Hawthorne while he fixes my heat." *Or heats my fix. Or something along those lines.*

"Now, you listen to me, MB. You get yourself back to bed the moment Tag's done, hear? And you stay there until you're better. Your clients won't die for lack of you. LaDawn's got you covered. Now, one of us will be over in the morning to check on you and make you some breakfast, okay?"

Marybell nodded again, finally loosening the lid on the jar.

"You hear, MB?"

"Yes! I can't wait. The more chicken soup for my flu-riddled soul, the better," she chirped. "And thank you again, Em. I really do appreciate you." She clicked the phone off before Em had her married to Tag and fixin' her heat for better or worse for an eternity.

Dropping the phone into her pocket, she glanced at her naked face in the mirror before driving her hand into the jar of green goo, taking a huge scoop of it and slathering it across her forehead and cheeks.

When she was done, she wrinkled her nose at her image, turning her head from side to side to be sure she'd covered every inch of her face. Flipping on the faucet, she rinsed her hands, toweled them off and grabbed a clip, pulling all of her hair up on the top of her head to imprison it there.

It wasn't a pointy Mohawk, but it was just as scary.

One last glance as the goo on her face began to harden. Okay, she assessed. This could work. Feeling only a shade less uneasy, she wrapped a towel around her neck and popped open the bathroom door, running right into Tag.

"Oh!" she yelped, putting her hands in front of her to find them flat on his chest.

Tag grabbed for her, wrapping his arm around her waist.

Marybell's head popped up and she'd swear, if she ever retold this story, when describing his reaction to the hardening green mass on her face, she'd call it horrified quickly followed by the world's worst acting job at covering up.

He grinned down at her, deep lines on either side of his mouth forming inviting grooves she had to stop herself from reaching up and touching to feel how deep they really were. "You okay?"

She closed her eyes for a moment, unsure if she was dizzy from the brush of their bodies or her cold. But the brush of his long length against hers, even with the flu, was a whoa moment.

Then, like every other moment she'd spent in his presence, the whoa factor passed and she remembered she was just a girl. Just a girl hiding for her life behind a flaking green face mask of goo.

Forcing herself to step out of his reach, Marybell nodded. "I'm fine, thank you. So, have you figured out the problem?"

He nodded, his eyes flickering over her face before resting on her mouth. "I have. You should be nice and toasty in three, two…one." Tag held up his index finger just as a rush of air from the vent on the floor blew up her bathrobe.

Marybell smiled in relief, sinking her spine into the wall behind her to avoid making contact with him in the narrow space. "What was it?"

"Pilot light. It was out."

She rolled her eyes in self-disgust, bringing on another wave of dizziness that left her groping for the wall in support. "Of course it was."

"It's an easy thing to miss."

"It was a dumb thing to miss."

"You're sick."

"Sick? Yes. Brain-dead? No."

His teeth flashed white in the darkened hall. "Don't be so hard on yourself."

She snorted, congested and gross. "You're too kind."

He stared down at her, making her wonder how many times he'd smiled just like this and how many times the recipient of that smile had been a woman. It appeared his boyish grin was Tag's standard default when he wanted his way.

Ridiculous thoughts likely brought on by her unstable, drugged brain.

"I also fixed the thermostat. The digital reader was broken. Anyway, I'll let you rest now. Em called to remind me to remind you to take your medicine and get as much rest as possible. Hope you feel better soon."

Suddenly he was leaving, just like that, his reign of unwitting terror over. And so soon. She put a hand on his arm, letting her fingers sink lightly into it. "Money," she garbled.

Tag turned, cocking his head. "The root of all evil?"

"No." She forced the word out, noting she'd left green

flakes of goo on the arm of his sweatshirt, covering the roped muscle of his arm.

"Are we free-associating here?"

"I meant, let me pay you."

"For igniting your pilot light?"

No. For lighting my hormone's pilot. "Well, yeah. Don't you charge an hourly wage?"

He chuckled. Rich. Thick. Slippery. "Not when Em's hiring."

But wait... "I can't just let you light my pilot for free." *Smooth, Marybell.* Since when did anyone do anything for free, especially a contractor? And what was this reluctance to let him leave? Twenty minutes ago, she been living for his exit.

Now she was every bit Thumper eyes and lobbing money at him.

He backed away, deftly avoiding her black bag with the silver spikes on it, lying on the floor in the nook of the sharp right turn into the living room. "You can, and you will. Feel better, Marybell," he called out, the sound of the wind and then the door muffling his voice as it closed, greeting her ears.

Her shoulders slumped.

But they were warm when they did.

She wandered back into the living room, hands in her pockets, feeling strangely empty.

Tag had filled up an entire room, and when he'd left, which was exactly what she'd wanted him to do from the moment he entered, the space felt void of something.

Something.

As she pondered the something, she sat back down on the couch, pulling the throw over her legs, and that's when she noticed it.

A freshly made cup of tea, sitting beside the bowl of decorative balls on her coffee table, complete with tendrils of steam lifting off the amber liquid in wispy waves of heat.

Tag Hawthorne had made her tea.

The corner of Marybell's lips tilted upward in a reluctant smile, somehow evolving into butterflies in her stomach. Her schoolgirl smile cracked the thick layer of her green face mask until chunks of it fell into her lap.

Then she caught herself, the butterflies accumulating in the pit of her belly fleeing, replaced with dread. The green chunks were a warning. A symbol of what could happen.

Liking Taggart Hawthorne, even a little, would crack her carefully guarded life, turning it into a steaming pile of similar face-mask goo.

Nothing, especially not the temptation of a good-looking man, would ever entice her enough to do that.

Three

Marybell gasped low and long, making his spine stiffen. "Ohhh, Fredrico! The things you do to me!" She cooed the words, following up with a customary moan Tag had become familiar with since he'd started eavesdropping at her office door like a stray dog hungry for scraps.

These constant thoughts about Marybell, this mystique he wanted to unveil, with no sense to it at all, were damn inconvenient. Unwarranted, and totally unwelcome.

Yet here he was, a week after meeting Marybell for the first time, exercising his right to curiosity.

From the moment he'd left her apartment, he couldn't shake the crazy need to see what she really looked like without the big ridiculous hat and that green mess she'd put on her face.

What drove her to go to such lengths to keep him from seeing what she looked like, anyway? It wasn't as if he hadn't seen her before, whether she knew it or not. Not up close and personal, but he'd seen her around.

They'd even met briefly once a few months ago in Em's office, Marybell on her way out, him on his way in.

He'd concocted an answer for that while he thought about her nonstop since they'd met.

The answer was easy. He'd discovered a thing or two about the women here in Plum Orchard. They didn't like to be caught without their pretties, as Em called them. Marybell had been really sick, so it stood to reason that catching her at such a bad time would make her run for cover if she was anything at all like Em. She was Em's friend. They were bound to be on the same wavelength. Though Marybell's makeup and hairstyle were a little more over-the-top than Em's, they were clearly what made her feel pretty. He'd taken care of lumping their motivations together in his mind quite nicely.

That handled, he still had no answers.

This strange fixation on Marybell wasn't like him. Not since Alison, anyway… No one had interested him even a little since Alison.

He couldn't pinpoint his curiosity, couldn't reason with it. So he'd chalked it up to Marybell's voice, sugary-sweet and light as air even nasally with congestion, and those enormous eyes, looking up at him in the midst of the crusty stuff surrounding them. She'd sparked his curiosity, and since he'd fixed her heat, he hadn't stopped wondering what Marybell Lyman really looked like.

When Em mentioned they needed some work done around the guesthouse at Call Girls, he'd done everything but jump up and down with his hand in the air, yelling, "Pick me!"

Now, as he hovered around her office door, pretending to fix an outlet that didn't need fixing, he found

himself glued to her every word through the door sep-
arating them. And whoever the hell Fredrico was, he
already didn't like the bastard.

Which was irrational at best. Why his back was up
over a phone call with a stranger, one of the twenty or
so he'd heard her take since he'd started his "behave like
an ass" campaign, was a question Tag wasn't ready to
find the answer for.

You couldn't be jealous about a guy you didn't even
know for having an intimate conversation with a woman
you didn't know, either. Could you?

Shit.

If she'd just show her face, he'd probably find out she
wasn't his type and then this hunt for Marybell Lyman
would be done. End of irrational.

But it was as if she was hiding from him. Every time
he thought he had her cornered, and she was going to
walk out of her office door at any second, she didn't.

Then Em, being the kind of GM she was, a stickler
for details, would hunt his ass down and drag him off
to another project to complete before he had the chance
to pin Marybell down.

"Tag?"

Em's voice cut into his thoughts, making him drop
the screwdriver in guilt. It clattered to the floor, smack-
ing into his toolbox. Damn. Caught again.

Tag dragged his eyes upward, meeting Em's inquisitive gaze. "Yes, ma'am?" he drawled, hoping he'd managed to keep his voice level.

"How do you keep ending up here?"

*Here as in parked in front of Marybell Lyman's of-
fice? Or here as in here way past the time most contrac-*

tors call it quitting time, here? Play dumb, Hawthorne.
"Here?" Tag lifted his knit cap and scratched his head.

Em pursed her lips, her eyes not amused. He knew that look. It was the "there'll be no plum pie for you" look—the one she gave to her sons and his niece, Maizy, when they misbehaved. "Yes. Here." She pointed to the hallway, swishing her finger around. "Whenever I wonder where you are, I don't have to wonder long. Somehow we always end up here. What is your fixation with this hallway?"

It was Marybell Lyman's hallway? Probably not the answer she'd want to hear. Though why should he feel guilty for his interest in a woman? He was a single, mostly healthy, thirty-four-year-old man. He was allowed to be interested.

Except whenever he came to do any work at all at Call Girls, there was always the residual Neanderthal concept he felt ridiculously compelled to silently defend.

Women talked dirty in these here parts. Men liked to hear women talk dirty. There was always the natural assumption he was voyeuristically living out a caveman's dream under the guise of "fixing" things.

If he were completely honest, hearing Marybell say some of the things she said did make him hot. They damn well did. But the heat was always tempered with the reminder that this was her job, and she likely filed her nails and caught up on her reading while she did it. Not quite as hot.

Yet this quest to meet Marybell wasn't about her words. Not at all. This was about finding out if she was still just as cute without the floppy hat and flakey goop. If her hair was buttery blond all over, or just at the tips, leading to the question: *Why don't you just ring her doorbell and meet her right and proper, Hawthorne?*

Answer? He wasn't sure if he was ready for that yet. Calling on her was an unspoken commitment he wasn't prepared to offer. A gesture he wasn't sure he'd properly be able to follow up with anything more than his curiosity. He'd only just begun to get his life back on track—complications, especially with a woman, were the last thing he needed.

So instead, he skulked around the fringes of her doorway on the off chance he could take the easy way out and catch a glimpse of her—in the effort to rule out any possible attraction, of course.

Em poked his shoulder, bringing her once more into focus. "Tag?"

He shrugged casually, straightening. "I thought you said you needed me to fix the outlet." Em had said fix the outlet. She'd said the one in the entryway to the guesthouse, but he said tomato; she said tomahto. At least that was the explanation he'd go with if push came to shove.

Em nodded her dark head, patting him on the arm as if he were ten. "I did, but not the outlet here in the hall. The outlet in the *entryway.* You know, that pretty room with all the lush green plants you're always complainin' remind you of the rain forest section of the zoo? The one out there, not in *here?*"

Right. The room which damn well wasn't anywhere near Marybell's office. "Right. Sorry. Must've misunderstood you."

She planted her hands on her hips, cocking her head. "All week long? I swear, it's like I'm speakin' in a foreign language!"

Movement in Marybell's office took his attention away from Em's clear impatience with him. Tag stopped just shy of holding up his hand to quiet her in order to listen uninterrupted.

Marybell's chair creaked. There was the rustling of paper and then the typical nothing. No door opening. No blare of trumpets playing, signaling that the elusive Marybell had finally strolled out of her office door to grace them with her presence.

Em snapped her fingers under his nose, the clicking interfering with what was going on in Marybell's office. "Taggart Hawthorne, where are you?"

He blinked to refocus, catching Em's confused gaze. Tag let his head hang low to show appropriate shame. Em had given him work he damn well needed, and he was too busy hunting Marybell like prey to pay attention. "Sorry, Em. Just distracted. Won't happen again."

Em's finger rose in lecture pose just as he heard another noise coming from Marybell's office, blotting out everything else.

Her office window. He'd know the sound of a latch snapping unhinged on a window from a hundred paces.

Oh, the hell she'd escape him this time. That thought made him spring into action. He swooped down and grabbed his toolbox, skirting around an annoyed Em with a grin of apology. "Entryway. I'm on it."

She fell into a thorny bush just outside the window of her office, catching her nose ring on the brittle end of one of the limbs before dropping into the mulch surrounding it with a grunt she tried to muffle.

Her shaking fingers reached up to attempt to untwist the small hoop when she heard an amused "Good thing

I brought my chain saw. I'm happy to help. Just say the word, and I'll rev her up. Vroom-vroom."

Surely there was no one looking out for her up there. Hadn't she just expressly prayed for the umpteenth time in the past week, to whoever was in charge, to allow her an easy escape? Or had she been slacking off? She'd lost count of the times she'd sent skyward the pleading wish to avoid Taggart Hawthorne.

Knock-knock, is anyone home?

Would he ever be done with whatever it was he was doing and go away? What kind of contractor was he if it took him this long to do what Em had labeled "minor repairs"?

The sheer terror she'd fought all week long while Tag banged around outside her office door rose in her throat like cream to the top of a cup of coffee.

But you have the "people shield" on, Marybell. Relax.

How could she relax when her entire life was a lie? Seeing Tag confirmed that, drove that point home as sure as he was the hammer and she was the nail.

Since she'd recovered from the flu, and reasoned her fears away without the influence of cold medication, she'd taken a deep breath about the situation with Tag and had decided avoiding him was better all around.

There was no reason why she couldn't do it, she'd told herself. Even though she and Em were friends, and there'd be occasions when she'd have no choice but to mingle with him, it didn't have to be difficult if she didn't make it difficult.

Except Tag had made it difficult, probably without even realizing he had. First, she hadn't been able to stop thinking about him and his tea, which tasted awful. But the gesture still made her heart quicken and soften.

Second, it wasn't just his awful tea lingering in her house. Tag's rugged sexy had hung around long after he was gone, and she couldn't shake it. Every time she thought she had her lusty thoughts contained, the fantasies of his calloused hands on her flesh, sweeping along her skin to part her thighs, reared their ugly heads in the way of an erotic dream or seven—if she kept count.

She'd spent hours wondering what his lips tasted like—felt like. Was he a sloppy kisser, his tongue doing that awkward slap at hers? Or was he an expert with a tongue like the god of sex and sin?

Since Em had told them all he'd be doing some work around the office, she'd been on pins and needles, avoiding him at every turn while he breezed in and out of Call Girls. Not just because he might somehow recognize her even with her "people shield" in place, but because just the sound of his voice beyond her door made her knees weak.

"Marybell?' Tag rustled his way into the bush, sitting on his haunches and leaning over to bring his face into her line of vision.

It was such a great face. Almost classically handsome, but not quite. Angled, defined, *rough*. That was the word that came to mind every time she thought about him.

His sharp jaw caught the light of the half-moon, his eyes, heavily fringed with black lashes, full of playful amusement. "Here, let me," he offered deep and delicious, lifting that calloused hand to her nose, the one she'd spent a ridiculous amount of time recalling.

Swallowing her hysteria, Marybell protested, raising a finger to ward him off. It was trembling, but she waved it for all it was worth, anyway. "No, no. I've got this."

Tag grinned, infuriatingly wide, deepening his boyish dimples, that were a stark contradiction to the rest of his face. "You're pretty hooked on that limb. One move the wrong way and you're gonna lose a nostril."

She attempted to twist her finger up under the hoop to no avail. "Nostrils are overrated. I can always breathe through my mouth."

His hand went to her nose, anyway, shooing hers out of the way. "You should always have backup," he teased, far too gravelly and sex-on-a-stick-ish for her panic's comfort. With easy fingers, Tag plucked the limb from her nose ring and grinned again with his success.

Free from the limb, Marybell scrambled to her feet, cursing her clunky work boots when she tripped over the cement Buddha statue Sanjeev, Dixie's friend and house manager, insisted each of the Call Girls have beneath their office windows.

Tag's hands, strong, so incredibly solid, went to either side of her waist, settling there to right her. An unfamiliar thrill shot straight to places Marybell was unused to having thrills.

She flattened a palm against his chest to protest— a chest like a hard wall of granite. This would be so much easier if his chest was more on par with something mushy—say a bowlful of Jell-O maybe. Yet the firm surface of muscle through the wall of his thermal shirt set her palm on fire.

Tag's breathing picked up, shooting a stream of condensation from his hard line of a mouth, slicing the chilly night air. Had that hitch in his breath happened because of her hand? She marveled at the notion.

No. It couldn't be. Marybell dismissed the thought entirely. She was a sex-starved fool. That's what she was. There was no siren in her, no unique song she sang that brought droves of men to flounder at her feet as they did at gorgeous Dixie's.

She wasn't carved-in-stone pretty. She was gothic and dark with a touch of glam to motivate her to continue this charade she'd long since outgrown.

Then Tag's skin was touching hers, his long fingers, as calloused as she'd remembered them, snaked around her wrist in a loose hold. "You have nice hands," he commented clear as day. "Interesting color choice for nail polish." He inspected her fingers one by one, holding them so close to his lips Marybell shivered.

"You don't like gunmetal with gold flecks?" she croaked, acutely aware this hard, rough man was sucking her into his blatantly sexy aura.

"Oh, no. I like gunmetal, but I really love gold flecks," he teased. "I like the green and red in your hair, too. I also like that you still have a nostril because of me. It evens out your face. Why don't you thank me for saving it over dinner?"

Marybell's breathing became rapid and choppy similar to the function of her brain. "It's ten o' clock. Too late for dinner." No, no, no. No dinner. No tea. No contact.

But he doesn't recognize me...

And we're going to keep it that way. How do you feel about losing everything plus putting the people you love in a circus of media?

While she battled internally, they had somehow become pressed impossibly close together. His breath on her face, warm and minty. His thighs touching hers—thick and insanely hard. His scent—so Tag, clean, spicy. Tag's everything mingled with her everything.

Was there no mercy tonight?

"But isn't that what you were sneaking off to grab when you climbed out the window? Your dinner break is at ten, right?"

"What makes you think I was sneaking off at all?" There was no sneaking about this. She was flat-out in hiding.

"Simple deductive reasoning. It's gotta be easier to get to the lunchroom by just opening the door of the phone-sexing room than by way of your office window, right?" he asked, his hips blending with hers and settling against them until the outline of him through her suddenly too-thin, zebra-striped leggings heated her whole body. "All that climbing out, climbing back in. Hard on the thighs."

Hard thighs. Lots of that to go round here.

"Challenge is my middle name. I like a good one. The window seemed as good as any."

"So you're not avoiding me or anything, right? Because even though your office window presents a good workout, it's a little extreme."

"It's hard to fit exercise in between takin' calls. It was the obvious choice."

He shook his head. "That's not what I asked you."

"What did you ask me?"

"I asked you if you were avoiding me. I'd find it hard to believe, because who'd want to avoid a nice guy like me, but there it is. I think you're avoiding me."

His point-blank stare was what was impossible to

avoid. He'd pinned her with it, and he wasn't letting her gaze go.

Blatantly lying wasn't her strong suit. Her strengths lay in running away. But here went nothin'. "I don't even know you. Why would I do that?"

"Only you have the answer to that, Marybell Lyman. What could the answer be?"

Her silence deafened even her.

"So, about saving your nostril…" he murmured, slow and easy, his gaze now roving over her face, taking in each feature with all-seeing eyes.

Marybell nodded, forcing her voice to project around a thick knot in her throat. "It was amazing. So heroic and chivalrous. We should give you a superhero name. Nostril saving is hard work. It deserves at least a cape."

"You bet it does, and don't the damsels in distress always have dinner with their superheroes?"

A giggle almost erupted from her throat before she remembered hanging out with the subject you wanted to avoid and gushing about him isn't exactly avoidance. Admiring the way their bodies fit together, soaking in his maleness like a sponge, wasn't dodging disaster, either.

She went slack in Tag's arms, hoping, maybe even praying, he'd take the obvious hint. Because she couldn't do this. This wasn't allowed. It was just Marybell for always. No one was permitted in. Not even casually.

She shrugged. "Do they? I thought they never did normal things with their superheroes because of the identity thing. It was always on the DL, full of subterfuge and innuendo." *Oh, the parallels to be had.*

"Then it's a good thing I'm not like every other superhero, because I'm definitely available for dinner, and for the record, I don't care if you tell people I'm the one who saved your nostril. No subterfuge here."

"You have chivalry down to a science, but I'm not dat—"

Tag's lips were on hers before she'd even formulated the rest of her sentence. Greedy. Hot. Firm. Demanding. Knee-buckling hungry. Tasting like mint and man.

So much man. More man than even she'd dreamed up.

Before her brain got in the way, Marybell was returning his kiss, melting against the solid wall of his chest, her nipples taut and rigid, pushing with need at her leather jacket.

Tag's breath mingled with hers when she inhaled sharply, acutely aware of every sensation he aroused in every nerve ending she owned.

Her breasts swelled in her bra, driving against the material until her nipples tightened even harder. Things began to happen between her legs, too, wet, swollen things she'd long since left behind.

Tag's tongue slipped into her mouth on a low groan, silky and taut, driving, tasting, deepening their kiss. With his arm around her waist, he hauled her tight to his body until Marybell had to dig her fingers into his thick shoulders to keep from tipping them over.

His arms tightened when her fingers sought the fringe of his hair at the bottom edge of his knit hat, the muscles in them flexing in firm ripples. She rolled the soft wisps between her digits, touching, memorizing the strands.

Tag's kiss was everything, forcing her to see, hear, feel only him.

There was nothing but this kiss. This breath-stealing,

mind-melding kiss. Everything about this kiss was wrong, but right. So right.

No. So wrong, Marybell.

But this kiss...

Tag's lips were leaving hers in a sudden release of suction and air, allowing the sounds of the chilly night to crowd around her.

He looked down at her as though he wasn't exactly sure what had just happened, either, but the emotion flickered and died, swiftly replaced with a grin that made the corners of his eyes wrinkle upward. "Dinner. Tomorrow night on your break. I'll make it. All you have to do is show up. Bring your nostrils," he said on a husky chuckle.

There was no chance for protest. No time for regret. No time to do anything but watch Tag's broad back exit the bushes, hear his footsteps hard on the pathway that led back to the guesthouse.

Shaken, Marybell reached for the side of the house, pulling air into her lungs. It hit her chest in sharp, razor-like pangs.

Panic began its deep dive into her stomach, clawing and burning until she almost choked on it.

She couldn't have dinner with Tag Hawthorne. She couldn't have anything with him—ever.

In fact, if he found out exactly who she was, her head would be a selection on the menu—not a dinner date.

She'd seen him angry. In the one comment he'd made to a reporter at the courthouse just before the trial. Knew what true contained rage looked like in Tag's eyes—in the clench of his fists. Marybell shivered at that rage.

Like her, everything had once been taken from him.

She understood what that did to you. Her core hurt from what that did to her.

But Tag was unknowingly toying with the alleged enemy, and she had to find a way to keep him at bay.

Her panic evolved into bitter disappointment.

All because of that kiss.

Four

"You did what?" his brother, Jax, asked.

"I said I kissed her."

"Marybell? Marybell Lyman—the one with the Mohawk?" Jax did a thing with his hands in the air over his head.

"That's the one." The one who'd, with just one quick kiss, set him on fire—reminded him he was still a man with working parts.

"Can I ask why?"

"Can I ask why you'd ask why?"

Jax scruffed his hand over his jaw and frowned at Tag. "Because it's sort of out of the blue and really random, especially with you lately. You'd just as soon bite someone's head off than kiss her."

"Sometimes kisses are like that. Random." It had taken him by surprise, too. But there she was, smelling amazing, her back up, her luscious lips covered in some crazy metallic-blue lipstick, and he couldn't resist.

At first he'd kissed her because he didn't want to hear that she wasn't dating right now. He didn't know why those words were so unacceptable to him. It wasn't as if he hadn't been turned down for a date before. It wasn't as if he wasn't still stinging from a long-term relationship not so long ago. He had baggage. He didn't want more.

Yet somehow those words were just unacceptable coming from her shiny-blue lips. So he'd kissed her—he wasn't even sure if he'd expected the kiss to be especially good. But it was.

And yep, it was definitely uncharacteristic of him as of late. It was more like the old Tag. The one he couldn't seem to dig out in the rubble of his life—forgive the past. Maybe that was why he was so fixated on Marybell. Because she shook something up in him—something that kept him on his toes—something that felt real.

"You don't even know her, and you just laid one on her?" Jax pressed.

"I met her when I lit her pilot light for Em."

"Is there some kind of magic involved in lighting a woman's pilot light all these years I've been missing? I'd have lit one a long time ago."

Tag grinned. "No, you wouldn't have. You were waiting for Em to come along. And ya done good, brother."

Jax smiled, that smile he always smiled whenever Em's name was mentioned. Kind of stupid and head over heels, but nice. "Damn right I did. But that doesn't explain how, after one light of a pilot, you were kissing Marybell."

"I like Miss Marybell. She always makes me paper dolls when we go to Miss Dixie's house for pool parties. Her hair is so cool," his niece, Maizy, chimed from the playroom adjoining the kitchen where Tag was expending an infinite amount of time making bologna sandwiches for the date Marybell had never officially agreed to.

"She's nice, right, A-Maizy?" Tag confirmed. He smiled and winked at her. He didn't know why seeing Marybell was making him stupidly happy. But it was.

He'd woken up today with a smaller knot in his chest than usual. His financial worries, his life issues didn't seem as daunting this morning, and when he thought about that, Marybell's face had popped into his head.

"Does Em know you kissed her?"

Tag stuffed a sandwich into a Zip-Loc bag and frowned. "Why does Em have to know I kissed her?"

"Kissed who?" Em asked, floating into the kitchen to settle herself against Jax's side with a sigh and a squeeze of his brother's hand while her boys, Clifton Junior and Gareth, flew into the playroom to join Maizy. She dropped a plate of brownies on the counter for them. One of the many perks of Emmaline Amos.

He liked Em. She'd changed everything for Jax and Maizy. She was a pear-scented whirlwind of hugs and kisses, freshly baked pies, well-balanced meals for Maizy, and one of the biggest badasses with a band saw he'd ever seen.

Truth be told, he and his younger brother, Gage, were probably needed a whole lot less in Maizy's case since Em had come into their lives. They'd both come to Plum Orchard for their own reasons, but the biggest one had been helping Jax take care of his best friend's daughter.

Now Em did all the things they'd once done to help Jax, and she did them a damn sight better than the two of them ever had.

But Em wouldn't hear of them leaving Georgia— even though a small part of the reason he'd come to

Plum Orchard, to help Jax renovate their aunt's old house, was no longer a valid reason. The house was mostly done, and this was due in part to Em who'd organized and planned until it was exactly the way Jax claimed he'd envisioned it.

He should be out trying to get some contracting work. Unfortunately, his tarnished reputation made that almost impossible, and here in Plum Orchard, there wasn't a huge call for contractors. So he took side jobs that paid little but kept him doing what he loved to do more than most anything else. Building things.

He'd thought for sure now that Jax had Em, he and Gage would just be in the way of the eventual blending of their two families.

But Em had sat both men down and firmly said, with a teasing smile, "Ya'll don't become less important to Maizy and Jax because the house is finished. You're all she's ever known since birth. You're family. Why should that change because of me and my interferin'? You both stay put until you want otherwise. I can work around you."

He'd been surprised by her attitude. Thought for sure, even the nicest of women wouldn't want two messy, loud roughnecks with more issues than a stack of magazines hanging around. But not Em. Em had embraced them as hard as they'd embraced her, but most of all, she'd brought all the things to Maizy's life not one of the Hawthorne brothers could.

Hair ribbons and sparkly dresses and pink castles made out of life-size LEGOs. Nail polish, facials, bedtime stories of evil queens vanquished with the power of love, girl time once a week with Em and the women at Call Girls and a million hugs and kisses.

"So, who are you kissing, Tag?"

"He kissed Marybell," Jax teased.

Em's blue eyes went wide as she pulled off her coat and scarf. "My Marybell?"

"Did you have dibs on her, Em?" Tag teased, reaching for the bag of chips he'd dug out of the pantry.

Em made a face at him, her fingers going to her throat in a gesture he knew well. It was a signal she was concerned. "Oh, hush. I'm just surprised."

"That she'd let a schlub like me kiss her?"

"That she'd let anyone kiss her. Marybell's…"

Tag's ears instantly went on alert. "Marybell's what?"

Em sighed, her eyes thoughtful and cautious. "I don't know. She's very private. I just get the impression she's had some troubles, though I don't know what, and even if I did, I wouldn't be tellin' tales out of school. So you mind yourself, Taggart Hawthorne. I won't have you upsettin' my girl with your unspeakable charms."

Yeah. He got that Marybell was private—closed off somehow; he just didn't know from what. But he wanted to. "My unspeakable charms?"

Jax slapped him on the back. "It's a Hawthorne trait. Ask Em. She couldn't resist."

Em gave his brother a flirty smile and a peck on the lips. "It was not, either. It was all the power tools you're related to by familial connections that grabbed on to me and just wouldn't let go."

"Just ask me. Can't get her to give up that darn belt sander to save my soul," Gage joked, breezing into the kitchen to grab a brownie from the plate Em had brought over. He held it up after taking a bite. "Have I mentioned how much I love having you in our lives, Em?"

Em's chuckle filled the kitchen. "That belt sander is almost better than a manicure."

Tag packed up the last of his dinner, the only sort of dinner he could afford at this point, and stuffed it into a backpack. "Don't you worry, Em. I'll be on my best behavior. Gotta run, guys. Have a couple of things to do before tonight. Have a good one."

"Wait!" Em yelled, a bottle of ginger ale in her hand. She caught him at the door and held it out to him. "Marybell likes ginger ale. Has it every night with her supper—which is what I'm assumin' the bologna sandwiches are about? Supper—you and her?"

The words made his chest tight again. Damn stupid, but it took his mind off the other stuff. The bad shit. He was tired of the bad shit. Marybell made him think of good things—so he was going with it. "Guilty."

Em's eyes gleamed. "Then you be sure and wow her with your uncanny intuition and take the ginger ale. I won't tell if you don't tell."

Tag looked down into her pretty face for signs of disapproval. "You okay with this? I know she's your employee. I don't want to cause trouble."

Em grinned—the kind of grin she and Maizy shared when they were up to their eyeballs in something. "How could courtin' Marybell cause trouble?"

Her heard the metaphoric skidding of brakes in his head. "Hold on there. I'm not courting anything. It's just some bologna sandwiches." He wasn't courting. Was he? Hell, no. He was testing. Testing his social skills. Testing his ability to interact with the world again. Testing a connection that had made him feel good—as though there was life still left to live.

"I saw the way you slathered that mayonnaise on

that bread like you were plastering a wall—you did it like you were da Vinci. That kind of care says courtin' to me."

"It's just a sandwich," he insisted. "I like my mayo to be even on all four corners of the bread. I just assume that's how everyone else likes it. That's not courting—that's for the love of a good sandwich."

"You call it whatever you like, Tag, but hear me clear, Marybell's a gentle, kind soul. She's one of the best hearts I know—one of the best friends I have—and I won't have you toyin' with her emotions. I don't know everything about her, but I do know, if I lost her at Call Girls because of some silly love spat with you, I'd likely snatch old Coon Ryder's gun from his gnarled grasp and hunt you down."

Just one more thing he loved about Em. She was fiercely loyal. She could have wrangled the Hawthorne men and Maizy together in a million ways that would have left some of them feeling displaced, but she'd do it without a single resentment from any of them. Slow and steady with a firm hand on the prize. The prize being family.

This fact about her was to be admired. "Swear on my carefully placed mayo, I'll be on my best behavior—a perfect gentleman."

She gave him a motherly pat on his cheek. "You see that you are. And one more thing."

"I know, I know. Coon's gun. You're not afraid to use it."

"Leave your baggage at the airport."

"My what?"

"Don't act like you don't know what I mean, Taggart. Leave all your broodin' and sufferin' out of this noncourtin'. Just for tonight, try to enjoy the company of another human being who isn't related to you and doesn't want to play Candy Land for twelve never-ending rounds."

Tag barked a laugh. "Is this your way of telling me you don't like Candy Land?"

Her face went soft. "I don't like that you've hurt for a very long time and you might mess up this opportunity to have a little fun by dredging up something that's long over. I've seen you do it before, but it wasn't with someone I care a great deal about."

Alison. She meant Alison. Fair. That was a fair assessment of his life at this point. He had things he was working out—coming to grips with. Sometimes they colored everything he did—or didn't do. "It's just a sandwich," he defended.

"One I hope you have the most amazin' time ever sharing with Marybell—baggage free." She gave him a quick pinch of the cheek before returning to the kitchen to Jax.

Propping the door open, he fought the envy the picture of Em and Jax made. He loved Jax, wanted him to be happy.

But maybe, after all this time, it was time for him to find some happiness, too. Even if it was just sharing a bologna sandwich with a woman who made his pulse kick up a notch.

Maybe.

Marybell took better care when she climbed out of her office window this time, avoiding the shrubs below it and hopping right over them only to get caught up on the gutter. "Damn!" she yelped into the night, grabbing for the side of the guesthouse to no avail.

Her fingers slipped and she crashed to the ground onto something hard. Not ground-hard, something that was softer hard. And grunted.

Her eyes, still adjusting to the light, gripped an arm, muscled and covered in flannel.

That arm came up around her waist and rolled her off him. Tag, covering her upper body with his, pressed her into the cold ground with his chest. He grinned, impossibly handsome, and her heart responded with impossible flutters. "If you squashed my carefully made bologna sandwiches, I'm going to be really upset with you. It took me two hours just to get the bread to rise."

Her heart pounded so hard she was sure Tag would feel it right through his jacket. *Don't panic. People shield is appropriately in place and it's dark.*

She scoffed at him, refusing to grin back, no matter how much she wanted to. "Two hours? Novice."

He nodded as if she'd just complimented him. "You make bread, too? Only someone who makes her own bread would know two hours is a ridiculous amount of time to make bread. But look at all the things we have in common. Wanna swap recipes?"

"I make trips to the grocery store to support the people who make it. Now let me up, please." *Before I die right here on this ground with you and all those hard muscles of yours pressed against me. Because it feels far too good—and uncomfortable—and good.*

"Is that any way to talk to the man who made you bologna sandwiches?"

Marybell gave him a nudge, even though she really didn't want to. In fact, what she really wanted was to lie right here with Tag, on the ground that didn't seem quite as cold, and watch the stars bobbing above their heads on this crisp night.

Instead, she let her arms rest limply at her sides. "Is pinning me to the ground any way to treat the woman you made the bologna sandwiches for?"

"I'll take that to mean you'll join me." He thrust upward to a sitting position and held out his hands to her.

Marybell ignored them and levered herself upward on her own, taking a good look at her surroundings. Tag had spread a blanket out beneath the window of her office right next to the garden gnome that Sanjeev, Dixie's right-hand man at the Big House, was so fond of. He'd laid out some paper plates and napkins, apparently, now scattered in every direction when she'd fallen on them. "What is this?"

Tag pulled some matches from his pocket and scraped one to ignite it. He held up a small candle and struck a match, illuminating his angular face and making his dark eyes look even darker. "This is dinner. Remember our date?"

For a couple of seconds, Marybell was speechless. No one had ever done something like this for her. Not in all her thirty years. The gesture stole her breath. It was sweet and thoughtful and utterly unexpected.

And under the window of her office. "I don't remember confirmin' our date."

He popped open a bag of chips and dumped them on her plate with another grin. "Ah, but you didn't deny it, either."

"So if I don't say no, it's automatically a date?"

"That's what the rule book says."

"Who wrote this rule book?"

"Probably some desperate guy who couldn't get a firm yes for a date."

She laughed, or maybe she giggled. The silly noise coming from her throat sounded suspiciously like a giggle. The kind of giggle a woman uses when she's enamored with a man. When everything he says is charming and a total orgasm to her ears. Marybell clamped her lips shut. "I thought I told you I wasn't dating."

Tag handed her a plate, complete with a sandwich cut neatly in a triangle, some fresh fruit and a pile of chips. "I don't think you got that far."

She hesitated. No food. She couldn't have a sandwich with this man. She'd been an unwitting party to ruining his life. You didn't have a sandwich with a man whose life you'd annihilated. "I'm not dating."

He ignored her and thrust the plate at her again along with a bottle of ginger ale. "I know this is your favorite."

He'd gone out of his way to find out what she liked to drink? Bits of the icy formation around her heart broke off like chunks of an overheated glacier. Marybell took the plate and the ginger ale and set them beside her on the blanket. "Thank…you."

Tag leaned back against the guesthouse and grinned again, letting his long legs unwind in front of him. "That's more like it. I like gratitude in the women I'm not dating."

She quashed the smile she was fighting with a vengeance. "As long as we're clear this isn't a date, I'll eat your bologna sandwich, but it's only because I'm starving and you've left me little choice now. Madge will be closin' up shop soon, which means I can only get whatever she has left. Usually that's eight-hour-old meat loaf."

Tag took an enormous bite of his sandwich and nodded, swallowing hard. "Bologna's better for you than meat loaf. All these by-products put hair on your chest."

Her laughter tinkled from her lips before she could stop it. She nibbled at a chip to keep from making any more unfamiliar mating noises, but her mind was racing. "Why did you do this?"

"Do what?"

Make me feel something for you. Make me fight a dreamy sigh. Make me want to twirl my Mohawk in centuries-old, ritualistic gestures of flirtation. "Here— this—under my office window."

He shrugged his wide shoulders. "Because I had a funny feeling you'd try to skip out on our nondate. I figured this was the best way to catch you skipping."

"I'm not dating."

"Anyone, or just me?"

"Anyone."

"Where do you come from, Marybell Lyman?"

"Did you just hear me?"

"Just because you're not dating doesn't mean you can't have polite conversation."

Everywhere and nowhere. "Atlanta." Atlanta was big. That seemed safe enough.

"Me, too. The last name Lyman isn't familiar, though."

That's because it's not really mine. "I get the feeling we didn't travel in the same social circles." *No truer words.*

"Did you go to college?"

She stiffened. He couldn't possibly know—could he? Why was he asking so many questions? *That's what people do when they want to get to know you, Mary-bell. They make conversation.* "Did you?"

"Yep. Got a degree in architecture."

"Which led you here to Plum Orchard where big buildings are just linin' the streets." She was doing her best to be surly, but Tag wasn't having it, and she was having trouble sustaining it because he was blatantly ignoring her efforts.

"Nope. My sister's death led me here."

Damn. Now she was just being a jerk. She knew from Em that his sister, Harper, had died, but she didn't know that was why he was in Plum Orchard. "I'm sorry. I didn't mean to be so rude."

"Sure you did. You want our nondate to be over. But you know what, Marybell Lyman, that's all right. To be rude, I mean—because we're on a nondate. If this were a real date, I'd make you pay the tab for being so rude."

"I think I can rustle up some spare change for the bologna sandwich." She stopped then. He wasn't attacking her safe place knowingly. He wasn't threatening everything she loved and held dear to be a malicious jackass.

Lighten up. At least enough to appear civil.

Marybell reached out and put her hand on his arm, softening her words. "And I really didn't mean to be rude about your sister. I just didn't know your reasons for comin' to the PO. I'm sorry for your loss." No one understood loss better than she did.

Tag grabbed her hand and used it to slide her closer. "I'm sorry, too. She was a great sister."

The brief flicker of pain in his eyes made her wonder what had happened beyond what Em had told them. It was deep and it was personal, if Tag's face lined with some raw emotion she couldn't pinpoint was any indication. But then he smiled without letting go of her hand. "Why phone sex?"

Her hand in his felt so good, so warm against her icy fingers, Marybell forgot to pull away. "Why not?" she said on a smile.

"Hey, no judgment here. Just curious. I mean, if we're honest, not many little girls dream they'll grow up and be phone sex operators."

Not this one, either. This one had wanted to grow up and be a ballerina and wear a pink tutu. "The economy stinks."

"And that's what led you to phone sex? Even in a bad economy, most people don't consider phone sex. McDonald's? Sure."

"Most people aren't me."

"Fair enough. How'd you know you'd be good at it?"

Desperation made me good at it. Desperation and the kindest man in the world who'd offered her an opportunity to live in a warm house free of vermin and filth. "I don't know. I just made it work because financially, I needed to."

"Desperate times, huh?"

And so many desperate measures. "That about sizes it up."

"Landon Wells, right? He's the man who owned Call Girls before Dixie and Caine?"

Her heart twisted in her chest at the mention of Landon's name. She'd loved him so much. He was the only person on earth who knew who she really was. The only person on earth who'd cared little about her past—who'd been willing to help her when the entire world wanted to spit in her face—and some had—literally.

"Yes." She damned her throat for closing up. Clearing it, she sat up straighter, acutely aware of Tag's thumb caressing her finger. "He was an amazing human being, and if not for him, I'd be livin' on the streets." She didn't care that she was revealing something so personal, so painful. Landon would always have her undying gratitude, and she'd never hesitate to say it out loud.

"No family to turn to?"

"Nope." Not a single soul.

"I'm sorry to hear that."

"Don't feel sorry for me." *Please.* "There are plenty of others who have it so much worse. For instance, just today I read one of the Kardashians broke a nail and Taylor Swift is never, *ever* getting back together with her boyfriend."

Tag chuckled. "I didn't mean it in a pity kind of way. I meant it in the 'Wow, it sucks that you don't have people nosing into your business twenty-four-seven' kind of way. So, where's your family?"

Marybell stared at him. This was getting too close for comfort. Yet she found herself repeating the words she repeated to everyone when they asked. "I was in the foster care system all my life. No family."

His grip on her hand tightened, and she knew she should yank hers back to safety, but it was so warm and…safe. Something about the calloused surface was safe. "Damn. This time I am sorry."

"Damn. I'd hoped you'd be more original."

"Original?"

"Everyone says they're sorry. I guess you're not the exception I'd hoped for," she teased, and smiled. She was used to the eyes full of sympathy, sad smiles, but it was all she'd ever known. She'd never truly realized what she'd missed until Landon came along.

Tag's eyes searched hers. "Not laughing. My family drives me crazy, but I couldn't live without them."

Marybell shrugged to hide all her childhood hopes dashed—all her Christmas wishes ignored. "You could if you didn't know what it was like to have one."

"So I gather the Call Girls are your family now? You all seem pretty tight."

There were times when she was almost afraid to acknowledge how she felt about them out loud. To say it was to throw it out into the universe and take the chance the universe would strike back.

If you didn't tell anyone you cared about something almost more than you cared about breathing, it wouldn't tempt the Fates to snatch it away. She kept her feelings about Em and the girls on the inside. "They're the closest thing to family I've ever had."

For all the years spent wondering what it was like to belong—really belong somewhere—she'd found that in the least likely place of all, and whether they knew it or not, she clung to their friendships. In silence, while she treasured them in ways she hoped they felt rather than heard.

She didn't want these friendships taken away when it had taken thirty years to find them. Tag had the ability to obliterate the only real thing she had, and he didn't even know it.

She faked looking at a watch that didn't exist on her wrist, pulling her other hand from his. Without looking at him, she rose to her feet, brushing the dead leaves from her torn jeans. "My break's almost over. I have to go."

Tag was up and on his feet, his large frame looming

above her. "So I bet you don't want to do this again, huh?"

Yes, she did. No. She wouldn't. "I'm not dating."

Tag tipped her chin up and smiled, his white teeth gleaming against his sun-weathered skin. "But you are eating. You need your energy for all that oohing and aahing."

Walk away now, Marybell. "Does what I do for a living bother you?"

"Nope. I won't tell you it's not a little weird to know you—"

"Get guys off over the phone?" Maybe if she was crude, he'd go away. He had to go away.

Tag didn't miss a beat. "Okay, if you want to put it that way. Then, yeah. But that's not something that'd scare me off."

What would scare him off? If her outlandish makeup and hair didn't do it, surely her job was cause to rethink pursuing her.

Tag gripped her shoulders. "Is that what you want? To scare me off?"

That's what she should want, but she wanted that far less than she wanted to throw her arms around his neck and kiss him again the way he'd kissed her last night. Taking a step back and out of his reach, she kept her tone indifferent. "I want to go back to work."

Tag latched his fingers together and held them out, hitching his sharp jaw at her office window. "You want a lift?"

She laughed, even though she knew she shouldn't. Marybell pointed to the path that led back around to the front of the guesthouse. "I'll take the long way. Thanks for dinner. G'night, Tag." She made her way along the cobbled path, passing the neatly manicured topiaries with twinkling lights on them, her chest heavy and tight.

It was time to find a new escape route to avoid Tag.

"G'night, Marybell," he called after her, his deep voice swirling in her ears.

Goodbye, Tag.

Five

Em clinked her wineglass as they sat around the break room at Call Girls on Even Phone Sex Operators Have Pizza Night. "Attention, Marybell Lyman!"

Marybell froze, midslice of gooey pepperoni. She lifted her eyes to meet Em's devilish ones.

"I hear someone's been kissin' a Hawthorne? Dish, MB!"

It really was true all the bad press small towns got for gossip. Nothing was sacred.

Dixie's head popped up from her *Brides* magazine, her eyes zeroing in on Marybell. "Ohhh, juicy—share!"

LaDawn sputtered, setting down the wine bottle she chugged from because she always said using a glass was a waste of dish washing liquid. "You been kissin' a Hawthorne? Dang. Which one?"

"Tag!" Em said on a laugh, swirling the red liquid in her tumbler. "She kissed Taggart."

"And you know this how, Emmaline Amos?" Dixie asked, closing her magazine.

Em winked at Marybell. "Because he said as much. And he was smilin' when he did."

Marybell had to fight the urge to run and hide. This was what girlfriends did, Landon had once told her. They shared secrets. They braided each other's hair, had sleepovers, shopped and stuck their noses in your beeswax.

Always done with love, but still done. You could say anything to your girlfriend, even if it was something unflattering, but God save the fool outsider if she took it upon herself to insult your BFF.

She didn't always understand the mechanics of a close relationship, friendships or otherwise. She'd never had a relationship that lasted much longer than six months before she was moved to a new foster home. It was barely long enough for her to adjust to her new surroundings, let alone forge bonds.

But Landon had taught her bonds could be forged virtually overnight. He'd taught her that not everyone had one foot holding the door open for her exit, and not everyone betrayed you.

The girlfriend thing she was still feeling her way around in the dark about.

If you let just one person in, Marybell, it eases the burden of your own troubles some because then y'all share them. I hope someday, when you decide we're not all bottom-feeders, you'll do just that.

She'd held those words to her heart when she'd taken the leap and decided to move with LaDawn, Cat and the others to Landon's small hometown instead of staying in Atlanta. He'd prepared them for the kind of snobbery they'd be up against, but he'd also promised them if they moved with the company, there'd always be more love than hate.

And for the most part, he'd been right. Still, the security and friends he'd given her far outweighed the problems they'd faced in Plum Orchard.

"Why so quiet, Miss MB?" Cat, so beautiful in her last month of pregnancy, asked. She rubbed her swollen belly and batted her eyelashes.

So, what to say? *It was amazing. I haven't stopped thinking about it since it happened. It can't ever happen again because I'm allegedly responsible for the downward spiral his life has taken.*

She wiped her mouth with a paper napkin. How could she keep this girlfriendish enough to keep them happy, but not lead them to believe that kiss had been with her every waking moment? "It was no big deal."

Em threw her paper plate away and crossed the room to wrap her arms around Marybell's neck, giving it a squeeze. "No big deal? It most certainly is a big deal when the woman we know hardly ever even looks at a man. Now, out of the blue, she's kissin' one? That's big where I come from."

Marybell patted Em on the arm and gave it a squeeze before untangling herself. "Men don't really look at me, so why should I look at them?"

Dixie grinned. "Well, you been doin' just a little more than lookin' at Tag, now, haven't you? So, are you going to see him again?"

"I'm not really dating." Brief and to the point.

"But you are kissin'?" LaDawn snickered.

"It was just a kiss. No big deal."

"He made her bologna sandwiches," Em offered. "In all the months I've known Tag, he hasn't shown a lick of interest in a soul here in the PO, and now he's makin' bologna sandwiches for our Marybell like he's creatin' the Sistine Chapel with a knife and some mayonaise."

She warred with a secret smile of pleasure and her rising discomfort with their teasing. The half of her that had never had anyone give that much thought to making her anything wanted to preen. She wanted to tell them how amazing his kiss was. She wanted to gush and giggle the way they did. She wanted a happy ending just like Em's and Dixie's.

But the other half of her, the half that had to keep this from spinning out of control, just wanted everyone to leave it alone and stop drawing attention to it. She was good at indifference. Really good at it.

If you didn't let anyone know how important something was, they couldn't take it away from you. "I'm not interested. But the bologna sandwich was nice. Now, ladies, I have to get to work. Thanks for the pizza, Dixie. I'll see you guys later."

She ignored the looks her friends passed to each other and wiggled her fingers at them before almost running out of the break room. She stopped at Nella's desk and gave her the thumbs-up for calls and escaped to her office, shutting the door.

Putting on her headset, she clicked the on button and waited only a few seconds before her phone began to ring. A glance at her computer screen said the caller was unknown. Since Jax had restructured their entire call system, there was no guessing when it came to who was calling.

Each call was tagged with a label for recurring callers, regulars, newbs and the undecided. Meaning, either Nella didn't know what to do with them or their needs were unidentifiable.

Answering the phones was what had saved her four years ago—being someone else, pretending. She was good at it. She was good at compartmentalizing her feelings on the subject of the art of talking dirty. It was all just words—words she submersed herself in—worlds she created. They weren't conventional worlds, or appropriate in most minds, but they were hers.

She'd studied the art of naughty as if she were studying for the biggest test of her life. Learned the words, said them over and over in a mirror before she'd ever taken her first phone call so she'd sound as if she'd always said them. In fact, some of her regulars were the only long-term relationships she'd had before she became so close to Dixie and everyone else.

"This is Marybell," she cooed into the mouthpiece. "Who's this big, strong man callin' me up on this fine night?"

"Do guys really fall for that?"

Her heart fluttered. Tag. "Do you really want to know how gullible your gender is?"

He chuckled, rich and deep. "Ouch. Maybe not."

Here was a real opportunity to scare him off for good. Tag didn't come across as the kind of man who liked when a woman took charge. She knew how to keep a man in line. "So, what's your pleasure tonight, Taggart Hawthorne? You up for a spankin'? Because I have to tell you, LaDawn really is your girl, if that's your scene. She's the BDSM master. But I'm game if you are. Or how about some submissive play? You know, I'll be your dominatrix, you mop the floor clean with your toothbrush while I whisper dirty words in your ear. Or do you want to be the big mob boss and I'll be your beautiful but brainless trophy? Some role-playing, maybe?"

"Will you call me the Godfather? Because I have to admit, it's a crazy ego stoke."

She laughed. Damn him for making her laugh. For liking that he made her laugh. "Sure, Godfather. So what's your kink?"

"Well, I have one in my neck. Damn well twisted it fixing Elias Godfreed's track lighting. Does that count as a legitimate kink?"

"In my world, track lighting probably is someone's kink. But I get the feeling we're beatin' around the bush here, and time is money. Yours, of course. It is four ninety-nine a minute, after all." Bringing up the amount a call ran always scared the "just curious" off.

He whistled into the phone. "Wow. No wonder Landon was so rich. And I chose architecture. Anyway, where were we? Kinks, right?"

Marybell bristled. Shouldn't he be afraid now? It was time to play hardball. "Yes. Kinks. You know, fetishes. There are a million. Some we're forbidden to engage in, so tread carefully when choosin'."

"Do you have a list of them so I can decide? Do they cost more if I pick one but I want a side order of another? Maybe you could read them off to me? That'd be helpful," he said, his voice playful.

She was losing this round of take charge of the unruly man. Time to kick it up a notch. "Well, let's see—there's paraphilic infantilism. The fetish where you wear diapers. There's—"

"Whoa, whoa. Hold up. *Diapers?*"

Ah. Now she had him. He'd be ready to end this call in five seconds. "Well, yeah. You put on a diaper and wear it while I talk dirty to you." She had to fight from letting the giggle escape her throat.

"Huh. Had no idea. But you might be onto something here. Diapers could solve a lot of problems for the modern contractor. I don't have to climb down a fifty-foot ladder to use the facilities. I could keep right on working."

Marybell bit back a chuckle, wrinkling her nose. "Innovative."

"But then I think, will they come in my color? If I'm wetting my pants, I want them to be in a nice color. One that complements my coloring."

Marybell fought another snicker and made a face. If this was scaring him off, what was inviting him in? "Okay, no diapers. How about feet? Shoes, in particular. You like lickin' high heels?"

He sighed. "Not a fan of leather. It's tough and chewy and comes from animals and while I subscribe to the food-chain theory, I'm not a fan of wearing animals for show. Now, give me some good old-fashioned canvas, and we could have a plan. Or rubber. I hear Crocs have a distinct taste to them."

She couldn't hold it in anymore. She laughed—out loud—sort of barkish and ear-shattering. "Why don't you tell me what you really want, Tag?"

"I want you to go on another nondate with me."

"Did I mention I'm not only not dating, I'm also not nondating, either?"

"So you don't want any more friends? I hear you can never have too many."

"You didn't really just say that, did you? You have met Dixie, Em and LaDawn, right? My friend card is on full."

"But I'm an awesome friend to have. I fix things."

"Em fixes things."

"But can she build them from scratch?"

"I don't need anything built from scratch. I rent."

"Why do you resist me, resistant one?"

Okay, big guns, both-barrels-loaded rejection looked as though it was the only way to go. "I'm not resisting you." Marybell paused before she said the words—to be sure she'd get them out without her voice hitching or a shred of her real feelings creeping into them. "I'm just not interested."

"Did you hear that?"

"What?"

"The arrow through my heart."

Still, she had to ask why he was so interested in her. "Why me?"

"Why you what?"

"Why are you interested in me?" Of all the women in the world.

"If you're not interested, why do you care?"

"Just curious. I mean, I'm not exactly conventional. I always wonder what attracts a man to me."

"Your nose ring."

"You like my nose ring?"

"I'm fascinated by it. Did it hurt?"

"It pinched a little."

"And your hair."

"My hair…"

"Well, yeah. It's an art form. Isn't it like crafting a sculpture every single morning? That's gotta be a lot of work, and a fortune in hair gel."

If he only knew. An easy two hours a day between her makeup and hair. "It's just who I am." God, she was sick of saying that, sick of forcing herself to sound convincing. This wasn't who she was anymore. It once was, now it was just a way to keep the bad away.

"Listen, let's be honest here. No elephants in the room. No, there's nothing conventional about you. But conventional is everywhere. I can see conventional all over Plum Orchard, if I wanted to."

"Is this the part where you tell me how much other women want you in an effort to make me jealous?"

"Nope. What I meant was, I see the same cookie-cutter women all over this town. Most of them dress alike and sound alike. You don't sound or look like any of them, and you don't seem to care that those women don't like it. I like that you spit Plum Orchard in the eye. And c'mon, what kind of guy would I be if I didn't at least take a shot at a date with a woman whose job is as a phone sex operator? I'd be like a rock star with my friends if you'd just agree to another nondate."

Men. A truthful man. But still. Men. "That implied assumption should make me angry."

"I didn't imply anything. I was very direct and honest."

Marybell laughed again, cupping her chin in her hands—so tempted by his warm, chocolate-rich voice and his sense of humor.

You can't do this, Marybell. If you think life in the PO is hard now, just wait until they hear about who you used to be. "No nondates."

"All right, but I just bought some really good bologna. Not the generic stuff, either," he coaxed, grumbly and deep.

"Darn. Disappointment. It cuts like a knife."

He laughed. "I know the feeling. But I'm not giving up on you, Marybell Lyman. Because I know you like

me, too. So for now it's good night, but this isn't goodbye. Not by a long shot. You have a good night, phone
sex operator." Tag hung up without another word.

He should infuriate her with his pushy requests for
nondates and his stark honesty. Instead, Tag made her
long for him in the way one only can when they can't
have something they want.

Maybe that was why she was longing so hard?

Maybe if she had him, she'd decide she didn't want
him as much as she thought she did?

But maybe she'd like to try just to see.

But she absolutely could not.

Damn.

Marybell pushed her way through the doors of In a
Grind and headed straight for the counter. She loved
it here. Loved all the books lining the shelves above
the conversation area, loved the scent of flavored coffee brewing.

She loved the bright green and lemon-yellow overstuffed chairs and '70s-style flowered pillows. But she
never stayed here long. If she stayed long enough to
settle into one of those chairs with a book or her laptop, someone was bound to look at her just long enough
to make her worry they'd seen past her people shield.

She needed a good dose of caffeine to ward off her
maudlin thoughts and a sleepless night. She'd tossed
and turned the better part of it while bits and pieces of
her past haunted her.

Especially the bit involving Tag. Tag was conjur-
ing up all the images she'd tried hard to purge. He was
smiling now, but she'd seen him angry. Seething, spittin' mad, and deservedly so.

If only she could…

"Afternoon, Marybell. The usual?" Gordy Perkins asked with a smile. Gordy didn't seem to mind her hair and crazy makeup. He greeted her like everyone else, and that left her grateful. She wasn't up to fighting demons today.

"With extra whipped cream and sprinkles. I need the sugar today."

Gordy bobbed his red head. "Yeah. I can see that." He made a circle around her eye area. "You look tired today."

"Rough night slingin' sex, Marybell?" Louella asked sweetly, leaning against the counter in all her blond perfection.

Speaking of demons. Marybell popped her lips. She was in no mood for Louella Palmer. "Sorry you can't say the same, Louella?"

Louella's eyebrow rose. "Why are you all still here, Marybell? What's it gonna take to get Call Girls gone?"

"What's it gonna take to get you to find a new hobby? First it was cross-dresser shaming. Then it was birth-certificate tamperin'. Have you tried quilting? I hear it's like music. It soothes the savage beast."

Louella and the Magnolias, the town's group of snotty upper-crust socialites, had been hot on Call Girls heels with the wish to rid Plum Orchard of the apparent evil Dixie's company brought. So far, they'd been unsuccessful. When Landon had said he'd covered every possible technicality before moving the company here, he hadn't been kidding.

But it hadn't stopped Louella and crew rounding up people to sign petitions to have them run out of town. She'd balked at how Call Girls was ruining Plum Orchard's chances for better tourism. Because when you thought of exciting things to do, sleepy Plum Orchard was the first thing that came to mind. Right.

Louella's eyes narrowed when her transgressions were on the table. "You're all bad influences. The lot of you."

"Do you mean like the kind of influence that trashes little boys' lives and gets you a new nose courtesy of Johnsonville's finest plastic surgeon?" Marybell asked just as sweetly.

A few months ago, when Louella, in a jealous rage over Dixie's return, had revealed pictures of Emmaline's cross-dressing ex-husband in front of the whole town in the hopes Em would think Dixie was responsible, Louella and Dixie had had what Dixie called a tussle. That tussle had resulted in a broken nose.

Unfortunately, the result of that night had made for some hellish experiences at school for Em's boys.

It had died down now, mostly because Jax had taken on the school board like a gladiator, but it didn't change the fact that the Mags still had it out for them.

Louella's hand went to her nose in subconscious response and then her eyes narrowed. "I have no idea what you're talkin' about."

Marybell eyed her. "Really? Has your fast-and-loose memory forgotten that you dug up dirt on Em's mother and Dixie's father?"

In round two of "rid Plum Orchard of Call Girls," Louella had also been the party responsible for sending Em her real birth certificate, revealing she was Dixie's half sister and exposing her mother Clora's affair with Dixie's father all those years ago.

Thankfully, Dixie and Em were the truest of friends,

and neither had missed a beat when they'd found out. But everything Louella did was geared toward trying to create a rift between the women, and no one was immune.

Louella ran her tongue over her glossy lips, but shame, if she had any at all, didn't stop her from reminding Marybell she wanted them gone. "We'll find a way, Marybell. Might not be today, or maybe it will, but we'll find a way to rid this town of your kind of filth. You mark my words."

"Find a way to what?" Tag asked, wedging his way between the two women with a grin.

Oh, he smelled so good. "Shut us down."

Tag frowned, the lines in his forehead creasing beneath the edge of his knit hat. "Shut down Call Girls?"

Louella smiled, pretty, pink-lipped. She placed a hand on Tag's arm, curling her fingers into it. Marybell fought the urge to peel them away one by one. "Surely, bein' an uncle to a young, impressionable girl, you can't support such an establishment, Tag. Please tell me you're the sane one over in the Hawthorne household."

Tag looked down at Louella's hand, then directly into her eyes. "I support people who're just trying to make a living and go out of their way to keep their interaction with the impressionable youth of this town squeaky clean. I also support minding your own business."

Marybell's eyes flew open. He was taking up for her. Right here in front of everyone in the coffee shop. He absolutely had to stop being so attractive in almost every imaginable way. And she had to get away from him before she said as much.

Gordy placed her coffee on the counter and eyeballed

the three of them with a tentative glance. He was no stranger to coffee shop confrontations between the Call Girls and the Mags. "Can I get you something, Tag?"

Marybell threw a ten-dollar bill on the counter. "Whatever he's havin', it's on me. Keep the change, Gordy." She turned to Louella, leaned in and growled at her, "Good sparring with you, Louella." She snapped her teeth for good measure, pivoting on her heel and sauntering toward the door of the coffee shop.

"Hey!" Tag called after her, his wide hand engulfing a foam cup. "Wait up."

Marybell pretended she didn't hear him until he was right next to her outside the coffee shop. Big and rangy, he was even more handsome in broad daylight.

He leaped into focus in ways that made for loud, chest-thumping exclamations of "Look at me. I'm all rock-hard man, sent to tempt you with my chiseled beauty."

She pushed her eyes back to the ground to avoid consuming him with them. That unfamiliar beat to her heart began, thump-thump-thumping out an uneven rhythm that belonged solely to Tag. She hadn't dated a lot in her lifetime, but she'd definitely had a relationship or two, and none of them ever made her feel quite the way just standing next to him did.

Tag grabbed her hand and stuck it through his arm. "You didn't let me thank you properly for the coffee."

She tried to pull it away without drawing more attention to them. Though just the sight of freakish Marybell Lyman with a studly Hawthorne was enough to make the folks in the square gawk.

She knew what they were all thinking. Why would a perfectly good man tangle with the likes of her when there were plenty of single, respectable ladies in town to tangle with?

Tag tightened his grip, nodding at Kitty Palmer, Louella's mother, as they strolled past her. "So, thanks for the coffee. You didn't have to."

"You didn't have to take up for me with Louella. I don't think I've ever seen her hush her mouth so quick. I should be buyin' you a drink."

He stiffened, ever so slightly, his hand tensing and flexing before it relaxed. "Don't drink."

Marybell stopped walking, turning to face him. "Let go of my hand. People are staring."

He grinned—so warm—so perfectly adorable in all those gruff angles, her pulse managed a cartwheel. "Like you're not used to that. I mean, you have a nose ring. Let 'em stare."

She rolled her eyes. "Are you ever going to leave me alone?"

He hitched his unshaven jaw at her. "Are you ever going to go out with me again?"

"I already told you no."

"Then unless restraining orders are involved, it could be a while."

The cold wind ruffled through the stiff points on her hair, sending a chill of warning along her spine. *Remain indifferent but attempt to negotiate.* "What will it take to make you go away?"

"Ahh, negotiations," he said with a dazzling smile. "One more date. If you're not thoroughly impressed with me, I'll leave you alone forever."

Marybell gave him an arched eyebrow of disbelief. "Forever?"

"Yep. Act like you don't even exist. Walk-into-a-room, look-right-through-you don't exist."

Marybell hesitated. "What are we going to do on this date?"

"I'll cook."

"At your house?" She'd turned down every invitation in the book when Jax and Em invited her to their gatherings just to avoid seeing Tag. Now she was going to walk right into his lion's den?

"I was hoping you'd let me come to your house. Jax's isn't exactly conducive to privacy. Plus, I can't properly charm you if my family's in the mix. They're a nosy crew. Promise I'll even take dish duty."

She waffled, shuffling her feet while her hand stayed firmly ensconced in his. "But what will Blanche say?" Blanche hadn't been keen on renting her basement apartment to Marybell until Caine and his mother, Jo-Lynne, had intervened on her behalf. Now they shared a strange acceptance of one another.

Sometimes Blanche would drop off a piece of pie at her door. She never acknowledged it was from her, but Marybell knew, and she'd nod her thanks if they passed each other on their way into their separate entries to the house. No one could miss the enticing scent of Blanche baking one of her blackberry pies.

She mowed Blanche's lawn so she wouldn't have to pay an unreliable teenager, and Blanche acknowledged that by leaving her cold pitchers of lemonade on the front stoop.

She understood why Blanche kept her distance. As far as the Mags were concerned, she was consorting with a member of Team Sin. Marybell couldn't afford to rock the boat, and having a man over would surely rock the boat.

"Don't you worry about Blanche. She loves me."

Rules. They needed rules. "No funny business?"

He wiggled a dark eyebrow, the lines around his eyes crinkling upward. "Define funny."

"You know what I mean."

"Just awesome conversation."

Blowing out a breath, she decided she had two choices. One, let him keep chasing her until he ran out of steam. Apparently he had a lot of steam. He also had a lot of sex appeal. If he kept hanging around, she didn't know how long she could resist him, and resist she must.

Two, let him have this date and blow his mind with as much leather, makeup and mayhem as she could rustle up. "Fine. When?"

"Tomorrow night. You're off then, right?"

How did he know what her days off were?

"Em," he said, answering her silent question. "I asked very casually."

"The way you told them you kissed me. Was that casual?"

"It was a heat-of-the-moment confession. It'll never happen again."

"Swear?"

"Pinky-swear."

"Okay, tomorrow, my house, eight o'clock. You cook, we talk, I remain unimpressed, you clean up, you go home. For good."

"Done deal."

She stuck her free hand out to shake on it.

Tag grabbed it and used it to pull her close, clamping his lips to hers with a brief-but-searing kiss. His lips…she could get lost in his lips, warm, firm yet soft.

Just as her fingers were about to curl into his jacket, just as she was about to sink into all that muscle, someone whistled, reminding her where they were. Marybell dragged her mouth from his, taking a step backward, outwardly hanging on to everything she had to keep from letting him see how rattled his kisses made her. "The deal didn't include kissing."

"We Hawthornes seal all our deals with kisses. It's the Hawthorne family way. Do the Lymans do it differently?"

She wanted to be mad at him for catching her off guard, for practically shouting to the world what was going on between them.

But he was so doggone cute with her blue metallic lipstick smeared all over his lips she didn't have the heart. "An addendum to our deal."

He sipped his coffee and nodded, the long column of his throat working as he swallowed.

"No kissing."

"You're a fun stomper for sure, Marybell Lyman."

"Deal?"

"Deal." He tipped an imaginary hat at her. "See you tomorrow at eight."

On impulse, she pulled a tissue from her pocket and stood on tiptoe. "You have a little something ri-i-ight there," she teased, flattening her hand and dabbing at his mouth. She grabbed his fingers and put the crumpled tissue with smears of blue lipstick in his palm. "See you at eight."

Marybell hid her smile until she turned around, but the grin spread as she made her way across the square.

And then she remembered, she had to make this the worst date of his life.

That wiped the grin right off her face.

Six

"Are you payin' attention, Taggart Hawthorne, or are you daydreamin' about Marybell?" Em poked him in the ribs with an elbow and laughed.

"Uncle Tag?"

The mention of Marybell made Tag instantly fish for the tissue he'd stuffed in the pocket of his jeans and remember the smirk on her face when she'd wiped his mouth.

"Uncle Tag!" Maizy yanked on the edge of his hoodie.

His eyes finally found focus. He stared down at his niece, her fiery hair a red glow in the last remnants of afternoon sun streaming through the kitchen windows. "Yes, Miss A-Maizy?"

"You're not listening to Em, and she says if you burn the lasagna, it'll be your own fault. I bet Miss Marybell doesn't like burned lasagna. If you like her, you better pay attention, because that's what makes you not self-ish. When you pay attention to what other people like."

He swiped a finger down her cute nose. "Sorry. I was distracted." With thoughts of Marybell. All of his thoughts since she'd turned him down cold on the phone had been of Marybell. *Why?* Why couldn't he get her out of his head? "So, where were we?"

Em snickered. "We were at the part where you have to confess to Marybell that you can't cook."

He took the package of no-bake noodles from Em and shook them. "Of course I can cook. Or at least I'll be able to after you show me how."

Em wiped her hands on her apron and pulled Maizy in for a squeeze. "Would you go dig Gareth out for me, please, sugar? I just know your poor uncle Gage needs a break from all those questions he's been askin' lately."

Maizy nodded and skipped out of the kitchen, making Tag smile. For the most part, Maizy had managed to accept Gareth and Clifton Junior with open arms. They'd all worried that Maizy, being an only child, would struggle with Jax and Em's attention spread three ways. They'd worried that the boys, who'd only just adjusted to their father's departure a year prior, would struggle, too.

But Maizy and both boys had rallied with a little help from Em, and that only made Tag respect her more. She was a damn good mother. "She really loves Gareth and Clifton Junior. I'm pretty impressed at how seamlessly you've managed to blend this bunch."

Em stirred the sauce she'd shown him how to make in three easy steps. "Slow and steady wins the race. If Jax and I keep taking this one step at a time, eventually they won't even remember a time they weren't all together."

He liked that. He liked that Jax and Em were so solid about their decision-making. He liked watching them becoming a family. He didn't like the small pangs of envy he'd been feeling about it lately. He'd been so full of anger for so long that these new softer feelings still felt foreign.

"I hope you know that I take all of you into consideration, Tag. Not just Maizy, but you and Gage, too. I don't ever want y'all to feel like we're takin over. This was your home first." Em still lived in her house with the boys, and Jax hadn't popped the question yet, but Tag was guessing it wouldn't be long. They were about as crazy about each other as he'd ever seen two people. He wanted that for his brother.

Lately, he wanted it for him, too. He couldn't pinpoint when it had happened. He attributed some of it to Em's presence, her influence, her silent-but-gentle demand he figure his shit out, and he was trying. Some of it he had locked down. The rest was slow going.

Tag dipped a spoon into the sauce and tested it. As always, it was amazing. Thank God for Em. "This wasn't a home until you used the oven. As far as I'm concerned, if you keep cooking for us all, you can take over the world."

Em pulled up a stool at the breakfast bar and patted the one next to her. "So, tell me where you stand. I'm guessin' the other night went well? The bologna sandwiches?"

Tag slid onto the stool, pulling his cup of hot chocolate toward him. "It was a disaster. She hated every second she spent with me." Still, he grinned. There was something there, and he wasn't alone. She could fight it, or she could come along for the ride.

Em braced her head on her hand. "Couldn't have been that bad. She's lettin' you, er, *me,* cook for her tonight."

"She's only doing that because she thinks it'll make me go away. I told her she had to give me one more date before she shuts the door completely on dating me."

"I don't want to pry, and you don't have to answer if you don't want to. You just say, 'Em, mind your p's and q's,' but you've been turned out by her. Why keep goin' back for more?"

He didn't have the answer to that, either. He kept thinking, if she'd just let him hang out with her, the challenge of getting her to give him the time of day would dry up and blow away.

But when she'd agreed, and he knew full well she was intent on making him hate every second he spent with her tonight, it just made him smile harder. "I don't know. I know it's cliché, but there's just something about Marybell. I like her. She's got a sharp tongue. She's also a mystery." He wanted to see what was under all that makeup and hair—like he'd never wanted to see anything else in his life.

"What about Alison?"

The reference to his ex-fiancée made him bristle. Em knew all about his downward spiral and why he'd come to Plum Orchard. To pick up the pieces of his crapped-out life. "What about her?"

"Are you totally over her?"

His jaw went hard when he stared down Em. "I was totally over her the second she told me she was leaving me for a guy who still had a checking account." Alison wasn't the woman he'd thought she was, and he'd turned into a man he never thought he was capable of becoming because of that.

That's just an excuse, Tag. No one made you drink until you were stupid. You did that. It's a choice.

She waved a finger under his nose. "Don't you get snippy with me. Yes, I'm bein' nosy, but I'm doin' it because I'm lookin' out for my friend."

Tag rolled his shoulders. Alison wasn't easy to talk about. He'd trusted her completely, so totally, he'd have handed everything he owned over to her without a blink of his eye.

They'd been together a long time—known each other all their lives—and then one day, she'd turned into someone he didn't know. A liar, a cheat. She'd blindsided him and, worst of all, she'd left him questioning his judgment. How could he have been so deeply in love with someone and never know what she was capable of?

It only proved to him you never really knew anyone. You were always just scratching the surface.

Em gave him the eye. "So, Alison?"

"I'm definitely over her. Not sure I'll ever be over the shock of finding out she was cheating on me. Of all the things she could've done to shock me, that was never even a consideration."

Em smiled her sympathetic smile. "Fair enough, but I'm gonna tell you true about Marybell because I love her. She's my friend. We've all thought somethin' troubles her. Dixie's been over and over all the letters and DVDs Landon left about Call Girls and each of our employees. She's questioned Sanjeev until she's blue in the face, but he didn't leave a clue as to why he helped her, or what he helped her with. Maybe he just gave her a job because she applied."

"Well, that makes the most sense," Tag said. Yet he wasn't sure he even believed it.

Em shook her head. "But knowing Landon and that enormous heart of his, I doubt it. Every one of the operators has a specific reason Landon hired 'em. But Marybell's the only one who hasn't said a word. We don't push, because we don't want her runnin' scared. It's hard enough in the PO with all the cruel things people say. I won't have her feeling like we're on her back, too."

"But?"

The lines around Em's crystal-clear blue eyes deepened. "But there's *something*." She punctuated that with a finger, like trying to place it on the invisible something. "Something we all handle with kid gloves even though we don't know what it is. There's a vulnerable side to Marybell that worries me greatly. It worries us all. I don't know if it was man trouble or something else. But who up and moves to a small town where everyone will stare at you and sometimes openly berate you on purpose? She came here knowing what she was in for. Landon told all the girls what it would be like before he moved the company here. Who does that?"

He shrugged. "LaDawn?"

"Ha! Now, there's what I mean when I say all of the operators are there for a reason. Landon wanted her off the streets of Atlanta. But LaDawn's an open book. Once a lady of the evenin', rescued by Landon. Not a lady of the evenin' anymore. LaDawn hides nothing about her old life, and we like her just that way. But we don't even know if Marybell has a family somewhere. Maybe someone she had a falling-out with? She's been with Call Girls for quite a while and no mention of it. She never talks about high school or college or anything before she began working for Landon in Atlanta and then here in the PO. It's like she didn't exist before then."

Curiouser and curiouser. "She did say she has no family. She was a foster kid all her life."

Em looked almost hurt by that revelation, but her eyes held sympathy. "I had no idea. I'm a little hurt by that, in fact. I always feel like she doesn't trust us. Sometimes I wanna shout, 'There's nothing you can tell us that will make us love you less.'"

"What makes you think she's keeping secrets?" He'd love Em's take on it because he felt much the same way. The way her words were short and stilted when he'd asked about her family. The way her body language changed from loose to stiff in just one question.

"I wish I knew what makes me think we girls don't have her full trust. It's just somethin'. Like when we're all gabbin' about men and talking about our past boy-friends or crushes, Marybell gets real quiet. That's not to say all it could be is she's very private. It's just some-thin'…"

"So, what's your point here, Em?"

"Here's my point. Marybell is an amazingly giving human being despite what I sense are trust issues, and if she's here because she's been hurt before, don't you chase after her just for the chasin'. Mean it if you want it, Tag. This is the first time you've stepped out on that limb o' yours after all your troubles these past couple of years, so you have to be careful, too. Go slow."

He understood why Em was nosing around. She was doing what she always did: looking out for the women she considered family. "Slow and steady wins the race."

"Right. And my lasagna. Now," she said with a smile, hopping off the chair and pointing to the white ceramic pan she'd lined with her sauce, "let's impress our girl."

Tag followed her back to the stove, but his mind was

racing with the things Marybell had chosen to tell him and not some of her closest friends.

That had to mean something, right?

Marybell fisted the pointy thatch of hair on her head and pulled it high when it began to slump. It was time to chop some more of it off if she hoped to keep this Mohawk up to standard.

Maybe she'd just shave it all off and give Plum Orchard something else to gawk at. She pressed a stray strand that had somehow managed to escape the wrath of her gel and hair spray back into place, then grabbed the can of red hair dye and sprayed it, deepening the color.

It would be so much easier if she were simply running a brush through it or clipping it up in a barrette. Sometimes, when she had time on her hands and she was at home alone, she re-created Dixie's and Em's hairstyles, just to see what it felt like to be what society dubbed the norm. She loved the long layers and beachy waves Dixie wore so often or when Em threw her dark locks up into what she called a messy updo.

But if she wanted to stay here, with the people she loved, she was going to look like this when she was sitting in a rocking chair at the Plum Orchard Senior Center. She was also going to have to pray her voice didn't change with age in order to keep her job because it didn't look as though she was ever going to do anything else but talk dirty.

Satisfied with her eerie reflection and the new heavy white foundation she'd ordered online that made her eyes look like two black holes in her head, she flipped the bathroom light off and padded to the living room, where she waited with a sinking feeling for Tag to arrive.

To set the mood for her "Freak Tag Out" mission, she flipped on some Marilyn Manson and lit the candles she had left over from Halloween. They were black and suited her mood.

She'd spent a solid afternoon trying to figure out what kept Tag coming back for more, and she still had no answers. He was handsome and available, funny and smart, and he was chasing after the woman everyone called a freak. If he'd just go away, lusting for him from afar would be a picnic.

The ring of her doorbell had her wiping her sweaty palms on her zebra-striped leggings. She'd added extra studs to her eyebrow and thrown on as many pleather-studded items as she could find in order to ensure that she was at her freakiest.

Propping the door open, she grinned, knowing her black lipstick made her teeth look especially white. "How's it goin'?"

But it didn't phase Tag. He grinned, perfect, solid, smelling like tomato sauce and the outdoors, and held out a white pan—one that suspiciously looked like the pan Em brought to work when she made them all tater-tot hot dish. "I see you've dressed for the occasion."

What did she have to do to freak him out—swallow a flaming sword? "I won't apologize for likin' pleather." She curtsied.

That earned her another smile. "And studs," he said, handing her a bowl and a loaf of bread wrapped in tinfoil. "I like them on you. I especially like the trouble you went to in the eyebrow section of your face. Really shiny. I like shiny, too."

She took the bowl and loaf of bread without another word, walking to the kitchen, making sure her ugly green-and-black work boots made extra, unladylike noise.

Tag followed, dropping the pan on the counter. He let out a low whistle when he took a look around at the eerie glow she'd created with the candles. "Wow, are we sacrificing an animal tonight? You didn't say it'd be that kind of date. If only I knew, I would have brought my chalice and my voodoo dolls."

When she turned to face him, she had to cover the skip in her breathing and clear her throat. God. He was so roughly beautiful. Like one of those hand-carved wood statues with craggy edges and dark lines. "It's okay. I gave up ritual sacrifice. It's messy."

"Okay, but just so you know, I'm open to new experiences." Tag pulled his cap from his head and placed it alongside the white dish.

She'd never seen him without his knit cap. He had amazing hair. Probably considered too long for Plum Orchard, but thick and shiny and curling over the edges of his collar. She clenched her fists to stop herself from reaching out and brushing the strands from his eyes. "So, Em cooked, I see?"

He shook off his down jacket and hung it on the rack near the door, giving her a view of his incredible butt. He was officially killing her. "No. She *helped* me cook. I figured, if I premade stuff, I wouldn't have to spend all my time in the kitchen, slaving over a hot stove, and that means we have more time to talk."

Marybell stuck her hands in the pockets of her pleather vest. "A resourceful man. Good on you."

He rubbed his hands together. "So, I'll just stick this

in the oven, you turn up Marilyn Manson and then while the lasagna cooks, we can plan our grassroots attempt at cult leadership. That work?"

Of course he knew Marilyn Manson. What self-respecting god of beauty and insane body didn't? He was making it harder and harder to maintain a hefty level of indifference. She shrugged and wandered into the kitchen, popping open the door to her fridge. "Wine?"

He shook his head, his broad back to her. "Nope. Don't drink. Water's good."

Marybell pulled the bottle of Chardonnay out of the fridge and poured a healthy glassful. She'd drink straight from the bottle at this point, but she needed her wits about her to pull this thing off. "What's with the not drinking?"

He turned to face her, pot holders on his hands and looked her square in the eye. "Alcoholic."

Nice. You want to get rid of him, not dredge up his demons. "I'm sorry…I didn't…"

"Know? It's not like I advertise it. It is what it is. I'm past the point of shame, and just focused on staying on track." He turned back to the stove, pushing the pan into it without another word.

She forgot to stomp when she made her way to the living room because of his confession. He was all kinds of open book, and she was one big ball of secrets. Dropping to the couch, she sat quietly, the way she always did when she was in unfamiliar waters.

Tag was suddenly sinking into the couch right beside her, rocking her carefully balanced dinghy. He turned to face her, scanning her eyes. "You feel awkward now."

Bingo. "I didn't mean to pry or put you on the spot."

"I don't feel put on the spot. It's something you'll need to know for date two. You know, when I'm done impressing the life out of you."

"What made you drink?" *Snap out of it, Marybell! This is not the way to fly your indifferent flag.*

"What makes anyone drink? Escape, a way to numb the pain."

His words touched her—made her identify. It wasn't the tone of his voice or the words themselves. It was the brutal honesty he was so effortlessly laying on the table. If she'd had more money in her darker days, drinking might have been a solution she'd have considered. Now she hid it with hair gel and black eyeliner. "Pain?"

Tag shook an adorably crooked finger at her and smiled, the brackets around his mouth deepening so deliciously she wanted to run her fingers over them. "Uh-uh-uh. I get a question now."

She swirled the wine in her glass and sighed as if it made no difference to her. "Okay."

"Did you like kissing me?"

What woman, with lips on her face, wouldn't like kissing him? "It was okay."

"Rate it."

"I thought I got another question."

"That wasn't a question. It was a demand."

"On a scale of one to ten, or with letters?"

"Whichever you prefer."

"It was a solid four."

"You lie."

She bit her lip to keep from doing that giggle. "Well, it was really a three, but I don't want to trash your manhood in one fell swoop."

He lifted a raven eyebrow. "You're crazy generous. Okay, your turn."

"Pain. You said there was pain involved in your drinking." Why was she digging? To an outsider, it would appear she was taking some kind of perverse pleasure in his admission, knowing what she knew, but that wasn't the case. She needed to hear it as a reminder to stay away from Tag so she wouldn't invariably cause him more pain.

"I said it numbs pain. Not that I had any pain."

"So then it was escape?"

"That's two questions. My turn."

She rolled her hand for him to proceed, the studded bracelet she wore catching the glow of the candlelight, reminding her she'd dressed this way to scare him off.

"Why did Landon give you a job at Call Girls?"

"Because I'm really good at phone sex, and have you heard my voice? It brings all the boys to my yard." She ramped her Southern drawl up a notch.

He acknowledged her with nothing more than a nod. "Your turn."

"The escape. Was drinking a way to escape?"

"It absolutely was. I didn't want to be me anymore. When I drank, I definitely wasn't me."

She'd done that to him. Not directly, but indirectly. She was responsible for being too naive and stupid to know what she'd gotten herself into until it was all too late. Her chest became so tight she had to move away from him, move away from her guilt or she'd explode.

"Beautiful People" thumped out its angry beat and she leaped on the opportunity to move off the couch and turn it up, hoping it would block out her pain— Tag's pain.

Marybell kept her back to him, clenching her teeth to ward off tears.

"It's your turn," Tag whispered in her ear, his lips brushing against the eight or so studs she had in her lobes.

Tag's hot breath sent a wave of shivery delight skittering along her spine, making her nipples spike. Her fists pressed into her thighs to keep from leaning back against him, letting her head lie against the solid wall of his chest. Swallowing hard, she muttered, "I'm good for now."

Tag apparently wasn't done. He planted his hands on her hips and turned her around to face him. "Hit a nerve?"

Do it, Marybell. Tell him. Just say it. Then there'll be no more secrets. He might leave hating your guts, but at least he won't be chasing after a lie.

No. Don't do it. He'll tell Dixie and you'll get fired so fast you won't know your corn bread from your chicken-fried steak. Then, you'll be run out of town so quick your head'll spin around Exorcist-*style, and you'll lose everything you've worked so hard for—again.*

Remember the streets, Marybell? That's what will happen if you tell Tag. You don't have enough money in your savings account to last you more than a year. Landon pays you well, but life's expensive. The streets will eventually be your playground again. No one hires someone lookin' like you. Not for a respectable job with benefits and a retirement plan, at least.

She affected a cocky expression, stiffening in his embrace, ignoring the strength of his hands and the havoc that wreaked. "Nerve? I've got lots of it, but not much hits one."

Tag stared down at her so hard, surely his gaze would leave a mark. "I think that's what you'd like everyone to think, and you're pretty good at it."

"But you see the real me," she said dryly.

"I think I do."

He tugged her closer, their hips meeting until Marybell didn't think she could hold her breath any longer. The closer he brought their bodies, the harder it was to resist him. Instead of pushing her way out of his embrace, she reacted with her heart, not her head when she asked, "What do you see?"

He leaned in low, letting his lips hover at a very tender spot on her neck, his breath warm against her skin. "I see a nerve I'm about to hit."

And then Tag nibbled, splaying his hands across her back until their chests touched and his lips were skimming over the sensitive flesh, slow, hot, achingly gentle.

Her hands were supposed to go to his shoulders to give him a shove the way all girls should who weren't supposed to rub up against the men whose lives they'd been a part of trashing. But Tag made her forget everything and instead her fingers sank into the caps of his shoulder, clinging to him as her eyes slid closed.

She'd promised herself that no matter how manly, sexy, irresistible he was, she'd stick to the hands-off plan.

When his lips traveled along the column of her neck, leaving her swollen and achy in places she had no right to ache, she managed to forget everything.

Everything.

So much for sticking to the plan.

Seven

"Note," he mumbled when he skirted her jaw, "I'm not kissing you."

Why? Why aren't you kissing me? she wanted to scream in frustration when his hands strayed to the back of her head. That he got a handful of stiff spikes of her hair didn't deter him.

It didn't deter Marybell, either. She arched her back, letting the heat of his chest seep into hers, sighing when Tag licked just behind her ear, a shiver of longing pulsing through her body.

"Still not kissing you. I could, you know, if you wanted me to. But no pressure."

His rumbly voice, thick in her ear, slow and lazy against her flesh was her undoing.

Marybell didn't think. She didn't process. She didn't debate. She reacted by putting her hands on either side of his jaw and dragging his head upward. Her fingers sank into his thick hair as she planted her mouth on his with a sigh of instant pleasure at his grunt of surprise.

Firm, yet soft, delicious and perfect, she explored

Tag's lips, burrowed closer when he widened his stance and invited her between his hard thighs.

He was an amazing kisser, thorough, intense. "I'm kissing you," he murmured teasingly between the duel their tongues were having.

She didn't care. Nothing mattered but his lips. Nothing mattered when she put her arms around his neck and molded her body to his, loving every hard ridge, every dip and plane in his stomach.

Nothing mattered when her hands suddenly weren't in full cooperation with her brain and began to pop open the buttons on his fitted shirt.

Nothing mattered, not even when Tag began to make comical protests against her lips. She couldn't hear them. She couldn't see anything but Tag naked.

Without another word, she pulled Tag toward her bedroom, ignoring everything but the dull throb between her legs, a humming need for satisfaction.

The soft glow of her robin's-egg-blue lamp cast a romantic hue on her one luxury. A king-size bed covered in white-and-blue pillows with a thick white duvet she snuggled under every night was the only furniture aside from the whitewashed nightstand she'd bought at a yard sale.

Tag made her room look small—he made everything look small.

Marybell didn't waste any time. She peeled her vest off, dropping it on the floor, vaguely wishing she had cute underwear on, or at least a lacy bra. All she had was some Hanes, white and practical.

When she dragged her black T-shirt over her head, Tag hissed, moving in closer, the heat of his body matching hers. Circling her waist, he knelt in front of her, brushing his mouth along her naked belly before bending his head and untying her work boots.

It was a small gesture, nothing big or overly romantic, but this big man, at her feet, unlacing her shoes brought a sting to her eyes. A stinging she attributed to the overload of emotions racing through her, but still, they stung.

So Marybell closed her eyes and sought the place she'd been in just moments ago—the place where Tag made love to her, his muscles scraping against her skin, his mouth hot and wet on her, all over her.

Tag dragged her zebra-striped leggings downward, taking her underwear with them. He carefully lifted each foot out of them until she stood in nothing but her bra.

She wasn't ashamed of his scrutiny, or his assessments. She had small breasts, a narrow waist and more back end than she'd like. But she was okay with her body—she worked enough at it to know she was in fairly decent shape.

What she wasn't okay with was his next question. "Who's Doby?" He fingered the tattoo just above her hipbone, making her angry and hot simultaneously.

Marybell wobbled until he firmed up the grip he had on her waist. "He was my dog." A long time ago when she'd lived on the streets. A stray she'd found, knew she couldn't possibly keep when she couldn't even feed herself but kept, anyway. They'd spent five months together—five amazing months in alleyways and abandoned buildings.

The answer seemed to satisfy him. "He must have been a pretty great dog to earn a tatt."

Her throat tightened. The best dog ever. She'd gotten

the tattoo after she'd landed the job with Landon—in honor of the one living, breathing thing on the planet that had accepted her as is.

A deep breath later, she was looking down at the top of his head, mesmerized by his tanned fingers running over her fair skin.

He dipped them between her legs, slipping into her cleft, parting her flesh with such agonizing care her eyes rolled to the back of her head. No preamble, no skirting the issue, Tag's lovemaking was as straight up as he was.

Marybell widened her stance, allowing his surprisingly gentle fingers to roam, but when he slid the pad of his thumb over her clit she had to find the tops of his shoulders to steady herself. His tongue slipped into her as easily as his fingers, rough and soft at the same time, circling the aching nub with a wisp of a touch.

The groan that escaped her throat was husky and thick. It had been a long time since she'd been this close to a man, and if she'd even entertained reservations before, they flew out the window when Tag drove a finger inside her.

Her teeth clenched tight and her hips bucked forward as his tongue lashed against the sensitive bud. A deep ache in the pit of her stomach grew, hot like a liquid fire, spreading to every nerve, reminding her she was still alive.

Tag stroked her with his tongue, with his finger, until her legs began to weaken and her nipples tightened, scraping against her bra. She pulled him closer, luxuriating in the feel of his hair against her belly, his silken mouth exploring the most intimate place on her body.

The first vestiges of her orgasm were vague, a fleeting tingle of bubbling awareness, making her rock forward until it grew, wending its way across her flesh, forcing her to acknowledge her need to climax.

Marybell bit her lip to keep from crying out, to keep from begging Tag to keep doing what he was doing. Keep stroking, licking, torturing her. But she didn't need to; he sensed the tightening of her muscles and kept pushing until her toes curled.

When she came, it was, for lack of a better word, like enlightenment. Hot and sweet, a sharp sting, a full-bodied shudder of release.

That was her moan, one she tried to stifle, but it was still hers, low and hoarse. She clung to Tag's shoulders and rode it out.

Tag's arms tightened around her waist, his tongue buried deep inside her as she swayed until the moment passed and her vision cleared.

But that wasn't enough. It wasn't enough that he'd made her come—she wanted more. She wanted him naked, she wanted to see what was inside those jeans. She wanted all of it—now.

Giving his shoulders a tug, she pulled him upward, unbuttoning the rest of his shirt as he slid along her naked flesh, dying to run her hands over his chest, her palms itching to feel his skin.

Tag cupped her face, skimming his tongue over her lips, reviving the heat between her legs. "Bad news."

"No, no, *no*. No bad news allowed," she said, and she meant it. She wanted this, more than she was able to apply reason to. More than was like her.

"No condoms."

"Oh. I thought it was actual bad news. No worries— I have some."

His hands cupped her naked breasts, tweaking her nipples. "Do this often, then?"

She sighed into his neck, her spine arching her breasts toward his hands. "What if I did?"

"I'd have to wonder with who. There are all of three available men in Plum Orchard. I think one of them is Sanjeev."

She wrapped her arms around his neck, letting her body stretch the length of his. "Dixie sponsored a health class on safe sex for Plum Orchard High. The condom company sent boxes and boxes. She shared."

Tag nudged her jaw upward, raining kisses under her chin, blending their bodies together until she felt the hard ridge of his cock, pressing against his jeans. "Boxes and boxes? So much pressure."

As he unhooked her bra, she teased back. "You're letting me down here, Hawthorne. Don't blow it. They're in the nightstand."

"Well, then, let's do 'dis," he said in a comical New York accent, setting her away from him and unbuttoning his jeans while kicking off his shoes.

Marybell knelt on the bed, yanking open the nightstand drawer and pulling the box out. She grabbed one and planned to throw it at him until she caught a glimpse of Tag naked.

It left her struggling to breathe or even move. He was, of course, as close to perfection as she'd ever seen. His shoulders were wide, covered in muscles, his abs tight and defined, his hipbones sharp and even more defined.

Narrow hips led to thighs that bulged, thick and sprinkled with dark hair. They were the thighs of a man who spent many hours going up and down a ladder.

She didn't look away when she glimpsed his hard cock. Thick and erect, it gave her giddy pleasure knowing she'd inspired that.

But Tag's forearms, as thick and as rigid with muscle as his everything else, caught her attention. They held myriad tattoos—a snake, winding its way up toward his elbow, his sister Harper's name—and a Chinese symbol.

When he knelt on the bed, she ran her finger over the black ink, the pads of her digits skimming through the dark hair. "What does that mean?"

He slid one of those forearms under her waist and hauled her close. "Family," he whispered. "I got it when I got sober."

Her heart shuddered. *Family.*

She shivered when their flesh finally met, letting her hands roam over his broad back. Hiking her leg up over his hips, she handed him the condom. "You have a nice one."

Tag settled at the throb between her legs, slipping the head of his cock into her folds with a low groan. "I do. I have an amazing one. And right now they're all up in my attempts to get busy. I'll tell you all about them after," he grunted when she reached between them and stroked his long length.

Tugging at her lips, he slipped his tongue between them, cupping her breasts and tweaking her nipples until she moaned.

She was slick, wet and so ready when he trailed kisses along her neck and down to her collarbone. The heat of his mouth, the friction of their skin throbbed in her veins with a need long unfulfilled.

She wanted him in her, hard and thick—now. Until his lips surrounded her nipple, then she wanted him

in her doing that thing with his tongue, flicking over
the hard peak until sizzling heat thrummed through
her veins.

Bright colors flashed behind her eyes when he
wrapped an arm around her leg and lifted it higher,
poised at her entrance. She was greedy. She wanted
this. Wanted it so much.

"This is bigger than kissing," he husked against her
heated flesh. "Much bigger."

Marybell lifted her hips and reached between them
in answer. She didn't care what it was. She only knew,
if she didn't have it, she'd probably die. Or something
equally as dramatic. Twining her fingers around his
cock, she savored the hard length for only a moment
before she thrust downward.

Tag's grunt rang out in her small bedroom, raw and
husky, his hands sank into the flesh of her hip, his lips
sought hers, kissing her hard, sliding his tongue into
her mouth with hot spears that tasted of mint and man.

It took a moment to adjust. Her body pulling back
signaled Tag. He stared down at her, the heat in his eyes
turning her on. "It's been a while?"

A long, long while. "Yes."

He gritted his perfect white teeth. "Then don't move
much or we're goners. I'll try to go slow."

She didn't acknowledge it when she'd met him and
he'd kissed her the first time. She'd tried to ignore it,
fought to keep it at bay, but Tag inside her was what she
wanted. The rest be damned right now. All there was
was him, shifting his hips in a slow circle, cupping her
butt, holding her close.

Their bodies gyrated together, blended, fused in
a measured grind, letting Marybell adjust until she

couldn't take it anymore. Until she thought the sensations coursing through her would set off the ticking time bomb of hormones locked inside her.

Burrowing into his body, she pushed her hands up under his upper arms and clung to him, rolling against his lower body until he picked up the pace.

Tag nurtured the hot burn of orgasm building in her belly. He stroked her back, ran the heels of his hands over her shoulders, let his smooth chest create a delicious friction of skin on skin.

The wet ache between her legs throbbed, begging for release, and when he slipped a finger between them and stroked her clit, it happened.

A low humming noise sounded in her ears. Her thoughts got all jumbled and twisted until everything was blocked out but the delicious pulse of Tag in her— deep. So deep she lost her breath.

Her hands went to his hair, clutching the dark strands as she came, biting her lip to keep from screaming what felt like victory.

Tag's breathing became harsh and raspy, his thrusts wild and fast until he whispered her name against her lips and jutted his hips upward one last time before he came, too.

The room came back into focus for her in a vivid rush of dim lights and whitewashed walls. But when her guilt returned, it was in black, angry slashes and red, remorseful hues.

Her brain began to compartmentalize. Tag goes here—under "never again." Lies go there—under "will have to be told if you allow this to go any further."

Get out now while the gettin's good, Marybell. Say something rude, do something awful, but ship him off

*while you still can without getting any deeper. Tag isn't
the kind of man you can toy with.*

But Tag sensed she was pulling away—whether she
was physically, she didn't know. So he pulled her closer.
"Are you going to spoil the afterglow with all sorts of
protests?"

She looked over his shoulder at the picture on her
wall. A painting of a beach with bright whitecaps and
vanilla-colored sand. "I shouldn't have done this."

"I think we should do it again," he growled in her ear.

She shoved the fresh wave of excitement he stoked
in her aside and focused. "You have to go home now."

"Is it because of your landlord, Blanche? You're an
adult. You can have male visitors."

"No. It's because this shouldn't have happened."

Clearly, he wasn't getting it. He didn't move. Instead,
he nuzzled her neck. "Okay, I'll give you it was a whole
lot earlier than I anticipated. Yay for surprises, but to
say it shouldn't have happened is kinda harsh."

She shook her head. "I can't be involved with you."

"Why not?"

"Because I'm not available."

"You know, you've said that once or twice since we
met."

"Now I'm sayin' it again." She gave his rock-hard
shoulder a shove.

"Give me one good reason why you can't be involved
with me. One."

Ha. She could give him a hundred. "I'm emotionally
unavailable. I have issues I can't discuss."

"Now, this is interesting. Issues you can't discuss?
Physical or mental?"

"Both."

"You look pretty good to me physically," Tag purred in her ear.

"Then it's mental. Mentally, I'm incapable of having a relationship."

"So the issues you can't discuss are mental?"

"Yes. I'm off my rocker. You do not want a piece of that."

"Maybe I like women with off-their-rocker issues."

Maybe you should stop being so confident and go home—forever. Her heart didn't like that, apparently, because it jiggled in her chest. But Marybell ignored it. This couldn't go on. "You say that now, but that's what all the boys say in the beginning. Until…"

He leaned back, tilting her chin to force her gaze to meet his. "Now you're just trying to scare me off. So let's knock off the witty banter and get to the real issue. What happened? Did a boyfriend do something shitty to you? Cheat? Lie? Am I getting the backdraft of past failed relationships?"

She sighed a grating sigh and hardened her eyes for show. "Get dressed. Go home. Forget this ever happened." *Please.*

"Not gonna happen. I mean, I'll go home now. But I'm not forgetting that." He swished his finger in a circular motion.

"Fine. Then don't forget it, but it's never happening again."

"That's what you said about us kissing," he teased.

"Do you want this to end badly?"

"End badly how?"

"With me throwing you and your clothes out the door in front of the whole neighborhood."

He frowned. So adorable. "That is bad. Wow. You're mean."

"I can get meaner. Now go home."

Tag made a comical face at her, pulling from within her and moving away. He sat up on the edge of the bed. "Fine, but I'm taking my lasagna with me."

"That's fine by me. I have a spare body part in the fridge somewhere I can heat up…" Her voice trailed off when she caught sight of his back, and it wasn't just the incredible amount of bunched muscle catching her off guard.

He looked over his shoulder at her. "Now what?"

She had to put a hand over her mouth to keep from laughing out loud. "You have a Little Mermaid tattoo on your back," she said around her fingers.

He made another face, only this one wasn't as comical. "It's only as big as a billboard. Good eyes."

"I have to know. Why?"

"You're kicking me out of your house, but you want to know something personal like why I have a Little Mermaid tattoo on my back? You are off your rocker." He didn't have that teasing tone to his voice this time as he pulled his shirt from the pile of their clothes on the floor and slipped his arms into it.

Marybell rolled to the edge of the bed. "That's fair."

"Maizy," he shot back, stuffing his gorgeous thighs into his jeans and zipping them up.

Pulling the sheet around her, she frowned when she hopped off the bed. "Maizy wanted you to get a Little Mermaid tattoo?"

He planted his hands on his hips. "No. Not exactly. Though she likes it. Both she and the Little Mermaid have red hair."

"You're purposely bein' evasive and obtuse."

"Maizy loves the Little Mermaid. She was who I was thinking about when I got it. At least, that's what I think."

"You think?"

"I was drunk. All-nighter. Hit the tattoo shop and the one friend I had left at the time said I demanded a Little Mermaid tattoo. He's not my friend anymore."

"Because he let you get the tattoo?" she asked, tightening the sheet around her.

"No. Because I was an asshole to him like I was everyone else, and I wouldn't listen to him when he told me not to do it."

"And the artist gave it to you, anyway? When you were drunk? Isn't that illegal?"

"Artist is a subjective word. He wasn't exactly totally on the up-and-up. Plus, I did have cash."

"So now you have to live with a tatt of the Little Mermaid almost as big as Maizy on your back forever?"

He turned his back on her and grabbed his boots, shoving his feet into them. "Now, don't exaggerate. She's almost two inches shorter than Maizy. And that's the price you pay for being a drunk. Sometimes your choices last a lifetime." Tag strode out of her bedroom and toward the living room.

She followed, fascinated by how open he was about something so personal. "So it's a form of punishment?"

"No. It's a reminder of how one drink can turn your life into a nightmare of Disney princesses." Jamming his arms into his jacket, he grabbed his knit cap and headed for the door.

He was going to leave angry. He should leave angry. She was sending him packing as if he was meaningless. But she hated to do it. Wanted to apologize for it. Explain it. Yet she knew she couldn't. "The lasagna."

Tag paused by the door, all bulky and angry. But then, out of the blue, he smiled. As if he had some secret. "Keep it. It's better for you than spare body parts."

He popped the door wide-open, letting his image, bathed in the moonlight, be her last visual of him.

Eight

Damn it all. He should have waited. They should have waited until he was sure Marybell wouldn't throw up one of her walls.

That's what she did. Every time he thought she was letting him open the door a crack, she got out her trowel and her plaster and built another wall—higher than the last. They'd had four conversations to date, and in each one, she'd added more bricks.

Now she'd booted his ass out of her apartment as if he were some cheap thrill. But he knew it wasn't because she was into casual sex.

Really, Tag? And how do you know that? What are you all of a sudden—a mind reader? Stop applying all your AA theories to Marybell's life. That was your life. Not everyone was as screwed up as you.

No. For all her bluster and glib remarks, she was a lot deeper than she let on.

There was pain there. He knew that kind of pain. He was finding his way to the end of that kind of pain right now, and Marybell was like this bright light of challenge at the end of a tunnel he wanted to get to the end of.

That made no damn sense. He only knew he liked her. He liked her screw-the-conservatives attitude. He liked her smart-ass comebacks. He liked that she'd been the first woman he'd made love to after a long period of celibacy and it had been as sweet as anything he'd ever experienced.

He liked that they'd made love. He liked her soft skin, her full hips, the cinnamony taste of her. He liked that she had little to no inhibitions about her delectable body—he even liked her practical white underwear.

But he'd still moved too fast.

He'd hoped his sharing about his alcoholism would garner one from her. Instead, she'd clammed up tighter than ever before.

What would it take to get Marybell to go deeper with him? Why did he care? Why did he want to draw her out? She played tough, but there were glimpses of vulnerability. Moments when he wanted to gather her in his arms and tell her everything was going to be okay. But then she tucked back into that turtle shell and hid whatever it was she was hiding.

Was it shame? Was it fear? What made Marybell tick? Being around her was like playing a game of Ping-Pong. They went back and forth, back and forth until they wore each other down.

"What is that shit all over your face?" Gage asked.

He was in no mood for Gage and his jokes tonight, but his brother's words stopped him at the mirror in the entryway.

He grimaced. The mark of Marybell Lyman. A battle hard won. A war still raging. "Makeup."

Gage looked over his shoulder and nodded. "Yeah. So, something you want to share with me—or is this our little secret? Because if that's your new thing, I'm tentatively supportive."

"Tentatively?" he asked, digging in his coat pocket for a napkin to wipe his face.

Gage grinned, flashing his teeth. "You'd have to be a whole lot better at applying makeup than that before I could jump in with both feet."

Tag hardened is jaw. "Not in the mood."

Gage, the prettiest of the three of them, rolled his eyes. "Are we back to brooding again? Just when I thought you were getting it together, too."

"Bad night."

"With a door-to-door cosmetics saleslady?"

Finally Tag laughed, too, pulling off his jacket and hanging it up on the rack by the door. "Something like that." He padded into the kitchen, fighting the urge for a beer and grabbing a bottled water instead.

A beer would go down really sweet right now.

Almost a year and a half sober, buddy. Don't blow it. He tightened his grip around the bottle.

Gage followed behind, hopping up onto the counter. "You wanna talk?"

"Not yet. It's still too much to process."

"One more thing before I leave you to your brood."

"I'm not brooding. I'm just thinking. Anyway, shoot."

Gage made direct eye contact with him. "You hear old man Falsom's selling his mill?"

Tag's ears pricked in interest. "I heard."

"I think I might want to buy it from him."

"So you wanna stay here in Plum Orchard?"

Gage's eyes had that look they used to have when they'd bid on a new project together. He grinned. "I think I do. I like having Jax and Maizy here, but it won't be long now before Em and Jax get married. I don't want to intrude on that. Plus, I'd like a place of my own. You know, some privacy. It's time. Question is, do you want to stay?"

Tag nodded. It was definitely getting to be about that time. "I'm not sure yet." He sure didn't want to go back to Atlanta. He'd burned a lot of bridges there.

"Well, give it some more thought, and let me know. Because it'd be great if you went in on it with me."

He took a swig of his water before replying, "I don't have the money to go in on anything, Gage. That plays a big role in this." Tag was just barely making ends meet at the moment with the odd jobs he did around town. Buying into another business was the last thing he could afford to do.

Gage waved a dismissive hand at him. "Look, I'm tired of your pride. You keep going on and on about how you don't have any money, but I still do."

Tag was damn tired of his brothers offering to dig him out of this hole. "You were smart, kiddo, socking it away like you did."

"You paid me well. But that's not my point. My point is, you got screwed, and it sucked."

"Yep. I got trashed and then—even after I was trashed, I spent what I had socked away on booze and bullshit. I could've survived a decent amount of time until I found another job to keep me afloat."

"So you don't deserve another chance now that you're clean? You'd deny yourself the opportunity to stay here near Maizy and Jax and the kids and Em and do something that you love just because you still want to punish yourself?"

"It's not a punishment." *But it is, Tag. Being poor is your reminder. It's the bookmark in your life, the folded edge of the paper where you left off and your life went to shit.*

"Whatever you're calling it, it's keeping you from getting off your ass and doing something. Do something with me. Just like we used to. Remember when we built houses together?"

"You mean before Leon Kazinski stole every penny I invested?"

Gage's eyes narrowed. "Here we go with the I'm-such-an-idiot thing again. We had a nice long reprieve from that for a while, but look, it's back with a vengeance. *Yes,* Tag, before that. Before you got caught up in a Ponzi scheme and lost Hawthorne Brothers, twenty employees and a dozen or so subcontractors. Does my saying it out loud make it better or worse? Does it drive the knife of punishment as deep as you want it to go? Or do you want me to go deeper? Maybe bring up Alison?"

Tag's brother's anger with him was justified. He'd milked this long road back from perdition for a long time. Maybe it was rubbing him especially raw today because he wanted to date Marybell, and dating cost money, something he didn't have a lot of.

His personal anger only came in flashes lately, but it came hot and hard when it did, especially when the mention of the people he'd had to let go came up.

That was worse than losing his own money. "Sorry. Sometimes it still crops up. But that's not all of it, Gage. What if the mill didn't work out? I don't want you going down again because of me."

"I didn't go down the first time because of you. I wish like hell you'd separate those two issues in your head. Not. Your. Fault. Either way, we were a good team, bud. A really good team, which is why I have so much money in the bank. You'd do the same for me if our roles were reversed. So because I don't want to rile your crabby ass up, I'll leave it at that for now, but Falsom's gonna put it on the market soon, and I want in before anyone else. So make it quick with all that brooding you're so good at and make a decision."

Gage slid off the counter and slapped Tag on the shoulder before taking his leave.

Gage was right. He was still stuck. Stuck somewhere between finding his way out of the mess he'd been in, accepting that it had happened and moving on.

He was almost there. Sometimes he thought he was there.

There were days when he didn't get that slice of searing pain in his gut thinking about how stupidly blind he'd been about Alison or about his sister Harper's death. In fact, a couple of weeks could go by before something reminded him of his sister.

But he still wasn't past having everything he'd worked almost his entire life for taken away from him by a greedy, scumbag son of a bitch like Leon Kazinski, and his even greedier intern, or femme fatale as the press had dubbed her, Carson Chapman.

They'd taken off with his money, disappeared as if they'd never existed and left him with nothing but the money in his savings account.

So hell, yeah. That still stung like a bitch.

Marybell's mouth dropped open as she crossed the street from the square and headed toward Call Girls.

A dozen or so people were assembled, tucked into

winter jackets, their heads in an array of colorful caps, holding signs as they paced along the sidewalk.

Signs that read Keep Plum Orchard Pure!

They were picketing Call Girls? Priceless.

Marybell skirted the crowd gathering and pushed her way toward the path that led to the guesthouse, pleased with the sound of the clank of the chains at her waist.

Leading the pack was none other than Louella Palmer. Marybell sidled up beside her and growled. To her maniacal delight, Louella jumped. "Gee, Louella, didn't you get that hobby we were talkin' about the other day? Or is knit one, pearl two too complicated?"

Louella swung around, her fluffy blond hair catching on one of Marybell's eyebrow rings. She tugged at it with a hard yank, and irate eyes. "I'm just doin' the right thing. You women are bringing filth to this town. You're all a bad influence on our youth, deflowerin' their innocence. And me and the Mags here are determined to see you all gone, sooner rather than later."

Annabelle Pruitt and Lesta-Sue Arnold stopped their endless motion and came to stand behind Louella.

Marybell crossed her arms over her chest and grinned, the kind of grin that made her makeup look as if it came fresh out of someone's worst nightmare. "You spelled fornication wrong, Annabelle." She flicked the homemade sign with a finger, successfully making three Mags jump at once.

Lesta-Sue made a face, from far enough away that she felt safe, but still it was a face full of scorn. "You take your Satan-worhippin' self elsewhere, Marybell Lyman. We're picketing your establishment and all it stands for!"

"Fornication!" she yelled into the crowd, placing a

finger under the word on Annabelle's sign. "*F-O-R-N-I-C-A-T-I-O-N!* Forn-i-ca-tion!" Tapping the sign, she said, "It's not *F-O-R-N-I-C-A-S-H-U-N.* An easy mistake. You just sounded it out wrong, Annabelle."

Annabelle's face went sour, her cheeks bright red. "Go away."

She clucked her tongue and made a sad face. "That's not very inclusive of you, Annabelle."

"You are not welcome here, Satan worshipper," Lesta-Sue whisper-yelled, her eyes fierce and fiery.

There were rumors in town Marybell worshipped Satan because of the music she blared from her car and her crazy out-of-place makeup and hair.

She didn't tell anyone otherwise, but she did show up at church every single Sunday, even if she'd worked the night shift the evening before.

It was her personal, but very public, stab at their scorn. "You're a mean one, Lesta-Sue. Cuts me right to the core, but at least your spellin's better than Annabelle's. You got the word *deflower* down. Up top on that." She held her hand up to a glacial response.

"We've got a petition going, you know. Won't be long now before we have enough signatures to take it to Mayor Hale, and then he'll have to listen, and not even all of Landon's money will save you lot," Louella said, dropping her sunglasses back down over her eyes.

Marybell cocked an eyebrow at one of Plum Orchard's finest. She'd practiced in the mirror, raising an eyebrow with all the goop on her face, and her eyebrow rings made her look like the epitome of creepy. "I hope you didn't let Annabelle write it. Who knows what you'd end up petitioning?"

Among the crowd, she saw Blanche duck under the

cover of a towering oak, avoiding Marybell's eyes. It didn't hurt her feelings that her own landlord didn't acknowledge her.

The pressure of the Mags was intense with all their decades-old rules for decorous behavior. Renting to Marybell via the blackmail of Caine and Dixie's money was one thing, doing it of her own free will quite another.

Nanette Pruitt adjusted her fancy hat with the feathers and shook her sign at Marybell, repeating her daughter's words, pious indignation in her eyes. "Satan worshipper!"

Marybell laughed. "Nice one, Mrs. P, but can you spell it?"

"Nanette Pruitt, for shame," Tag drawled from behind Marybell. "Are you pickin' on my girlfriend?"

Yeah. Are you picking on his—his—wait, his what? She was ready to turn around and protest, but Tag draped an arm around her shoulders, pulling her to his side, and she forgot to protest because he smelled so amazing. Looked so amazing.

Nanette's face screwed up, but her eyes softened in Tag's direction. "Your girlfriend? Have we lost another Hawthorne to the likes of these Jezebels?"

Tag grinned down at her. "Lost? I don't feel lost."

"Surely you're lost, Taggart, if you're datin' the likes o' her."

"Then I like being lost, Miss Nanette."

She harrumphed him, the rolls of her neck jiggling against the pearls she wore around it, and stomped off.

Tag squeezed her tighter. "So, how are we today, Marybell Lyman? Still basking in the glow of the other night? Ready to do it again?"

She gave him her elbow. She'd thought of nothing but Tag since he walked out of her door the other night. Tag and his lips. Tag and his muscles. Tag, Tag, Tag.

"I'm not your girlfriend. Stop givin' people the wrong impression." Especially all of these people. People who'd just as soon see her strung up in the town square than corrupting one of the rare bachelors in town.

He looked down at her, his blue eyes sparkly and amused among all those thick lashes. "You know, that hurts. You don't care if people think you worship Satan, but letting them think you're my girlfriend is the worse of the two evils?" He pounded his fist against his heart. "Ouch."

"You know," she mimicked him, shading her eyes from the bright sunlight, "you'd think after the other night, you'd be too embarrassed to be within a hundred paces of me." And angry. How could he not be angry with her for booting him out of her apartment?

"Why? Because we had amazing sex and you not only kicked me out, but kept my lasagna I worked so hard to impress you with?"

"Shhh!" Marybell stood on tiptoe and pressed her hand to his mouth, still surprised he was in such good spirits where she was concerned. "Blanche is here. If she finds out you were at my place—"

"Making amazing love to you—"

"Stop! Clearly, you can see, I have plenty of trouble without you adding to it."

"Only if you agree to have a real dinner with me again. Otherwise, I'm telling everyone in the square we—"

"Okay!" she yelped. Anything to hush him.

He nibbled at her fingers, making her giggle. Tag placed a finger over her mouth now. "Shhh! You don't want people to actually believe you're enjoying yourself, do you? Next you'll have them believing the sunlight doesn't hurt."

Marybell bit her lip hard to keep from laughing out loud. "This is blackmail."

"Yeah. Of the worst kind. The food kind."

"Name your terms."

Tag rocked back on his heels, clearly smugly satisfied with himself. "Madge's, tonight."

"That's it?"

"Well, the last time I named my terms, look what happened. We ended up sleep—"

"Shhh! Okay, okay. Madge's. What time?"

"Six sharp. Make sure you wear extra hair gel."

"Why?"

"Because I plan to make it curl and that would ruin your spikes." Swooping down, he dropped a kiss on her lips. "See you tonight."

The stares of the most disapproving in Plum Orchard bored holes in her back as she made her way to the guesthouse, but she couldn't hide the smile on her face.

Which, if she were a smart woman, she'd wipe directly off her face this instant.

She'd agreed to another date with him.

What had made her do that? What had possessed her to encourage being found out? She couldn't keep dating Tag. It was one big fat lie. She'd have to lie to him every moment she spent with him. She knew beyond a shadow of a doubt, if she truly wanted Tag to stop pursuing her, he would. Because he was a gentleman.

Which meant she had to either give in or really take a

stand. A real stand. Not the kind of stand where she let her needs send the mixed message she'd been sending.

Tell him. Just do it.

No. I'll lose everything. Everything I have. Millions of people didn't believe me—why would my friends feel any differently than millions of people?

Millions of people don't know you. Dixie and the girls do.

No. No, they don't. They don't know the Marybell before Landon. They don't know the woman who had no place to live. Who lost her scholarship and ended up sleeping in abandoned buildings and alleyways.

They don't know the woman who dug food out of Dumpsters.

You're ashamed.

Of course I'm ashamed. I sank so low. The lowest I've ever been. Dixie and the girls know Marybell the phone sex operator with the youthful, innocent voice and the spiked hair who thumbs her nose at propriety. They don't know she was a homeless squatter.

If she could just get Tag to go away—leave her alone—move on.

Because you did a stand-up job of that, didn't you? Sleeping with a man doesn't succinctly say, "Go away." Now you've agreed to another date. You're sending out mixed messages, and that makes you a tease. Add to that, you're a liar. What's your trifecta?

Just one more date. One more and she'd call it quits. Hang up her datin' shoes and become a spinster.

Just one more.

Nine

Sliding into the booth at Madge's while she waited for Tag, she winked at Essie Guthrie, one of the older Magnolias, and waved. While she mostly liked to keep a low profile, she hated the way the Mags treated Dixie.

It made her act out in ways she wasn't always proud of. From behind her people shield, fighting back was much easier, though. She used that protective cloak to loosen up the part of her that normally remained silent in the face of injustice.

Essie turned her nose up at Marybell, making her chuckle. She grabbed a menu and tried to focus on how she was going to end this madness. Every second she spent with him was every second she spent lying to him.

You're doing that whether you're with him or not, Marybell.

Tag breezed in, lifting a hand to Coon Ryder before swinging around, a bouquet of yellow-and-purple flowers in his hand. He handed them to her with one of his delicious grins. "I imagine you'll probably pluck the heads off these, but at least it'll remind you of me when you're doing it."

Rolling her eyes, she took them from him. She loved flowers. No one had ever bought her flowers before. It might seem unoriginal to the more experienced dater, but to her, it made her breath hitch. Still, she caught herself before she gushed. "Thank you. What made you choose yellow and purple?"

"They didn't have any black?"

Marybell cracked her knuckles. "Okay, so we're here. Let's eat and get this over with."

Tag walked his fingers across the table and snatched her hand up. "Don't make me call you my girlfriend again. Now play nice and decide what you want to eat, cranky."

She snatched her hand away and shoved it under the table. "Stop calling me your girlfriend. You can't make me be your girlfriend if I don't want to be." The mature response, of course.

He held up a finger, and mimicked her voice. "Shhh! Stop using the word *girlfriend*."

There was no stopping her giggle of laughter, which was probably some type of encouragement she shouldn't indulge in. "Fine. Let's just order and be done."

Tag fanned the menu out in front of him with a snap. "So, what do you like to eat, Marybell Lyman? The freshly plucked wings of moths? Souls, perhaps?"

"Moths are for the ill-informed novice. Butterfly wings, now—butterfly wings, they're for the true connoisseur." Staring down at the menu, she kept her eyes on the shiny plastic and off his incredibly gorgeous face.

"I doubt Madge has any of those. I think they're too delicate to dip in gravy."

"Pity. Guess I'll have to settle for a cheeseburger with bacon."

"Favorite food?"

"Lobster thermidor."

He whistled. "Fancy, Ms. Lyman."

"Landon. He taught me a lot about food. Your favorite?"

"Hot dogs dripping in chili and onions and cheese. I know, not the most health-conscious choice, but there it is. Favorite color?"

"Pink."

He dropped the menu, giving her a comical look of disbelief. "It is not."

"It is, too." She loved pink. She'd wear more of it if her people-shield clothes came in any other color but black and deep reds with the occasional splash of purple thrown in.

"I've never seen you wear a single pink thing."

"Who said I had to wear it on my body to like it?"

"I was stereotyping, wasn't I?"

"It's to be expected. Your favorite color?"

"Green. Dark green, not the minty frilly kind that looks like a SweeTart. A manly green." Tag wiggled his eyebrows over the menu.

"Favorite movie?"

"The Notebook."

Marybell snorted, making a few heads snap up in the surrounding booths. "Stop."

"Okay. Never saw that. I was trying to be a sensitive male. Truth is, anything that blows things up or makes me laugh. Yours?"

She shrugged. There wasn't much TV watching when you were a foster, and certainly no extra money to see a movie. Being a poor college student, then homeless didn't lend itself to many movies, either. "I don't really have one. I haven't seen very many."

"Not a fan of the movies?"

"No. I love them. Just haven't gotten around to seeing very many." *Nosy.*

"So you've never seen *The Little Mermaid? Cinderella? Beauty and the Beast?*" He gasped in that goofy way he had. "I'm sure they'll all offend every feminist sensibility you own, but all little girls should at least see the classics once if for nothing else than to scoff derisively at them. Not even *Snow White?*"

She shook her head. "Not a single Disney princess."

He made a disgusted face, scrunching up his nose. "Well, we'll just have to fix that."

And here she was, being sucked in again. She slammed her mental brakes on. "This is our last date. No fixin'."

"Right. Tell me that after you've seen *Aladdin* with me. There's nothing like a little Jasmine to change your life."

"You've seen them all?"

"Don't be ridiculous. Of course I have. I live with the ultimate princess. You know, Maizy?"

He watched Disney movies with Maizy? Her heart fluttered. She'd seen him with Maizy a time or two at town events. They were sweet to watch together. But she hadn't realize he was so involved with her.

"Princess night is a big deal at our house. We all have to wear fluffy boas and crowns on our heads. We make popcorn and milk shakes. I've seen them all. I call you're a *Mulan* girl. A badass who dresses up like a boy to save her country."

"Bet you're glad Em's around now so you can retire

your boa." *Cynicism. Good on you. Keep that candle burning, Marybell.*

Tag shook his head. "Oh, no. I wouldn't miss princess night for the world. It makes Maizy happy. It makes her happier that Em joins us. That's all that matters."

No matter how hard she tried to knock him down, he just kept getting back up again, and when he was on his feet, he was right back to making her heart do jumpy things in her chest.

Their waitress, Carlene Clement, approached their table as if she were approaching alien life-forms. Marybell was used to it. She did, after all, growl at Louella on a regular basis.

But Tag smiled at her, warm and reassuring. "It's okay, Carlene. She doesn't bite. Satan worshippers only snarl. All bark, you know?"

She couldn't hold it in anymore. Her mouth opened wide and she laughed, scaring poor Carlene. She clapped a hand over her lips before saying, "Sorry, Carlene, but I promise, I really don't bite." And then she laughed some more.

"Look who it is. Marybell and Tag." Louella strolled up behind Tag's shoulder to center herself beside their table.

Tag leaned forward over the table and whispered, "Enter the evil queen. You wanna hide your face in my chest like Maizy does?"

Marybell snickered. "I think I have this." She turned toward Louella, perfectly coiffed, perfectly outfitted for a night of dastardly dealings, holding a steaming cup of coffee in one hand and a book in the other. "Look who it is, the petition starter. Did you get enough names to go to Mayor Hale today, Louella?"

Her pink lips flattened, meaning no. But she rallied in the face of adversity "We're very close. You women better watch out. You'll be out of business in no time."

"Optimism is healthy, Louella. I hear it's good for the skin," Tag said, keeping his face so serious it was hard for Marybell not to scream with laughter again.

Louella smiled. "Never you fear, Taggart. We'll get Plum Orchard cleaned up, if it's the last thing we do so your niece Maizy can be raised up right."

"Never you fear, Louella. Maizy's raisin' up just fine."

Louella pursed her glossy lips, and then her brow furrowed. "Did you get another eyebrow ring, Marybell? Heavens, how many can you fit on that little head of yours?" she asked, leaning in to look closer, bumping into the table and dumping hot coffee all over Marybell's jacket and down the front of her tank top.

Marybell jumped up out of the booth, trying to stifle a screech of pain and pull off her pleather jacket. Tag was at her side in an instant, using his napkin to mop up the mess.

Louella held up another napkin and waved it, her eyes assessing the damage. "Oh! So sorry, Marybell. It was an accident."

Marybell leaned over Tag's shoulder and snarled at her.

"Now, now," he whispered against her ear. "Never let the evil queen see you sweat."

Grabbing more napkins from the table, she wiped off her bare arms as Louella made her way out the door. "I'm soaked." *Damn Louella Palmer.*

Tag bobbed his head. "You sure are."

Disgusted, she threw the napkin on the table and

grabbed her soaking-wet jacket. "This was a mistake, Tag. I have to go."

He grabbed her arm and shook his head, looking down at her sodden shirt. "Oh, no. No way am I letting you go out into the cold night air with nothing more than a wet tank top on. You'll get sick. Take my jacket and I'll walk you home. You can give it back to me when we get there."

"You don't have to." She'd lived through far worse than a cold walk home to her warm, dry apartment.

"No. I have to. Em would have my head. Besides, I like you. You like me. We like each other. What beats a nice moonlit walk home between two people who like each other? Nothing, I say. Also, I need my jacket for tomorrow." He nabbed his jacket and held it up for her.

She sighed, shivering, but allowing her arms to slide into it. "Fine."

All eyes were on her and Tag as they made their way out of Madge's and into the chilly night. She stomped down the sidewalk, tucking Tag's jacket around her. It smelled like man and laundry detergent. It was all she could do not to burrow her nose in it.

"Hey, wait up. I didn't dump the coffee on you. It was the evil queen. I'm the handsome prince."

She slowed her pace, sending him an apologetic look. "Sorry. Sometimes it's all I can do not to resort to physical violence with that woman."

Tag grabbed her hand, letting it swing between them as they crossed the square. "She's a mean one. You think that petition she's got going will cause trouble for all of you?"

"In a town this size, I imagine it wouldn't take many to get the mayor's attention, but Landon was a pretty thorough man. I have to doubt he left many openings for the Mags. He knew what they were like."

"Good. I'd hate to think of you all losing your jobs. I often wonder if Landon didn't bring Call Girls here as a slap in the face to some of the backward thinking that goes on."

She shook her head, feeling one of her spiky strands of hair fall to the side of her face. "I'm sure some of it had to do with that, but mostly he said it was because he wanted to know we'd all be taken care of. He knew Sanjeev and everyone at the big house would look after us. Secretly, I think he wanted to incite change. We could all be doin' this phone sex thing from our bedrooms and no one in Plum Orchard would ever be the wiser. I'm convinced it had to do with lighting fires under their stodgy butts."

Tag didn't say anything; instead, he held her hand in his, warm and secure, passing the houses in her neighborhood in peaceful silence.

When they got to her door, Marybell placed a finger over her mouth so they didn't alert Blanche and her poodle, Taffy. She dug her key out of her wet jacket pocket and jammed it into the keyhole, flipping on the light in her living room.

Worming her way out of his jacket, she handed it to him with a smile. "Thanks. Prince Charming has nothing on you."

He took it, but instead of putting it on, he threw it on the hook by the door, inching closer to her until they were almost close enough to touch. "You do realize, all princesses feed their princes."

Ah, she saw what he was angling for. "I'm not your princess." When she was younger, one of her foster parents had called his daughter princess, and she'd always wondered what it would be like to be daddy's little girl.

"Fair enough. But you did promise me dinner."

Pulling her shirt from her torso, she made a face. "And look how that turned out."

"Tell you what. You go grab a shower and wash off all that coffee. I'll heat up the lasagna from the other night. Still have it in the fridge?"

"If I say yes, will my obligations be fulfilled?"

"You bet."

"Okay, but dinner and you're gone."

"Yeah, yeah. Go shower—you stink," he teased, dropping a light kiss on her lips.

She padded to her bathroom, wondering how she was going to avoid washing all her makeup off if she showered.

Her people shield was becoming an enormous drag.

Twenty minutes later, Marybell reappeared. Makeup still in place. He'd hoped to finally see what was behind all that makeup, but she was working pretty hard to keep him from seeing it. But he was pleased to see she'd thrown on a simple T-shirt and a pair of jeans that made her ass look amazing.

His mouth began to water, and it wasn't because he was hungry for lasagna. He was hungry for her. Hungry to get her to get past whatever was keeping her from going out with him. Every time she loosened up, she just reined it in tighter.

Setting out the plates at her small breakfast bar, he folded some napkins and placed silverware on each one. "Sit," he directed, smiling when he noted the humid shower had made her spiky Mohawk sag to one side.

"Smells good," she commented, folding her hands on the breakfast bar. She was back to stiff and uncomfortable. Another brick in her wall.

He dug out the pot holders and opened the oven, pulling the lasagna out and placing it on top of the stove. "And I made it myself." He grabbed their plates and put a healthy portion on each of them.

Her hazel eyes, shrouded by black glittery lids and a white stripe in the crease, acknowledged his efforts, but nothing more. She jammed a forkful of the lasagna into her mouth, dabbing daintily at her dark purple lips with the napkin. "Hmm."

"See? So, where were we before Louella showed up?"

"Boas and tiaras," she offered, sipping from the glass of wine he'd poured her.

"You should join us on princess night. I think you'd like it. We have an extra pink boa."

She scoffed the way all tough girls did when it came to frilly things. "I'm not much of a pink boa, tiara girl."

Thwarted again, Hawthorne. "Books? Do you read?"

"I do. This probably won't surprise you, but I'm a horror fan."

"Stephen King?"

She nodded, jamming more lasagna in her mouth as if it were a lasagna-eating contest, but she couldn't hide her smile.

He held up his fist to her to bump. "Huge fan. Also like a good medical thriller."

Now her eyes lit up when she fist-bumped him back. "Me, too. Have you read James Patterson?"

"Alex Cross. All-time favorite. You tried any Robin Cook?"

"Coma!" they said together. She laughed and nod-

ded. Now the other Marybell was back. The one he damn well knew wanted to participate.

The one who liked a good laugh.

"You've got sauce on the side of your mouth." He leaned forward to wipe it away, but even that crazy dark purple lipstick was irresistible. The hitch in her breath when he moved in close, even more irresistible. It made him hard in his jeans, uncomfortably so.

He didn't want to eat lasagna. That was the thought that fueled him when he kissed her harder, letting his tongue slide between those delicious full lips. When she sighed into his mouth, he wrapped an arm around her waist and pulled her in close, knocking his stool over in the process.

In his defense, she let him, dropping her fork and wrapping her arms around his neck, melting into him until he hiked her legs up around his waist.

All he wanted was her naked. Naked and his mouth on her—all over her. He wanted to be deep inside her, so deep she'd scream his name.

He grabbed at the edges of her T-shirt, more than a little pleased she wore no bra. He cupped the undersides of her breasts, pushing them upward until his fingers found the rigid peaks of her nipples. He tweaked at the tight buds, hearing her gasp of air, her low moan of pleasure.

Marybell's fingers found his buckle, pulling his belt out and popping the button holding his jeans together. She unzipped him in a matter of moments and swept his jeans and underwear down over his hips until there was nothing between them but her clothes.

Wrapping her fingers around his cock, she began a slow stroke, forcing him to thrust forward into the soft flesh of her hand. He had to grit his teeth to keep from coming right then and there. So he focused on getting her jeans off, shoving them away so he could get his fingers inside her, stroke her hot flesh, feel her squirm when he spread her.

Everything about her was fiery, from her personality to her body, and as she slid along his frame and positioned herself between his thighs, he found her mouth was, too.

She wasted no time when she pushed him back against the breakfast bar and yanked his boots and jeans off. Then it was nothing but him in a shirt and a pair of socks.

The first lick she took of his shaft made him dizzy, left him clinging to the red-and-green spikes in her hair. Her tongue was soft, silky on him, easy, but hitting all the right pressure points. When she enveloped all of him while he watched, cupped his balls with gentle fingers, stroked that spot on his cock just beneath the head, he had to make her stop.

Hauling her upward by her arms, Tag lifted her straight up and off her feet, planting his mouth on hers and kissing her until she melted against him again—soft, hot—pliable. "Condom. Wallet, back pocket of my jeans," was all he could manage while she scooped his jeans up and retrieved his wallet.

Tag reached blindly for the one stool still standing and positioned it under him while she unbuttoned his shirt, spreading it open, kneading his pecs, rolling her palms over his flesh while he ripped the foil packet and stroked the condom on.

Then she climbed into his lap, straddling her legs around him so willingly he couldn't see straight for this goddamn need to be inside her. It tore at him, rippled through him with such force he had to slow down or he'd hurt her. Planting his hands on her hips, he stroked her silky flesh, ran his flat palms over her ass, felt her lean into him, drop kisses on his neck.

She gripped his shoulders, lifted her hips, waited until the unbearable sexiness of her couldn't be kept at bay any longer.

He thrust upward with the sound of her hiss of pleasure as her head fell back on her shoulders and her thighs gripped him tight around the waist. She was wet and tight, drawing him inward to her deepest depths.

Tag's lips found the long column of her neck, nipping at the flesh until her nipples beaded and scraped against his chest and her hands thrust into his hair.

That hot, uncontrollable wave of need filled his balls, drove him upward into her until he almost couldn't breathe from the tension flooding him.

Her hips began to rock back and forth, rolling, writhing against him, her breathing coming in short pants. She was on the edge—he knew the signs from the night before—but he wanted more. He wanted her to explode, to scream, so he slipped his hand between them, spreading her flesh and stroking her clit.

Marybell whimpered, her head falling forward on his shoulder, her muscles tightening in tune with his.

Tag dug his heels into the carpet when he came, keeping her as close to him as possible, holding on until Marybell slowed her movements and sank into him, driving her arms up under his and surrounding his back.

The moment caught him off guard, her leaning against him for support when she had to be the strongest woman he knew. He cupped the back of her head and sat very still, memorizing this scene, snapping a mental picture of it in his head so he'd always have it with him.

He really liked this Marybell.

And that made him smile.

Ten

"You had a condom in your back pocket," she accused with a weak laugh, her breathing still ragged. She'd tried to keep her mouth busy with lasagna. Eat fast, say thank you and goodbye. End date.

Yet another plan foiled by Tag and his delectable lips and chiseled body.

He chuckled, the rumble beneath her cheek vibrating from his chest inviting her to stay awhile. "Are you presuming that had something to do with you, pretty lady?"

She grinned, sated and happy. In this moment, she was happy. "I am."

"Bold."

"Truth."

"Look, I won't tell you I didn't hope it would happen again. I just didn't expect it to be so soon. Which makes you a little tiger, huh?" He snatched a kiss to her cheek before she batted him away

Lifting her head, she shot him a direct gaze. "You kissed me first."

Tag shook his dark head, reaching up and twirling

one of the many earrings in her ear. "We had no rules about kissing tonight. None."

Using her index finger, she swiped at his cheek. "You have my makeup all over your face."

"Your eyeliner is smeared." He used a thumb to wipe under her eyes, his eyes moving to her shoulder. "How did I miss this tattoo the other night?" he asked, dropping a kiss on it.

It was the first tattoo she'd ever gotten in celebration of earning a full scholarship to school. A small thumbs-up sign with a pink fingernail. She wanted to pull away in response to the painful memory the ink brought, but Tag had been pretty open about his Little Mermaid tattoo. "Told you I liked pink."

"Does it mean something?"

"Yep. It was my first tatt. I got it when I got a scholarship to college."

You're going to get caught.

"Well, well. Ms. Lyman's an educated woman, is she? What did you study?"

Whoa. Pull back, Marybell. "Nothing and everything. I got booted out before I was there long enough to make a difference."

Tag's eyes flashed surprise. "After getting a scholarship? Are you a bad girl, Marybell?"

"I'll never tell. But we have definitely done a bad thing." *It doesn't feel bad,* she wanted to yell. But she had to stop encouraging him.

"Does bad feel like this?" He gave her butt a squeeze.

When the glow passed, it always came down to the same thing. This dangerous line she was walking. "I can't date you, Tag."

"But you can have sex with me?"

"Yes. No. No! I shouldn't have sex with you, either."
This was getting too deep. Going too far. She'd pay for
these lies. She'd pay hard.

He sighed, lifting her from his lap to stand in front
of her. "You're like a Katy Perry song."

She cocked her head, hands on hips, utterly naked.
"You know who Katy Perry is?"

He gave her an exaggerated roll of his eyes. "I live
with Maizy. 'Hot And Cold' and 'Roar' are like her
anthems." Tag, completely, deliciously, devastatingly
naked, made his way to the bathroom where he shut
the door on her.

"You're a pretty good uncle, Tag." She heard the
water run and the flush of the toilet.

He opened the door again, leaning in the frame of it
with one arm propped in the doorway. "But obviously,
not a pretty good dater," he offered with a chuckle, holding his hand up as he made his way back to the breakfast bar and pulled his jeans on. "It's okay, Marybell
Lyman. You go on thinking you don't want to date me,
and I'll let you."

"You'll *let* me?"

He grinned so devilishly she fought a sigh. "Yep.
But I'm telling you, it won't be long till you beat down
my door and ask me for a date."

"That's plumb crazy."

"I'm plumb right. So for now, until you beat down
my door, it's goodbye." He scooped her up, naked as
the day she was born, and planted a long, delicious kiss
on her lips before setting her back down, giving her a
wink and strolling back out the door.

Marybell looked up at the ceiling, regret burrowing a hole in her chest. "Why? Why now when, for

the most part, everything was goin' so well? You have any thoughts on that, Landon Wells? Maybe you could drop that question in the box reserved for girls with sordid pasts?"

She began to scoop up her clothes, realizing in the cluster of fabric on the floor, Tag had left his hat. Pressing it against her nose, she inhaled the scent of his shampoo, which only reminded her of the scent of his cologne, and the domino effect on her thoughts began, leaving her sad.

At least you left things light. No harm, no foul. All neat and tidy.

She wasn't ever going to ask Tag out on a date, because she couldn't. It stung less knowing they'd at least wrapped it up on decent terms.

But it didn't stop the sadness from creeping in, from settling in the pit of her stomach. It would pass. She'd left plenty of people and things in her lifetime.

Tag was no exception.

She took another glance at his hat before setting it on her head, and pulling it over her Mohawk.

She decided to keep it, much the way she'd done with other small mementos from important events in her life. Things that were light and easy to pack at a moment's notice—sometimes a moment was all you had.

Marybell let her head rest on her desk in her office, trying to block out the incessant banging until she couldn't take it anymore. It had been a week since she'd seen Tag. A week full of wishing she were anyone else but who she was.

Seven days of fantasizing about him and all those muscles. Torturous thoughts of him naked, bronzed, smiling, gorgeous followed her at every turn.

All of a sudden, everything reminded her of Tag. From the place where he'd sat on her couch to the book she'd grabbed at the library, and he'd kept his promise that she'd have to ask him out next. He'd waved cheerfully to her at the office while he made repairs on the pool house outside, but he didn't approach her.

He'd called a "Hey!" to her as he shared a sandwich (a bologna sandwich, no less) with LaDawn before he'd gone back to helping her with her crossword puzzle. He'd waved and smiled as he drove by on his way to Lucky Judson's Hardware store.

He'd even wiggled his fingers in her direction while none other than Kitty Palmer, who wanted a deck built in her backyard next summer, ushered him off.

She'd readied all her tired old excuses each time she saw him, preparing to send him packing yet again, but there was no need.

Clearly, he was sticking to his guns—no more chasing down Marybell Lyman for him. Not for a week.

An entire week.

She couldn't concentrate for thinking about him. It was driving her right out of her mind. She missed sparring with him. She missed making nondate deals with him. She missed the smell of him, his silly grin. His clever comebacks, his hands. Definitely missed his hands. She missed smiling about him, laughing with him.

And the pounding down the hall didn't help.

Pulling off her headset, Marybell threw it on her desk and went in search of the banging. She poked her head out her door and listened. It was 11:00 p.m., for gravy's sake. How was she ever going to get someone's sexy on if she couldn't think straight?

Dixie's office. It was coming from there. Loud, abrasive, not sexy background noise.

Stalking down the long hallway, she caught the flash of a hand in Dixie's office. Before thinking, she pushed the door open and said, "Are you going to be done soon? This is—"

"As I live and breathe, it's Marybell Lyman." He grinned. That grin that made her stomach flutter like the wings of a butterfly.

She had to catch her breath it was so good to see him for longer than ten seconds. It filled up all the empty spaces inside her. "I came to ask you to stop making so much noise."

He made a funny pouty face. "And a girl can't get her naughty on with all this big bad noise?"

She threw her head back and laughed. "Yes!" she said, stomping her foot.

"I won't be much longer. I just have to finish up this baseboard, and I'm out. Promise." He grabbed the hammer and lifted it to swing.

That was it? *Aw, c'mon. No openings? No funny repartee? Nothing?* "How've you been?" she shouted, her cheeks turning red when she realized she was yelling.

Tag sat back on his haunches, the muscles of his thighs rippling beneath his jeans, and smiled some more. "Really good." He lifted the hammer again, preparing to knock out another nail.

Hold on, now. "You're not going to ask how I've been?"

He pursed his luscious lips. "Um, how've you been, Marybell?"

Bad. Very bad. "Good." She smiled, too. Just to show him she had it in her to be cheerful.

"Good. Now, if you want the banging to stop, I've got to finish up."

"But wait!" She leaned against the door frame and waffled. "How's Maizy?"

That brought more smiles. Pleasant, distant smiles. "She's great. Just got an A on her spelling test."

"That's awesome. How about Jax?"

Tag bobbed his head, one that had a brand-new hat on it. He hadn't even bothered to come back for his hat. "Jax is good, too."

"How's—"

"Everybody's great at the Hawthorne residence. Now, like I said—"

"Right. You need to finish. Sorry. But if you feel like talking or hanging out, I'm just down the hall." She pointed to "just down the hall" with a ringed finger over her shoulder. "Sunday nights are usually slower. Day of worship and all."

He yawned. "I'm kind of tired. It's been a long day, but thanks." He didn't bother to wait for her to respond. Instead, he hit the nail this time, the clang of it echoing in her head.

Feeling incredibly pouty on the inside, she slunk back to her office and dropped into her chair as if the popular kid in school had just turned her down.

Seeing Tag gave her sudden life. Ridiculous, no doubt, an odd sort of truthful inner confession, but the truth all the same. Seeing him reinforced how much she'd missed seeing him.

Something had to be done about that.

Soon.

Tag gave the last nail a satisfactory bounce from the head of his hammer, hoping Marybell heard it good and loud.

He smiled to himself as he cleaned up his tools. Marybell Lyman wanted him to come to her office and hang out.

Not gonna happen—even if he wanted to do that almost as much as he wanted to keep breathing. He understood the word *no*. Question was, did Marybell understand why she wasn't saying yes? What was she keeping so locked up inside her that it prevented her from enjoying herself?

He knew that place—a dark, empty dwelling. He understood the place where you didn't think you deserved to laugh or smile ever again. If you did, something bad would happen to punish you for it. You didn't deserve to laugh or smile when you'd done something unforgivable. He'd lived in that place when his sister, Harper, had died.

She'd been that thread that sewed them all together, and when she was gone and they were left with an empty chair at Thanksgiving dinner, left without her feminine guidance for Maizy, left without her unwavering love for them, he'd taken the worst dive of his life.

Because what he'd done when Harper died was unforgivable. That his brothers still spoke to him left him floored. But they did, because in some buried corner of his mind, he knew when they told him she'd want that, she really would have.

Was that what it was? Had Marybell done something

unforgivable? She'd said she lost her scholarship. Maybe wherever this closed-off vibe she threw went deeper than he'd first guessed?

He'd thought about her day and night for the past week. Wondered about all the things that made Marybell tick. Wondered why she'd never watched a Disney movie. Didn't all little girls like princesses? And even if they didn't, didn't they at least know they existed?

Hadn't Marybell been given the chance to decide whether she liked them or not? A strange sadness grabbed his heart when he considered she'd been a foster kid. Obviously, there'd been neglect on all fronts if she'd been bounced around, but he found himself aching for the things she must have missed. The things Maizy had should be the things all little girls had.

For some weird reason, he wanted to turn that around for her.

Wanted nothing more than to beat down her door, scoop her up and make more love to her—because it felt right. But he wasn't going to beg.

Something was up with Marybell. She didn't want to date, but she definitely enjoyed his company, if that exchange said anything about their relationship thus far.

He might be overconfident, but he sensed she missed him, too.

Good.

Now he just had to wait around until she made the next move. He was patient, though seeing her day after day, treating her like some distant acquaintance was killing him. And sometimes, after seeing the look on her face when he gave her a quick wave, secretly amusing him.

But she needed space to come to whatever conclusions or peace she had to make with herself. He didn't want to push her so far away she wouldn't come back.

Now, if she would just damn well come back.

All good things come to those who wait, Tag. His sister, Harper, had once said he was as impatient as a newborn, waiting on a midnight feeding.

Harper. It was getting easier to think about her these days. Maybe because his focus was lying elsewhere. When he woke up, he didn't have that sinking feeling in his stomach anymore. The dread that had followed the opening of his eyes for almost two years since Harper had passed was easing, ebbing and flowing more and more.

He was learning to forgive. Making his peace with what he couldn't change.

There was a seed of hope sprouting, and he kept watering the hell out of it. He just had to wait for it to grow. Some seeds took longer to root than others.

Obviously, Marybell was one of those types of seeds.

She was giving him yet another reason to stay out of the dark recesses of his mind. He wanted something for the first time in a long while. He wanted to get his shit totally together. He wanted to laugh. He wanted to look forward to things—all kinds of things.

He wanted Marybell Lyman.

Eleven

Marybell's stomach was a nervous ride on a Tilt-A-Whirl. Up, down, sideways, backward. She'd thought long and hard about this choice late into the morning after her shift was over. She'd hadn't slept much in the past three days, but she'd come to a sort of peace with her choice at about noon on day two, just before she clicked "ship to this address."

She'd kept right on thinking it through even after the package arrived. Then she'd waffled a little, but she rallied in the eleventh hour.

It was time to stop hiding. Time to stop fearing everything she loved would be ripped from her clinging hands.

It was time to stop wringing her hands, and figure this out. It would take a whole lot more than just resolutions and promises in her head, but she wanted to do this as clean as possible. As fast as possible. Figure out the almost impossible.

Tucking the package under her arm, she gripped it tighter with clammy fingers.

She found Tag out by the pool, working on the trellis. The gray day made his dark hair darker, his image against the cold sky warming her from the inside out.

A quick tap on his shoulder had him turning around, his eyes cautious when he realized it was her.

She hated that. Yet it wouldn't stop her. Marybell pulled the package from her arms. Metaphorically, she was dragging the tail from beneath her legs. "I brought you something." She held it out, rather proudly, almost like a cat handing over a mouse to its owner.

"For me?" he teased in a feminine tone. "I don't know what to say."

"Say you'll open it. I'm freezin'." Her teeth began to chatter.

"You always know all the right things to say to a man, Marybell. Don't let anyone tell you different."

The tension in her eased when Tag joked with her. "So open it."

He put the package on the glass table of the patio set and slit the box open with a knife from his tool belt. Peeling away the tape, he pulled out the first item. *"Beauty and the Beast?"*

Marybell's stomach did another nervous flip, so nervous she could only nod.

Tag riffled though the package, pulling the rest of the DVDs out and fanning them on the table. "Let's see, there's *Sleeping Beauty, Snow White and the Seven Dwarfs, Mulan, The Little Mermaid...*" He sighed.

She held her breath and looked away. It was too late.

"So, this is going to be one of those awkward gift-giving moments where I tell you I already have all of these, isn't it? It's like that diamond ring I got once. How do you tell a woman you already have one?"

She giggled—still an unfamiliar sound to her ears. "They're not really for you."

"Now you're just being fair-weathered. You give, you take away."

"They're so you can watch them with me. On our da...*date,*" she forced her lips to enunciate.

Tag raised an eyebrow in that comical way he had and gave her the eye. "Are you asking me out? *Me?* Because I gotta tell ya, it better be a real sell after all that rejection. You've let the pie sit out a long time, tiger."

She sucked her cheeks in to keep from laughing. "I need a guide to Disney princesses. I figured you were my best bet with all that experience."

He barked a laugh. "Oh, now it's a guide you need? Not a date? Well, then, I just might have to turn you down, Ms. Lyman. Unless you want to call it a date. That—" he paused, pointing at her "—could change everything."

"What's the difference what I call it?"

"Oh, I dunno. What's the difference when a man calls it sex and a woman calls it *making love?* What's the difference when a man calls it his lifeblood and a woman calls it just a silly game with a bunch of loud roughnecks in tight pants? It's huge. So call it a date or call it nothing." He ended with a flirty challenge of a smile.

"Fine. It's a date."

He shook a finger. "Oh, no, it is not. You have to ask me first."

Marybell narrowed her eyes at him. "I just did."

"No. You declared it one before you even asked. Overconfident much?"

"Do you want me on bended knee, too?"

"No, that's more like the marriage question and far too presumptuous at this early stage of the game. So quit being so stalkery and ask politely."

Taking a deep breath to keep from giggling more, she said, "Will you, Taggart Hawthorne, come to my house and watch Disney princess movies with me on a real, live, honest-to-God *date?*"

He scooped her up and planted his lips directly on hers, kissing her so hard their teeth almost collided.

Just as she was melting back into his incredible warmth, his delicious muscles, he pulled away, looking down at her. "Yep."

"Put me down! Someone will see," she said, though her protest sounded weak.

He rolled his eyes. "Are we going to start that again? Because if this is a secret date, I'm out. If you're embarrassed by me, then I just won't be able to go on."

Embarrassed by him? Who'd ever be embarrassed by Tag? She gave a tug to the collar of his denim jacket. "I'm not embarrassed by you. If anythin', it should be the other way around."

The light in his eyes went out like a doused fire. "Don't ever say that. Ever. As long as we date, never say that. Okay?"

Now she was the one coaxing him by planting her hands on the sides of his face. "Easy, there. I'm just stating a fact. Going into this, you should know people will question your motives about dating me when there are perfectly good Southern belles who fit the norm just waiting to be dated."

He gripped her hands, running his thumbs over them. "If I was interested in them, I'd have dated them by now. But I'm not. So no more talk of embarrassment."

It was easy to search his eyes from behind her people shield. When she wore it, she felt less exposed, less like someone could look beyond her curtains and right into the window of her soul. "Fair enough. Now put me down. I have to go clean my apartment because I have a *date*."

He was light again, all smiles and teasing. "Does this date include food? What kind of date are we talking about?"

"How does pizza grab you? It's a marathon date, by the by. As many princess movies as we can fit into one evening."

Tag grabbed a handful of her butt, reminding her how talented those hands were. "Then I'll bring my comfy slippers and pipe."

She leaned into him and kissed the edge of his mouth, and it felt good. So good to do something spontaneous. "Bring popcorn, too." She squirmed out of his embrace with reluctance and sauntered toward the guesthouse. "Tonight, seven or so. Don't be late, Hawthorne!" she called over her shoulder, her heart lighter than air, her stomach anxious with anticipation.

She'd done it. Phase one complete. *Yay!*

Now for the hard part.

Boo-hiss.

Tag rang her doorbell at seven sharp, shaking the box of microwave popcorn at her. Tonight wasn't the first time she hated putting on the people shield, but it was with the hope that soon she wouldn't have to put it on at all.

Her nerves about embarking on dating Tag were a mixture of excitement and fear. The people shield gave her courage. The makeup, the hair, all of it left her bolder than she'd once been before the people shield existed.

Or maybe it was just life that had done that? Would she be as sassy without her spray-on hair dye from a can or the thick eyeliner?

She'd like to think she'd be just as bold if her face was naked and her hair was in a ponytail. Those things came naturally to her. They were things she really liked. Maybe she'd just keep them.

Tag didn't give her much time to think about it. He swooped in the front door and pulled her to him, forcing her to look up at him. "I'm positively giddy, Ms. Lyman. Like a debutante at her coming-out ball."

She was giddy, too. Giddy and more giddy. "Giddy? Would that be attributed to a man as big and brawny as you?"

"Are you sexist?"

"Not on your life."

"Then I can be giddy, too. Even big and brawny. Look." He held up a plastic bag. "I brought you a gift."

She tried to pluck it from his hands, but he held it out of her reach. "Not until we watch the movies. So let's get this date started. You grab the pizza, I'll warm up the DVD player and we'll cuddle up on the couch."

"You mean eat on the couch?"

He dropped a kiss on her lips before nodding. "Hell, yeah, I mean eat on the couch. When you watch movies, don't you sit on the couch?"

Marybell tugged at her leopard leggings, embarrassed by her knee-jerk reaction. Sometimes she forgot she could live by her own rules, or if someone or something spilled food on her couch, the answer was simple—she could clean it.

Possessions, things she was always afraid would disappear right under her nose, became a territorial issue for her when she least expected them to. She had trouble letting go of her control of them, and as a child, she'd never been in anyone's home where she was allowed to eat on the couch or have things of her own.

She'd worked hard for these things, as sparse as they were, and she was always afraid she was going to lose them.

But Tag almost looked as though he understood. "You know what? Tonight's for breaking rules. We're gonna break 'em all. Just like you broke the one about not asking me out."

"It wasn't a rule...." Her throat tried to close up on her.

"Was so. It might not have been a written one, but it was one you'd made up in your head. Doesn't make a difference. Tonight, rules go out the window and we walk on the edge. So you get the pizza and some plates and napkins and I'll get the DVD player ready. Any thoughts on what you'd like to watch first?"

She grabbed the pizza box and the plates and napkins. "I'm a little at a loss. What's your suggestion, Disney princess guru?"

Tag dug out the DVDs from the bag. "You know, I'd say we go straight for *Mulan,* because if we were to compare you to a Disney princess, my bet's on her. But let's ease you into this slowly and save the impact watching for later."

Placing the pizza on the coffee table, she was careful not to disturb the bowl of balls she'd so carefully placed there. "What's your favorite one?"

Tag scooped the bowl of balls up and set them on the floor. "I gotta confess, I really like *Aladdin*. Robin Williams cracked me up."

She ignored the bowl of decorative balls. Because they were breaking rules tonight. "Then *Aladdin* it is."

Putting the DVD in the player, he clicked it on and then dropped down beside her and opened the pizza box, grabbing a slice and putting it on a paper plate. "Now, come sit next to me, and I'll show you all the pros to eating pizza on the couch with your date. Grab one of those perfectly folded throw blankets and cuddle up right here." He pointed to his side and grinned.

She pulled the throw off the back of the couch and sat next to him, picking up the napkins to hold under his plate.

Tag pushed them away and held the slice of pizza to her mouth. "Bite. I'll press Play."

The intimate gesture, one she'd seen a hundred times before between Dixie and Caine, or Jax and Em, was so easy for him, and with each bite he fed her, while the swells of a Disney musical score played in the background, it became easier for her, too.

"Wait! Press Pause," he ordered, a mouthful of pizza. "I almost forgot. How could I forget? We'd get kicked out of the Disney princess school for forgetting if Maizy knew." He reached behind the sofa and got the plastic bag, rooting around in it. "Close your eyes."

"No," she said around a gooey bite of pepperoni and cheese and a laugh.

"If you don't, our date will have to be over."

"What's in the bag?"

He put his fingers over her eyelids. "Close your eyes, Marybell. Be a good dater. Why is everything with you like pulling teeth?"

She chuckled, closing her eyes to the tune of the rustle of the bag and something thrown around her neck.

"Okay, open."

When Tag came into focus, Marybell giggled. *Again.* So much giggling when he was around. "Pink's your color."

He chuckled, easy and deep. "Ya think?"

She threaded her fingers through the feathers around her neck. "You brought me a boa. That's…" Out of nowhere, she was choking up, her words running out.

Tag leaned in and kissed her with soft lips. "All princesses should have one when they watch princess movies." Pulling her tight to his side, he sat back and pressed Play.

Marybell blinked back the threat of a tear. How had she missed all these incredible movies? Tag held her hand, snuggling under the blanket with her, feeding her popcorn while they'd watched *Aladdin*. But *Mulan* had become serious. The movie brought up all sorts of feelings, all sorts of questions.

Why had Tag compared her to Mulan? Did he think she was hiding like Mulan because of her makeup and hair? A small tingle of fear crept into her thoughts. She forced them to calm. He couldn't know her motivation for the people shield or he wouldn't be still sitting right next to her. His comparisons likely lay in her flippant attitude and outspokenness.

She took one last breath before she banished those thoughts.

Sitting on the couch with Tag, his arm around her, sometimes his head somehow among all her spikes, resting on top of hers as she burrowed down next to him, had been magical.

If he could only know just how magical something as simple as this was to someone like her.

He gave her a nudge as the credits rolled. "Hey, you awake down there?"

She nodded, still wondering at his comparisons.

"I think I got some pepperoni on the couch."

"It's okay," she murmured against his chest, pulling her boa tighter around her neck.

"This from the woman who couldn't even eat on the couch a few short hours ago. It's the magic of a Disney princess movie. Told you."

No. It was the magic of Tag. The easy comfort he brought. The laughter. "Thank you," she whispered.

He tipped her chin up. "For?"

She had to gulp. *For not caring about my Mohawk or my silver lipstick or the fact that I've never watched a princess movie. That all the things that make a person whole, all the memories, all the special cheese sandwiches cut into triangles, all the marks on the wall to measure your height, birthday parties and proms, are devoid in my life. For not making me feel half of something, instead of all of something.* Instead, she just said, "For princess night."

"You make an amazing princess."

Now she rolled her eyes, the lump in her throat easing. "Princesses don't look like me. Maybe princesses of darkness," she joked, referring back to their banter. Banter was easier than all these feelings.

He leaned down, letting his nose brush hers. "You're

the hottest damn princess of darkness ever, then," he said before capturing her lips.

Everything welled up in her at once. Their rule breaking, cuddling on the couch, popcorn and princesses and boas, making her reach up and wrap her arms around his neck, pulling him tight to her.

Tag reacted by closing his arms around her and pulling her into his lap. He rocked her, and the tired Marybell, the one who always had her guard up, rested for just a little bit.

Tag carried her into her bedroom, dragging the fluffy comforter down along the bed and setting her carefully on it.

When she'd climbed into his lap tonight, as if he were all there was left in the world, something inside him cracked. If he knew anything, he knew for sure Marybell had lacked so many of the things he took for granted in his life.

He didn't know what she'd missed, maybe more than even he suspected. He didn't know how much she'd tell him about her life in the foster care system, but he wanted to be the one she told.

He wanted to protect her. Fix whatever was broken, even when he knew you couldn't fix anyone. They had to fix themselves.

He wanted to give her princess movies by the dozen. Dinner on the couch. More pink boas than she knew what to do with.

That meant getting his life in shape. Like real shape. Starting with Gage's offer.

Marybell stirred, rolling to her side. Her eyes popped

open, the pretty hazel of them no less beautiful with the makeup surrounding them. "What time is it?"

He brushed one of her fallen spikes off her cheek. "Almost two. I'd better go. You're tired, and we don't want Blanche to talk."

She grabbed his hand and said, "She won't start talking until at least five.... That gives you two hours to wow me."

He grew hard as a damn rock just hearing the words. But he wasn't up to light banter right now. Now he wanted to bury himself deep inside her and never leave. He wanted to show her that Taggart Hawthorne wasn't just in this for the laughs.

Rather than answer her, he began pulling his clothes off while she watched from the bed, until he was naked, and then he slipped his hands under her cute T-shirt with the slashes in it and cupped her breasts.

Her moan made his cock stand at attention, hard and ready for her. But tonight, he wanted to savor her—savor the taste of her on his tongue, the feel of her silky flesh against his.

When he bent his head down to capture a pink nipple, he loved the way she raised her arms above her head and arched her back. Open, willing, so different from the way she communicated her thoughts. He licked at the tight buds, blowing on them, nipping them, running his tongue over and over them until she hissed and lifted her hips.

She pulled him onto the bed, her fingers clutching at his hair, her hands following the path of his belly until she grasped his shaft and began to stroke it, long and firm.

Tag wrapped his hand over hers, thwarting her motion. His teeth clenched tight, but he managed to find words. "Pull those hot leggings off so I can get my tongue between your legs or I'll rip them off you."

She shuddered against him, whimpered in his ear as she wiggled her way out of them.

Tag clamped his mouth over hers, slipping his tongue between her lips, tasting all the things that made up Marybell while his fingers found her wet flesh. He spread her without hesitation, and she let her legs fall open wide, her hand at his wrist, her lower torso lifting up.

He loved kissing her almost as much as he loved licking her, and that was the thought that made him pull away and nibble a trail over her collarbone, along the soft swell of her belly, along each silky thigh.

Hovering for a moment, he slid her to him, hooking her ankles at his neck before he dipped into the sweet core of her, slow at first. A lazy stroke of his tongue here, a wet kiss there.

Marybell moaned low from above him when he broadened his strokes, driving deeper, going longer, circling her clit, thrusting a finger into her, then two. She contracted around his digits when he flattened his tongue and made her come.

Her body heaved beneath him, her knees tightening against his head. When she bucked upward, Tag smiled against her, trailed his fingers in the wet heat of her until she gasped for breath.

Marybell's hands reached down, pulling at his shoulders, threading her fingers through his hair, clutching it, redirecting him upward until their lips met again. Her arms were strong when she wrapped them around him and rolled him to his back and settled herself on his hips.

Tag kept his eyes open when she reached over him to the nightstand drawer to grab a condom. He watched her lithe form move, the skin along her sides stretch until he could count every bone in her ribs. The swell of her hip, the indent of her waist, her breasts, full and so perfect for his hands. He ate her up with his eyes, drank in her hands slipping the condom over him, stroking it downward over his cock, her hazel eyes gleaming.

Leaning forward, she kissed him, long and slow, using her tongue to tease, letting his hard shaft slip in and out of her wet flesh, rolling against him until he reached around her and sank his fingers into her ass as he slipped inside her.

Tight, she was so tight and slick it made his mouth water and his head reel. It was almost impossible to gather his senses and focus on her when she was so damn delicious.

But Marybell clearly wanted some control. Pushing herself off with the heels of her hands on his chest, she sat up and leaned back, bracing herself on his thighs. Her head fell back on her shoulders, exposing the long column of her neck, fair and so different from the heavy foundation she wore on her face.

He heard her whimper at his stroke upward, make another small sound when his fingers delved between her folds. She stiffened, her muscles flexed, her hips rolled in a slow rhythm, her nipples became hard points he needed his mouth on.

Reaching up, he slipped his arms under hers and pulled her to him, taking a nipple in his mouth and sipping at it until she hissed in his ear, gasped for breath, drove her lower body against his in a hard grind.

The rhythm they'd found grew impatient, demanding, the heat of their skin leaving a fine sheen of sweat that glued them together.

And then he was lost, lost to her wetness, lost deep inside her, lost to that hot wave of the climb toward release. Their chests crashed against each other's, their hands explored in smooth glides and clenches of flesh, their lips found each other's again, their tongues lashed.

Tag couldn't breathe from the explosive rush of his blood, pushing through his veins, couldn't hear anything but his own growl when he came, pumping into her until he was drained and Marybell shuddered.

She curled into him, fisting her hands under her chin and firing up his protective instincts again. He tightened his hold on her, listening to the sound of his heartbeat slow in his ears, thinking about how much he wanted to wake up next to her tomorrow morning.

As if she read his mind, she mumbled, "Don't let me fall asleep. We don't want to get in trouble with Blanche."

Tag smiled. "I promise to be out of here in plenty of time to keep the Mags from wagging their tongues."

"It's not that I don't want you to stay…."

Now, that was certainly progress from a week ago when all she wanted to do was get rid of him. "I get it. No hard feelings."

"Don't let me fall asleep…" she muttered again before she fell asleep. Her chest rose and fell against his, slow and steady.

Tag lay there for a little while, holding her close to him, knowing something had happened tonight—some-

thing inside him. Knowing this was bigger than he'd
first thought.

Simply knowing.

Twelve

She read the text from Tag and smiled, scrolling through it to read it again. He'd left her last night on time as promised, though, she didn't remember when. He'd cleaned up their dishes and tucked her in, and written her a note on the counter with a strict warning not to watch any more princess movies without him.

Just those small acts left her so warm on the inside and at the same time, so afraid. Yet she found the warm was outweighing the fear. Warm might win if not for this thing between them that could ruin everything.

These were unfamiliar waters—sometimes calm, sometimes choppy. All these feelings all at once should have left her on overload. But she was finding it was getting easier—if she let it. If she soothed herself with the plan she intended to execute, it made her moral dilemma with Tag less frightening.

She read his text again, smiling at his promise to meet her for a late lunch as she sipped her coffee on the bench in the square.

"What are you doin' out here in this chill, Marybell Lyman? It's almost sundown and you have that flimsy jacket on. Don't I pay you enough to buy yourself something warmer?"

Marybell smiled up at Dixie and her mothering. "You and Caine better procreate soon so you'll stop nagging me."

Dixie nudged her over on the bench and set a greasy white paper bag on her lap. "I'm wedding-planning eating. Have some of this enormous doughnut with me so I'm not in it alone." She dug the doughnut out and waved it under her nose.

"Wedding-plannin' eating?"

Dixie nodded. "It's like stress-eating but with gowns and doves and matching cocktail napkins."

"You're going to have doves?"

"Over my dead body. I know Caine wants all the fuss because of his mama, but—"

"There's all those bad memories associated with the first time around?"

Dixie stabbed the air with a pink-gloved finger. "Yes! Oh, Marybell, it was dreadful. I think I have post-traumatic-wedding disorder because of it."

A snicker slipped from her lips. "Landon told us." She remembered his face distinctly as he'd given them all the gory details. He'd been smiling, now leading her to believe he'd been cooking up that contest between Dixie and Caine even then.

"Oh, that man! I bet he was laughing at us."

Marybell nodded. "There was laughter. But it's all going to be okay. You do know that, right? Caine loves you something fierce. Not even the plannin' of a wedding could change that."

She turned to look at Marybell, a question on her

face. "You know, I don't think you've ever told us how you met Landon."

Don't clam up. This is the part where you begin to let everyone in. Dixie's one of the best people to start with. "Landon was the kindest soul ever. I don't know what kind of luck was shinin' down on me that day, or why I got so fortunate, but just when I didn't think I could take another step, go on a single second more, Landon showed up out of the blue." She didn't know it at the time, but he'd turned out to be the best thing to ever happen to her.

A tear slipped from Dixie's eye. "Sounds like my best friend. You don't have to tell me about what happened that day, but I'd love it if you would. Hearing stories about him always make me feel like he's right here with me." She patted the place on the cold bench next to her and stuck her arm through Marybell's.

Marybell let her head hang low, her throat so tight it was almost impossible to speak. "I was living on the streets, making a couple of bucks here and there by cocktail waitressing in some underground clubs."

Dixie tilted her head and patted Marybell's hand for reassurance. "Goth clubs, I take it?"

Marybell's laugh was dry and full of sarcasm. "Well, it wasn't at the country club, that's for sure. So, yes, goth clubs. I was workin' for a man who was pretty shady, but I needed the money, and he needed a waitress because one had just quit. I did a twelve-hour shift in that disgusting dive, and he tried to stiff me out of my pay. I got angry." Because she hadn't eaten in two days. Because that promised money had been like a ticket to the Fountain of Youth.

"So I have to ask, what was Landon doing at a seedy

goth bar? You do know he was far more Liberace than he was goth."

That wrung a smile out of her. "Oh, I remember. He wasn't at the bar, he was driving by, I was bleedin'. Good Samaritan type stuff."

Dixie gasped. "Is that what the scar is above your eyebrow? That man hit you?"

"Well, to be fair, when he said he wasn't going to pay me, I popped open the cash register and just took it. He chased me down and gave me a real shiner. Landon drivin' up scared him off—or so that's what Landon says. I was a little out of it until I woke up in the hospital."

Never, in all her life, would she ever forget Landon's smiling face, staring down at her as though she mattered. As though a couple of stitches and a fat lip were reason to call in the brain surgeons. He'd had nurses and doctors flying around that hospital room with nothing more than a twitch of his finger.

And it had overwhelmed her at first, threatened to swallow her whole.

That was the Landon who'd saved her. A big, handsome, generous man who only wanted to help, who was willing to extend a hand even in the face of her crude rejection.

Dixie ran her finger over the feathery scar just above her eyebrow, her eyes sad. She chucked Marybell under the chin. "I didn't know. But I bet he was in a limo, wasn't he?"

Marybell couldn't help smiling at the memory. She'd been petrified at the time. All sorts of unsavory characters roamed the darker side of the city, looking to score; she figured he was just one of the richer ones who hid his proclivities behind all his money. "A big, shiny black one that Sanjeev was apparently driving. Somehow they'd managed to get lost in my sordid neck of the woods. It was all just luck."

"And maybe a little heavenly intervention." Dixie pointed up at the inky-black sky. "Gracious knows I wouldn't be surprised to hear that man had connections upstairs. So what happened next? How did he manage to talk you into, of all things, phone sex?"

"It wasn't just the phone sex. It was the promise of a steady income." A warm place to sleep, a bed.

Marybell swallowed hard, her chest ready to burst. "I'm sure you know better than anyone, Landon can be very convincing, but it took more than him paying my hospital bill and some smooth-talkin'. I got away from him as fast as I could. I trusted no one, least of all a slick man with a limo and an ascot. There are a lot of crazies out there. But he found me again—not far from where he'd found me the first time—and offered to buy me lunch in a very public place."

"Because when my Landon wanted something, nothin' stopped him." Dixie chuckled at that.

Marybell folded her hands into a fist in her lap and nodded. It felt good to talk about Landon.

Good to tell someone how much love he'd given her in so little time. "To this day, I don't know what made me believe him, Dixie. I should have been utterly and totally freaked out when I found out he wanted me to work for his *phone sex* company. I mean, phone sex? C'mon. If that doesn't sound alarm bells, you have to be deaf. In fact, I stayed freaked out until I staked his so-called company out and watched the women who worked for him come and go."

She'd done exactly that. Spied on him and Sanjeev, grilled his doorman and the security guard, seen LaDawn before she ever even knew a Marybell Lyman existed. She'd watched skeptically for two solid days until she got up the nerve to ask the doorman to buzz her up.

"Even after he got me inside the penthouse in Atlanta where this all began, I still had reservations. There's always a catch. Nothing's too good to be true. Not where I come from. But Landon just had this thing about him…." She shrugged. That warmth in his eyes. That gentle tone. That easy smile. "Well, you know what I mean. It's the same thing you have. Charisma, maybe?"

Dixie made a face, offering Marybell some of her sugary doughnut. "It's persistence and the tenacity of a huntin' dog, is what it is. So when you found out it was all legit? What then?"

"That was more of a process. I was awful at phone sex first. Men called wanting things I just couldn't provide. But I was determined to make it work because no matter how skeptical I'd go to bed at night over how this was too Cinderella for me, I'd wake up the next morning to fresh peach muffins and Sanjeev pourin' us all coffee in that fancy kitchen Landon had."

"Did you know he was going to die, Marybell?" Dixie's voice skittered, hitching with a pain that was still so fresh for all of them.

She gulped, swallowing the fear and core-deep sadness those months had brought. "I did. He told us all like he was tellin' us he was going on one of his safaris or to London for some tea he liked in a pub he talked about all the time. We didn't know until almost the end—it all happened…so fast."

Dixie sniffed, pulling a tissue from her pocket and dabbing at her eyes.

Marybell grabbed her hand. "I'm sorry. I didn't mean to dredge up your pain."

"No, MB," Dixie admonished with a squeeze of her fingers. "That's a pain we share. Landon might not have been in your life as long as he was in mine, but you loved him as much. I know you did. I'm okay sharin' it, if you are."

Marybell stayed quiet, the lump in her throat refusing to budge.

"So y'all knew about us. Me and Caine and Em?"

Marybell smiled. Landon was a crafty man. This web of love he'd woven had been carefully orchestrated, and as it all began to unfold, she could only sit back and marvel. "We didn't know everythin'. We knew who you were, and that you'd be coming back for his funeral, and that he hoped you'd run his phone sex company. We didn't know he'd make you compete for it. He told us all sorts of stories about you two when you were kids." Stories Marybell had latched on to and lived vicariously through.

Stories of friendships she'd never had, events she'd never attended.

Dixie's sigh shuddered. "We had so many great times together. I wasn't the kindest person in the world, or the easiest to love, but somehow Landon managed to love me, anyway."

"He did mention you were a handful, but he really loved you." A love Marybell had envied until she'd met Dixie.

"How did he ever get you women to agree to come here?"

"We only knew he wanted to move the company here because this was his hometown, and he loved it. He left us one of his infamous DVDs like he did you and Caine. He told us how hard it would be to come here, and what we'd be up against, and if we wanted to bail, we could do it with a ridiculous amount of severance pay. But he'd told us so many stories about Plum Orchard—he had so many vivid memories. I think we all wanted to be in a place he loved so much. Maybe so he'd always be with us—closer somehow."

"As unkind as people can be, Landon always garnered respect. He didn't care that some people didn't agree with his lifestyle. He didn't care that they shut up about it because they loved the money he funneled into this town. He did it because he loved Plum Orchard."

"Most of us would've done anythin' for Landon, and he needed operators to keep this thing afloat until it was on its feet because, in his words on that DVD, 'phone sex is what's gonna save a couple of people who're dear to me, just like it did all of you.' We didn't know what it meant at the time, but once we met you and Caine, we guessed."

Dixie sighed, her breath feathering out from between her lips. "Can I ask you something?"

Marybell hesitated only a moment. "Sure."

"You know, I've been meanin' to ask you how you feel about a marketing position. Instead of answering calls. You're so good with social media, and you have some of the most clever ideas for drummin' up business. Is that somethin' you'd consider down the line?"

Give up answering calls? "Do marketing positions require a fancy suit and wearing my hair in a bun?" she joked to hide her interest. She'd stay an operator forever if it meant keeping these people in her life, but the chance to do something closer to what she'd once hoped to do was enticing.

Dixie laughed, slapping her thigh. "I don't care what you wear, MB. I think you know that. I just care that you're fulfilled. That doin' what you're doin' is enough."

Marybell squeezed Dixie's hand. Call Girls, no matter the capacity, would always be enough. "I'm fine, Dixie."

"Are you happy here, Marybell? At Call Girls. In Plum Orchard? Really happy?"

She hid her eyes, forcing them to her booted feet. "I'm happier than I've been in a long time. Landon gave me back the will to survive. He gave me security, a retirement fund, for gravy's sake. I'll always honor that."

Dixie's tongue clucked. "That's not what I asked you, sugar. I asked if you were happy here. With us. Answerin' phone calls? With your *life*."

She was still afraid to say it out loud. Afraid to put it out into the universe. "I think I don't always understand everyone's definition of happy. But this fits mine."

Dixie turned to her then, her glittery eyes searching her friend's face. "Happy is full up, honey. Happy is knowing who you can trust. Happy can be alone, or with someone, but it's living out loud. That's happy. I want that for you. I know something's troublin' you, MB. I don't know what. Maybe it's conflict over this new relationship with Tag—"

"We're not officially—"

"In a relationship. I know," she said with a wave of her gloved hand. "But whatever it is, no matter what it is, I'm always here. We're all always here, and I'll do whatever it is you need me to in order to help. All of us will."

So she was going to lie. Right through her teeth, and she was going to eat her guilt about it for the next three meals, but she was going to do it for the time being. Just until she could fix this.

Landon was a rare bird. He'd believed in her when no one else had—when she'd been massacred—but that couldn't happen twice in a lifetime. Not without some evidence to the contrary. No one was that lucky. "Y'all are plumb nuts. I don't know what you're seein' that I'm not, but I promise, I'm fine. Everything is fine. Now stop henpecking me and share this doughnut so our butts are equally flabby."

Dixie stared at her a few seconds more before her expression changed and she was smiling again. "Heaven forbid we only have one flabby butt among us." She ripped a piece of the doughnut off and handed the rest to Marybell.

She shoved it in her mouth to keep from saying anything else.

Staying hidden was hard.

Thank God for doughnuts.

"So it's a go, Gage," Tag said, hauling a two-by-four over his shoulder with a grunt.

They were in the middle of repairing Essie Guthrie's shed when he decided to go for it. Yeah. He was gonna go for it.

Gage looked at him over the rim on his thermos of coffee. "A go? What's a go?"

"The mill. Use your money, make a bid, do whatever it takes to get your hands on it. You own it. I work for you."

Gage's surprise swiftly changed to guarded eyes. "Uh, no. You own it, I work for you."

"Not gonna happen. When we get it up and running and we're banking some money, I'll buy into it. But until then, you're the boss."

Gage put his thermos down and spanned the space between them, his face read skeptical. "I don't know the first thing about running a business, Tag. You did all of that."

"Then I'll help you, but no freebies. I lost what little money I had left when everything went to shit. If I hadn't been so busy wading in my own crap, I could've gotten back on my feet again. I didn't. I drank and gambled. I don't want any handouts for fucking up. It just doesn't feel right. So I start at the bottom. You pay me a fair living wage. I work my ass off to get this up and running *with* you."

Gage paused, showing his hands in his flannel jacket. "So you're staying. No running away. No bullshit. Staying here in Plum Orchard, period."

Tag grinned, damn happy all over for the first time in a long while. "Yep. Right here."

"I hate to rock the boat, but why the sudden change of heart?"

Because the opportunity to start over kept banging him on the head. Talking with Marybell had forced him to see how he took advantage of always having a support system.

"I really like it here, and you guys are all here now, too. It's time to be an adult again. It's time to make a future for myself, and that means hard work and a consistent paycheck. Once things come together at the mill, I'm going to start looking for a place to hang my hat. I love Maizy and Jax, but we both know big brother's gonna ask Em to marry him soon. They'll have their hands full blending the kids. They don't need me hanging around."

"Damn glad to hear that."

Tag lifted his knit cap off and wiped his forehead. "It's time, don't you think? No more feeling sorry for myself. No more keeping all that anger about Harper and losing the business as an excuse not to get my shit together. I can't change what happened. I'll always regret it, but I know I have two choices. So I made one."

"Harper," Gage murmured. "I think about her every day. I wish she could see Maizy and how awesome she is."

Tag looked down at the dead grass beneath his feet. "I think about her every day, too. She was a huge part of our lives. She helped us all in one way or another. She helped Jax with Maizy. She helped me develop the software for the business. Managed to get your skinny ass through college by helping you study. I didn't realize all of that until it was too late. I don't want to do something like that where you're all concerned." Ever. He didn't ever want to forget how they'd stuck by him— still stood by him.

Their heavy moment passed and Gage grinned, slapping him on the back. "This is all good news, brother. But I can't help wondering if it has something to do with all that sneaking in at four-thirty in the morning and a woman named Marybell?"

"And if it does?"

"Then I want to buy her dinner. But first, I gotta ask."

Tag pointed a finger at him. "Go."

"The makeup. The hair. Does it bother you?"

"Nope. I won't say it's not different. Because it is. But that's who she is. I like *who* she is."

"Music to my ears, buddy. One more question?"

"One more and then we have to knock this out. I have a late lunch date I gotta get to." He liked saying that in reference to Marybell.

"Did you hear Alison was fishing around, asking questions about you?"

He didn't even stiffen. Not a single twitch. Her name no longer evoked the kind of anger it once had. "Says who?"

"Just some old friends I've kept in touch with since the move here. Apparently she broke off her engagement to what's-his-name."

"Ted Hardy. His name was Ted Hardy." Ted Hardy, rich lawyer.

"Yeah. Him. Anyway, she was asking about you and where you'd landed."

"Maybe she should have asked that back when she was dumping me for him because I didn't have any more money, and she needed some."

"Just figured I'd give you a heads-up. In case she calls or something. I like Tag right now. I didn't like Tag back then."

No one had liked Tag back then. Bitter, angry, ugly. But Gage was warning him. Keeping him from backsliding. "I get it. Alison is done. It was done when I found out she was cheating on me with Ted Hardy, rich lawyer extraordinaire."

"Cool. So, let's finish up so I can call Falsom, huh?"

Tag grinned again, forgetting about Alison and her questions about him. He was over Alison. He was over her betrayal. She'd run at the first sign of trouble and it had been downhill from there.

Not the kind of woman you wanted to spend the rest of your life with.

Now, Marybell on the other hand...

Whoa, Hawthorne. Slow and steady wins the race.

She said she had things to work out. You don't know what those things are yet.

She's not sick—that's all that matters. The rest will happen when she's ready.

Right. Slow and steady.

Thirteen

"Bologna *and* cheese this time? Be still, my foodie palette," Marybell chirped, smiling at Tag before rubbing her belly.

They'd been having a late lunch together every day for a week now. Lunches filled with so much laughter she even laughed over them when she was alone. She'd never been courted, but the girls had informed her this was how it was done.

Courting made you secretly smile, made you shiver when you remembered intimate moments. Courting gave your stomach a run for its money with all its fluttering. It made your heart race and your blood pump.

He sat across from her at the breakfast bar, cutting her sandwich into a triangle. If he only knew how something so small and insignificant was enormous in her world. "And lettuce. You'll need your vegetables if you plan to keep up with me and my insane desire to peel your clothes off right now."

She shivered. There had been plenty of late-afternoon lunches followed by late-afternoon lovemaking, turning late afternoon into her favorite part of the day.

"I'm on the pill." She blurted the words out without thinking. It wasn't the exact setup she'd rehearsed in her mind at all.

Tag looked up from his sandwich making. "Does this mean what I think it means, Ms. Lyman?"

She'd always been on the pill. She'd just been uncomfortable trusting him enough to tell him at first. "What do you think it means?"

"I think it means you want to be my girlfriend—like all exclusive."

She hid her smile in her sandwich. "It might," she teased.

Tag wiggled his eyebrows, popping a chip into her mouth. "Well, girlfriend, what brought this about?"

A week of serious thinking. A long week full of choices and talking herself down from the ledge she was on. This seesaw of ups and downs wherein one minute she was sure she could make this right and in another, certain she couldn't.

And him—everything about Tag had brought this about. His jokes, how hot on her heels he always was with a quip. Princess movies, and medical mysteries, and the promise of more kisses on the couch, more walks in the square, more laughter.

More. She wanted more. She only hoped he'd be willing to give her more with a few prerequisites.

Don't think about it anymore. Just do it.

"I have a confession, and it's part of the reason I was so reluctant to date you."

He sat up straight, mocking a serious face. "Confess."

Go on, Marybell. Just like you practiced in the mirror. "There's something I need to tell you, but I have to do it when the time is right. When I know the time is right, and not before. So before you agree to date me exclusively, I need to know you'll give me the time I need."

It might not be fair. It was probably all shades of wrong to get involved before telling him everything, but her efforts to go to him with proof had to mean something.

Concern lined Tag's face and he was up and out of his chair as fast as his legs could carry him. He pulled her from her chair, his muscled arms around her in an instant. "Are you sick? Jesus. You'd tell me if you're sick, wouldn't you?"

She stood on tiptoe and gave him a kiss, running her fingers over the creases in his brow, loving that he was so protectively worried about her. "I'm not sick, Tag. Promise. I just need..." She took a deep breath. "I just need some time to work something out. Is that okay with you or do you want to stop seeing each other altogether until I work things out?" As much as she hoped he didn't, it was only fair to offer him an out. Even if there was deception behind the out and he didn't know how big the deception was.

"As long as you're not sick, you work out whatever you need to. Unless it's another boyfriend. That won't work."

Tag wasn't often serious, but when he was, you knew it. Something had happened to him in a relationship somewhere along the way, and it involved cheating. She pressed her lips to his harder. "Never."

He leaned back and stared down at her, his teasing tone back. "So you're my girlfriend? I can tell people?

No more hiding—skulking around like I've done a bad, bad thing?"

"No more hidin'. Tell whoever you want. Just prepare for the backlash." *Prepare for everyone to gossip about you and that naughty Marybell Lyman, dirty, phone-sex-operating freak.*

Tag tipped her chin up so their eyes met. "You do know I don't give a rat's ass about that, right? I don't want you giving one, either."

"People talk. They talk a lot about me. They'll talk a lot about you. I don't want you or your family hurt. Especially Maizy."

"Maizy's a smart kid. Look at how she handled that business with Clifton Junior and all the teasing he was taking for his father's cross-dressing."

That had been hard to watch. As the subject of much mockery herself, she had been pained to see Em's boys suffer. Thank goodness, it had all died down. Jax demanded respect, and he'd stepped in and demanded some for Em, who'd then begun to demand her own.

"My job—"

"I'll admit, it was a little hot before this happened between us. But now I close my ears when I have to walk past your office. I definitely don't love hearing you talk to strange men like that. I get that it means nothing to you, but I wouldn't be human or a possessive knuckle dragger if it didn't make me want to punch something. So I'll stay out of it and not ask questions. Fair?"

She understood. Completely. She left all dirty talk out of the bedroom for that exact reason. That and because she liked the silence between them. The ease of it. She took more pleasure in the sounds their bodies made, the sighs, the low, husky moans. They meant more than words. "Very fair. More than fair. The fairest."

"Then I guess you have a boyfriend."

"Then I guess you have a girlfriend," she said on a grin. A silly, unfettered, incredibly happy grin.

Tag whooped and grabbed her up, throwing her over his shoulder and heading straight for the bedroom. He dropped her on the bed as though she weighed nothing and sank down on top of her, the hard ridge of his cock pressing against her thigh.

She sighed when his hands began pushing her clothes aside, when he found her nipple and stroked it through her bra. "You didn't let me finish my lunch, heathen," she whispered in his ear.

"Later. We have some celebrating to do," he whispered back against her lips.

Later was just fine by her.

"Did y'all hear?" Dixie asked, pointing to her computer as they all sat around the office on Wear Your Pajamas to Work Day.

"Are they takin' your favorite shoes off the market again, Dixie? Lawd, ha' mercy on us all. Never heard such weepin' and wailin' as when they stopped selling those wedges," LaDawn teased, ruffling her boss's hair.

Dixie made a face at LaDawn. "No. That scumbag Leon Kazinski's been spotted. Heavens, you'd think he was Elvis reincarnated for all the press he's getting." She turned her head from the left to the right. "The picture's a little blurry, so I'm not buyin' it totally, but if I had to compare it with a clearer image, it sure looks like him."

"Who?" LaDawn asked.

Oh, God. Fear gripped Marybell. *No. No, no, no. Not now.*

"The guy who bilked all those seniors and investors out of millions of dollars with that Ponzi scheme," Em responded, straightening her favorite adult onesie, a look of disgust on her face. "Oh, that was awful. All those poor people, puttin' their life savings in that vulture's hands only to be left with nothing in their retirement funds. I'd bet my britches he has a big fat account somewhere nobody knows about, and he's off sittin' on some beach, livin' like a king. I don't know how he sleeps at night."

"Oh, yeah. You mean the one with the cute blond intern who got off scot-free because she played the 'I'm pretty but stupid' card and no one's heard from or seen her since?" LaDawn crowed.

That would be the one. Marybell gripped the arms of her chair until her knuckles ached. *Breathe. Breathe often.*

Em nodded, her ponytail bobbing in time. "That's the one. I'll never believe she had nothing to do with it. She was his intern, for heaven's sake! All interns know everythin'. Not to mention, she was his concubine. Did you see that picture of her with him? What was her name again?"

Marybell forced her sheer terror to calm.

Em jumped up from her chair, her white fuzzy slippers clapping against the tile. "Chapman something, I think! Where'd she go, anyway? There was a time when you couldn't look at the cover of a rag-mag without seein' her face. She was gorgeous and blond. A petite little thing with a killer body. Could never figure out what she saw in that Leon. He was much too old for her.

But I guess the slimy are just naturally drawn to each other. Bet she has all that money stowed away somewhere, just waitin' on a day like this. You do know he was the one who left Tag bankrupt, right, Marybell?"

Marybell said nothing, merely moved her head. Words were impossible right now. Breathing was impossible. She was frozen in place, helpless to do anything but listen to them talk about her while she sat right in the room with them.

Their words hurt. They slashed at her heart. Would they be the same words if she just came clean? Or were they really her friends—the kind of friends Landon once claimed existed? Would they believe her when she said she knew nothing without having any proof she knew nothing?

No. No one had believed her before. She wasn't ready for this yet. Not yet. Everything was going so well. And she was happy. This was what she got for having the audacity to be happy.

Em winced, putting a hand on Marybell's arm and rubbing it. "Maybe I shouldn't have said as much. Tag lay pretty low during the whole mess in order to stay out of the limelight because that whole thing was some circus. But seein' as you two are gettin' so close, I'd imagine he's already told you."

Marybell froze. What could she say? Neither of them had talked about it. But Tag's confession was something you took slowly. Something you revealed a little at a time. Hers? Hers should have been revealed from the moment he'd asked her out the first time. "We haven't talked about it."

Em went back to smiling. "Well, I'm guessin' it won't be long before he does. It was a bad time for him. A really bad time. Right now you two are smack-dab in the middle of the good. When the honeymoon evens out, I'm sure he'll tell you all about it. Sometimes it just takes men longer to talk about their hurts than it does us yappy women."

Sometimes.

Em passed her one of the cookies Nella made, a frosty pink confection with gumdrops. "He's pretty smitten with you, Miss MB. Have I mentioned how nice it is to see you two strollin' the square?"

"Hoo, Lawd. The two of you canoodlin' makes me green with the jealous, MB. But the way he looks at you. Hmm-hmm," LaDawn hummed her approval, hiking up the thin straps of her lavender negligee. "I'm happy for you."

Marybell forced herself to smile. Forced herself to nod and listen to their chatter about Leon Kazinski sightings.

Leon Kazinski was a pig. A filthy, lying, cheating pig.

And someone had spotted him? Was Leon really back from wherever he'd scurried off to?

Panic set her feet in motion, moving toward her office as fast as she could in her black bootie slippers. She hit her browser, prepared to search for the picture, but she didn't have to. It was the trending topic.

The picture of Leon with his slimy intern second only to the alleged picture of him.

If not for the fear eating her from the inside out, she'd laugh at being a mere first runner-up.

Her fingers went to the screen, tracing the outline of the picture that had ruined her entire life. They trembled along with everything else on her body.

A Leon Kazinski sighting meant the nightmare would return, in full force.

But you have the people shield, Marybell. It protects you.

I don't want the people shield anymore! I want out. I want to tell Tag the truth. I want to tell my friends the truth. I want to stop pretending I'm someone I've long outgrown.

But the picture of her, lying on top of Leon Kazinski on the floor of his office, clear as day, glared back at her in all its ugly truth and wasn't going to let her do that.

Fear seeped into her bones, and her stomach gurgled as she read report after report speculating about her whereabouts. Her mouth went dry as she scrolled through rehashed picture after picture of herself.

Her trying to get a cup of coffee while flashbulbs popped in her face, blinding her. Her leaving her apartment, her expression of surprise misconstrued as smug and condescending.

Her, in the last stages of her old life just before she'd disappeared, leaning up against the side of a Dumpster after she'd riffled through it to find leftover food.

She gagged, her hands cold and clammy, her cheeks hot with embarrassment.

And finally a freshly written report with a picture of her in the cafeteria at school with the headline "Where in the world is Carson Chapman?"

Marybell gulped hard, her throat so tight it hurt.

She's here.

Right here in Plum Orchard, Georgia.

Fourteen

Marybell squinted at the laptop, her eyes grainy, her head sporting a dull ache. Proving her innocence wasn't going to be easy. In fact, it was looking like it was virtually impossible. Now that her fear had quieted, and she'd forced all the painful words the girls had said at the office from her mind, she was focused. Focused and fighting for her life.

How could she possibly prove that picture of her and Leon was an accident? How could she prove that she hadn't been smiling down at him while she was atop his bloated body, smelling the stench of scotch on his breath, but actually sneering at him and his last feeble attempt to get her into bed before her internship was complete?

She'd been his intern and nothing more. She wasn't privy to the inner workings of the Kazinski fortune. She took notes at meetings. She listened to him give speeches at charity functions. She'd ended up being nothing more than his gofer, but a recommendation from the kind of prestige someone like Leon once had was golden in the world of finance. So she'd stuck it out.

She'd fought off his crude advances, his drunken rants, his endless come-ons in order to make something of her life. Growing up in the manner she had, with no one to count on but herself, she'd learned what complaining got you.

Nothing. But sucking it up for the greater good almost always left you a winner. There was no one to turn to, anyway. It had always been just her. The very little information she had about her birth parents was so vague it was almost nonexistent.

Born in Carson City, Nevada, and somehow, dropped at the doors of Child Protective Services in a small town in Georgia when she was three months old with a note attached to her blanket reading *Carson*. She didn't even know where her last name had come from or if the people at Child Protective Services had made it up so she'd have one. In all her research, she'd never found her biological parents for confirmation one way or the other.

What she did know was an endless string of social workers and foster parents. None of them bad, per se. Yet none of them in the business of keeping her. She'd worked hard to find her way out of the system. Despite the jumble of endless homes and towns and schools she'd ended up in, she'd managed to keep her grades high enough to earn a full scholarship to college and then funding for graduate school.

She'd worked several part-time jobs while studying for her degree, saving every spare penny she could get her hands on for the day when she'd go out into the world and finally have something to call her own.

When she'd nabbed an elite internship with Leon Kazinski, she thought she had the world by the tail. In-

terning for him was a huge coup, and all that was left
was to graduate.

Then it was gone. All of it gone. The very little
money she'd saved went to hiding from the paparazzi
until she ran out and then she was homeless.

After six years of working her fingers to the bone
in school, almost on the cusp of having it all, it all just
evaporated.

But the two years she'd spent on the streets until
Landon came along and rescued her had taught her
how to survive. Looking at her life now, she realized
she didn't just want to survive—hide—lie.

She wanted everything back, damn it. She wanted
her reputation back. She wanted to go to Tag and beg
him to forgive her for not telling him sooner, but she
wanted to do it with proof that she was innocent.

Marybell stared at the picture again. *Who'd* taken
it? It had shown up under the guise of anonymous at a
rag-mag, two days after the story about Leon filching
all that investment money, and it had turned her into
the biggest scandal in the past five years.

She'd been compared to infamous presidential interns. They'd run polls on who was hotter, more devi-
ous, they'd Photoshopped her, said horrible things about
her. Speculated about her lack of family, made things
up about her until she'd almost burst at the seams from
keeping her mouth shut.

It had been a long time since she'd looked the image
up on the internet. For almost a year, it was the lead
story on Yahoo!. She couldn't walk past a newsstand
without seeing it. She couldn't surf the web without it
cropping up in her news feed, couldn't stand in a gro-

cery store line when she wasn't on the front page for months.

It was what had driven her into hiding. That and the paparazzi, chasing her down everywhere she went. Some of the less reputable journalists had actually posed as patients at her dentist's office just to get pictures of her. In her efforts to get away, another patient had almost been hurt.

People whispered about her even when she was right in the room, making Plum Orchard's idea of gossip child's play in comparison.

They'd pointed, they'd insulted, they'd thrown things at her until she was on the verge of having a nervous breakdown. And then came the day, shortly after the story broke, when the dean informed her she'd lost her funding because of her scandalous behavior.

She'd packed her things and skulked away without even saying goodbye to her roommate. Not that it mattered. Tara-Anne didn't talk to her anymore, anyway, and her classes had become unbearable. Walking the campus was a living nightmare of cold stares and lots of backs to her face.

After that, her life spiraled out of control. Employer after employer had turned her down, and what little money she'd managed to save tutoring while she was in school was gone within the first week spent at a grungy hotel.

She'd never forget handing over that key to the hotel room for the last time, knowing she had nowhere to sleep, no food. That was when the idea struck her to start using the goth scene as a way to hide, and in an hour of desperation and with a pointless interview at an underground goth club, she'd made a choice.

Goth had been her thing in college. She and her old roommate used to frequent the clubs often, spiking their hair, doing each other's makeup. So when she saw the sign for help wanted in one of her old haunts, she'd applied, goth-scene makeup and all, and the club owner never even recognized her. She'd found her escape.

Unfortunately, she didn't get the job—or any job after that, but her outlandish makeup and hair brought her peace. If not the kind involving three square meals and a warm bed, then the kind that left her minus the hateful glares and the heat of the press on her back. She'd worn it almost day and night, only occasionally washing it off in a dirty gas station bathroom at night, hiding in the shadows until she had to put it back on again.

Fear of exposure threatened to swallow her whole once more and forced her to focus on the fact that in this very moment, she was okay. She had the things she'd worked hard for and the money she'd been saving on the chance her entire life could fall apart all over.

Landon knew all about who Carson Chapman was. It took him a few months before he finally got it out of her, but he knew, and he believed.

The most important part in all of it was he'd believed. He'd been convinced if she shared with Cat and the others, they'd believe, too. But she hadn't been so convinced, and even though Dixie and the girls didn't know the entire story, their words today had cut her to the quick.

She couldn't face losing them. She couldn't face them looking at her the way the rest of the world had. As if Carson Chapman was the dirty thing you scraped from the bottom of your shoe on the sidewalk.

Her doorbell rang, making her slam the laptop shut in guilt. Her eyes flew to the clock on the DVR. Tag— it was Tag. She gave a quick glance in the mirror to ensure that everything was in place, took a deep breath and opened the door.

He smiled at her from under the porch light. "Did you add another earring to your ear just for me, *girl-friend?*" he teased, pulling her into a kiss.

"No. I added this." She stuck her tongue out at him to reveal a small gold bead embedded in it, then laughed at his expression.

Tag growled, deep and husky. "For me?"

She pulled him inside, closing the door and heading for the bedroom. "You'll just have to wait and see, Hawthorne!"

"Wow," Tag muttered against her lips. "Gotta say, I had my doubts about the tongue ring, but kudos."

Marybell chuckled from beneath him, luxuriating in the vestiges of their lovemaking. She arched upward, loving the feel of his rippled muscle pinning her to the bed, and sighed when he began kissing her still-flushed skin, working his way down toward her belly.

He made her forget this lie between them. He drowned out the noise.

Tag kissed the spot where her tattoo was. "Tell me about Doby?" He didn't demand she do it, and tonight, she didn't feel he was asking to seek information about who Marybell Lyman really was. Rather that he was interested.

"Doby was my dog."

"You said that."

Did she say he was the only reason she'd kept breathing? That she'd found him tied to a stairwell in an abandoned building in one of the places where she'd squatted when the nights got cold? Whining for freedom, his squiggly golden-furred tail wagging at her as if she could offer help was all it took to capture her heart.

Had she mentioned even though she'd had nothing, Doby'd given her everything?

Let him in, Marybell. Just a little. You don't have to tell him you were homeless. You can tell the truth without the gory details.

She swallowed hard. The memory of Doby still ached. "He was just a stray I found. I was going through a pretty rough time in my life. Doby helped."

He looked up at her, his eyes understanding. "Animals are amazing healers."

"At that point in my life, Doby was the only living, breathing thing that loved me."

Tag paused, his hands still. She saw him turn her words over in his head before he asked, "What happened to him?"

She'd kept him for six months. They'd hunted scraps together. They'd slept on the streets, under bridges, in condemned houses together. She'd loved Doby more than anything in her life ever. She lifted her shoulders in a shrug. "I had to give him away. I just couldn't take care of him. Take him to the vet, get him shots and checkups and all the things a dog like Doby needed. It wasn't fair to him. I gave him to a little girl and her family in front of a restaurant I used to… Parker's. It was called Parker's. I went there a lot."

A flashback of that day at the end of the alleyway, when Doby had gotten off his leash by one of their favorite restaurant garbage bin haunts and run toward a chubby-cheeked little girl as if he'd always known her, seized her.

The little girl's squeals of excitement, the hope in her voice when she'd asked her parents if she could keep him settled deep inside her. Reminded her she was incapable of taking care of herself, let alone Doby.

When the little girl's parents protested that her beloved dog belonged to someone else, Marybell had stepped in, telling them Doby was a stray she'd found, but he needed a good home with a big backyard and a warm bed and a nice little girl to snuggle with at night.

Not at all put off by her wild makeup and hair, they'd chatted with her for a little while and then agreed to take Doby. He was getting bigger every day, making it almost impossible to keep him well fed. She knew he was too skinny for his size just by comparing him to other dogs of his muttlike origins. The vague impression of his ribs said as much.

Saying goodbye to him, pretending she was happy he'd found a home, yet knowing he'd have all the things she couldn't give him from someone else, had taken a chunk of her soul. That first night without Doby giving her his back as a pillow had been the worst kind of torture.

That pain trumped being shuffled from foster homes, leaving behind the sparks of friendships she'd begun to make, losing her scholarship, going hungry.

Tears threatened to fall, but Tag stroked her skin, soothed her ache. "Did you keep in touch with the people who took him?"

"I lost track of them, but I know he's happy. At least, I have to believe that." Or she'd go out of her mind. Doby was running in the park, eating the best kibble money could buy, chasing a ball and tearing up rawhide bones by the dozen.

That little girl was scratching his back just the way he liked it, and giving him kisses before bedtime every night.

That had to be how it was. She'd accept nothing less.

"You must've really loved him to get a tattoo of his name."

Closing her eyes, she squeezed them tight, not caring that it would smudge her eyeliner. "I got it after I got the job at Call Girls. In his honor. Because he gave me so much when I had very little."

Tag was quiet for a bit, probably absorbing her words. They weren't light words. They weren't the funny words she and Tag shared. They were the words from inside her. Words she'd never shared—not even with Landon. "You're a good person, Marybell. Just plain good."

Tag slid back up her length and rolled her into his embrace, pulling her so close she almost couldn't breathe. Yet she burrowed into his solid strength, anyway, the myriad emotions Doby's name brought up made her feel.

The feelings hurt. Just like so many lately.

But they were feelings. Uncomfortable, disjointed, scary.

But indeed Marybell Lyman was feeling them.

After Tag left, she pulled the box from beneath her bed. The box that held all the things she treasured— things that were small and could be packed up at a moment's notice.

She sifted through the few items, her fingers shaky, her heart shakier. Her sixth-grade report card where the teacher had said she was a shining star and had stamped it with a happy face.

A piece of the baby blanket she'd been found under at Child Protective Services. Just a scrap of pink satin and white fur after years of dragging it behind her until it became too tattered and full of holes.

A grainy picture of her from ninth-grade algebra—a candid shot taken by the photography club and circulated in their school flyer just before she'd been plucked up and moved to a different foster family.

A shoelace given to her by one of her foster sisters, in her favorite color, pink, and the only time she'd had shoelaces that weren't white and secondhand.

And Doby's leash. A red-and-white nylon rope she'd acquired burns on her palms from when she'd first begun to teach him how to walk, not run beside her.

Marybell twisted it around her fingers, clenching it, remembering.

And then she saw Tag's hat, reminding her that every small tidbit she revealed about herself was a piece of her life puzzle. Tag hadn't asked questions, he hadn't pried, but she'd seen them in his eyes.

If she wanted a relationship with Tag, she was going to have to do something about it. Do something fast.

Tonight, when he'd realized Doby touched a still-raw nerve, he'd held her and let her mourn in silence.

That was the moment she'd decided she wanted a real relationship with Tag. Not just the fun, flirty variety, but a real one where she could finally unload this heavy weight and find out if Tag would understand why she'd asked for time.

Maybe he wouldn't understand. Maybe he'd hate her

for duping him thus far. Maybe even proof of her innocence wouldn't make up for all her lies so far.

Maybe he'd never forgive her.

But maybe, if he was falling in love with her the way she was with him—he'd find a way to understand.

Maybe.

Fifteen

Marybell headed across the square after grabbing plum fritters and coffee for the girls on her shift.

A crowd of noisy people with more picket signs than the last time followed a path behind Louella. As she got closer, she saw a news van from an Atlanta station, unloading gear. Cameras, lights, laptops. All things she was far too familiar with.

She knew that van. The people inside that van had hunted her mercilessly for months.

Her legs froze, her heart hit the top of her feet. The press was in Plum Orchard.

She'd been found.

How? How could they have figured out who she was? Someone had been digging. That had to be it. Since that picture of Leon had surfaced, everyone was speculating about her again, too.

Oh, God.

Clutching the coffee carrier, Marybell struggled to find an avenue of escape. Her eyes looked over heads, scanning the crowd, catching sight of Dave Davison, one of the sleaziest of the bunch who'd hunted her like a wounded animal.

He'd know her. He'd hear her voice and he'd know. No one had ever caught her speaking on camera but Dave Davison. He'd blocked her path the day she'd tried to leave the dentist office. At her wits' end, she'd threatened him by offering to take a shot between his legs if he didn't move.

He'd made a snide comment about her voice. He'd said he could almost understand Leon cheating on his wife with her because of her seductive, innocent voice.

She had to get away—run as fast as she could. Call in sick— *Do something, Marybell, instead of standing here like some deer caught in a pair of headlights.*

But suddenly she was swept up in the crowd, pushed forward, stumbling and spilling cups of coffee everywhere.

Then Louella Palmer was in her face, dragging Dave Davison behind her. "This is one of them, Dave. She works right in there with the rest of those filthy women."

Like the days of old, a microphone was thrust under her nose, and Dave Davison was looking her square in the eye. His sharp eyes roving over her face, judging her based on her makeup and hair, no doubt.

She held her breath, panic keeping her rooted to the spot. There was nothing left to do but raise the white flag. Everything inside her sank to her toes.

"This is Marybell Lyman. Marybell, this is an old friend of mine, Dave Davison. He's doing a human-interest story on the dirty little secret this small town's been hidin'. Care to comment?" she drawled, so sure, so cocky.

Strong hands landed on her shoulders, reassuring,

warm, safe. Tag grabbed the microphone from a speech-less Dave and spoke into it. "No, she doesn't care to comment, but I do. I don't know what you're up to now, Louella, but while you're busy here with your old friend Dave, isn't the bitter old maid society missing their leader?" He launched the mic like a football across the square and bent down low in Dave's face. "Go fetch."

Taking Marybell by the hand, he pushed his way through the crowd until they made it to the path leading to the guesthouse.

Sanjeev or Dixie must have worked some kind of magic, as four large WWE-looking men waited at the entrance with stern faces and bunched muscles.

Tag wasn't intimidated. He pointed at her. "She works here. I'm her boyfriend."

"Name?" the man with the shortly cropped hair asked.

She finally found her voice, weak from fear. "Mary… Marybell Lyman."

He looked over a list, then nodded, moving aside so they could pass. The moment they entered the foyer was the moment her legs threatened to give way. She took deep breaths of the warm, perfumed air, letting Tag lead her toward the reception area.

Call Girls wasn't in the chaos she'd expected to find. Instead, everyone's head was down, buried in something on their desks.

Marybell was still in too much shock to speak. Relief flooded through her when she realized the reporter wasn't here for Carson Chapman, and then anger took its place. They were going to wreak havoc in her friends' lives. Shred them, poke and prod until everything blew up, and somehow she had to warn them.

"What's goin' on?" she asked Em, her hands in the air.

Em flipped to the next page of her paper. "Louella. Again."

Marybell's eyes flew open in response to her very casual remark. "Is that *it?* Is that all you have to say?"

Em's face held confusion. She tucked her hair behind her ear. "What else would you like me to say, sugarplum? It's just Louella stirrin' the pot like she's always done. Nothin' new."

"The press is here!" she yelped, pulling away from Tag and clapping her hands on the desk Em sat behind.

Nella dropped her glasses in a clatter.

Dixie shot out from her office and into the entryway.

Em patted her hand to placate her. "I know, MB. We have it handled, or did you miss Big, Brawny, Brute and Brawnier just outside the door? We're safe in here."

She couldn't believe they were taking this so lightly. Did they have any idea what the press would do to their small town? A town, even with those heartless troublemakers, she happened to love. They'd take every little thing and turn it into something heinous and dirty. They'd blow things out of proportion, speculate, misinterpret. She wouldn't let that happen.

"We have to do something! Why are you all just sitting around like it's no big deal an Atlanta news station van is parked right outside, just waitin' to chew you all to bits?"

"Dave Davison? He's hardly Matt Lauer, Marybell," Em scoffed. "He's to be taken about as seriously as TMZ."

Tag put a hand on her arm and squeezed. "Honey, calm down."

Honey? Calm down? She shrugged him off with an angry shake. "No! I won't calm down. They're going to distort this company until you won't even recognize it and make us all look like pariahs."

Dixie barked a laugh from across the room. "MB, just in case you missed the memo, we are pariahs. Nothin' they do can hurt me. We know who we are. That's all that matters. It's business as usual."

She was sure they all could hear the furious, fear-riddled pounding of her heart. They couldn't just sit back and let this happen. She couldn't watch it happen. "It doesn't matter if you know who you are, Dixie! You won't if you let them get their hands on this and run with it. They'll pick at you like vultures until you're nothing but a carcass. I can't watch that happen to all of you!"

Silence took over the room in a heavy blanket, covering her in awkwardness. No one moved. No one batted an eye.

Em went into motion first, but Tag held up his hand to stop her. Surely, if anyone understood the press, it was Tag. His spotlight in the Kazinski case had been brief when you took into consideration he was young and healthy, and capable of earning back his retirement fund. The press had focused on the victims, the seniors Kazinski'd wiped out and the villainess—her.

Why wasn't anyone taking some action—hatching a plan?

Are they all going to put on crazy makeup, spike their hair and hide on the streets of Atlanta like you did?

"MB," he said in quiet tones. "It's all going to be okay. I won't let anyone hurt any of the women. Especially you. Okay?"

No. No, it wasn't okay. But she nodded, anyway.

Because as realization sank in, and the surprise on everyone's face at her outburst penetrated her panic, she realized she'd gone way over the top. The usually quiet Marybell had just plumb lost her fritters and no one knew what to say or do.

Looking down at her feet, she apologized. "I'm sorry. It was just so crazy out there, and I didn't expect it, and I worry about all of you...."

Em and Dixie rushed her, heedless of spatial issues, giving her hard, motherly hugs. "I sent you a text, Marybell," Dixie said. "You didn't answer your phone, but I wanted you to be prepared. I called Tag just in case. Now, never you mind Louella Palmer and her pathetic connections to that plastic-looking man, Dave Davison. He'll lose interest when he finds out we have nothing to say."

Em bounced her head in tune with Dixie. "I'm sorry you were caught so off guard, MB. But we have it under control. Promise. Let 'em dig all they want, say whatever they want. Nobody cares about a legal phone sex company anymore. There are much bigger fish to fry nowadays. It's not like phone sexin' hasn't existed forever. So I don't see what all the fuss is about. So relax, okay?" She rubbed Marybell's arm and gave it a squeeze. "You all right now?"

No. She had a sick feeling in her stomach, a certain dread that could only be attributed to trouble. Big trouble. Yet she held her tongue and nodded, letting Tag lead her to her office.

An hour later, her head clearer, her fears at bay, Marybell shuffled to Em's office on her fifteen-minute break, rapping her knuckles against the door. "Knock-knock." She poked her head in and smiled.

Em waved her in while nodding at the phone in her ear. "Yes, Mama. Of course I've heard all about it. They're all right outside the door." She motioned for Marybell to sit.

Em's mother, Clora Mitchell, if what the gossip and even Em herself said was true, was horrible. *Cranky, pious* and *disapproving* were words thrown about when it came to Clora. But since the day Em had found out Dixie's father was her father, too, she'd watched a shift in the dynamics of their relationship.

It was subtle, and for the most part Clora still disapproved of Em's job, but there were far fewer moments full of tension than there'd once been, and every once in a blue moon, Marybell caught Clora smiling. Surely the earth rumbled when her lips cracked one, but she smiled, and it seemed to make Em happy. In turn, that made Marybell happy for her.

"Yes, Mama. I'm fine. We're all fine. Thanks for callin'. See you for Sunday supper." She clicked off her phone and folded her hands in front of her on her desk with a sigh, smiling at Marybell. "What can I do for you today? Please don't tell me someone else is sick. If I have to let LaDawn take one more vanilla call, we're goin' down."

Marybell laughed out loud. LaDawn's specialties didn't lie in the subtler phone sex. They were shouty and in-your-face demands to perform. "No. No one's sick. So, how's Miss Clora?"

"Still crusty around the edges, but better. Thanks for askin'. So, what's up with you?"

"I came to apologize."

Em's brow wrinkled. "For what, honey?"

A squirm or two later in her chair, she said, "For my overreaction to what's goin' on out there. It was just so…"

"Much?" She waved her hand in a dismissive gesture. "Bah! Never you worry your pretty multicolored little head, MB. It took you by surprise. I understand. No apologies necessary. But we have it contained for now."

The phrase "for now" was what worried her the most. "So, how are you? I feel like I haven't had the chance to sit and talk with you since you and Jax jumped into the pond of commitment. Is everything goin' all right? The boys gettin' along with Maizy?"

Em's entire face lit up. "We've had some moments of adjustment. You know, sharing me, sharing Jax, but on the whole, everything's right as rain."

It warmed her inside and out that Em had found love and happiness. No one deserved it as much as she did. "I'm happy for you, Em. Really happy."

"How about you, MB? How are things with you and Tag and the relationship you're not having?" she teased.

Looking down at her lap, she fumbled with her words. Words she wanted to share to express the kind of giddy, light side to her Tag evoked.

This was what Landon had meant about letting people in, sharing your life, the good and the bad with them. So she tried it on for size. "I really like Tag."

Em was up in a flash, pulling her into a tight hug and squealing her approval. "I knew it! I just knew it. I told Dixie and LaDawn I know what fallin' in love looks like. I'm so happy for you, MB. Just bustin' with sunshine."

Was this what falling in love felt like? Real love? Seeing Em all dimples and twinkly eyes made her smile, too. "I said I *liked* him."

"Oh, like-schmike. Does he make your heart flutter and your tummy tingle? Does the sound of his voice make your arms all goose bumpy? Does he make you feel all gooey inside when you least expect it? Safe, happy, warm?"

From somewhere deep and buried inside her, a fizzle of Em's excitement triggered hers. She wanted to share these new emotions with her friends. She wanted to giggle and tell secrets to them. She wanted. "Yes…" she mumbled. Then louder, "Yes! He does all those things."

Em jumped up and down, taking Marybell with her. "I'm so excited for you! What a lovely, lovely thing to happen to a person as lovely as you!"

Lovely. No one had ever called her lovely. "Do you think I'm lovely, Em?"

She stopped jumping and hugging her and held her at arm's length. "Of course I do, MB. I think you're probably one of the kindest people I know. Wait, let me list the ways. Wasn't it you who held LaDawn's hair back while she dumped her intestines into that toilet after she got food poisonin' from Gaylan Foxner's chicken wings at the fair and stayed with her till the fever passed?"

She was still green just thinking about it. What a mess. "You'd have done the same, Em."

"But we're talking about you. Isn't it you who instituted give-Em-a-break day and took the boys off my hands every Saturday mornin' for a play date in the park for an entire month while I worked up the new Call Girl's operator policy? After workin' an eight-hour shift, no less?"

She averted her eyes, looking to the floor. "I love Gareth and Clifton Junior."

"And they love you. But wait, there's more. Wasn't that you who dropped everything and took Sanjeev to the doctor when he had kidney stones? Isn't it you who makes that special blend of tea none of us can copy for Dixie just because you know she likes it? Wasn't it you who dressed up as Binky the Clown when the real Binky canceled for Gareth's party just two hours before our guests were due to arrive?"

Marybell shrugged. "Well, I do have the makeup for it."

"That's not the point. The point is, you're a terrific friend. One of the best I've ever had. Of course, I think you're lovely, MB, and I want lovely things for you because of it."

She didn't know how to respond or how to get past the lump in her throat. So instead, she stared at Em for a beat before saying, "Thank you, Em."

Her lips instantly pursed. "Did that Louella Palmer say somethin' to you to make you doubt what a kind, generous person you are? Because if she did, you might want to mention to her that it was you who shoveled her mean old mother's driveway when Kitty was havin' foot surgery and you were worried she'd slip on wet leaves. Louella was too busy takin' her mean lessons that day to care what happened to her own mother."

Praise was always murky for her. It was a foreign concept she always felt uncomfortable accepting—even when it was lavished upon her by Em. She just wanted to know that somehow, even if she struggled to share her appreciation, these people, who'd grown so important to her, knew she cared.

Shooting Em an amused gaze, she covered herself. "Now, you know Louella better 'n that. All I have to do is snarl at her, and she's in a corner huffing. She didn't say anything to me. I don't know why I asked you that."

One pat to Marybell's arm, and the concern fled Em's face. "Good. Now, let's dish boys. Tell me everything!"

Easy. She felt easy and lighter, and as Em encouraged her to chat about Tag, she found a new aspect to her inner workings.

There was a part of her that liked having someone to sigh with over how adorable Tag could be.

And that was nice.

Tag took a hearty bite of one of the cookies Em had left them on the counter and tried to sort through Marybell's strange reaction today.

She'd been utterly panicked, her eyes wild, her hands shaking. It didn't make any sense. She'd nearly bitten Em's head off over a low-life reporter as if he had the power to take Dixie and crew down single-handedly.

He was far less worried about Call Girls than he was about Marybell. He'd felt her panic. He'd seen it in her eyes.

Jax grabbed a cookie from the plate and nodded a greeting at Tag. "Some kind of crazy over there at Call Girls, huh?"

"Yeah. No kidding. Em okay?"

Jax smiled. "My Em? The one who's suddenly all teeth and snarl? She's fine. I'll go pick her up when she's done for the day. She's gotten pretty tough, but

I'll be damned if I'm going to let some asshole stick a mic in her face. MB all right?"

No. He had the strangest feeling she wasn't. He just couldn't figure why. "She was pretty shaken up, but she's okay now. I'm going to do the same and get her after her shift. Just to be sure that dick isn't lurking somewhere in the bushes. Can't figure why any reporter worth his salt would listen to Louella Palmer."

"You mean Davison? I hear she got him here by telling him about Landon and the contest between Dixie and Caine. Even I have to admit, it's pretty damn crazy how they ended up with the company. It's interesting enough, but will it do what Louella wants it to do—run the girls out of business? Especially in this day and age where everyone outside Plum Orchard won't find this nearly as appalling as some do here."

"Guess it doesn't matter now. Louella still managed to get someone here. It must have been worthy enough for them to bring a camera crew."

Jax stuffed another cookie in his mouth. "But I think she forgets who she's jacking around. She's messing with Dixie Davis. I think just because Dixie's gone good, Louella forgets who she's playing this game with. Add in LaDawn, and I have to think this won't last long."

He hoped to hell not. Marybell would have a cow if it did.

"So, are you okay?" Jax asked, peering at his brother over his coffee cup.

"Sure. Why wouldn't I be?"

"You've had your own go-round with the press."

Tag shrugged. "I was a big nobody in that mess. They wouldn't even remember my name. Most of the sympathy and spotlight, rightly so, went to the seniors that jack-off stole from. I managed to lie low except for that one day after they took my deposition. You know, because I was too busy drinking myself into a stupor."

"You heard he's supposedly been seen, right?"

The fury associated with Leon and what he'd done to Tag's thriving company had once left him seeing red. But if he allowed all the crap he'd been reading as of late to get to him, he'd be right back where he was—drinking at his endless pity parties, missing the things that were important. "I saw, and I'm fine. I've given up hope anyone's ever going to actually find him or his intern or all that money. But I've made my peace with it. I think I can safely say, I've moved on." Yeah. He was saying that.

"Good to hear. And Harper? I know it's a touchy subject for you, but this is me, touching base."

There'd been a time when he didn't know how to address Harper with anyone but the therapist he'd seen and the mirror he had to look in every morning. Yet, after talking with Gage, it was becoming easier. His response was honest. "I miss her."

Jax grimaced, rubbing his jaw. "Me, too, buddy. She was sort of our glue, huh?"

The best kind of glue there was. Pretty, levelheaded, smart, protective glue. She'd always been the soothing balm to their brotherly arguments, the voice of reason, the first one to chip in when Jax kept Maizy after his best friend left her to him when he died. "She was."

"But you know, I'd like to think we learned how to make our own glue without her here. She taught us well. It took a lot of manpower, and one helluva learning curve, but I think we're back on track." Jax's smile was fond, just like always whenever Harper's name came up.

Tag's head dipped, his eyes focused on the floor. "I didn't help that much. Have I ever said how sorry I am for what happened?" Jesus, he was sorry.

"You have," was his brother's husky reply. "I don't want your apologies. I just want you to feel good again. Start over, get your life back into the game again. That's the best way to honor Harper, you know. It's what she would have demanded from you had it been me or Gage."

He did know. It was slow to sink in, but it was happening in small spurts.

"So, Gage tells me you two are making a bid for Falsom's mill."

A deep sense of satisfaction welled up in him, and the pain of remembering Harper eased. "That's the safely-moving-on part."

Jax slapped him on the back. "Proud of you," he said, wandering out of the kitchen with a smile.

For the first time in a long time when bringing up the state of his life, he and Jax managed to get through a conversation without any angry words shooting out of their mouths, and it felt good.

It was pretty safe to say, that, too, was all part of moving on.

Tag waited for her just outside the guesthouse doors when her shift was done, a hot chocolate in his hands and a kiss on her lips. "You feel better tonight?"

His eyes were fraught with concern. Why wouldn't they be? She'd behaved like a raving lunatic. With time to gather her senses, she'd talked herself back off that ledge she teetered on lately.

Today, and her reaction to today, was a perfect opening to the discussion they had to have. Yet she clammed up tighter than a drum, too afraid. But the incident had also motivated her to find a private investigator. He was expensive. It would cost her a chunk of her savings, but finding out who took that picture of her would be money well spent.

He draped an arm around her shoulder and began to walk toward the square. "So, I'll ask again, you okay?"

She sipped the hot chocolate, grateful for the warmth on her hands. "I overreacted. I'm sorry. I was overwhelmed and it set my mouth to runnin', and… Anyway, I'm sorry. I hope I didn't embarrass you."

"Rest your pretty spiked head, there's nothing you can do to embarrass me that I haven't done myself."

Leaning into him, letting his warmth pick away at the icy layer of fear she'd carried around all night, made her curious. "I can't imagine you embarrassing yourself."

"That's because you've never seen me drunk."

She heard the pain in his words, the effort to pull them from his throat. "Bad subject?"

"Not so much anymore. I'm an alcoholic. I always will be. I'm an alcoholic because I let myself be."

"Why?"

He stopped walking and stared her right in the eye. "Because my life fell right apart, Marybell Lyman, and I was too lazy to pick up the pieces. Buying booze was easier."

The word *How?* slipped from her mouth before she

could put any sensitive thought behind it. "Wait. Stop. I'm prying. If you're uncomfortable, don't—"

"I lost my business, got completely ripped off. Then I lost my fiancée." More directness. It was refreshing considering that she lived a life full of secrets. Yet it frightened her because she couldn't live her life without her secrets. Not yet.

Her antennas went on alert when she considered his fiancée. He'd lost a fiancée, too. There was no end to this havoc. "I didn't know you had a fiancée."

His smile was wry under the moonlight as they began to walk again. "She apparently didn't, either. Alison and I grew up together and eventually became college sweethearts. We'd been together a long time. She left me at the beginning of my downward spiral— just after I lost all my investments and my company and when she realized if we were still going do this thing, it was going to be on the cheap. There'd be no cathedral weddings and ten K in wedding dresses. There'd be no honeymoon, either."

She couldn't ask him how he'd lost his money and manage to stay comfortably in her skin. To play dumb and behave as though she didn't know the intimate details of his financial downfall made her want to vomit. That was going too far.

So she chose to stick to the parts she didn't know. Alison leaving him. It was when people stayed that counted. Maybe that's where this understanding between them came from—this connection? "So she left you at the worst point in your life?"

"I can't really blame Alison. I was pretty shitty up to the point that she left. But she was cheating on me before I shut everyone in my life out. My drinking was the perfect escape for her."

"That's awfully fair of you." What had a drunken Tag been like? She'd encountered her fair share of drunks on the seedier side of Atlanta, but she'd never been involved with one. He was so funny and playful, she couldn't imagine him any other way.

"I'm a mean drunk. I don't mean physically abusive, but I was definitely surly and difficult. That's how I got a Little Mermaid tattoo, remember? Alison was halfway out the door when I lost my company, but she'd been lying to me for a long time. She nailed me with her cheating, completely floored me. It was the last thing I expected, finding out she wasn't who I thought she was. The drinking was just my excuse to feel sorry for myself."

Finding out Alison wasn't who he thought she was. The words made her want to confess right then and there. They instilled fear in her, panic for the time when she'd have to tell him who she was. Instead, she said, "Sounds like something right out of AA."

He nodded his head in the shadows. "It is. Maybe not word for word, but it's what I took away from it."

They stopped at the pathway leading to her apartment. "What made you turn the corner?" She stopped him before he could answer. She was asking him to reveal his innermost demons—she was asking for full disclosure, yet she was hiding. Unfair. "Don't answer. I'm just pryin' again."

Wrapping an arm around her waist, Tag fused his hips with hers. "Well, you are my girlfriend. Girlfriends can ask questions."

"But...I..."

He read her mind. "You'll tell me whatever you need to all in due time. Until then, I'll be the open book. My big shot in the head, when I finally got a grip on myself, was when my sister, Harper, died."

Tragedy, the bucket of ice water over your head. Yet she didn't know what to say, how to make the flash of pain in his eyes better.

How did you make someone's death better? You didn't. You waited it out. You prayed it would ease. She'd never experienced sorrow like when Landon died, and while it probably wasn't the same as your sibling dying, it was a hurt she understood.

"I'm sorry," she offered, putting her free hand on his chest, feeling feeble and stupid.

"I was sorry, too. I was sorry that I was passed out cold in a hotel room, my cell phone shut off because I didn't pay the bill. I missed Jax's phone call when he called to tell me Harper'd been mugged and stabbed."

Tag paused for a moment while Marybell waited, instinctively knowing there was more.

His sigh was ragged, his body tense. "But what I'm sorriest about is the final phone call I missed when the doctors realized she wasn't going to make it, and I screwed up my last chance to say goodbye to her."

Marybell stared up at him, her heart crashing in her chest, her throat tight. "Because you were too drunk."

Tag stared right at her, no hiding. No plays for sympathy in his eyes—just dead-on and matter-of-fact. "Because I was too drunk. I was a goddamn drunk, and that's who Taggart Hawthorne was just a couple of years ago."

Tag was opening his scars and bleeding right out in the open.

Now, more than ever, she wanted to tell him she knew what it was like to bleed, too.

Sixteen

When the words were directed at Marybell, Tag was surprised to find that when he finally said them, they came out far less venomous than they had in a long time. He'd said them only in angry rants to a therapist, to his brothers, to his mother, to himself.

He'd almost choked on the pain of those words more times than he cared to remember. The impact of Harper's passing, the last opportunity to tell her how much he loved her got all fucked up because he was lying in a puddle of his own damn vomit.

That was the truth. He'd never forget the pounding of his head when Jax and Gage finally reached him. That ache, that incessant drone of sound in his head, compounded by a massive hangover. He almost hadn't been able to process the words for the ache in his head.

He'd never forget when they'd broken his door down that next day, thinking he was dead, too. He'd never forget the worry on their faces until they realized he was doing nothing more than drowning in his own damn misery.

Then he'd never forget their cold, angry faces. The

yelling. The punch he'd taken to the jaw by none other than Gage.

But most of all, he'd never forget their disappointment—so deep it was as if they'd used a knife to cut his flesh.

They'd been on a long road to recovery since then, mending fences, Gage and Jax going to see a therapist with him, sharing their pain not just over the loss of Harper, but over the loss of him.

They'd never once faltered in their disappointment, their hurt and anger that he'd missed the last moments of Harper's life, but they were also the kind of men who made him own it, do something about it.

And it had been hard to watch them fight to keep those emotions out of their disagreements, off their faces, but they'd done it, and somehow found a way to support his road back to recovery.

Now, looking down at Marybell, his ugly secret between them, he didn't want her pity. He didn't want her to tell him it was okay. He just wanted honesty. As much as he could give her, so she'd know what he'd done.

Marybell was silent for a few beats, but then she said, "I feel like you wanted to shock me."

"Did it shock you?"

"Yes. It was the last thing I expected."

"And how do you feel about it? No sugary coatings, please."

Her blue, shiny lips went thin. "I want to say it was a mistake and we all make them, Tag. But that's not how I really feel."

"Then tell me how you really feel."

"I feel a little angry with you. Your family is amazing. I'm bettin' Harper was amazing, too. To not be there…"

"She sure was. They sure are."

"To ignore that, take it for granted, it's huge. So much bigger than I…"

"Yep. For a while, it was bigger than me. After Harper died, when I had no choice but to get sober if I was going to attend her funeral, because Jax and Gage made it clear they'd keep me out if I wasn't, I knew I was at rock bottom."

Her eyes had grown wide, shiny with unshed tears, and he hated it. But he had to own his failures if he wanted to live in truth. She should know what he'd done. What he was once capable of. "How do you *live* with it?" she finally asked.

Tag heard the rasp in her sweet voice, the ragged edge to her question, and he wondered if she hadn't had some similar experience somewhere along the way. That whatever she couldn't tell him right now was a lot like what he'd just told her. "I had to find a way to forgive myself. That's a tricky word, *forgiveness.* I don't know that I'll ever totally forgive myself, but I accept that I did it. I accepted responsibility. I got sober. I went into therapy. I raged. I stumbled around for a while. I was eaten up with anger and guilt. It affected everything I did, everyone I was around. Then I learned that sometimes the only thing you can do is go on or give up. There were more things to go on for than there were reasons to give up."

Marybell said nothing, nearly killing him, but this was his reality. It was only fair she know it. If she wanted to walk away from a man who'd done something like that, it would kill him, but he wouldn't blame her. He was deeply flawed—that came with a price.

When she spoke, she looked him square in the eye. "I'm sorry you made such a huge mistake, Tag. I'm sorry you hurt the people you love. I'm sorry you were lost. I'm sorry if my honesty hurts your feelin's, or if you expected me to tell you what you did was okay."

Tag looked down at her, watched her eyes filter her thoughts before they skittered to a focal point on his chest. "I'm not. It will never be okay. But can you accept it? Accept me so flawed?"

Because he needed to know. He needed to know she understood he wasn't in this for her to "poor baby" him or minimize what he'd done. He'd told her so the part of him that he'd held back until now was free. No surprises.

She lifted her chin, cupping his jaw, and simply said, "Yes."

Then she smiled up at him and took his hand and led him inside her apartment.

Tag wasn't sure if the breath he took in relief was audible, but his chest shifted, heaved hard, easing the tight tension.

Marybell pulled him all the way inside, closing the door and taking his cup of hot chocolate from him. She set it on the counter along with hers and without a word, led him down the short hallway to her bedroom.

Her heart ached for what he'd done, what Tag could never run away from, what he'd live with forever.

It was far more unbearable than anything she lived with. At first, she didn't know how anyone could live with it. She didn't know how to respond other than truthfully.

What he'd allowed his life to become, so steeped in alcohol, was taking for granted some of the most precious gifts life can give you. He'd done wrong. So wrong.

And then she saw his eyes, eyes waiting to see if she'd reject him, call him all the names he'd likely already called himself, and she couldn't do it.

Wouldn't do it.

He'd shown her his soul, in all its weaknesses. He'd shown her there was more to Tag than just a quip. He'd shown her his pain.

She'd felt his pain.

Now she wanted to ease it, soothe him the way he soothed her.

Her hands went to his jacket, tugging it off his shoulders and setting it on the edge of the bed. She untucked his shirt and popped the buttons on it, pulled his belt and jeans off. Pushed him to the edge of the bed and removed his work boots and socks.

Tag went willingly, his limbs pliable, his beautiful face devoid of the amused expression he always wore, as though his confession, maybe even the worry she'd reject him, had exhausted him.

Marybell swept the pillows away and lifted his feet, putting her hand flat on his chest to push him onto the bed. She dragged the covers up over him, not even sparing the usual moment or two to admire his gorgeous body before pressing a kiss to his forehead.

Pulling off her own shoes and clothes, she put her nightgown on and climbed in beside him, tucking herself next to him and wrapping her arms around his shoulders so her head lay on his chest.

And then she closed her eyes, stroking his hair, loving the feel of his strong body curved into hers. Loving his willingness to relax into her, take a deep breath and close his eyes.

Tonight, she let the pressure of her fears, her secrets, wash away.

Tomorrow she'd think about hiring a private investigator and reclaiming her life.

Tonight she wanted to lie with Tag and fall deeper in love.

The sunlight hit her face, tearing her from the comfort of Tag's embrace. Her eyes flew open to find her alarm clock.

Ten a.m. *No, no, no.* Tag had spent the night. How was she ever going to get him out of here before Blanche caught sight of him?

"We've done it now," Tag teased from his place at her chest, nipping at her flesh.

"Blanche is gonna have a chicken," she moaned.

Tag nibbled the flesh along her collarbone, sweeping his tongue across her skin. "Never you worry your pretty little head. I know a back way out of here even Blanche doesn't know about. Caine told me all about it."

She pretended to be affronted while she leaned into his attentions and sighed. "Have you been discussin' our activities with Caine?"

He chuckled, rich and deep, cupping her breast, using his index finger to circle her nipple. "I just made mention we engage in late-night visits because of your shift and Blanche might object to my calling on you. He suggested alternative routes out of here."

"Do they involve tramplin' on Blanche's roses? Because that's cause for eviction," she whispered on a gasp as he licked at her nipple.

"No trampling. Now, are you going to be quiet and let me have my way with you, or do I have more convincing to do?"

She shivered against him when he slid his fingers inside her panties and spread her flesh, arching into his hand, loving his rough fingertips inside her. "We have to make it quick. Really quick. I have a bake sale to attend at the VFW Hall to raise money for the bowling league's trip."

Tag grabbed her hand and dragged it over his erection, moaning when her fingernails scraped it lightly through the fabric of his underwear. "Does this feel like it should be treated quickly, Lyman?"

Marybell pulled his boxer-briefs from his hips and enveloped his cock in her grip with a smile. "This is Dixie we're talkin' about. If I'm late for the bake sale, your insatiable needs will be the least of my worries. Besides, what big strapping man turns down a quickie? Now hurry it up, Hawthorne," she demanded on a laugh, rolling to her back and pulling him over her.

Tag positioned himself between her legs, slipping inside her with a slow thrust.

Her whimper was low, coming from way down in her chest. The intense satisfaction she drew from him so deep within her always touched her at her core, left her breathless and needy. Each time they made love, it solidified that feeling.

Tag's muscles flexed as he settled into her. The now-familiar ripple of his muscles against her flesh set her on fire.

She responded by wrapping her legs around his waist, sliding under him and lifting her hips, cradling him close until her nose was buried in his neck and they became one entity.

His strokes became more powerful, his lips finding hers, fusing them together as she clung to his broad back and the heat he never failed to create in her began its steady climb.

White-hot pangs of need stabbed at her, rising, falling, sharply turning until she was desperate for release. *"Please,"* she whispered. *"I need you."*

He settled deeper. The delicious friction of her clit rubbing against his pubic hair made her writhe beneath him.

Tag thrust long, slow, grinding against her until that well of heat building inside her surfaced, sparking an orgasm that clutched not just her body, but her heart, squeezing it until she stiffened and her muscles tightened to almost unbearable.

His big body shuddered above her in tune with hers until she heard his hiss of satisfaction, felt the release of his breath against her ear.

Lips nuzzled at her neck, kissing along her jaw. "I think I'm a little in like with you, MB. What do you have to say to that?"

She smiled against his neck, so incredibly warm inside. "I think a little is understating things."

"Saucy," he whispered, nipping the top of her ear, the only place she didn't have earrings.

"You really like me as is? Makeup and hair and zebra-striped leggings?"

"Affirmative. I especially like the Marybell with the black shiny leggings. Makes me hard as a rock. Though I will admit, someday, I hope you'll let me see Marybell in the shower. Naked and soapy."

And without makeup. "Under all this goop lies a troll. Someday, when I show you that Marybell, you'd better not hit the ground runnin'."

"I promise to leave my shoelaces untied," he teased, lifting her chin so he could see her eyes. "You'll show me when you're ready. Until then, I think I've proven I don't care what you look like."

She planted her lips on his, kissing him hard. He had. In spades. He'd shown her all his cards. She'd eventually have to show him hers. "For the record, I like you, too. Now I need to get in the shower, and you need to plan your escape route."

Running his thumb over her breast, he muttered against her lips, "Sure I can't wash your back for you?"

She squirmed under him, wishing they could stay in bed forever—just like this. "We'll never get to the bake sale that way. Now, out, Hawthorne, or know the wrath of Dixie."

He lifted up and off the bed, his thick body even more amazing in the sunlight than it was in the dim light of their usual meetings. He had makeup all over his face from their lovemaking, and his hair was sticking up, and still, he was like some hard-chiseled god.

He began to pull on his clothes while she hopped off the bed and grabbed something to wear from her drawers. They worked in silence, as though they'd done this a million times before. Stepping over each other, moving around each other as if it were a familiar route they took every day.

This was what she longed for. These routine day-to-day habits she could look to for comfort.

Tag swatted her on the butt, grabbing her around the waist and pulling her tight to him. He rained kisses along the side of her neck, making her giggle. "You'd better save me a cookie, Lyman."

She spun around, wrapping her arms around his neck. "After what just happened in that bed, I'll save you two. Now go, before Blanche gets out the Holy Water."

He chuckled. "See you at the VFW Hall." Planting one last kiss on her lips, he left the bedroom in all his big-framed, tightly put together swagger.

He made her sigh, smile, feel giddy and excited.

She pondered that as she made her way to the bathroom, catching a glimpse of her face, her makeup smeared, the eye shadow on her eyes smudged almost to her hairline, the spikes in her hair crooked and stiff from all the gel and hair spray.

The real Carson Chapman aka Marybell Lyman wanted out. She wanted out so desperately it had started to hurt. She wanted Tag. She wanted to love him, and let him love her. She wanted more than this half-life she'd been living, kidding herself that she could hide behind clothes and makeup forever.

Tag's words last night about Alison frightened her more than she'd like to admit. *It was the last thing I expected. She lied.*

She was going to be the last thing he expected, too. She'd been lying.

It had to end.

She wanted total freedom. And there was only one way to get that.

Grabbing her phone from the pocket of her discarded jacket, she dialed the number of the private investigator she'd bookmarked.

"Larry Roberts, private investigator, how can I help you?"

"My name is Marybell Lyman.... Um, sorry. This is Carson Chapman...."

Seventeen

The VFW Hall was crowded to capacity, people milling from table to table, eyeing the cookies and cakes. Parents swatted at errant children's hands, people grouped off in batches, laughing and talking, Mayor Hale blustered in and out, shaking hands and smiling.

This was what she loved about Plum Orchard. The sense of community. She often wondered, if the Mags were taken out of the equation, with their pot stirring and the gossip, what the town would be like minus their almost bullyish influence. As she looked around at so many happy people, all willing to pitch in and have a bake sale so the bowling team could go to Atlanta, she had to believe there was more good than bad.

She even wondered if the Mags didn't instill a sense of unspoken threats in folks' morality. Most of the time, everyone was decent to her, if they didn't completely avoid her altogether.

But when a Mag showed up, she got noses in the air and backs to her face, leading her to believe not everyone thought they were ruining Plum Orchard one dirty call at a time, but rather, putting on a good show so the Mags wouldn't turn their attentions on them.

Still, she loved Plum Orchard, and she wanted to clear her name so she could live in truth again. She'd set up an appointment with the private investigator for next week, giving her enough time to write a timeline of events and list everyone she'd worked with at the time.

"Well, well." Em waved and smiled coyly as she made her way to the Call Girls table. "Look who decided to sell cupcakes and cookies today. Are you plumb tuckered from your nighttime activities?"

Marybell giggled. "I'm five minutes late, and that's only because it took me five minutes to get across the room. Good showing today, huh?"

"You're five minutes too late to see Gage Hawthorne turn down Annabelle Pruitt's invitation to the Midwinter Dance, too," LaDawn said, fluffing her platinum hair.

Marybell's eyes went wide. "He did not."

"He did, too," Dixie said on a chuckle from her folding chair behind the table. "Turned her down flat. Said he had a date with our Nella."

"Nella?" Marybell asked. "Our Nella? Quiet-until-provoked Nella? I had no idea he was even interested."

Em fanned herself and giggled. "I don't know that Nella does, either, but Lawd, Gage said it clear as day. We all heard it. Annabelle's over there in the corner mopin' right now." She pointed a shiny red nail to the far corner of the room.

Maizy popped out from behind Em and waved at Marybell, her fiery-red hair enhanced by the sunlight streaming in through the windows. "Hi, Miss Marybell."

Marybell wiggled a finger at her and grinned. "Oh, my goodness, it's Princess Maizy Hawthorne, standin' right here before me." She curtsied to the tune of Maizy's infectious giggles.

"I'm not a princess, Miss Marybell. I'm just me."

Marybell wrinkled her nose and made a silly frown. "No? I woulda sworn with all that pretty hair and those shiny shoes you have on, you were a princess. When I go home, I'm going to look in my big book of princesses to see. Bet I'll find your name there."

Maizy grabbed her hand and fiddled with one of her many bracelets. "Will you make paper dolls with me again soon? Maybe we can make princess dolls?"

"You bet, with crowns and everything. Why don't we see if your uncle Tag wants to make it a date sometime? We'll all have grilled cheese and Cheetos and make a million paper dolls. Deal?" She held out her fist to Maizy.

Maizy fist-bumped it and grinned her infamous Hawthorne grin. "Deal!" she chirped before skipping off across the room to her father, her shiny shoes tapping out a happy rhythm.

Em tapped her on the shoulder. "Dates with the family included? Well, well, Miss We're Not in a Relationship. I'd say someone's denyin' a little too much," she teased.

That got a chuckle out of her, a chuckle and one of those secret, silly smiles. She wanted Tag. She wanted to be in a full-blown relationship with him. She wanted to be a part of his life, the lives of the people he loved.

Cat came up behind her and tugged on one of her spikes, prompting Marybell to turn around and give her a hug. "How're you feelin'? I haven't seen you in forever." She placed a hand over Cat's belly and rubbed, smiling when the baby kicked back.

She smiled, her cheeks flushed, but her eyes bright with happiness. "I'm exhausted, so my eyes are closed more than they're open these days, and I'm so ready to be done. But this little bugger just won't get out. I keep tellin' her she's got all these women she needs to meet, but she's a stubborn one."

Marybell laughed. "Like mother, like daughter? Or are we forgettin' Flynn?" she asked, referring to a time not so long ago when Cat and Flynn, two very different people, were going around in circles without realizing they belonged together.

Cat swatted at her arm playfully. "Oh, you just hush. I came round when the time was right. Got myself knocked up to boot to seal the deal. Now, tell me all about you and a Hawthorne boy, Miss MB. I hear ya'll been givin' purpose to these gossip' ninnies." She pointed at Dixie and Em and fluttered her eyelashes, snatching a cookie from one of the plates.

"I meant to call you, but things have been so hectic."

"Well, I'll tell you what, you and me, we need a sit-down next week. Late lunch at Madge's on Wednesday?"

"It's a date. Now go sit before you burst." She grabbed a chair for Cat and led her to it.

Cat settled in and folded her hands over her belly in a protective manner. "So, I hear Louella's been stirrin' up trouble, picketing and bringing the newspeople from Atlanta here. What's that about, Dixie?"

Dixie rolled her pretty eyes. "Just Louella bein' Louella, Cat. She dragged that poor plastic man, Dave Davison, all the way here for a whole lotta nothin'. Word is, she was hoping to get people all in an outrage over our little town harboring a bunch of dirty talkers. I think she forgets, outside our little burg, the big bad world awaits, and phone sex is hardly news. No matter where it's done."

Cat chuckled. "Oh, that woman. She really picketed?"

Marybell nodded, rearranging the cookies on the plate. "Spellin' errors and all. It was quite a sight for a little while, but we locked down tight and kept our mouths shut. Dave Davison seems to have lost interest. Haven't seen him lurking around for a couple of days now." Making that one less issue she had to worry about.

"Uh-oh," Cat mumbled from behind the curtain of her shiny hair. "Speakin' of our intrepid gossiper. Incoming, girls. Fake smiles all round, now."

"So, ladies, I see the Call Girls made a contribution. Who knew women who did what y'all do for a living would want to help raise money for a bowling team's trip to Atlanta? Have too much money in the furry handcuff fund that you have money to spare?" Louella drawled, smoothing a hand over her blond hair.

"We're equal opportunity fund-raisers," Dixie said with a sweet smile.

LaDawn held up the plate of cookies and wafted them under Louella's nose. "And look, Louella. We did ya proud. They're not even in the shape of man parts."

Marybell fought a giggle when Em slapped at LaDawn's hands and took the plate of cookies away.

"Ladies," she whispered, fighting a smile. "We will remain ladies."

"Ladies," Louella murmured. "What a funny word

when attributed to all of you. Most especially Marybell."

Marybell yawned, digging her heels into the VFW Hall's floor, contemplating whether a *lady* would snarl at Louella. "Are you going to attack my lady-hood now, too? You can't have it all, Louella. First it's my hair, then my nails and then it's my love of Satan. Choose one path and stick to it."

"I don't have to attack your lady-hood."

Dixie began to rise from her metal chair behind the table of cookies, but Marybell held up her hand. "Then what are you attacking today, Louella? Hurry up, already. We have cookies to sell."

Louella wagged a finger at a figure lurking in the crowd. He strode over to them, his suit a bit wrinkled, but his hair gleaming and dark under the lights of the VFW Hall.

Dave Davison. Perfect. *Keep your mouth shut, Marybell. Keep it shut tight. He knows your voice.*

A cameraman followed him, hiking the heavy camera on top of his shoulder.

Across the room, she caught sight of Tag, who began pushing his way through the crowd, his eyes on her. Obviously he felt she needed protecting.

The look in the reporter's eye made her uncomfortable. It was penetrative and beady, as though he were looking for something else, investigating some hidden facet to her.

Relax, MB. He has no clue who you are. Just don't say anything.

In that moment, the one when she wondered why she was so fascinating to him, a chill of apprehension, so bone-deep she had to grit her teeth, raced along Marybell's spine.

Louella smiled at her, her wide eyes flashing before she turned that smile on the reporter. "This is Dave Davison from Channel 7 Cable Network News in Atlanta. You've met him. He has a question for you, Marybell."

She relaxed a little. He probably wanted a comment on the petition to shut Call Girls down. Louella had probably pressured him to come back.

But why did they want a comment from her? Dixie was the woman in charge. She glanced up at Dave Davison and the microphone he'd shoved in her face and said nothing.

Dave's sharp eyes roamed over her face, as if he was seeing something impossible.

She considered growling at him the way she did Louella, but thought better of it when Em's reminder to behave like a lady prevented her.

When Dave spoke, his smooth voice washed over her, a voice perfect for television broadcasting. Perfect diction, perfect timing. "Is it true, Ms. Lyman, that underneath all the hair and makeup, you're really Leon Kazinski's intern, Carson Chapman?"

A bulb popped in her face. Then another as Dave Davison's camera crew took her picture.

Everything faded away. The crowd of people milling about the VFW Hall. The gasps of her friends. The delicious aroma of cookies and pies. The only thing that remained was Tag's face.

His shock. His narrowed eyes and the immediate flash of rage in them.

And she knew she had to run. Run far, run fast.

Run.

* * *

Tag felt as if he'd just been run over by a semi as he watched Marybell flee the VFW Hall. He didn't know which way to go first, chase after Marybell or punt-kick Dave Davison's head off his shoulders.

He cornered Dave Davison, looming over him until he shifted uncomfortably. "Where the hell did you get that information?"

"He got it from me," Louella offered from behind, a phony smile plastered across her face.

Dixie was the first to react, her eyes shooting daggers at Louella. "You'd do anything to get rid of us, wouldn't you? Even concoct a crazy lie. What kind of a leap did your brain cells suffer for that one, Louella? Does your head hurt now?"

Louella shrugged, folding her fingers behind her back. "I didn't have to work at all. I just had to find the tattoo."

Tag's head would explode. Right here, right off his shoulders. He spun around to look Louella in the eye. "The tattoo?"

"Well, yes. Carson Chapman has a tattoo on her left shoulder. You can see it right in this picture here." She pulled the infamous picture of Leon Kazinski's alleged mistress out of her purse and pointed. "I magnified it, of course, for truth-seeking purposes, but when it began to circulate again, you know, with all the supposed Leon sightings all over the internet, it looked so familiar. I admit, it took me a little while, but then I remembered last summer, when Marybell was wearing those oh-so-fashionable tank tops day after hot day, she had a tattoo on her left shoulder, too, just like this one." She held up the picture, jamming it in Tag's face. "Imagine the coincidence that she has the very same tattoo as Carson Chapman. So when I accidentally spilled that coffee on your Marybell at Madge's, and offered to clean her musty jacket, I couldn't believe my eyes. Her tattoo is identical to Carson Chapman's. You remember her, right, Tag? The woman who helped steal all those retirees' money? You couldn't have missed it—it was global news. Just ask Marybell. I mean, Carson…"

How could he have missed something so significant? He'd seen that picture of Carson with Leon a million times, and it had never clicked. The thumbs-up with the pink fingernail…

A haze of red filled his eyes, and if he didn't punch someone, hard, square in the head, he'd lose his mind.

Em was there then, placing a hand on his arm. "Tag, I need you to go with Jax now before they realize who you are, please. Please don't make this worse."

What she really meant was, *Don't make a scene. Don't make a bigger ass out of yourself than you already did once before.*

Em gripped harder, her voice urgent. "Walk away, Tag. Right now. I will not have you make a scene when there are children present. Especially Maizy and the boys. Please leave like a gentleman."

Jax clamped a hand on his rigid shoulder, forcing him to reenter the VFW Hall. "Tag. *Now*."

Gage was suddenly in his line of vision, his eyes flashing warnings at Dave Davison and Louella. "Take it elsewhere, buddy. You stick that microphone in his face, and you'll never sit right again."

Jax and Gage surrounded him, grabbing him on either shoulder and dragging him out of the VFW into the cold day. The harsh glare of sunlight prevented him from seeing clearly until he heard a scuffle of feet and shouting.

"There he is!" someone yelled.

"Fuck," Jax muttered. "Head down, brother, keep moving. We can't keep them from finding out who you are, if you don't move your ass."

Gage began dragging him, coaxing and prodding his numb feet to move. "You put that in his face and you'll be eating it for supper," he growled. "Move, Tag. Move fast."

Gage's urgent warning set in, pushing the haze of red in his brain around, allowing the buzz of noise full focus.

Jesus. There were people littering the square, vans parked up and down the street, men and women with microphones, screaming his name.

All of them asking the same questions. Did he know Carson Chapman? Was he really dating her? And was Marybell Lyman actually Carson Chapman?

Marybell flew into her apartment, slamming the door so hard the bowl of balls on her coffee table shook, her breathing ragged, her heart crashing so painfully it made her chest hurt.

They knew. Oh, God, they knew.

Don't let panic set in. Don't do it. Move your feet. They haven't found out where you live yet, but it won't be long. Go! Go now. Get your emergency bag, and get in your car and go!

Where! she wanted to scream. *Where can I go? They know what I look like now. There's nowhere to hide.*

Her feet were frozen in her heavy boots, but she forced them to her hall closet, yanking out her suitcase and throwing it in the hall. Then to the bathroom, trying to make a list of what she could feasibly carry and still make a hasty escape.

Marybell didn't think; she just began pulling things off the shelf, her hands shaking so violently she kept knocking things over. The green face mask cream she'd put on to keep Tag from recognizing her the first time they'd met fell to the floor, smashing in thick bits of goo and glass.

She brushed them aside with her boot and grabbed an overnight bag, stuffing her pounds of acquired makeup into it, her hair gel, her spray-in hair dye, and hauled it over her shoulder.

The bedroom. Grab clothes from the bedroom, as many as you can stuff in a suitcase and run, Carson Chapman. Run until you can't run anymore.

She turned to make a break for her bedroom, ticking off items in her head to bring with her. In her haste, she slipped in the green goop, and crashed to the floor, landing on a piece of sharp glass. It sliced the heel of her hand, cutting the skin cleanly, leaving a gash and a bloody trail dripping to the floor.

As she looked at the bloody mess, the fear that had been a part of her life for so long assaulted her. Clawed at her, made her angry, made her want to hit something, hurt anything in her path. It welled up, bubbled to the surface in a furious boil and exploded.

She grabbed the bag with her people shield and hurled it against the shower curtain, screaming a raw, hoarse yell of frustration, heedless of the crash of the curtain's rod as it clattered to the floor.

She rose to her knees and screamed louder, piercing the empty silence with her long-overdue rage. Cleansing herself of it, pushing it out of her heart, ridding herself of the lies, the half-truths, the hiding. Tears sprang to her eyes, hot tears of shame and loss.

And as they began to fall to the tiled floor, inky-black with mascara, she doubled over, pressing her face into her knees, and sobbed for the first time since she was five.

"Open this door right now, Marybell Lyman, or I swear to you, I'll pull my skirt up around my waist and climb in that doggone window! If the press gets a picture of my backside, you're on my bad list!" Em yelled from outside.

Someone pounded on the door and then Dixie, "Do you see this purse, you maggot? It doesn't just hold my pretties. It's considered a lethal weapon. Now back off or I'll show you what some good ol' Southern rage is!"

There was the screech of metal, distant and far off to Marybell from the floor of the bathroom. Her ears heard it, but she couldn't move. Nothing on her body would move.

A sharp crack filtered the thick haze she was lost in and then more Em. "I told you, y'all better move on outta here! I am not afraid to use this umbrella!"

Her window in the living room crashed shut to the tune of pounding footsteps. "MB!" Dixie screamed. "Where are you, honey?"

"MB, you answer me this instant!" Em was in her bedroom, riffling around, and still, she couldn't move.

A nudge on the bathroom door pushed at her hip. "In here!" Dixie called. "Honey, let me in. Please, please let me in. Em, there's blood on the floor!"

"Move, Dixie!" Em ordered, yanking the door open

and falling to her knees, hauling Marybell up in her arms. "Oh, heaven, MB. What have you done? Oh, sugarplum!"

Hands were touching her, dragging her out of the bathroom and she knew she had to speak, but her throat was raw. She held up her hand to the tune of Dixie's sigh of relief.

She knelt down in front of her, her eyes wild, but her words, her words were calm. Dixie-calm. "MB, oh, MB. Give me your hand. Let me see." She lifted MB's hand up to the light in the hall and winced. "She's got a pretty bad cut, Em. She needs stitches."

Marybell began to squirm, shaking her head, forcing her words to string together. "No stitches. No hospital. I just slipped and fell on some glass."

Em rocked her, hugging her so hard she couldn't breathe. "MB, oh, MB. You scared me so bad. Let me help you up. C'mon, let's get you cleaned up."

Marybell let Em help her off the floor, catching the worried gaze passing between her and Dixie. "I'm sorry. I'm sorry." What else was there? What other words made this all better?

Dixie was a flurry of high heels and movement while Em brought her to the couch and set her down. "Close those curtains, Dixie! And peroxide, find some. We need peroxide and a cool cloth for her face and bandages. Get some bandages."

She was limp, limp and too weak to protest. Not even the angry buzz of voices just outside her door motivated her.

Em forced her chin up, wiping away the streaks of makeup from her face with a tissue from her purse. "Talk to me, Marybell. You had us sick with worry.

You talk to me right now. Never you mind those animals outside, but you talk to me, tell me how we can make this better."

Tears began to flow again, harsh and rushing down her cheeks. "I lied to you. All of you. For so long...I lied."

Em was always so warm, so gentle, and now was no exception. "You sure did, but why? Why didn't you come to us? We're friends, honey. We're your friends, and all this time you've been hidin' like this. Why?"

Defeat punched her in the gut, hard and sharp. "How do you tell someone something like this, Em? *How* could I tell you I was Carson Chapman? I've been painted like some Jezebel for so long, why would you believe any different?"

Dixie handed Em a cool cloth and some peroxide. "Because we're your friends, Marybell Lyman. We know *who* you are. That's how. You tell us and we find a way to help you. That's how friendship works." She came around the couch and nudged Marybell over, taking the bottle of peroxide from Em and ordering her to hold her hand still.

Em put the cloth under her hand while Dixie held the bottle up. "This will sting, but not nearly as much as it stings to know you didn't trust us enough to let us help you. We made complete asses of ourselves talkin' all that nonsense about you and Leon right in front of you and you never said a word. Not one." Dixie poured the liquid over her open wound with thin lips, making Marybell hiss.

Em closed the cloth around her palm, her eyes filling up. "That's why you do this, isn't it?" She circled

Marybell's face with a finger. "Because you were afraid we'd recognize you."

She tucked her chin to her chest as more tears fell. "Terrified." That felt so good to say. Whether it was going to work in her favor or not, the terror of discovery was gone and all that was left was the fear of rejection.

"Oh, MB. Why didn't you tell us?" Em soothed, pulling out a pile of tissues and wiping her face with tender fingers. "We love you. You don't really think we'd believe you had anything to do with stealin' people's money, do you? *Do you?*"

She swiped at a tear with her thumb. "Is this the girlfriend card?"

Em gave her shoulder a hard shove. "This is the *family* card, MB. Don't you use that against me. I won't have it. I love you—we all love you like you're kin. I love you more than some of my kin, and you know my kin. So don't you go crackin' wise about my hurt feelings. There isn't anything you can't tell me—not ever—and had I known you were sufferin' like this for all this time, I'd have made it my mission to figure it out. I knew somethin' was wrong."

Marybell took a deep breath. Everything she'd feared, exposing not just herself, but her friends, was all becoming a reality. "I didn't tell you and now look. Your lives have been invaded. Plum Orchard is a three-ring circus out there because of me, and if you think it's going to get better, it'll just get worse." Her voice began to rise, her muscles stiffening again.

Dixie clucked her tongue while she wrapped a long bandage around the heel of her hand. "Honey, I play on a field where Louella Palmer is the captain o' the team. You can't think the press scares me, can you? I'd hope you think me a whole lot stronger than that. And just you wait till I get my hands on her. It's time to bring out the big guns."

The tightness in Marybell's chest was beginning to ease. She shot Dixie a glance of disbelief. "Now you're insulted that I didn't invite the press to hound you?"

"I'm insulted that you think we wouldn't go to bat for you. I have a lot of money, Marybell Lyman, er…Carson Chapman. Oh, whoever you are. If you had come to me, we'd have seen our way to findin' a lawyer or a mob hit, or *somethin'* that would clear your name. Let us help you."

No. She shook her head hard. "You can't help me, Dixie. No one can help. Do you see what it's like out there? They'll ruin your lives. They ruined mine. They ruined it. I lost everything. Every single thing I ever had. I lost a scholarship I worked all my life to get. I lost a place to live. I lost my dignity. When Landon met me, I was eatin' out of Dumpsters! I was homeless for a long, long time. People spit on me, Dixie. I won't let that happen to all of you while you're tryin' to protect me. I won't allow anyone to treat you that way."

A crash against her front door startled them all, that familiar panic, the one where flashes went off in her face and microphones were stuck under her nose began to smother her.

"I said you get the hell off this lawn or I'm gonna show you what a can of some good old-fashioned companionator whoop-ass is, you bunch o' flesh-eating vultures!" LaDawn yelled, pushing her way inside the apartment door. Her eyes were wild and angry when she flipped the lock and turned to face them.

She held up a crushed cup carrier, dripping coffee.

"It's a nuthouse out there, but I brought fuel. Let's plot a death or ten."

Em rushed over with a hand towel and began to wipe, her expression grim. "We can't plot a death if Mary-bell won't let us."

That's when LaDawn spied the suitcases. Her mouth fell open and she gasped. "You were just gonna up and leave in the middle of the night like we were some lot of one-night stands?"

"If I leave, they leave." She used a thumb to point at the ruckus right outside her door.

LaDawn clamped her hands on her hips, the jangle of her bracelets echoing in Marybell's tiny apartment. "You did not just say that to me, Carson Chapman! That's right. I called you by your given name because that's damn well who you are, and the *H-E*-double hockey sticks I'm gonna let you run away like we all never meant nuthin' to you. You'll stay right here, and you'll fight for your right to live your life in peace. You're not leavin' me alone so I'm the only one they stare at. We do that as a couple. End of."

Marybell shook her head, making it pound harder. "Do you have any idea what they did to me, LaDawn? I'll say it one more time, they virtually ruined my life. My entire life. I couldn't even go to the dentist without them showin' up. They harassed everyone around me until no one wanted to be around me anymore. No way am I going to let them ruin your lives, too. What will they do when they get wind of the fact that I've been working for a phone sex company all this time? Or that you were once a companionator? You'll never find a moment's peace."

LaDawn's eyes went wide. "Whose damn life is it?

It's mine, and if I want to let them ruin it, that's up to me. Not you."

Now the panic thrummed through her veins, plucked them until they were so tight she thought she'd burst wide open from it. "Please, *please* hear me. I promise you, you won't feel that way when they take pictures of you picking your nose or some equally unflatterin' photo. *Please.* I appreciate all of you, but, Em, you have children, and, Dixie, you have a phone sex company. You know what the press can do to something that appears so innocent. If I leave Plum Orchard, they'll follow me and leave you all out of it."

"Stop!" Em yelped. "Stop this now. Back when this all happened, you didn't have us. But you do now, and we're going to get to the bottom of this, if it's the last thing we do. You are not leaving this town, Marybell— Carson—whatever your name is. I won't allow it."

Marybell gaped at her. "How do you propose we prove I had nothin' to do with any of this? It's my word against an idea in everyone's head that's been blown out of proportion over and over. There's been so much speculation about my involvement—and it wasn't good speculation—that there's no turnin' the tides now. Never mind the fact that I went into hiding. How does that make me look? Guilty. It makes me look guilty."

"You were cleared by the D.A., right?" Dixie asked as she took another cloth from LaDawn and began wiping at Marybell's face.

After the millionth grilling. "Yes, but that didn't change the public's perception of me. Not one iota. Everyone thinks I helped Leon run off with that money because of that stupid picture of us together. Now that this story has been dredged up again by this supposed sighting of him, the press probably thinks we're waiting to meet up and spend all those millions together."

"Explain the picture of you two," Dixie demanded, her eyes hard bits of blue.

Her sigh was ragged, but she closed her eyes and told the story again. "I was working late, filin' papers, and Leon came back to his office from a party drunk. He never made any bones about the fact that he found me attractive, but I'd managed to skirt his attentions up to that point. I know you're all wonderin' why I stayed when he was so aggressive, but my internship was almost up, and interning at Kazinski's was a huge coup on my résumé. I needed the prestige it brought. So I toughed it out."

Dixie nodded, tucking her hair behind her ears. "So, why were you sprawled on top of him on the floor, Marybell?"

Her words were slow to come. She'd explained this at least a hundred times and it always led to the same looks of suspicion. Sure, they couldn't prove she knew anything, but that didn't mean they didn't think she was lying through her teeth.

A sigh escaped her lips, harsh and tired. "Because he pulled me onto his lap, and the chair he was in fell over and I fell on top of him. If you look closely at that stupid picture, you can see the leg of an overturned chair. It's hard to see until it's pointed out, but it's there. I don't know who took the picture. I don't know why. I just know I didn't know he was stealin' money from anyone, and *I did not have an affair with Leon Kazinski.*"

Dixie nodded, patting her on the knee. "Then that's all I need to know."

"What?"

"I said that's all I need to know."

"Ditto," LaDawn muttered.

Em slapped her hands on her thighs with a smile. "Meeting adjourned."

Marybell sat on the couch, frozen, her hands ice-cold. "That's it?"

"What's it?" Em asked, confusion in her blue eyes.

"You all believe me?" They believed her? No proof. No hard-core evidence? No grilling? They just believed?

LaDawn nudged her from behind. "Course we do, MB."

Dixie flashed a finger upward. "Now we just have to set our minds to provin' it."

Eighteen

Sanjeev poured everyone cups of tea: tea he promised would ease Marybell's sore throat and her pained heart. The moment Dixie had called him was almost the exact moment he'd shown up at the door, armed with food and fighting off the press, cursing the helicopter now hovering over her house. "It's almost like they've discovered Elvis alive and well and living in Plum Orchard," he mused.

Em smiled gratefully at him, taking her cup. "Honestly, who would have thought one little ol' sex scandal could drum up so much noise?"

Marybell reentered the room after a long, hot shower at the insistence of the girls. The people who believed in her. All of them, in one room.

Instinct had her tucking her chin to her chest, but LaDawn propped her chin up with a finger. "No more hidin' even though I hate how doggone pretty you are, no more fixin' your eyes to the ground. Hear me, Carson Chapman?"

She lifted her eyes, letting her friends see her for the first time without makeup and eye masks and all manner of people shields. Her hair down around her face, almost touching her shoulders, she stood rooted to the spot.

Em stuck her tongue out at her from between crimson lips. "Had I known you were this gorgeous naturally, I'd have told you to keep that makeup on your face. Forgive if I hate for just a minute or two. It'll pass."

"Why, if it isn't Carson Chapman," Dixie murmured softly when she looked up from a ream of paper sitting on her lap. "You are the prettiest thing." She patted the place on the couch next to her. "Now let's figure this out."

The entire time she'd showered, all while she'd scrubbed her face clean and rinsed her hair, she'd alternated between elation that Dixie and the girls believed her and anxiety over how to approach Tag.

She couldn't get his face out of her mind. The hard lines of it, the shock, the red anger flushing his cheeks. Would he listen as they had? Or would he hate her for lying all this time the way Alison had?

Her hands fisted tight against her sides. She couldn't even bring herself to ask them if anyone had heard from him. Every time she tried, her throat closed up again.

She looked at the laptops lying around, pictures of her running from the press and even one of her lying against a Dumpster just before she'd disappeared, glared at her. The humiliation of that time in her life, the ugly truth of her, backpack at her feet, torn skirt, greasy hair, propped up against a garbage can, her eyes sunken and red, made her want to curl up into a ball of shame.

Dixie's voice cut into her thoughts. "So Landon hired someone to poke around Kazinski's life?"

Sanjeev's nod was a brisk bounce of his dark head.

"He did. The moment he hired Carson, or *Marybell,* he told me he smelled fish."

"Something fishy," Dixie interjected.

"Can one *smell* something wrong?"

Dixie laughed. "Only in America where metaphors and euphemisms abound. Forget that, Sanjeev. Landon knew MB was tellin' the truth all along? You knew who she was all along? Why didn't you tell us?"

His black eyes admonished. "That was not for me to share. MB lost many things, Dixie. One of which was her pride, her dignity. She lived on the streets. She's suffered indignities the likes of which I can't even imagine, yet I can identify with. I lived on the streets, too, Dixie. You have no idea what that does to your soul, and I hope you never will. To reveal such anguish is a journey one must make alone, and each journey is different. I am not the exposer of journeys. Landon asked that I never reveal what I know, and as always, I honor his requests. My apologies to you, Marybell."

Marybell sat next to Dixie, still in shock, unable to articulate how true Sanjeev's words were. How stunned she was to find Landon had fished around on her behalf. It was so like him to want to make everything better.

Yes. Landon had known about Leon. He'd found her at her worst, and her most mistrustful, but he'd poked and coaxed and prodded for several months until she'd finally told him everything. Yet she'd had no idea he'd looked any deeper than her confession.

Dixie pursed her lips. "But, Sanjeev—this is a huge secret to hide from us. Maybe I could have done something before any of this happened."

Sanjeev blustered, waving his hands in the air. "You

don't propose to tell me you could have done something Landon couldn't, do you? That's preposterous."

"Okay, fine. That's probably true. So forget not tellin' me and just tell me what his investigators did find."

Sanjeev's mouth flatlined. "Nothing. No trail to the money he stole. No proof our Marybell wasn't at the center of this in cahoots with him. If you give this thought, Mr. Kazinski's plan was quite foolproof, and above all, simple. All he needed was somewhere to hide that money, if, in fact, he still has it, and disappear. Maybe he planned to escape where there are no extradition laws? The United States can apply to have one extradited, but that doesn't mean the country will approve it. If those pictures really were taken in Morocco where Leon was allegedly sighted, they are a country, in fact, that has no treaty with the United States."

"How do you hide out for all this time, Sanjeev, without someone recognizing you? Kazinski was global news, for gravy's sake!" Em said, letting her cup clatter against the coffee table.

Sanjeev shrugged. "You have connections?"

"Who?" Dixie said, frustration in her tone. "His wife didn't seem to have the answer. She bailed ten days after he was indicted because she thought he was cheatin' on her with MB. His employees? All of whom are now working low-end jobs and just managing to make ends meet, if this investigator's reports are correct. Wow, when this Kazinski ran, he ran hard."

As if she hadn't asked herself this a million times. Where had he hidden the money? Who had taken that damning picture of her?

Dixie flipped through some more papers, handing stacks to Marybell and LaDawn. "You know what, I hate to say it, but the logistics of this make no difference to me. I don't understand how he managed to funnel all that money wherever he funneled it to. It's like trying to decipher the Da Vinci Code. I don't care. I just care that we find something to prove Marybell wasn't cattin' around with that thief. Proof so these vultures will go away. We need to find whoever took that picture. I believe with all my heart they know the truth. If it just turned up anonymously, it was done to either make money or get some kind of revenge. That's always what somethin' like this is about."

LaDawn's eyes narrowed. "Maybe it was his wife? I mean, I'd be in a snit to top all snits if I found out my husband was havin' an affair with someone that looks like our Marybell does."

Marybell shifted on the couch, her hands folded in her lap, thinking, rehashing.

Em cupped her chin in her hand. "Very true, but if she did take it, she lied to the investigators. Says here she denied any knowledge of MB messin' with her husband. And if it was her, would she ever admit it, anyway?"

No. It wasn't Leon's wife. She couldn't say why she didn't believe it, but she'd never believed Helene was capable of getting up enough nerve to do something like that. She'd been miserable with Leon, everyone saw that, but she was also afraid of him.

Marybell shook her head. "Helene was always so kind to me. I have to believe she wasn't capable of being so vengeful. Leon was awful to her the entire time I worked for him. I think what he did was the excuse she needed to leave him. She was afraid of him. Every time he spoke, she cringed."

LaDawn made a face. "Jealousy does crazy things to women, MB."

Dixie's head popped up. She held up a finger as though she were piecing something together. "Who in tarnation is Tara-Anne Baker?"

No. Never. "Why do you ask?"

Dixie tapped the papers in her lap. "Tara-Anne Baker. It's right here. She's listed as an employee of Kazinski's. I don't see a deposition from her in this list of ruled-out suspects anywhere."

Marybell sat up straight, a foreboding tingle running along her spine. "Tara-Anne Baker was my roommate in college. I got her a job cleaning offices at Kazinski's...."

Dixie's eyes narrowed when she tapped the list of employees. "Then why wasn't she questioned?"

Her head was reeling. What had happened to Tara-Anne? She'd skulked off campus the moment the dean told her she'd lost her scholarship and never looked back. It wasn't as though she kept in touch with anyone. Virtually all of her past life had been erased because of Landon, and she'd worked hard to put it all behind her.

"So you haven't seen or heard from her since you were booted out of college?"

"Well, I guess I wouldn't. I mean, it's not like I left a forwardin' address, Dixie. I ran away, and Landon helped me cover my tracks."

Dixie jumped up from the couch, her boots clacking against the hardwood floor. "Sanjeev? Call up that fancy private investigator and tell him he missed a suspect!"

Marybell's head was spinning. All she wanted to do was run away—far away, hide under the covers, pretend this had never happened.

Do you want to do that next to a Dumpster, Mary-bell? Or do you want to hike up those britches and fight for your life?

Yet she voiced her fears. "Tara-Anne's a long shot, if you ask me. All she did was clean the offices." Wasn't it?

Dixie gave her a pointed look. "They questioned the security guard, the bathroom attendant, MB. How did they miss the cleaning lady? Somethin' ain't right. This is where we smell fish. Now let's find this woman. No stone unturned, I say."

Dixie had the men who'd guarded Call Girls come to stand outside her door. Their angry faces and big bodies kept the reporters at bay for the moment.

After the girls and Sanjeev left, the silence of doing nothing but waiting crept in. The flurry of activity now gone left her with her fear.

She had to call Tag. She had to explain. He had to let her explain. Scooping her phone up, she scrolled for new texts and found a big fat nothing. She'd texted him, almost begging him to talk to her—his silence was the most telling of all.

What had she been thinking when she thought she could keep this all together? Where had all her big brains gone when she thought stalling him until she had some proof she was innocent and a confession were going to make up for all the lies she'd told him from the very beginning?

She couldn't get the picture of his face at the VFW Hall out of her head. She couldn't forget how different that Tag was compared to that of the funny, easygoing Tag she'd fallen in love with.

The quiet of her apartment sat in her bones, gave her too much time to remember Tag's arms around her while they watched Disney movies, late lunches with bologna sanwiches, his amazing smile.

A knock at the door had her jumping off the couch, her legs shaking. One of the security guards stuck his head inside, his stern gaze looking her over. "Miss Lyman, a Tag Hawthorne here to see you."

Her heart began a brisk thump, her throat drying up. The moment he entered the door, so perfect, so solid and secure, she wanted to run to him. Bury her face in his neck, beg him to forgive her.

But Tag's shoulders were stiff when he crossed the room. His face masked in anger. "So this is the real Marybell Lyman?" Tag said, dripping sarcasm. "Did you forget where you put your hair gel?"

Her hand went self-consciously to her freshly washed hair. He was here to get his licks in, and it was the least she could offer him for all the lying she'd been doing.

Pulse pounding in her ears, her head throbbing, she knew it was truth time. Time to face the one person she should have told before anyone else. Time to face the music.

He wasn't here to listen. That fact was in his posture. In his harsh tone. He wanted to vent. To rage.

She turned her back to him and walked farther into the living room, all the anxiety, all the secrets, all the hiding was coming to the surface again. Spinning around, her arms open wide, she offered an invitation to gut her. "Have at it, Tag. Give it to me good."

Tag was in front of her in seconds. "So it's really true."

Her stomach roiled, her bravado waffled. "Yes," she whispered.

His face, always so easygoing and open, was a closed mask of tension and fury. "*Why?* Why the hell didn't you tell me?"

Look at him, Marybell. Look at him and tell the truth. Tell him you didn't expect to fall in love with him. You didn't expect him to wear you down until you gave in. She lifted her chin. "I was trying to find proof so that when I finally told you, I'd have some kind of evidence I had nothin' to do with what Leon did."

"So while you were searching for this evidence, you lied. You. Lied. Over and over. All that bullshit secrecy over your family and where you grew up was because you're a goddamn liar. You helped that prick Leon steal my money—you helped him steal money from people who'd never have another chance to earn more. *You* did that," he said, his fists clenched, his jaw hard.

No. No more. No more accusations. He could call her a liar, but she wasn't a thief. "And where is all that money, Tag? With all that money I chose to become a phone sex operator in a town where everyone thinks I worship the devil. Can I get just a little credit here, please? If I'm some kind of brilliant mastermind when I'm stealin' other people's money, the least you could do is consider I'd be in some country without extradition laws by now. Not right here in Plum Orchard, right under your nose."

His eyes flashed, hot and dark. "Maybe Leon promised you things the same way he did everyone else, and then he stiffed you, too?"

"Okay, good theory. Let's explore that. So I've been stiffed now by Leon, too. Why would I get involved with

you of all people? One of the people he stiffed? Was I
going to hide behind my makeup and my hair until either we broke up or you asked me to marry you? Where
does Taggart Hawthorne fit into this? What do I gain
being involved with you?"

He paused for a beat, one she almost allowed herself
to feel hope in. Until he dashed that. "I don't know, and I
mostly don't care. The point is, you lied. You were never
who I thought you were. The rest almost doesn't matter."

She bit the inside of her cheek to keep her lip from
trembling, her flash of anger replaced with so much regret, it was a physical pain. *Calm, just find some calm
and tell him the truth.* "I wanted to tell you. I can't tell
you how many times I almost did, Tag. I hired a private investigator just this morning because I wanted to
somehow find proof that I'm innocent. So I could show
you. Prove it to you. But as I stand here, I did not have
a hand in stealin' your money."

"So, why did you hide like this, Marybell Lyman?
Why did you run off where no one could ever find you?
Why did you wear all that crap on your face—because
you were innocent?"

She fought a hoarse sob. The pressure of keeping
this secret, of being hounded daily for almost a year of
her life before she'd gone into hiding, broke. It broke
off in big chunks of frustration. "Because no one would
believe me!" she shrieked, more humiliating tears falling from her eyes.

His body language said he didn't believe her. Not a
word. It said, *don't touch me. Don't get any closer.* Yet
somehow she needed to believe their connection, everything they'd shared so far, would cut through his anger.

Marybell gulped in another breath, her legs shaking. "I did not ever sleep with Leon Kazinski. He was a vile man I interned for. I didn't know he was pilfering money from people. I didn't know anythin' about what he was doing. You can hurl accusations at me until you're blue in the face. You can badger me, but I'll die before I admit to something I didn't do."

"So, if you didn't sleep with Kazinski, how about explaining that picture of you?"

The crass image Tag portrayed almost made her gag. "That picture doomed me from Jump Street."

"Yeah, that picture. You mean the one of you lying on top of Leon Kazinski?"

"If you'll just let me explain it. If you'll just listen to my side of the story." Just one more time.

He shook his head, his face so hard, so far removed from the fun, lighthearted man she'd fallen in love with. "So you can lie some more? The. Hell. You had me hook, line and sinker. All this time I've been chasing you around and you've been stringing me along. 'No, Tag. I can't go out with you. I have issues. No, Tag. I don't want to date anyone,'" he mocked. "But that damn well didn't keep you from being with me, did it?"

If he'd taken a hot poker and seared her straight through her heart, his words couldn't have hurt more. How could she explain how torn she'd been? How afraid to confide in him? How could she explain the lies?

How could she explain how devastated she was to find out she'd been right about him? That she'd known all along he'd never simply take her word for it?

Marybell fought more tears until her eyes were on fire and her face felt as if it would crack. "So, are you done? Do you want more? Do you want to humiliate me, call me names—whaddya got left in you, Tag? What do you have that the rest of the world hasn't flung my way?"

He held up his hands, his eyes vacant. "Nothing. I have nothing left." Letting his palms fall to his sides, he walked out the door.

Everything inside her, all the pieces of herself she'd kept gluing back together, toppled like a house of cards.

Numb, she found her couch and watched as they fell.

He sat in the dark, trying to think. Trying to understand.

"Uncle Tag?" Maizy pushed her way onto the couch and snuggled against his side, letting her head rest on his chest.

He twisted a strand of her fiery red hair around his finger and nuzzled the top of her head, closing his eyes and breathing. "Yes, ma'am?"

"You don't feel good."

"No. I feel okay, Maizy-moo." No. He felt like shit. Like total shit.

"I don't mean on the outside. I mean on the inside. You're sad. That makes me sad."

Kids, Maizy especially, were so sensitive to emotions it freaked him out. He didn't want her to worry about him. "Why do you think I'm sad, sweetie?" he asked into the darkness.

"Because of all the mean things they're sayin' about Miss Marybell. I heard Ralphie's mom talking about it today at school."

Damn these people. Damn the press. Damn all of it.

Tag forced himself to keep his voice calm. "Don't listen to the mean things they say. That's called gossip, and it's wrong." Even if they were true.

"I told Ralphie he was a jerk because he said mean things about Miss Marybell, too, and then I put my fingers in my ears so I didn't have to listen. I like Miss Marybell. She's funny."

He closed his eyes tight. Funny, and beautiful, and a liar. "You're a good egg, kiddo."

"Do you think a story will make you feel better? Em always reads me one when I'm sad."

"I'd love a story."

"Maybe it will make you feel gooder on the inside?"

"I bet it will."

She hopped off the couch, but not before dropping a kiss on his cheek. "I love you a lot, Uncle Tag. Please feel better, and don't believe the bad goss…goss…"

"Gossip," he helped.

She nodded with a smile. "Uh-huh. Do what I do and put your fingers in your ears. Then you just can't hear it," she advised before she skipped off to find a book to read him.

Maybe, if he just stuck his fingers in his ears, he could shut it all out. The lies, the questions, the sick feeling in his stomach.

And the love.

He wanted to turn off the fact that in all this, he'd fallen in love with Marybell Lyman.

Nineteen

Tag took another swig of his coffee, wishing it were laced with whiskey.

No, pal. No booze to solve your problems. You've done that before. This time, you do it straight up.

He'd slept little last night. Marybell's face, the way she'd hoarsely screamed no one believed her story, was still driving a hole straight through his heart.

This was what she'd meant when she said she had something to straighten out, something she wanted to tell him. It damn well could have been anything but this.

He'd wanted to believe her. But he'd believed before, and this time, he was gun-shy. Infuriated. He'd been infuriated when that reporter had stuck a microphone in her face and asked her if she was Carson Chapman.

Infuriated and humiliated all over again, followed by stunned. Stunned he'd been so easily fooled. Everything he'd said to her last night had been based on gut reaction. He hadn't given it much thought before he'd gone over there. He'd stewed, simmered until he was ready to explode and then struck out as hard as his words could hurt.

And there was her face in his head again, so beautiful he almost couldn't speak, so astonishingly different from the Marybell he'd fallen in love with that it only made him angrier last night.

But today, in the cold light of day, he was sore all over. He ached inside and out. He'd told her his deepest, ugliest shame, and she'd still chosen not to reveal hers. He'd trusted her.

Would it have been any better if she'd done it then? When would have been the optimal time for her to tell you who she was?

From the very start.

He ran a hand over his jaw, not even able to touch the idea that she'd been Leon Kazinski's lover. It made his stomach pitch and roll.

Do you really believe that, Tag? Do you really believe she slept with Kazinski?

The picture of her says she did.

The picture of her says nothing of the sort, jackass. It says plenty of things, but they all have no definitive conclusions.

A slap on his shoulder made him jump from his deep thoughts. "You okay today, buddy?" Jax asked.

Tag slammed his lips shut.

Jax nudged him. "Don't do that, man. Don't clam up. I get you're pissed, but talk to me. Let's talk this out."

Every time he tried to formulate some words, he could only manage one thought. *"She lied."* Fuck that hurt. He'd worked hard to gain her trust, and he didn't even know why he was working so damn hard. Now he knew, and it damn well hurt.

Jax stared down at his coffee cup, swishing the liquid around with a slow turn of his wrist. "Yeah. She did."

"She was allegedly Kazinski's lover," he said between clenched teeth. Those words, the ones that likely hurt the most, made him want to smash Kazinski's face on something hard and sharp.

Jax paused for a moment, then shook his head. "You don't know that, Tag. Em says differently."

"Em?" he groused. "What does Em know? Marybell lied to her, too."

Em was there, out of the blue, pushing her way around Jax, and headed straight for Tag, shoving her finger under his nose. "I'll tell you what Em knows. She knows you're a damn fool, Taggart Hawthorne, to believe such filth of the woman you were falling in love with. Did you see those pictures of her on the news today? Did you? Did you see the one where she was sleeping up against a Dumpster? Before she put all that makeup on her face and hid away like some pariah? Before she was someone else besides Carson Chapman? How dare you see those images and still have the audacity to decide, without definitive proof, she's a lying thief!"

He'd been taken for a ride once before. Never again. "I've fallen in love with the wrong woman before. What I want to know is, how can you defend her? She lied to you all, too." Was it just him? Was he just being a complete asshole? Or was he so hurt he couldn't see past it to find his way to the truth?

Em's eyes went wide and wild, but her words were dipped in ice. "I will not allow you to speak that way about my friend—ever. Understand me? Marybell lied to protect not just herself but all of us. Do you see what's going on out there, Tag? Did you happen to crawl out of your selfish pity party long enough to watch the news shred my friend? See the news vans and vultures all over Plum Orchard, lookin' to cut her to ribbons all over again? Everyone knows she's here now. That means they know about you, too, you utter fool!"

He ground his teeth together to keep from slugging something. All the little things he'd come up with to keep himself protected, all the justifications he'd made in his head to make Marybell the bad guy, the ones that had kept him up all last night, needed vetting. "She didn't start out lying to protect us."

Em threw a towel on the counter, her hard eyes unlike anything he'd ever seen from her before. "You hear me, and you hear me well, Taggart Hawthorne. She did what she had to in order to survive. She lived on the streets. She ate from garbage cans! Would you risk a warm bed and food on your plate just to live in this truth you're always preachin' when you didn't do anything wrong, but not a soul on earth would believe you? Would you lie in order to exist? Would you? Survivin' meant losing every single thing in her life. *Everything.* Do you have any idea what losing everything is like and having no one to turn to?"

"Yeah. I sort of do, Em." He fisted his hands, jamming them into his pockets, a measure of reason beginning to force its way to the surface of his layer upon layer of anger.

And that was what really set her off. She went toe-to-toe with him, seething and hungry for his throat. "I don't give a hound dog about your issues or your pain or your whining about all your pain. Hear me? Marybell lived without anyone for years. All her life, in fact. And then, when she finally had something, a chance at an education, a stable living environment at school, she lost it all. You, Taggart, had the luxury of a family that loved you. You chose to spit on that. You drank and gambled yourself into stupid. You didn't even try to pick yourself back up again. But you darn well didn't do it alone. That's *your* problem. Marybell didn't keep you from the truth with malice in her heart. You'd do well to remember she has nothing to gain by lyin' to you. It's not like you have millions lyin' around she was just waitin' on stealing. You *don't* know what it's like to lose everything, Tag. It was only you—*you* kept you from *everything!*"

Jax put a hand on Em's shoulder and squeezed. "Honey, please."

But Em threw it off with a disgusted grunt, her limbs shaking. "Don't you please me, Jax. I will not stand by and allow him to slander my friend with ugly words like *liar.* She lied. She is not, nor will she ever be, a liar. If you say it again, Taggart, I'll stuff the first bar of soap I find handy down your throat!"

"Em," Jax soothed. "Let's try and rationally talk about this—calmly."

"I will not speak to someone who's so willing to persecute and judge when he has no right to judge anyone—ever! If you sat down and really paid attention to what happened instead of allowing your judgment to be clouded by your ridiculous need to hang on to this baggage, you'd see you've made the biggest mistake of your life, Tag. Now, I have a friend who needs my help. First, don't you dare try and come with me to protect me from those vultures out there because rest assured, I have a handle on that. And second, don't you dare tell me I'm wrong or that I shouldn't stand by Marybell, Jax, because I will ever so promptly tell you to eff off, too!" With that, she whirled out of the kitchen, her heels clacking on the hardwood until they both heard the door slam and Em scream a warning to the press to back off or she'd run them over then put it in Reverse.

Jax leaned back against the counter and sighed, his face lined from the same sleepless night they'd all enjoyed thanks to the media frenzy.

Tag did the same, bumping shoulders with his brother. To see Em so enraged had eaten up all of his anger. "I'm sorry."

"You know what, bro? I thought you were really getting past all the 'poor me, Alison lied and cheated on me,' with Marybell as a weird kind of guide. I really thought she was the light at the end of your damn tunnel. But you're not past pitying yourself. You're not past the hurt of being betrayed and it's messing with what's right in front of your eyes, you moron."

He'd really thought he was over it. But finding out Marybell was Carson Chapman brought it all to a head. All while he'd told her about losing his company, she'd known who he was. "My employees lost their jobs, their retirement funds because of what that asshole Leon did, Jax. Marybell was a part of that."

Jax's face went hard. "Was she? Do you know, beyond a shadow of a doubt, MB slept with him, knew he was stealing money? Where's your logic in this, asshole? Because I want you to take a good hard look at the facts minus your crap. Who the hell disappears like she did, and becomes homeless because they don't want to give up where some money is hidden? At least in jail, you get three squares and a bed, jackass. C'mon, Tag!"

When Jax said it out loud, it made more sense than

the justifications in his head. "People have done worse for less."

"Yeah, yeah. So explain why she'd get involved with you if she didn't really give a shit about you? If she was guilty, you'd think she'd be running the other way. The kind of deviousness you've credited her with says she'd split and be homeless again before hooking up with someone so closely related to Kazinski just for fear of getting caught. So what's she gaining in all this? Tell me her angle. I can't wait to hear how you rationalize this."

He didn't know. His head was a fucked-up mess of conflicting feelings. "I don't know. I just know she lied to me all this time."

"And you feel like a fool. Boo-hoo. You know, this here's your problem." He tapped the countertop to make his point. "While you could be off keeping this from turning into a total disaster, you don't. You blame. You react. Back when you drank, all that time you could have been fixing everything after the company went bust, you spent feeling sorry for yourself. I'd have given you the money to fix it, Tag. To help."

"I don't want your damn money."

"And I don't want your damn bullshit." Jax seethed. "I'm tired of it. You upset my woman. That upsets me. I want to smash your face in right now. The only reason I haven't is that Maizy'll be home any minute and I know Em would ground me for life if Maizy saw your blood all over the kitchen floor."

"What the hell was that all about?" Gage asked, strolling into the kitchen. "Em just tore outta here like she was on fire, nearly took out that reporter in the badass suit. Did you guys have a fight?"

Tag exhaled. "No, Em and I had a fight."

Gage whistled, shoving his hands in his pockets. "Hoo, boy. So I guess you said something stupid about Marybell?"

Tag closed his eyes and sighed. "No… Well, maybe. Okay, *yes*."

"He called her a liar," Jax offered, jamming his face in Tag's.

Gage used the heel of his hand to thump his brother's shoulder. "In front of Em? Jesus, asshole. You must not like livin'."

"She did, you know. She did lie to me." She did, and it hurt like goddamn hell. Maybe she'd even laughed at him behind his back.

Christ, even he had trouble believing that.

Gage rolled his shoulders, crossing his arms over his chest. "I'd lie to you, too, if I thought I was going to lose all my shit. She wasn't hurting anyone with the lie till you came along, Tag. Look, she was flat-out wrong to not tell you who she was when the two of you got so into each other, I'll give you that. But look at the fucking circus over at Call Girls, dude. Look at it right outside here. They want a piece of you just because they know you were dating her. Ask yourself this. What if they find out that not only are you dating her, but you're the Taggart Hawthorne who was screwed by Kazinski, and they find out you're involved with Marybell, Carson, whatever we're calling her? Imagine the story that shit would make. It's a reporter's wet dream. Then imagine them invading every part of your life, every day, all day. Imagine having no one to turn to. No family. No friends. No place to hide. Ever wonder how terrifying having them on your ass all the time must be?"

He'd thought about it all last night and into the early

hours of the morning. How afraid she must have been.
How hungry, cold, alone. It made everything inside him
hurt. "I just don't want to get screwed again, Gage."

Gage's dark head bobbed. "Yeah. I get it. The Alison comparison. She sucked. She still sucks. But she's
not Marybell. MB didn't abandon you. You abandoned
her as far as I'm concerned."

"So you'd just let it go? Like it was no big deal the
woman you'd fallen in love with was involved with a
man who stole everything you owned and could quite
possibly know where he is and what he did with that
money?"

"First, do you really believe MB's capable of that
much deception?"

"Because I'm such a good judge of character, Gage."

That was the issue in a nutshell. His instincts had
been shot to hell once, and now he second-guessed himself at every turn. It was safer to err on the side of the
worst-case scenario than to believe. That was the problem. He was afraid to believe, to let go and just fall.
He'd let his guard so far down with Marybell, to find
out this was why she didn't want to date him made him
feel exposed—stupid.

"Okay, so what does that say about you? That you're
really that much of an idiot? Look, Alison threw you
for a loop. I get it. You guys had been together forever.
We were all surprised by it—by her. You're afraid to
trust MB only to have it blow the hell up in your face.
So you have two choices. Believe either she lied to protect herself and anyone she ever got involved with or
she lied because she's an evil bitch."

Tag rose from the chair at the breakfast bar. The side
of him that wanted to believe in Marybell was winning.

The half of him that wanted to protect her, keep her safe. "*Never* call her a bitch. I'll break your damn face."

Gage threw his hands up in the air, egging him on. "Why not? Isn't that what she'd be if she was lying just to fuck with you?"

He sat back down. Gage's common sense burst his bubble. It all just clicked. "Okay. Fair. But she did lie. It's a sticking point with me. One I can't seem to let go of. Would you be okay with it, Gage?"

"For a shot at someone as awesome as MB? Yep. I'm not saying we wouldn't have to work on full disclosure as a couple, but yep. In a heartbeat. Do you see what they're doing to her? What they're saying about her? She's all over the news, pal. All because she was some fuckup's intern. That seem more than fair to you? Hiding here in the P.O. at a phone sex company was resourcefulness at its best, if you're asking. So, yeah. I'd find a way to get past the bit about fighting for some peace in her life, because she didn't lie to be malicious and conniving like Alison did. She lied to save her life. *Her life.* Not her bank account or her status with all her fancy friends."

There was a heavy silence between the three of them, Tag processing Gage's words and Em's rightful anger.

Jax broke it by pushing off the counter. "I have to go tell my woman I think you're a shithead, and I'm one hundred percent on her side. It'll probably cost me a couple of days' setback with that big proposal I was planning on, thanks to you. So I'm gonna go grapple. Figure this out, Tag. Really figure it out this time. If you want to trash this thing with Marybell because your issues with women are greater than the big picture—do it alone, okay? Because I'm with Gage on this one. I don't believe that picture that's circulating is what really happened, and I don't believe MB is involved. Sorry, bro. If you stew with this like you do everything else, you're in the pot alone." He gave Gage a thump on the shoulder and strode out of the kitchen.

Fuck. He'd blown it. It all sank in, dropped like an anchor in his stomach. As sure as the day was long, instead of giving her the benefit of the doubt, he'd been so caught off guard he'd blown it.

Like an utter jackass.

Gage stuck a juice box under his nose before planting it in his palm. "So, plan?"

"What makes you think I have a plan?"

"It's written all over your face. You know you're wrong. We just had to wait until you did, too. The question is, did MB wait? If she did, you gotta have a plan."

He'd been formulating a plan before this had all gone down, something he'd wanted to surprise her with. Something to heal an old wound and because he loved to see her smile. "She hates my guts."

Gage grinned and popped a straw into his own juice box. "She should. So, like I said, a plan?"

"How do you plan anything when you're as screwed as I am?" Remorse hit him squarely in the gut, twisting its searing knife into it until he squirmed. What the hell had he done?

Gage sighed. "Let's get past the 'what the hell did I do?' stage and spring into action here, huh? We only have so much time before the iron gets cold, and so does MB. Not to mention, we have to ditch the press, because they're gonna come for you, brother."

"I apologize." *Yeah. Because that'll make up for calling her a liar.*

Gage nodded. "Begging and scraping are always part of the plan, but that can't be all of the plan. You have to show her you believe her even though everything points to the contrary."

"How the hell do I do that?"

"You throw yourself on the mercy of Em and the girls and beg them to help you with those big wads of money Dixie has."

"I don't want Dixie's money, Gage."

"You don't want anyone's money but yours, *Tag*. But guess what? That shit's gone with Kazinski. This isn't about you. It's about exonerating MB."

Right then, he knew. He. Knew. "I don't need her exoneration."

"You moron, you really are going to let a good thing go, aren't you?"

He waved his hand, impatient now. "No. That's not what I mean. I mean, I don't need her to prove she had nothing to do with Kazinski. I believe her."

Gage grinned at him. "And now we have a plan."

Twenty

Marybell cringed at the sound of the knock on her door, until she remembered the security guards posted outside her door with strict instructions to look after her and Blanche. Exhaustion after a long, sleepless night left her dragging. The buzz of a helicopter, the endless voices outside her door and Tag's rejection had left her wearier than any day on the streets had.

Dixie poked her head through the door. The fine lines around her eyes told Marybell she hadn't slept, either. Their support left her humbled. Their unwavering belief had eased some of the pain Tag's words had left.

But she knew she couldn't stay in Plum Orchard. At three in the morning, she'd pulled up her big-girl panties and made an adult decision. No more whining. No more crying. No more letting everyone have their way with her life.

She was innocent, and the people who believed her were all that mattered. But she couldn't stay here and see Tag day after day, knowing how much she loved him. She couldn't do it. It was one thing to face persecution from the people in town; it was another to see what she'd seen on Tag's face last night.

Gone was the fun, easygoing man who was quick to tease, quick to comfort, replaced with someone who'd called her a liar.

Yes, she'd lied. Yes. It was wrong. But she'd needed his faith in her. It was the final key to unlocking her heart. And he'd turned her away.

Dixie approached her with caution, her eyes warm and Em and LaDawn in tow. "You all right, sugarplum?"

She let them hug her, forced the thought of more tears out. "I'm going to be okay. Promise."

LaDawn pointed to the suitcases, still in the hall. "Why am I still seein' suitcases?"

Marybell found her feet again. "I have to move on. Even if it's just to get the madness of the press to stop. They'll follow me, and they'll leave y'all alone. Before you get upset, please think about this logically. You're all connected to me because of this. Em and Jax have children. You don't really think I'd let the press near them, do you? And Tag. If they found out he was involved with me…" Fear formed its newest knot in her stomach. She swallowed the lump in her throat. "They don't know about him yet, do they?" She'd been too afraid to look.

Dixie shook her head. "No. I don't know if it's because Louella doesn't know Tag was scammed by Kazinsky because he was a low priority for the press on the list of all those people Leon stole from, but so far, no mention of Tag other than he was involved with you here in Plum Orchard. But the Hawthorne boys have a plan to throw them off the trail. Though, if Louella knew about Tag and Kazinski, I wouldn't put it past her to tip them off about him just to really tie your misery up in a neat package."

Marybell took a deep breath. For now, he was safe. "Just make sure he lies low, please? I'll get out of here as fast as I can, and hopefully they'll never get wind of the fact that he's here, too."

LaDawn grabbed at her hand. "I'm not lettin' you go like this, MB. Like you did somethin' wrong."

"You've seen what they're capable of, LaDawn. Please don't ask me to put children in harm's way. I just won't do it."

LaDawn's purple-lined lips went hard. "Then we'll go together. Like Thelma and Louise. You ain't leavin' me here all alone, and I'm not lettin' you go out there alone. So consider this my resignation, Dixie."

Dixie held up a hand. "Before ya'll leave me like I mean as much to you as day-old bread, let's discuss what we came here to discuss."

Em nodded, her eyes fraught with concern when she looked at Marybell. "Please listen first."

Dixie's chest rose and fell before she began. "Now, I need you to just trust me, okay, MB? I know that's not an easy thing for you to do, sugar, but before you get angry, just listen to why we've done what we've done."

Her heart throbbed in her chest, and her hands grew clammy and cold. "What have you done?"

"We found the person who sold your picture to that first magazine," Dixie said.

Fear swept along her spine, in all its icy tingles. "Who?" she whispered, her voice so faint she almost didn't hear it. Her legs shook so hard she almost couldn't stand.

Dixie wrapped an arm around her waist. "Tara-Anne."

No. Her ears wouldn't hear it. They refused. No. They'd been friends. Tara-Anne was the first person she'd shared a space with for longer than a few months. They'd laughed. They'd studied. They'd partied.

No.

Marybell shook her head so violently her ears rang.

Em cupped her jaw, smoothing away the tears. "Darlin', *yes.*"

She knew her eyes were wild, her face slack with shock, but she couldn't process it. "No."

LaDawn came into her line of vision. "Yes, MB. She was doin' Kazinski, all along thinkin' he was gonna leave his wife for her and they were gonna share his ill-gotten millions."

"No!" Hysteria rose and fell, high tide, low tide. She gripped the back of the couch.

LaDawn shoved Em out of the way, grabbing her shoulders with firm hands. "MB, listen to me. She was havin' an affair with him. A big, ugly, dirty affair until she caught him with you that night. She was angry, and hurt, and she took that picture of you and sold it to the tabloids because she wanted some revenge. It was Tara-Anne. You hear me?"

"How? How did you find out?" She was suddenly raw, shredded as surely as someone had run her through a wood chipper. Every moment she'd been alone, homeless, broken, she now had a face to place blame on, and she couldn't even stand up.

Dixie tightened her grip on her waist. "Does it really matter, honey? All that matters is the truth. We can prove it."

Proof. After all this time, they had proof. Funny, when absolution came along, it came in the way of one simple word. Proof. "Proof...what..."

Dixie nodded. "Tara-Anne has the original picture, and she was stupid enough to keep all the emails she shared with the reporter who broke the first story. It's definitive. Now it's up to you what we do with it. But please don't think about that right now. Think about telling Tag."

Em popped her lips. "I know you're angry with him right now, MB. I know he did wrong, and after I gave him what-for today, I tried to see his side of things. He was blindsided just like you. He was wrong to react the way he did, but after talkin' with Jax, I see where he was comin' from. Doesn't mean I approve, just means he should've taken more time before he came over here, guns loaded. Please talk to him, MB. Don't let this go without at least talking to him."

"No! Don't tell Tag!"

Em's eyes grew saucerlike. "Don't tell him? Honey, this proves you knew nothing about what Leon was doing. How could you not want to tell him?"

"Faith," she croaked. "He had no faith in me. Not a shred. When I bared my soul to him, he walked away, right out the door like bein' with me, seeing me, talking to me wasn't enough proof that I'd never do somethin' like that." She'd needed him to believe so much—so much it became an ache. And he'd walked away.

Dixie's eyes grew soft and warm. "There's nothin' in the world I understand more than needing one person to believe in you, MB. Especially the man you love, but please consider this. Tag's reaction was stupid and rash, but it came from a place of fear. Just like your hidin' did. There was more proof than not that you were involved with Leon."

Now she was angry. Angry at Tara-Anne, angry at the endless filth of the streets she'd endured, the stench, the fear. Angry at Tag for shutting her out. Red-hot fury fell from her lips. "No! You all believed me. You all took me on faith."

LaDawn shook her head. "We aren't in love with you, cookie. It's a whole different perspective when your friend takes up with a married man than it is when you think your lover did. You're not talkin' sense right now, because you hurt. You deserve to hurt. But don't hurt long, MB. Don't walk away from somethin' that made you so happy."

She couldn't hear about Tag's merits right now. She couldn't hear about perspective and pain. "Does the press know about Tara-Anne yet?"

Em shook her dark cascade of curls. "We decided as a group to let you choose where we go from here. It's not our place to run roughshod over you and do what we think is best. We just want you to know we'll handle it if you can't."

She shook her head, panic rising in her chest. "Don't say anything. Not to the press, and especially not to Tag—ever."

Dixie's brow furrowed. "Honey, that's not fair. To him, to you or to us. Please don't ask us to keep a secret that big. He's hurtin', too."

"Then don't. Tell him. Do whatever you see fit to make Tag all better."

LaDawn grabbed her hand, her eyes flashing. "Stop. You stop right now. I won't have this. I've been as good a friend as any to you, and I won't let you hurt yourself or Tag like this. You do what you want with this information, but don't behave like a spiteful child with it, and I'm not gonna let you leave it in our laps like that. I call unfair."

"Tag is going to be Em's brother-in-law, honey. It's wrong to put her in the middle like this," Dixie said.

They were right. It was wrong. It was unfair to ask them to make promises that only created more secrets. He could find out after she was gone. "Then just give me a day or so."

"To do what?" LaDawn demanded with a tap of her glittery purple nail to the countertop.

To breathe, she wanted to scream. To process the entirety of the whole mess her life had once been. To pack up and leave Plum Orchard so she never had to see Tag again. "I just need to figure out how to go about exonerating myself—in the right way."

"The right way?" Em asked, her tone full of caution.

Marybell ignored Em's question. "Where is Tara-Anne?"

"She lives in Atlanta still. She's married and has a little one. But she wants to see you, MB. She wants to apologize," Dixie soothed.

"Okay. So just give me a day—to get my head together—and then you can tell Tag whatever you want. *Please.*"

Dixie nodded and then put a hand on LaDawn's arm. "Could you ask Caine to prepare a bag for me? I'll stay here with MB."

Don't! she almost yelled before sucking in a gulp of air. "I need…to be alone. Please just let me be alone."

She watched as they all passed concerned looks at each other before Em said, "You don't have to be alone anymore, MB. We're here. Let us help you. Please let us help."

No. No one could help this empty hole in her stomach, the numb, almost out-of-body feeling. Marybell forced herself to soften her tone. These were people that loved her, and she wanted to honor that, but if she didn't get some time to herself, she'd crawl right out of her skin.

"I know you're here. If y'all knew how much I've appreciated that, you'd double over with the weight of my gratitude. But I was alone for a long time, and even though I know I can count on you at a moment's notice, I need time to wrap my head around this."

LaDawn finally smiled and bobbed her platinum head. "Without all our mindless yappin'."

Dixie gathered her in a hug so hard she had to squeeze her eyes shut. "You call me, understand? I won't have you alone if you need me. Doesn't matter what time."

Marybell nodded, reaching for Em and LaDawn and squeezing them, too.

"You heard Dixie," Em said, rubbing circles on her back. "Doesn't matter what time."

"Thank you. Thank you all. I…" She couldn't finish the words. She didn't always know how to express her gratitude, but if she knew what the words were to express how important their faith in her was, she'd use them.

"Say no more," LaDawn soothed. "You rest now, sugar. Enjoy a free day from all that slop on your face."

And with those words, they were gone in clusters of varied perfumes and high heels, and there was nothing left but the silence and the ringing in her ears.

* * *

"Tara-Anne?" Marybell fought to keep her voice calm, to keep her anger in check.

"Carson." There was fear in her reply, the kind of fear she'd lived with for years now. That she'd be found out. That the nightmare would start all over again.

Marybell clutched the phone in her hand. "Are you all right? You, your husband, the baby?"

She choked on her next words. "I can't believe you'd ask me that. I don't deserve it. I don't."

Marybell shook her head as though Tara-Anne were in the room with her. No recriminations, no apologies. Just an answer after all this time. She needed to hear it from her mouth. "I just want to know one thing, and that's all."

"Anything. Anything. I'm sorry, Carson. I can't ever tell you how sorry I really am."

Marybell couldn't hear apologies. How did you apologize for taking so much from a person? For stealing the very life out of her? "Why?" She had to stuff a fist in her mouth to keep from screeching the question.

"I was jealous. I was so sick with jealousy I couldn't see straight. I want to blame that on youth or stupidity, but it was just a blind rage. He'd made so many promises to me for so long. Then to see you two… I didn't ask questions. I didn't do anything but see all sorts of colors. And the next day, I found the sleaziest reporter I could, one who was hanging around Leon's office, hoping to get a scoop, and I handed him the picture of you, took his money once he verified it wasn't altered and sent you off to slaughter like… I had no idea…" Her hoarse words cracked, her voice rose. "Oh, my God, Carson. I had no *idea!*"

A blanket of peace fell over her. As easy as a feather, fluttering to the ground. "Okay."

"Then you disappeared, and I thought surely you'd run off with Leon, and I sat in my anger and waded through my money, and then I saw the news last week and how you lived for so long and…God forgive me, Carson, I'm sorry!" she screamed, ragged and raw, her sobs rising, her baby crying in the background.

Peace. Somehow she found peace in Tara-Anne's words. In her remorse, the hysteria in her words, the panic. "It's okay."

"Okay?" Her voice cracked with disbelief. "No! None of this is okay, Carson! I've lived with the guilt of this for so long that when your friends found me, it was almost a relief. If you'll just let me tell my husband and family, let me gather my thoughts, I'll make this right."

"No, Tara-Anne! Don't. Don't ever tell another livin' soul, or if you have to, only tell someone you can truly trust. Your secret's safe with me and my friends. I promise you. Don't do it."

Tara-Anne inhaled with a sharp wheeze. "I have to, Carson. You've been persecuted for so long, and now there've been Leon sightings. I can't let them chase you like this anymore. *I won't.*"

No more. *"Don't do it.* It'll ruin your baby's life forever. I don't want that. I want you to go right on doing what you've always done, but please don't go to the press. You have no idea what it's like." She bit back a sob. "I don't want the baby hurt. I don't want you hurt." No more hurt.

"I…I don't know what to say."

"Just say goodbye. Don't thank me. Don't apologize

to me. Just say goodbye and know that I'll go to my grave with this."

There was a long pause, one Marybell was certain was steeped in indecision before she whispered in a trembling phrase, "Goodbye, Carson."

Marybell hung up the phone, her hands shaking, but the burden of betrayal so much less like an anchor in her chest.

Twenty-One

When she woke the next morning, the empty hole in her stomach hadn't lessened, but her resolve was beginning to fill it.

As the day went on, and she packed as much as she thought she could fit into her car, she realized the drone of voices outside her door was virtually gone. Venturing a quick peek outside the window, she noted her security was still present but not a car in sight.

She went to the door and opened it. "They're gone?" she squeaked to the nearest guard. Everything the reporters had trampled had been replaced; all the lawn ornaments Blanche was so fond of were returned to their rightful places.

Blanche sent her a wave from just behind one immense guard. "How are you, dear?"

Marybell didn't know what to say. Blanche almost never spoke to her. "Fine, Miss…Miss Blanche, and you?" No way could she keep the disbelief out of her voice.

"May I come in?"

As in inside her apartment? The security guard

stepped aside while Blanche waited for permission. "Um…yes. I mean yes."

Blanche smiled at her, but her smile turned to something else when she saw the boxes stacked up. There hadn't been much to pack in the way of possessions, but it added up. "You're leavin'?" She breathed the question.

That tug on Marybell's heart tugged harder. "Yes. I was going to give you notice just after I found a safe way out of here, but everyone's gone."

"Mmm," Blanche hummed, tucking her purse under her arm. "I hear they think they've found that Leon—somewhere in Idaho was the last bit of speculation. Guess he's bigger fish to fry 'n you, but it won't be long before they're back, beatin' on your door. For now, they've all gone off to chase a new story."

Marybell's eyes flew open wide. Idaho? "But…"

Blanche patted her arm in motherly fashion. "That means you're no longer the story. So you won't need to give me notice, dear."

No. Even if they'd truly found Leon, she couldn't stay here with Tag. She couldn't. Plum Orchard was too small; her heart was too battered. "No, Miss Blanche. I won't be stayin', but thank you for rentin' me the apartment. I know Caine talked you into it, but I appreciated it just the same."

Blanche adjusted her purse in the crook of her elbow, her eyes inquisitive. "So you're just gonna run off? Why would you do that when you have a perfectly fine life right here?"

"But you hate us—me…" She felt as if she'd just been dropped into an episode of *The Twilight Zone*.

Blanche sighed, her face softening. "I don't hate you.

That's not to say I approve of what y'all are doin' back there in the guesthouse, but I don't hate you."

"But you picketed…"

"I'm weak, Marybell. So weak, I'm too afraid to speak out against the Mags. But I admire you. The way you've shown us bunch o' biddies what's what. We talk a big game, but not all of us feel like Louella and Kitty do. Some of us are just too pathetic to buck a system that's been in place longer than you've been on this earth. I don't admire that trait in myself, but that's the plain truth of it. So before you go off thinkin' it's better for you to run away, maybe you should keep right on takin' that stand you took when you were wearin' the devil's uniform." She turned on her heel and began to leave, but not before she said, "Good luck, dear."

Marybell stood in the middle of her apartment, her mouth wide-open. Blanche Carter had just given her the thumbs-up.

And the press was off looking for Leon in Idaho.

This was definitely an episode of *The Twilight Zone*.

"That was Gage drivin' through town like Coon Ryder was pointin' his old double-barrel at him, pretending to be you?" Dixie asked, her red eyes full of disbelief.

At Tag's request, they'd convened at Call Girls and gathered around the break room table.

To keep the press at bay long enough for Tag to get out of the house and institute "the plan" to win MB back, Jax and Gage had come up with the plan to send Gage out as a decoy, leading the press on a wild-goose chase. He looked enough like Tag to pull it off from a distance. Gordy playing Marybell had taken some convincing, though.

Tag directed his nod at Dixie. "Yep. It was Gage's idea, too. He figured if he could get the press to believe Gordy was Marybell, and Gage was me, he could get them to follow him at least to the airport in Atlanta and keep them busy for a while. We made flight reservations in both Marybell's name, and mine, too. It might not hold the paparazzi off for long, but at least it buys us a little time to figure out what to do next."

"Gordy? From the coffee shop Gordy? How did you talk him into putting all those spikes in his hair so he'd look like MB?" LaDawn crowed.

"We promised him a job at the mill. Full-time, with benefits, and it helps that he really likes Marybell."

Em leaned forward, clearly still very angry with him, her eyes as red as Dixie's. "Was it you who tipped them off about Leon being in Idaho?"

Tag shook his head. "That wasn't us, but it can't hurt. Last I heard from Gage, the line of cars following them on the road to Atlanta had lessened considerably."

"Why didn't we think of that?" Dixie mumbled, blowing her nose.

LaDawn popped her lips. "Because we're sittin' around here like a bunch of sissy girls and our heads just aren't on straight."

"And now, thanks to you, MB's leavin'." Em poked Tag in the chest. "Later this afternoon. She already called and told us all she wanted to come in and say goodbye. Not a one of us could talk her out of it. I blame you, Taggart Hawthorne."

She was right, but he had a plan. And he needed help.

If he focused on Marybell walking away from him, he wouldn't be able to keep his head on straight. "I need to see her, Em. I know I shouldn't ask you. I know you're angry with me right now, but I need you all to help me. *Please*." There. He was laying his guts out on the table, right there in front of them all.

Dixie perked up, blowing her nose into a tissue. "Well, spit it out. My eyes are all dried out from cryin'. If you have a way to fix it, you'd better speak up."

LaDawn dropped a Snickers bar on the table and pulled out a chair. "I sure hope it works, because I'm not lookin' forward to explainin' my bronzed flogger to the moving men."

Tag looked at her with surprise. "You're going with her?"

"You don't think I'd let my girl go out and face this alone, do you? Unlike *you,* that is."

"I deserve that." He did. But there was just one thing he wanted to do for her. If she was going to leave, and his begging and scraping didn't change her mind, he had one thing he needed Marybell to have before she left.

"You sure do. So tell us this plan and hurry up. Those movin' men need a two-hour window if I'm cancelin'."

Tag looked them all in the eye. Everyone that cared about Marybell. "I don't believe she knew what Kazinski was doing. I don't believe she was having an affair with him." He needed to set the record straight now, before he told them he needed their help.

A collective sigh swept the room. All the women looked at each other, but he couldn't guess what they were communicating with their eyes.

Em's shoulders dropped. "Thank heaven. I don't know if I could've lived with you if you did."

Dixie wiped her eyes with her thumb. "The plan. Tell us the plan. We'll do whatever you need us to do."

"This was something I was working on before all this went down. But now...now, even if she still decides to leave, I need her to have this. I just need to speed things up." And hope. He needed to hope he hadn't just fucked up the best thing to come into his life in forever.

Em clapped her hands. "All right, girls. It sounds like we have a plan!"

Marybell propped the door of her car open and gathered up the bag of plum fritters she'd purchased at Madge's. One last time before she left, she wanted to sit with her friends, laugh, girl-talk and eat doughnuts.

She didn't want to cry over Tag anymore. She didn't want to think too long on leaving—never seeing him smile again. She just wanted to be with the people she loved before she moved on.

Shoving the door shut with her foot, she almost laughed at the two or three people in the park, gaping at her. She'd garnered the same reaction at Madge's. Without her people shield, she found she wasn't interested in being bold. She didn't snarl at Louella Palmer when she passed her on her way out, and she didn't give her the hell she deserved for exposing her.

She'd simply waved to her and wished her well. In hindsight, Louella had done her a favor. She'd opened a door to the truth without meaning to, and for the moment, she was actually able to breathe. Marybell had no desire to tussle with her over it.

She'd rather Louella stew in her own soup, and wonder if Marybell Lyman was ever going to snarl at her again.

As she walked past the spot where Tag had kissed her that time right under the tree, the hot press of tears threatened to fall before she gulped in the chilly air of late afternoon and forced her feet to move.

The sooner she left, the sooner she could find ways to begin to heal. Right now it was too fresh.

"Marybell?"

Her hand tightened on the sack of doughnuts, but she kept walking, for surely she was dreaming up Tag's voice. She'd done it all night long—why would daylight be any different?

"Marybell, wait."

She stopped again, cocking her head, listening to heavy footsteps approach her from behind. When she turned around, she saw the old Tag. The Tag before he thought she was a money-stealing tramp. His eyes looked tired, but his smile was in place, that grin that made her chest tingle and her toes curl.

He reached out a hand for her, but she pulled away. "Wait. Please. Just hear me out."

It would be so easy to lob an insult at him, to ask him why she should wait when he didn't wait to judge her. But she didn't have it in her today. She just wanted to go.

Yet she stayed. Waited.

He took a small step closer, hedging his movement, using care with his words. "Will you hear me out?"

She closed her eyes and breathed again before opening them. "As long as you hurry. I don't want to be on the road late at night." *I want to be here with you. The one person I needed most in the world to believe me.*

He put a cautious hand on her arm. "Don't go. Just listen and then decide if you still want to go."

Had the girls told him about Tara-Anne? No. They'd promised. She believed they'd never give her up. "Why are you here?"

He ran a finger over her cheek, his smile apologetic. "I came to tell you I'm sorry. I was blinded by one bad experience, what happened to me with Alison. I know you're angry with me right now. I know I said some shitty things to you, but I'm here to tell you I love you, Marybell Lyman, or Carson Chapman, or whomever you choose to be from this moment on. I believe you. I don't care what the press says. I don't care what the people in Plum Orchard say. I don't care how many pictures they dredge up of you with that scum Leon. I believe you when you say you had nothing to do with it."

A million thoughts flew through her head. Thoughts preventing her from doing anything more than stammering, "But…"

Tag cupped her chin, stroking her jaw. "Oh, you don't have to but me. I've but the hell out of myself. I reacted, MB. I didn't think. I didn't reason. I reacted. It was such a goddamn shock to find out that's what you'd been hiding all this time, I just lost it. Doesn't make it right. Now, you can tell me to go straight to hell for doubting you. I won't talk you out of it, but I won't let you leave here without hearing that I love you. I want you in my damn life. I want to read books with you and listen to Marilyn Manson while we do it. I want to make love with you. I want to watch more princess movies with you while we feed each other popcorn. I want to stain your couch with spaghetti sauce. I want you to let me into your life, and I want you to do it all the way."

"But what about the press? They'll ruin your life. I can't let that happen. I won't."

He traced a finger over her lips, tender, soft. "How about we face that together when the time comes? For now, we have some peace. But nothing can ruin *us* if I don't let it. And I damn well won't let it, Marybell."

Her heart slammed into her chest, the roar in her ears drowning almost everything else out. They must have told him. "Did they tell you?"

Tag inched in a little closer. "Did who tell me what?"

"Dixie, Em, LaDawn, did they tell you about Tara-Anne?"

His genuine confusion was the best gift ever. Hope welled up in her. "Tara-Anne. Did they tell you she was the one who took that picture of me and Leon?"

Tag shook his head, his eyes determined. "I don't care about the picture. I don't care about anything but that you forget what an ass I was and we start over."

"You don't know…" He didn't know. He was offering her his trust and he didn't know. She had to show him.

"I don't care, honey. I love you. Period."

Marybell dropped the plum fritters right there in the square and hurled herself at him, wrapping her arms around his neck, knocking him back a step before he got his feet under him. "You don't know," she whispered. "I can't believe you don't know."

Arms, steady, solid, secure, wrapped around her and pulled her close. "I don't care about whatever I don't know. Just tell me you love me back."

More tears sprang to her eyes. Everything melted away. All the hurt, the agonizing pain of leaving him fell away. She buried her face in his neck, inhaled his scent. "I love you, Taggart Hawthorne. I love you, I love you, I love you."

His body shuddered against hers. "Okay. That's good. Now I have one more thing to show you. But you have to let go for just a sec."

No. She was never, ever letting go. Marybell slid down his long frame and dropped to the ground, but she kept a tight grip on his hand.

"You ready?" he asked.

She nodded, almost too dazed to understand what could possibly be next.

Tag let out a whistle. "C'mere, Doby! C'mon, pal!"

Doby?

From the shadow of the trees in the middle of the square, Doby bounded toward them.

Doby.

"Doby?" Tears sprang to her eyes. He was older now, a bit of gray powdering his golden forehead, his jowls puffy from age, his skin beginning to sag. Tag let him off the leash and he bounded toward her.

Marybell dropped to her knees when he went into sitting position—images of teaching him that command flashing like brilliant bits of an instant replay. She reached a trembling hand out and placed it on his cheek. Doby curled into it, just as he'd always done, waiting for her to call him to her. "Come."

She patted her thighs, fat tears falling down her face. "Come, Doby."

Doby dropped his full weight on her, burrowing

his wet nose in her jacket. "Oh, Doby," she whispered, wrapping her arms around his thick neck. "I can't believe it's you.…" She buried her face in his neck and rocked him, inhaled the scent that had comforted her for so many long nights. She reveled in his warmth, remembered all the nights she'd used his soft fur as a pillow, his big body for shelter.

Tag sat on his haunches and put his hand over hers, warm, secure.

"*Why?* Why did you do this?" she squeaked.

"That night when you told me Doby was the only living, breathing thing that had ever loved you sort of broke me. I don't know what it's like not to have someone to lean on, even if I was too much of an ass to realize it at the time. You said you always wondered what happened to him, and if he was happy with the family you gave him to for safekeeping. I didn't know everything behind the story of Doby at the time. I just wanted you to know for sure that Doby had his happy ending. You gave him one. I wanted you to have yours, too."

"How? How in the world did you find him?" She'd never known what happened to Doby. After she'd given him to the little girl and her family, she'd moved off to another part of the city, and shortly thereafter, Landon had found her.

Tag brushed her hair from her forehead, his eyes so different from the other night—tender, gentle. "Dixie and her wads of money could find a needle in a haystack. The Watsons frequent that restaurant you mentioned in front of the alley. We started there, and it all just fell into place. One of the waiters knew exactly who we meant, and he was decent enough to call them and ask them if we could connect."

The once-little girl at the end of an alleyway was now a pretty teenager. Chestnut-haired and dark-eyed, she was willowy and tall. So different from the chubby child with a long braid down her back. She and her parents stood by the big oak tree in the square, waiting with kind eyes full of hesitation.

Marybell's throat tightened until she almost couldn't breathe. "No one has ever… No one but Landon… I…" The tears she'd held for so long just wouldn't stop now. They fell into her lap, wetting Doby's head. "I loved him so, so much. Giving him away was the hardest thing I've ever done. I just couldn't take care of him…." She choked on her words, the sob raw and painful in her scratchy throat.

Tag swiped at her tears, cupping her chin. "I know, honey. But I swear on all the bologna sandwiches in the world, if you'll forgive me, I'll take care of you. I'll always take care of you. Me, and Jax, and Em, and Gage, and the girls, and Maizy, too. All of us. You just have to promise to stay and trust that I'll never let the past interfere with our future again. Trust that I'll talk to you before I shoot off my big mouth."

Marybell pressed her fists to her eyes, unable to stop the tears, the gut-wrenching pain of losing Doby. Giving Doby away had symbolized the end of all hope, and now here he was, happy and healthy, representing a new beginning.

Tag pulled her close, keeping Doby nestled safe between them. He rocked her then, swaying in the cold afternoon, helping her let go. "I'm sorry, honey. Jesus,

I'm so damn sorry. I didn't know what happened to you. I didn't understand. But I do now. I understand why you were so afraid. But you don't have to be afraid with me. Just let me be here for you. Trust me, and I'll trust you. Team Broken for the win."

Marybell's hands reached upward, under his arms, clinging to them with stiff fingers. And she cried. She cried for the child who'd never known a permanent home, who'd never had her own room or even her own clothes. Who'd never had loving parents.

She cried for the teenager who'd wanted so badly to fit in, but was never in one place long enough to make friends and find what fit.

She cried for the young adult who'd fought long and hard to overcome her poor beginnings and thought she'd finally found her place only to have that place in the world ripped out from under her.

She cried for the woman who ran away from life, who went hungry, who ate from a Dumpster.

She cried for all the years she'd missed with Doby.

She cried for Landon who'd believed when no one else had. When no one should have for all the overwhelming evidence against her.

And then she let Tag dry her tears. She leaned on him. She melted against him and let him carry the burden.

And it was good. So very, very good.

Tag leaned back and smiled at her—so handsome in the fading sunlight, so perfect.

Marybell latched on to Doby's leash, her hands shaking. "I don't know if I can let him go again, Tag," she muttered hoarsely. How could she let him go again? The idea of it was like severing a limb, cutting a vital artery.

"Miss Lyman?"

Her heart throbbed in her chest as she swiped at her tear-streaked face. Tag gave her a gentle tug upward. "Jody, right?" she whispered.

Jody smiled and nodded, reaching down to stroke Doby's head without ever taking her eyes off Marybell's. She was afraid. But she was here. Here, letting Marybell reunite with the dog that had become hers. "Yes, Jody. I...I just wanted to say thank you to you—for all those years ago when you gave us Doby. I was kind of a misfit in school. Nobody really liked me, but Doby gave me something to look forward to when I came home. He changed everything for me. If...if you want him back, I'd totally understand. He really loves you. I can see that. He knew...he knew exactly who you were." Her wide eyes filled with the tears only the expectation of separation can conjure.

Doby nudged Jody's hand, consoling in the way only her Doby knew how.

Marybell shook her head, wiping at her cheeks. "No. No, Jody. I'd never take him." Her voice hitched and Tag squeezed her hand, encouraging her. She cleared her throat. "I'd never take him from you. You've been so good to him, taken such amazing care of him. It's obvious he loves you, too. I'm so glad he helped you. Thank you, Jody, and your mom and dad, too." She held out the leash to the once young, awkward girl who'd turned into such a pretty young woman.

Jody's mother held out her hand, petite and dark-haired, her eyes warm. "Thank *you,* Miss Lyman. It's so good to see you so happy and healthy. We looked for you for what seemed like months, so you'd know Doby was okay, but we never did find you."

Marybell shook her head. "I moved...."

"Doby's the best dog anyone could ask for, and Jody's right. He changed her world. Watching her suffer day after day at school... Well, suffice it to say, Doby was better than any cookies and milk I could ever whip up. I can't ever thank you enough for that, but we hope to pay it forward."

Jody's father walked toward them, a smaller version of Doby in black on a leash in his hand. He came to stand next to Jody with a smile.

Jody's mother pointed at the excited mini-Doby, dark and wiggly. "This is Joe. Because of Doby, and how you came about him, we decided to foster. Thinking about Doby before you found him, wanderin' the streets, hungry and alone, broke our hearts. So we decided to do something about it. Doby brought so much good to our home, we believe everyone should have a Doby. So we became fosters a while back. Joe reminded us so much of Doby's personality, we jumped on the chance to take him in. Can you even believe someone would abandon this precious angel and leave him tied to a pole in the park? He needs a home, and we hear Plum Orchard's *your* home—it's so quaint here. And this square, it'd be a great place to walk him, don't you think?"

Marybell bent down and let Joe nuzzle her neck, lapping sloppy kisses on her face, and then he curled his face into her hand—so much the way Doby once had. It was a coincidence—surely, all dogs did it—but to her, it was a sign.

This was home.

Tag rocked back on his heels and grinned down at her. "I dunno, MB. You think we need another team member? Joe makes three."

"And as Doby's biological mom, I'd love to have you drop by and pay him regular visits. We all would. Maybe you'd consider babysittin' when we go out of town? He could play with Joe. They get along so well. Doby's a great big brother."

Tag dropped a kiss on her lips. "I'll help you potty-train," he teased, smiling at her. "Course, that means you have to stay here. You know, with *me*."

"Yes," she husked out around more tears. On tiptoe, she pulled Tag in for a kiss. A kiss that meant she never had to run away again. "Yes."

Cheers echoed from somewhere far off, making Marybell squint.

Cat, Em, Dixie and LaDawn bounded out from behind the square's gazebo, followed by Caine, Jax and the children. Their faces held smiles; their hands held picnic baskets.

Em was the first to rush up to her and drag her into a hug. "We have food—because you know nothin' worth celebratin' is celebrated without my fried chicken." She dropped a kiss on Marybell's cheek and scurried off to gather up Gareth and Clifton Junior.

Dixie held her arms out. "Phew, honey. It was touch-and-go there for a minute. Don't you ever keep somethin' like this from me again, okay? You promise, now."

Marybell, whose face was once more covered in tears, nodded against her shoulder, squeezing her eyes tight, savoring Dixie's familiar scent. "Promise."

Dixie leaned back and dabbed at her cheeks with a tissue. "And come Monday, once you two are done—" she paused and batted her eyelashes "—potty training, pay me a visit in my office, would you? We'll talk about that director-of-marketing thing, okay?"

Marybell nodded—so grateful she could only nod.

LaDawn twisted one of her curls around her finger. "You were gonna leave me here, Marybell Lyman. Persecuted and alone. I'm not gonna lie when I say that hurt." She pointed a pink, glittery nail at her heart. "We started this together. You, me, Cat and Landon. That's all there was back in the day."

Marybell hurled herself at LaDawn, hugging her hard. "I'm sorry. I was so afraid. I didn't want to leave you, but I didn't want you to suffer because of me."

LaDawn gave her a "sure, fine" smile and shooed her off. "You go on and be with your new man. You can buy me doughnuts later to make up for it."

She planted a kiss, an apologetic kiss, on LaDawn's cheek. "Glazed with pink frostin'—just for you."

"A dozen. Only a dozen will make this right," LaDawn joked, tucking her chin into her fake fur wrap and making her way to the tables everyone was setting up in the gazebo.

Jax slapped Tag on the back and dropped a kiss on Marybell's cheek. "There was no talkin' Em out of a celebration—which, if you know Em, involves a boat-load of food, but if you guys want to slip off somewhere—I get it. I'll cover for you."

Marybell shook her head. This was where she wanted to be right at this second. With her family and Tag, celebrating what family was sometimes about—injecting themselves into your life. And she loved it—every second of it. "So, what do you say, Joe? How do you feel about some fried chicken and potato salad?"

"Does this mean we're keeping him?"

"We are. *We* definitely are." She lifted her lips for a kiss. That amazing, toe-tingling kiss before turning to the Watsons. "You'll join us, won't you? You and Doby?"

Mrs. Watson squeezed her hand. "We'd love to."

"Ohh!" someone screamed. Cat came into focus, waddling toward them with Flynn holding her up. "It's time! Get the car!" she yelled, moving toward Marybell with a crablike walk, her arms under her belly. "Give me a hug before I head off to that hospital. Just so I know you're okay."

Marybell gave her a quick hug, and placed a gentle hand on her belly. "Go have that baby and make me an auntie," she said on a laugh. Flynn pulled their car around and bundled Cat into it. Cat grabbed her hand. "Don't you ever think about leavin' us, MB. I'd miss you so. We started this. By hell, we'll finish it." She blew her a kiss before Flynn revved the engine and took off toward the hospital in Johnsonville.

Tag took Joe's leash. "So, should I call you MB or Carson?"

She smiled, giving it only a moment's thought. "Marybell was a rebirth for me. Landon gave the name to me because he once had a friend in some foreign country whose name translated to Marybell. He saw to all the legal changes, and it protected me all this time. I left Carson behind, I guess. Becoming Marybell was like sheddin' my skin—skin that was strangling me.

So I think I'll keep it. In honor of Landon and this new life he offered me."

Tag held out the crook of his arm. "Well, then, Marybell, whaddya say we go start that new life with some of Em's fried chicken? New beginnings scream a celebration with fried chicken."

"Not bologna sandwiches?"

"Nope. That's only for nondates, and I think we're past the point of no return when it comes to those."

She threaded her arm in Tag's, snuggling close to him. "What point are we at? What comes after nondates?"

"They didn't tell you?"

"Who?"

"The nondate people."

"Missed that memo."

"How about I tell you later? You know, when we're alone?" He wiggled his eyebrows, making her toes curl.

Marybell smiled back at him, free. So free. "It's a date, Hawthorne."

Joe settled at the end of Marybell's bed, curling up on a pillow Tag had given him. Fed and walked, he was quickly making her fall hard for him with his gentle nature and his sloppy puppy kisses.

Gage and Gordy were safe for now, and enjoying a night out at some sports bar while the press chased after ghosts at the Atlanta Airport.

She'd told Tag the details involving Tara-Anne. To her dismay, he'd first wanted her prosecuted, but she'd managed to convince him that it didn't matter where the blame lay—in the press or otherwise. That he believed her was all that mattered to her.

"How is it we're on the floor and Joe's on the bed?" Tag asked on a chuckle, dipping his fingers into her panties.

She lifted her hips, savoring the slow slide he made into her wet flesh. "Are you gonna give me grief or are you going to have your way with me, right here on this floor?"

Tag peeled the straps of her new pink camisole from her shoulders. Em had given it to her, in honor of her love of the color pink, and to signify the change her life was about to take. "I just know you like all things sparkly and fluffy, MB," she'd said. "I've seen it from time to time when we were shoppin' and such. I just never understood why you didn't wear any of the stuff you liked. Now that I do, I figured you'd need a head start on a new wardrobe."

She'd handed Marybell the box, fancifully wrapped in all shades of pink with a smile and an Em hug.

Tag slipped the straps off her shoulder, pulling her down for a kiss. "I guess if I have to, I'll have my way with you," he teased, running the palms of his hand along her sides and over her spine.

She shivered, pressing into his length, her nipples beading tight. "Then we'd better get to it, huh? Joe will have to go out in another hour or so, and we are potty-trainin'."

"Always with the 'hurry up, Tag.' You are a hard woman to please."

She giggled, tucking her hair behind her ear before urging him to pull his T-shirt off. She didn't hide her sigh at the beauty of his body this time. This time, she openly admired him.

He twirled a piece of her hair around his finger. "Have I told you how much I love your hair? It's soft. I like."

"You didn't like my spikes?" She'd be hurt, but she had to admit, she liked her normal hair, too.

Bending low, he pulled a nipple to his lips, flicking his tongue over it. "I loved your spikes. But I think I love this more."

Marybell moaned against the top of his head, arching into the heat of his mouth while tugging at the button on the top of his jeans.

Somehow they managed to find their way out of their clothes, and naked, Tag sat up against the bed, his shaft hard when she reached for him and straddled his lap.

She stroked him, letting her lips glide along his neck, over his jaw until their mouths met. "Hmm, that's good," he breathed out, clamping his hand over her wrist. "You have amazing lips, Ms. Lyman."

She mirrored his sigh when he lifted her and settled her on his cock, sliding down along it until she sat completely on his lap and filled her up. "You have amazing everything."

Tag's hands kneaded her hips, the rhythm they'd found with each other easy, slow. "It feels like it's been a hundred years since we did this last," he muttered, hissing when she rolled in a circle.

Her arms went around his neck, her cheek on his head when she smiled. "It's only been two days."

Tag cupped the undersides of her breasts, rolling his

fingers over her nipples. "Let's make sure we never go that long again. It was torture."

She giggled just before biting her lip at the exquisite pleasure of his agonizingly slow thrusts. "Well, we can't have that, can we?" she asked; then her breath hitched and the stingy sweet push of release swept over her.

Tag's thigh muscles flexed, tensing and releasing until he groaned in her ear and she knew he was satisfied, too. He squeezed her tight. "Never, ever again."

Marybell nodded. Never again. "Hey, you forgot to tell me what comes after nondates."

He lifted his head and grinned her favorite grin ever. "The memo, right?"

"Yeah, I didn't get that one. So, what comes after nondates?"

Pressing his lips to hers, Tag gave her a soft kiss. *"Forever."*

She smiled up at him, finally understanding what Dixie meant by being so happy you were full up.

She was full up.

Full up forever.

* * * * *

Wonder where it all began?
Turn the page for TALK THIS WAY,
the Call Girls prequel novella,
available for the first time in print!

One

"*Y*ou work here?" Flynn McGrady asked, giving the small coffee shop a once-over.

Catherine Butler fought a hard roll of her eyes, putting a fake smile on her face just in case her cranky boss was watching her. "*Ogres* drink coffee?"

"Only the ones who eat little kids." He rubbed his flat stomach with the width of his tanned hand and almost grinned. "We have to wash them down with something. Bones have sharp edges."

Oh, heavens no. No way was Flynn McGrady ever going to make up for being the biggest ass-hat this side of the county line. Not even with his devastatingly dimpled almost smile.

Nope. She clutched her pen and pad to quell the rumble he evoked in the pit of her belly, looking down at the Formica table he sat at to avoid his eyes. "Then what can I get for you?" *You fun-stomper.*

"What do you suggest?"

Someone far braver than I yank out whatever's stuck

up your incredibly hard, drool-worthy backside? "Depends on what you like. There's a menu board right over there."

"But I'm asking what *you* like." He gave her a view of his rock-hard jaw in all its defiance.

"I like customers who can read." She pointed to the chalk menu board she'd spent an hour drawing on happy faces bouncing above steaming cups of coffee that was sitting on the shiny silver counter.

More rock-hard jaw, plus the added tic of aggravation, equaled his teeth clenching. As much as she hated to admit it, he made her pulse flex its underused muscles, and had from the first day she'd laid eyes on him at the Oakdale Nursing Home, where both their mothers were temporary residents.

"And I like baristas who are helpful," he groused up at her.

Arlo, her boss and resident tyrant, came into her line of vision, beefy arms folded over his chest, sourpuss intact. Damn. She'd been on his watch-like-a-hawk list ever since she'd tried to talk a senior customer out of the triple mocha latte that wasn't really a triple at all.

Arlo was a cheapskate and Howard, one of her favorite customers, was on a fixed income. He came in every day at noon while his wife was across the way at Oakdale in physical therapy to have a cup of coffee and a sandwich he brought from home, and Cat had fallen in love with his dedication to their marriage.

Howard's words about his love for his wife, his devotion to her, touched her. Made her yearn for something that had been elusive to her thus far.

Love. And a relationship that lasted longer than a

few months before she lost interest and took off onto the next shiny thing that caught her eye.

So, she couldn't just stand by and watch Arlo overcharge him by fifty cents for absolutely nothing. But encouraging his employees to stiff the customers was just one of the perks of working for Arlo. That and his grabby paws.

While she needed this job desperately in order to help pay for her mother's care at Oakdale, she wasn't willing to sacrifice her conscience over it.

Cat shuffled her feet when Arlo glared her way, keeping her voice low. "Listen, Mr. McGrady, I realize we've had our differences at the nursing home. I meant no harm when I brought your mama those alleged 'racy' novels. But you have to admit, it's helped her remember her words."

Flynn opened his pretty mouth to speak.

But Cat's hand flapped up before Mr. Pissy Pants could jump in and protest. "I realize the words leaned toward the colorful, but they're still words, right? After a stroke, it's important to be able to express yourself. Just ask Dr. Fairlane. He said as much. Now, the nursing home is one thing. But this is my job. Please, save your grudge for the proper venue."

Please. After today and her chat with Oakdale's administrator, who'd reminded her she was behind on her mama's bill, she was already on ice so thin you could see through it.

Oakdale was a privately owned nursing facility, one of the best in the country. It was exclusive and provided not just permanent residence, but temporary situations for short-term rehabilitation. And it cost a small fortune.

Medicaid had shot down the idea of a stay at Oakdale,

but with her mother's diabetes impeding her healing process, and the fact that she couldn't be with her around the clock, Cat wasn't willing to take any more chances with her recuperation. They'd sold her mother's home for a small profit, and decided to worry about where they'd live once she was healthy again.

After a whole lot of sweet-talking, and all of her meager savings, Cat had managed to secure a spot for her mother, and she wasn't letting go. Even if she had to hook for cash to keep it.

She could admit she wasn't very good at keeping jobs. Just ask her twelve or so former employers of the past several years. But this one? She needed this one more than any job she'd ever had in her entire life.

"Words are very important. On this we agree, Miss Butler. It's the type of words we disagree on. Couldn't you have at least brought her something tame? Maybe some Dr. Seuss?"

Cat secretly smiled remembering Flynn McGrady's mother, Della, forcing the words from her immobile lips while sitting in the middle of the crowded rec center. "Oh, c'mon. *Green Eggs and Ham* isn't nearly as rich with expression as 'Spank me harder!' Now that was a statement chock with emotion, crystal clear and perfectly executed. Relax, already."

He visibly cringed, the tips of his ears turning red. "I can't believe they let you mingle with the other patients."

Cat bristled, though, she had to admit, if her mother said something so racy, she'd probably cringe, too. "I can't believe you're not over-the-moon that your mama spoke for the first time today since she had her stroke."

He fiddled with the corners of the paper napkin on

his table, his nimble fingers folding the edges neatly. "You're taking credit for her ongoing recovery now?"

"I'm takin' credit for lightening up an otherwise depressing situation. Nothing more."

Flynn looked up at her, all deep blue eyes and thick, gravelly voice. "And you think hanging posters of romance novels with half-naked men on her walls is uplifting?"

Cat arched an eyebrow meant to shower him in haughty attitude. "Well, maybe not to the insecure male. But other than you and your blusterin', there have been no complaints, especially from Della. You must have known she loved romance novels before her stroke. That there wasn't a single one of her beloved books for her to read when you brought her to Oakdale astounds me."

"We didn't know she could still read."

Her cheeks sucked inward while Arlo hovered and her damn phone vibrated in her pocket. Probably Oakdale again, wondering where her payment was.

Yet, she couldn't let this go. Flynn had made all sorts of stink when his mother had chirped those words, as if Cat had brought Della something illicit from the naughty store.

She'd only given her what made her happy, and for the first time in the three months since Cat had met Della at Oakdale, when Cat handed her a copy of *The Sheik's Alien Twin Babies' Nanny* or some title she couldn't remember, Della's lips had lifted in a lopsided smile. She'd looked right at Cat, her once dull, defeated eyes full of what she was convinced was hope.

So too daggone bad on her cranky, ill-mannered, hotter-'n-sin son. No racing heartbeat and sweaty palms were going to deter her from encouraging Della.

"You didn't exactly check, either. All I did was surround her with the things she loved before her stroke. I asked your cousin Emmaline...Amos, is it?"

Flynn nodded his dark head with a grating sigh. "That's her."

"She's lovely, and sweet, and *helpful*. Em, as she asked me to call her, told me everything she knew that might make your mama happy when she was passing through Atlanta and dropped in to pay Della a visit. Maybe, instead of always ordering everyone around, if you stopped and paid attention once in a while, you'd know in her recovery, your mama needs the things that used to comfort her. Romance novels bein' high on the list."

You're going too far, Catherine Butler....

Flynn's eyebrows rose. "Now you're questioning my intentions for my mother's rehabilitation?"

Stop now, Cat. Stop before you draw attention to yourself simply because you never know when to hush your mouth. It's his mother, for mercy's sake. It's not like he never visits her or spends all of his time ogling pretty nurses when he does. He's just disagreeing with your unconventional methods.

Cat sucked in some fresh air and focused on not losing job number thirteen. "No. Now I'm questioning what your order is."

"Is there a problem here, Mr. McGrady?" Arlo sidled up alongside her, his beefy body and moon-shaped face infiltrating her view. "We've had some complaints about Cat, so if she's givin' you some kind o' trouble, you speak up. I like to see my customers leave here satisfied."

Cat stiffened. That wasn't true. No one had complained. Wait. Maybe one customer had, but he'd been horrible to the new mother, who had been frazzled and tired, and trying desperately to soothe her crying baby.

So she'd slipped and spilled coffee on his fancy new suit? Accidents happened. She'd offered to pay to have it cleaned. He'd declined and called her a clumsy bitch, but he'd left and after that, everything was right as rain.

Arlo put his equally beefy hands on his hips, just waiting. "Mr. McGrady?"

Hush now, Cat. How many times do I have to remind you, sometimes you have to catch flies with honey 'cos the vinegar will send you to the unemployment line?

Her mother's words. Words to live by, surely.

"There's no trouble here, Arlo," Cat insisted.

"No trouble at all, Arlo," Flynn repeated, staring Arlo down with his intense eyes and granite expression.

Arlo pursed his thick lips, obviously unconvinced. "You sure now? Don't cover up for her. She can be pretty sassy with that mouth o' hers, always disruptin' folk, buckin' authority like she knows how to run this place."

Cat's mouth fell open. She never bucked anything. In fact, she'd probably been the quietest she'd been in her entire life during her employment with Arlo.

Could she be accused of being overly passionate about the unfairness of overcharging seniors for weak, watered-down coffee? Or defending a new mother just trying to catch her breath without the jeers and eye-rolling of an insensitive, rude caveman?

Yes. But that was hardly bucking the system. Mostly she'd been nonbucking.

Still, what happened next was due only to the fact

that she'd always had trouble heeding her mother's infamous words.

She had no honey left in her pot to catch a fly with.
It was all just vinegar.

There went unlucky job number thirteen hot on the
heels of an incoming call from the Oakdale administrator, Casper Reynolds.

Shit.

The last thing he'd meant to do when he'd wandered
into the coffee shop was get the only person at the nursing home who'd been able to coax his mother into re-
sponding to anything in three solid months fired.

Nothing he'd said could change that tyrant Arlo's
mind, either. He'd bargained, offered to pay her salary
for six months and threatened to report him to the labor
board, but all with no luck.

Arlo was a caged tiger, and he'd latched on to firing
Cat like she was his only source of protein.

Flynn McGrady watched from his rental car as Cat's
long legs ate up the parking lot of the coffee shop connected to the nursing home. Her chestnut-brown hair
billowed behind her in thick streams streaked with gold,
her cheeks were fiery red and her chest heaved beneath
the snugly fitting blue T-shirt she wore.

In that moment, he realized how beautiful she
was, with her creamy skin, full peachy lips and bright
almond-shaped eyes. He'd never taken the time to really
look at her. She was always excusing herself and rushing
off somewhere when he came to visit Della.

Cat Butler was like Mother Teresa at Oakdale. Everyone loved her. There wasn't a patient in the connecting health-care facilities or senior in the nursing home

who didn't. She baked cupcakes when someone graduated from a wheelchair to a walker and turned it into a ceremony where she presented the lucky graduate with a certificate they could frame, and she encouraged everyone to join the party.

She played board games and cards with all the seniors, and made sure everyone was always included. She'd brought costumes in for an impromptu costume party and organized a senior parade along the halls.

In review, Cat was loveable, and he was an asshole. He'd overreacted to what his mother said.

He wanted to go and apologize to her. Smooth this over. Get her job back for her somehow.

She dropped down on a bench under a tree, resting her face in her hands. It looked as if her shoulders quivered while the sunlight slipped between the trees, casting shadows along her spine.

Perfect, and you made her cry, jerk.

He'd been a surly asshole with her from the moment he'd sat down at that table and realized she was the saintly angel from Oakdale. Since his mother's stroke, if he listened to his sister, Adeline, he'd been an asshole period.

It was the endless commute back and forth from his home in New York to Atlanta to see his mother each weekend and find she'd made little progress, as he tried to manage his internet-based company from two places at once, and also juggle her health care, that left him so cranky. At least he kept telling himself that.

Not a good enough excuse, Flynn.

He'd only egged on Cat because she'd managed to get his mother interested in something—finally. He was almost resentful. Nothing he'd bribed Della with, bartered with her for, had garnered the effect on her like Cat's idea about those romance novels had.

And in fairness, he'd been a little embarrassed, too. It was, after all, his mother garbling out the words *Spank me harder!* in front of a roomful of people.

Now he had to find a way to make this right. Cat was his mother's favorite visitor. They'd forged this bond, this secret sort of means of communication that made Della's face light up, even if her lips still couldn't unite a smile with her emotional state.

For the past three months, he'd made weekend trips to Atlanta to see his mother since she'd been admitted to Oakdale. He'd watched Cat and Della interact from afar when they were engrossed in a jigsaw puzzle, or watching a television show. He'd actually admired the ease with which Cat soothed Della when she was frustrated, by simply touching her hand, leaning in close and whispering something in her ear that settled her right down.

Pretty Cat had all the qualifications to help heal Della that he apparently lacked.

How was he supposed to know his mother read that kind of fiction? In fact, he'd never seen her with anything but a knitting book in her lap in all of his thirty-seven years.

Damn, he wished Adeline were here. She'd know how to help, but she was on active duty in Afghanistan with only the occasional Skype session or phone call to ease his uncertainties.

The last thing he wanted was for his mother to slip back into her deafening silence. If she found out he was part of the reason Cat had been fired, leaving all her Oakdale time eaten up to pound the pavement looking for work, Della would slay him with that sour look she'd perfected since her stroke.

Flynn gripped the steering wheel while he stared at Cat's back. Now what?

Anything. He'd do anything to help get back his mother's will to live. The doctors all said she was perfectly capable of becoming fully functional again. They said she had to *want* to fully function. Somewhere between Adeline leaving for Afghanistan and his father's passing, Della had just lost interest in the business of living.

When it had happened, he couldn't pinpoint, but it was clearer each time he visited her, which made the decision to leave New York, at least temporarily, an easy one.

The stroke had brought new focus; shed light on some underlying issues causing his mother to suffer. He'd been too blind to see them—too busy with work and his own life.

But he was here now. He'd leased an apartment, he had wheels and he was going to make it right.

With his mother and with Cat.

Two

"Cat?"

Swiping the tears from her eyes with her thumb, Cat looked up to find one of her all-time favorite former patients at Oakdale's Cancer Center, Landon Wells, staring down at her, his handsome face so elegant and understated, his eyes sharper than they'd been in a while.

Landon was in his early- to-mid-thirties, she guessed. He wasn't construction-worker hot with ripped abs and miles of hard tanned flesh. He was distinguished, the epitome of a Southern gentleman, with all the outward qualities the image evoked, and they'd struck up a friendship over the course of his recovery that she treasured.

She loved his drawl, his upbeat personality, but mostly, she loved their conversations that often spanned hours as she waited for her mother to finish her therapy and he wiled away early mornings and afternoons in his recuperation from chemotherapy. He'd wheel himself along the long corridor connecting the cancer center to the nursing home specifically to find her.

There was always something going on in his private wing as laughter spilled out into the hallways and Liberace's music filtered softly between the chatter.

Colorful people strolled in and out during visiting hours, and he never lacked for dozens and dozens of flower deliveries, which he always donated to the other patients' rooms.

When he'd found out she worked at the connecting coffee shop, he'd coaxed her—with his charming wit—into bringing him coffee every morning by telling her the coffee in-house tasted like piss-water.

From that day on, Cat brought him his favorite cinnamon latte each morning before she stopped to see her mother and head off to work.

Cat chuckled every time she recalled the exchange they'd had several months ago when he'd come to Oakdale and exactly five visits into their early-morning, caffeine-laced affair.

"I'm gay, just so you know." He made mention of it like he was commenting on the weather, leaning over the edge of his wheelchair, his expensive silk pajamas pressed and crisp.

She'd fought one of many grins he inspired. His honesty was refreshing, if not unnecessary. "I'm not. Just so you know."

He gave the newspaper he held a sharp snap before opening it and said, "Just keepin' you informed. I didn't want you to think our chats and my request to have you personally make my coffee had anything to do with unbridled lust or the desire to sweep you off your feet. I just like the way you make the swirls in my whipped cream look like puffy clouds of white perfection. There'll be no nursing-home affair here. So don't you go fallin' in love with me, hear?"

Cat had dramatically sighed, throwing a hand over her forehead while fighting a fit of laughter. "Thank goodness. I was gettin' worried I'd have to lose a few pounds just so you could do the sweeping," she'd joked as she rubbed her belly.

Landon had cocked his sandy brown head full of hair, which gleamed under the bright lights of the rec room, and asked, "Are you disappointed?"

"That I don't have to lose a few pounds?"

"That I'm gay."

"Are you disappointed I'm not?"

"Not even a little."

"Ditto. So, a game of checkers?"

Since that day, they'd found a contentment with one another, a morning banter Cat looked forward to, so much so that she woke with a smile of anticipation, knowing Landon would be in the rec room each morning while her mother was in therapy. He'd sit at the same table in the corner by the big picture window, and smile that same engaging smile.

More important, their mornings together reminded her decent people still existed. And Landon was surely a front-runner in that category.

Landon's specialty was kindness, and his genuine love of people. He'd sometimes sit for hours, chatting with the other patients or just watching people pass by the window on their way to some part of the facility. Didn't matter what walk of life you came from, Landon wanted to know you.

He listened to the family members of the patients— complete strangers. Really listened, to everyone from tired mothers visiting sick relatives, who rocked crying babies in strollers, and whose only form of adult conversation all day might be the words they had with him, right down to Hans, the janitor who was earnestly trying to learn to speak English. Landon spent two hours with Hans every week, tutoring him so he could pass his citizenship test.

Landon's benevolence at Oakdale was legend.

He donated not only large amounts of money to the chemotherapy wing, but also an extravagant amount of his time reading to the patients, playing the piano, strolling with them, pushing their wheelchairs when he'd grown strong enough and sharing meals with them.

Rumor also had it, he was filthy rich and just a little eccentric—or off his rocker if you listened to some of the meaner gossip at Oakdale. Judging by his clothes and Sanjeev, the man he called his "faithful friend in service," who brought Landon's visitors to see him in a shiny limousine each day, money wasn't a hurdle Landon had to jump.

But Cat never paid any attention to the rumors swirling around Landon—his soul was warm and deeper than the deepest well. His gobs of money were unimportant to her.

Money wasn't everything. Though today, it was something. It was something she needed buckets of if she hoped to continue to give her mother the best care in the state of Georgia.

"Move it on over, lady," he teased, dragging her back to her current predicament with a swish of a finger at the place beside her on the bench.

Cat slid an inch or so on the cool stone, leaving the long curtain of her hair to hide the profile of her tearstained face. "So how're you feelin', Landon Wells? Stronger these days, I'd suppose from the looks of that handsome face of yours."

He did look stronger, fuller in the face, and the color in his cheeks had returned.

Landon lifted his face to the sunshine and sighed. "I feel good, Kit-Cat. Life's good. So good. How you feelin'? How's your mama?"

About to be put out on the street? "She's mending. Seems like it takes such a long time with her diabetes in the mix, but you know Mama. She's a real trouper. So what're you doin' back here? I thought you were sprung last week?"

They'd thrown him a big party when he finished his last dose of chemo—Cat had blown up balloons and made a cake with the help of the staff and patients.

"Just a quick checkup to be sure all my parts are in workin' order."

She wrapped her arm around him and gave him a squeeze. "I never doubted we couldn't get rid o' the likes a you, Mr. Wells. I'm so glad you're stickin' around."

"So, I stopped by the coffee shop to get some of my Kit-Cat love, but you weren't there, and that Arlo was cowering in the corner while a big gorgeous man gave him what-for. Somethin' about you being fired. What gives?" he asked.

A gorgeous man yelling at Arlo? Huh.

Landon nudged her shoulder when she remained silent, the clean scent of his cologne drifting to her nose on the warm air. "Do you want to talk about it?"

She swallowed hard, so angry with herself. "Nope."

The crisp material of his suit rustled against his skin. Landon always wore suits and ascots in every color of the rainbow—even on the hottest of Atlanta days. "Surely you don't think I'd leave a damsel in distress, do you? It's obvious you've been cryin'. Cat and I can't have my favorite barista cryin'—so out with it."

"I'm not your barista anymore."

"Oh?"

"You heard me right. I managed to get myself fired."

Landon put his hands to his heart with a dramatic gesture and a comical pouty face. "Say it isn't so."

"I wish I could." It was very much so. What was she going to do? At one of the most crucial points in her life, where it was imperative she have a steady job, she'd still managed to dig herself a hole.

"Care to explain why?"

"My big mouth." There was no use sugaring it up. It was the truth. She could have let Arlo lie about her to Flynn McGrady. Surely her pride was nothing compared to how important it was to keep a steady income for her mother right now.

"Bah! You? A big mouth? I won't hear it. Your mouth is pretty as a picture and hardly big. It's just right for your face."

That made her smile for a moment. She tucked her hair behind her ear and looked over at him with eyes that teased. "Are you sure you're gay?"

"As sure as I am Liberace and I were somehow gypped out of an enduring, lifelong union by some insane mad scientist and his attempts at frozen embryonic separation."

Cat let her head fall back on her shoulders when she laughed. "Dream big or go home, I always say." She patted his arm and smiled her gratitude. "Thank you for making me feel better, kind sir. I want you to know, you always bring a ray of sunshine to my day. I'll always remember that."

Landon grabbed her hand, leaving a cool imprint on her palm, and tucked it under his arm. "Oh, no. You're not gettin' away that easy. We're friends. I never leave my friends cryin'. Besides, now that I'm sprung, what's gonna happen to me if you don't make my cinnamon latte at the coffee shop every mornin'? Nothing, and I do mean, nothing, will ever be the same for me. And don't you tell me that heathen Arlo will make 'em. He couldn't make a cup of coffee if Juan Valdez taught him himself. How will I ever go on?"

"Call Juan Valdez?" she teased, closing her eyes and allowing the warm breeze of early spring in Georgia soothe her.

"That's a brilliant idea. I'm sure I must know someone somewhere who knows him. Until then, what shall we do about your unemployment?"

His question startled her. "*We?* We don't have to do anything. I have to get online and start lookin' for work." Dread filled the pit of her stomach.

How was she ever going to find a job with her employment history? She'd hung on tooth and nail to her job with Arlo. She'd bitten her tongue more times than she cared to count, except when it really counted.

"What if I told you I can help?"

"I'd tell you to keep your bags o' money to yourself. Now, let's not kid each other here, Landon. I know you're rich. And if I didn't know, Sanjeev dropping by your room every day, driving a slick limo and bringin' the finest linen napkins my eyes have ever seen for you to wipe your mouth on, or all that fancy food you had flown in from Bobby Flay's personal kitchen when you were at the hospital, would have been a sure clue."

She didn't begrudge Landon his money or his fineries, but it wasn't as though she couldn't see with her own eyes he had plenty to spare.

People probably used him all the time because of it. She wasn't one of those people. He was a friend, not an ATM.

Landon gazed at her as the sunlight filtering through the big oak tree whispered across his smile. "Those napkins at Oakdale are scratchy and they chafe. You'd think for all the money they charge to stay there, we'd get better damn napkins. I won't apologize."

Cat chuckled. "Heaven forbid, I'd never ask you to. But if Sanjeev wasn't enough, the running tab at the coffee shop you keep for the women at the homeless shelter who go out job-huntin' every day would be." If she hadn't already been a smidge in love with Landon's heart, finding out that piece of information would have cinched the deal.

"Homeless women from the shelter need coffee, too."

"Do you have any idea how much the bill is each month?" Enormous. That's how much. But Landon had worked something out with Arlo, and each morning, no less than twenty women filed in to get their coffee and muffins, all courtesy of this kind man's gold-lined pockets.

He shrugged as though it was neither here nor there. "They need somethin' warm in their bellies to start their days. I can provide that. Besides, coffee and muffins always hits my spot. And do you have any idea how ripped off I'da been if you hadn't kept Arlo on the path of the righteous with that bill?"

She flushed. Arlo had tried to pad the bill, and when Cat caught him, she'd spoken up and threatened to tell Landon. Another one of her bucking-the-system moments.

"I suppose you didn't think I knew?"

"I…"

Landon nodded and smiled that handsome smile. "You don't think I got all this money because I threw it around without payin' attention to where it was goin', do you? But that right there—that's what makes you a good soul, Catherine Butler. Your heart's bigger than all of Texas. I know. I've been there. I've seen you with the people at Oakdale. Your mama told me all about what you did for Howard at Arlo's. You're a passionate, free spirit, always lookin' out for the little guy. Sometimes that gets in your way. I'm bettin' that free spirit of yours was what got you fired today."

That comment made Cat wince, her heart tightening in a ball. Her mother often called her just that— a free spirit, happy to enjoy what life doled out rather than forcing it to bend to her will. She'd floated most of her adult life—from job to job, just barely making ends meet. Jack-of-all-trades, master of none. But her life was her own, and she made all the rules.

And look where that got you today, free bird.

Cat peeked at Landon. "Do all free spirits have such big mouths and the employment history of a sixteen-year-old at the age of almost thirty?"

Landon barked a laugh, making the birds under the big oak tree scatter. "Free spirits sometimes need tethering, is all. Still free, just more centered while they're bobbin' around up there in the sky, reachin' for those stars."

Those tears of regret burned her eyes again. What was she going to do? She'd just barely been able to make the payments she'd managed to work out with Oakdale as it was. "I've made a real mess of things, Landon."

"That's why I asked you what you'd say to me helpin' you."

"I know what you asked me, but I don't want handouts. So I'd say thank you kindly, Landon Wells, but no thank you. I'm sure there are plenty o' other people out there willin' to abuse their friendships with you because you're rich. I'm not one of them."

"I know enough to know a good human bein' when I see one. Seen more than my share of bad. I can tell the difference."

She was here, at this place in her life, because she'd refused to conform to society's idea of what an adult should be. Turned out, society was right, and most people her age were at least able to help their aging parents if they did what society dictated and got good jobs, planned for the future. But her? Nah. She'd middle-fingered the notion.

For being such a complete idiot, she didn't deserve help. "No handouts."

Landon smiled again like he had some secret that amused him. "Okay, then. What about a hand up?"

"To?"

"You're gonna call me crazy," Landon joked, but his eyes twinkled.

"As if that's not a hyphen on your name?"

"So will you hear me out?"

Her throat went dry. "I'm almost afraid to answer that."

"Will you listen if it means you'll have security and a 401(k)?"

Cat fought a sharp inhale. All the things she'd never had. Resources she could have tapped into had she played by the rules. "How do you know I don't have one already?"

"I make it my business to know everything about the people I like—especially the people I like who are in a nasty pinch."

He didn't say it as though he had a leg up on her, or even like he was looking down his nose at her. "Have you been pryin' into my personal affairs, Wells? Using all that lovely money to research my sordid past?" she teased.

But Landon merely chuckled at her reaction. "Now don't go gettin' the wrong idea there, pretty lady. I'm not some crazy who wants to collect your skin to make a coat. I know our friendship hasn't extended outside of Oakdale, but my intentions are all on the up-and-up. So just say you'll hear my pitch, and if you don't like what I propose, you can get up and walk away, and never see me again. But not before you tell me the secret to those happy swirls of whipped cream." He winked.

Really. What did she have to lose but a few minutes of her time she'd only spend berating herself for this vicious cycle of unemployment she was caught up in? She was broke and desperate and all Landon required was her ears.

So what was the worst that could happen right here in broad daylight?

Three

Turned out, it hadn't been the worst thing to happen to her in broad daylight—not by a long shot. But plumb crazy? Yes, sir.

Landon had indeed offered her what he called help. He'd done it with flourish, lots of arcing hand gestures and that ever-present amused twinkle in his eyes.

As Cat made her way toward his home, the towering glass-and-chrome building where Landon had invited her to a home-cooked meal by Sanjeev, passing expensive shops and cars worth more than she'd make in a lifetime of work, she felt around the inside of her purse to be sure the can of pepper spray was where she could find it.

After the tale Landon had told her, she was more than a little skeptical. No. She was downright incredulous, leading her to wonder what she really knew about the real-world Landon Wells, anyway. Where did all his money come from?

She'd read all about the internet businesses he'd created, seen the occasional gossip article linking him with a prince in some far-off country. He'd certainly had his fair share of wild adventures.

So was he just eccentric-crazy, or crazy-crazy?

Please don't let him be a serial killer. Not after he's been so nice. Her day had already been ugly enough.

As a precaution, one she felt sick with guilt about even considering, she'd made sure her pepper spray was in her purse before leaving her place. There'd be no drugging an unsuspecting Cat Butler and stuffing her body parts into a black garbage bag and dumping her body at the local Winn-Dixie, thank you very much. That wouldn't pay her mother's hospital bills.

Yet, how could she possibly stay away after what he'd proposed to her? It was outrageous. She'd done nothing but think about it all afternoon long.

All while she'd dug out a dress for the dinner and taken a long, hot soak in the antiquated tub in her studio apartment. And while she'd blow-dried her hair and applied her makeup.

Now, as she gave the doorman her name, her legs trembled and her heart beat painfully hard.

The spry gentleman, dressed in an immaculate black suit with brass cuff links at his wrists and a gray tie, swept his arm toward the elevators. "This way, Miss Butler. Mr. Wells has a private entry elevator to his penthouse."

The buzz of her phone made her hold her finger up and dig it out of her purse.

Oakdale calling. Her heart began that heavy thud of dread in her chest, making her send up a silent prayer that Landon wasn't some crazy rich man who was prepping his prey. She pressed the decline button and stuffed her phone back in her purse.

If this job were for real, she'd be able to make that payment.

"Cat?"

She whirled around, stumbling in her heels. Flynn caught her by the elbow, sending a shot of electricity along her arm and a pool of warmth to her cheeks. Her first instinct was to fire off a warning shot. "Shouldn't you be off looking for someone else to get fired? Or are your plans more laid-back tonight? Maybe just an employee write-up or two on the agenda?"

Boo, Cat. That's totally unfair. It wasn't his fault he'd been the final straw for Arlo. It was just dumb luck. If it hadn't been him, it would have been someone else.

After some thought, Cat decided he had every right to look out for his mother's best interests. He might be narrow-minded about it, but he was doing it out of love.

Cat fully expected him to shoot a poison arrow back. Instead, he grinned, that grin that left her stomach wishy-washy and her pulse erratic. The one with the deep grooves on either side of his sexy mouth and lips she wanted to tug on with her teeth. "Still mad?"

Pulling her purse to her side, she looped her fingers into the strap and admitted defeat. "I'm not mad. It really wasn't your fault. You were just the catalyst to a long list of complaints Arlo had about me. Forget it ever happened." She turned to move toward the elevators, but he stuck his body between her and the up button.

Cat bit the inside of her cheek. That chest. Wide. Hard. Lightly tanned. A broad space where a girl could rest her head. Mercy, mercy.

If it were any other day but today, and he didn't want to see her skewered over a roaring flame for cor-

rupting his mother, she might have flirted with Flynn
McGrady—even as stuffy and conservative as he was.

But today wasn't that day.

Flynn looked down at her, his dark blue eyes melting her from the inside out. "Yeah. About that. I'd like
to apologize for goading you. I was out of line. I was
hoping maybe we could talk? Are you busy now?"

"I have an…appointment." A date with crazy. A li-
aison with lunacy.

"Here?" He didn't even try to hide his surprise.

She wondered if he was surprised because she was,
after all, headed up to a rich man's penthouse. In a red
dress and heels. But it was none of his business why
she was here. Let him think what he wanted. "Yes."

"Maybe when you're done we could talk? If you have
time after, that is."

Cat cocked her head, her brow furrowing. "I'm a
little confused. What do we have to talk about, Mr.
McGrady?"

"Flynn. Call me Flynn. I live in the building. Just
leased a place here for a few months to be closer to my
mother in her recovery. I was hoping we could talk."

Wait. Flynn lived in this building. Her libido would
never survive. "I thought you lived in New York?"

"I did. I do. But my company is internet-based. I can
work anywhere. The commute was keeping me from
seeing my mother as much as I'd like, so I decided, at
least for now, this was the best place for me to be. So
are you open to having a cup of coffee with me?"

Was he asking her out? After their spat? Oh, no. She
couldn't get to know Mr. Stuffy. Not with everything
she had on her plate right now. She didn't have time

for any distractions. Especially when they looked and smelled like Flynn. He was the kind of man distraction was made for. Sin and scandal. "For...?"

"For my mother's sake." He tacked on another grin.

Della. Of course, this was about Della. Cat crumbled at the mention of her. The folks at Oakdale had become like their family since her mother had been there, and Della was akin to a favorite aunt.

Rather than let her worry about Della's state show, she put a hand to her hip and affected a flirty pose. "Why, Flynn McGrady, did you just deal me a mom card?"

His smile was sheepish, but his eyes were determined. "I'm a desperate, desperate man."

Not a man in sight for over a year and suddenly, her dance card was full with a gay man who might murder her in his swanky penthouse, and a hunk who obviously wasn't poor if he lived here that wanted to talk about his mother.

Huh.

But it was Della, and he'd moved here to be with his mother in her recuperation. If he was a mama's boy, he was at least a good one. That gave her a fizzy feeling in her stomach she didn't want. "I'm due for dinner... with a friend. I don't know how long I'll be."

He backed up and began moving toward the common elevator, shoving his hands into the pockets of his jeans. "I'm up late most nights. Apartment 24-C. No funny stuff. Promise."

The elevator doors opened, and Flynn gave her a quick wave followed by another one of those delicious grins he'd apparently been saving up, before the doors closed and he was gone.

Cat stood for a moment in the cool silence of the ultramodern lobby of Landon's building and just breathed.

Could this day get any crazier?

She'd never, ever question the power of crazy again.

"Ah, Ms. Butler. Pleasure to see you," Sanjeev, Landon's faithful friend in whatever he'd titled him, said with a bow. Dressed in a pristine white kurta, he waved Cat inside Landon's penthouse.

Or palace, if one was to split hairs.

From the moment her heels hit the marble flooring, Cat knew she was gaping. She just didn't know how to stop. This wasn't an apartment; this was a monument to opulence. A decadent space full of rich colors in rust, red and dark green, amazing textures in luscious silks and all sorts of statues from every corner of the world.

Landon's couch alone, one she knew would swallow her whole if she sat on it, was probably worth more than her Prius. There were leather wing-backed chairs with lush throws, a baby grand piano by French doors leading out to a patio, rows of teak doors stained in dark walnut, one leading to a library with a bigger selection of books than the local used bookstore. Art covered the walls, art she knew had to be expensive.

Sanjeev leaned into her space just a bit. "It's a lot to take in all at once, yes?"

Cat slammed her mouth shut and simply nodded. A lot? It was more than a lot. It was a sensory overload. Was this really Landon's? Was he really that rich?

Sanjeev smiled, his white teeth a beautiful glow with the backdrop of his olive coloring. "Yes. Landon is really that rich. It will grow on you, I promise. For now, please follow me. Landon said you'd be dining on the terrace. It's a lovely night, don't you think? Not too hot just yet."

She hesitated when Sanjeev began to move away from the front door, her feet refusing to follow him. What if the real-world Landon really was some crazy murderer and his chemo had just slowed him down temporarily?

What if this was some elaborate ruse and she was too distracted by all the shiny, expensive things he had to look at to pay attention.

Sanjeev sighed. Cat didn't sense impatience, just a sort of acceptance. Like he'd been to this rodeo before. "I promise you, Ms. Butler, Landon is not a monster with your death as an item on the menu."

Cat winced. "Was I that obvious?"

"You all are."

"All?"

"Not a soul who works for Landon passed through these doors without the same mixture of fear and awe upon their faces. It comes with the territory and the job offer. Do you have an item in your purse you might club him with should this turn as ugly as your darkest fears lead you to believe?"

She stared at him, his expression as cool as a cucumber. "Um, pepper spray?"

He motioned to her purse with another smile. "Pull it out. If at any moment you feel the least bit uncomfortable, have it ready for use. Now, please do follow me. I've made a beautiful Chateaubriand accompanied by crisp fingerling potatoes and market-fresh green beans that will completely spoil if we wait another moment."

Sanjeev didn't wait for her compliance; he meandered through the beautiful furnishings and headed toward the twinkling lights out on the terrace.

So she followed, holding the pepper spray like it was a cross and Sanjeev was Lestat.

Four

Flynn picked up one of the books he'd confiscated from his mother's stash, courtesy of Cat, and flipped through it, forcing himself to focus on his mother's recovery and not the way Cat's ass had looked in that red dress.

Or the way her creamy skin picked up the glow of the sunset through the apartment building's lobby—or the scent of her hair, a fruity concoction that stayed with him long after she was in the elevator.

And who was she going to see? The desk refused to tell him who lived in the penthouse, discretion being the excuse, and one of the reasons he'd chosen this building.

Maybe it was some celebrity?

Why did he care?

Because she's sparked your interest, pal. Oh, and your mother likes her better than you.

Does not.

She does, too.

Damn. He had to find a way to make this right with Cat. If she stopped coming to see his mother...

He took a long pull from his beer and focused on try-ing to understand what his mother found so interesting about these romance novels. He needed a way to connect with her again—something they could talk about.

If reading about vampires and the women who loved them was his in, he'd take it, even if it made his eyeballs bleed.

Did Cat read these kinds of books?

Again, why do you care, McGrady?

Skimming the middle of a chapter, Flynn frowned. Oh, c'mon. No guy said stuff like this. Not any guys he knew, anyway.

You're the reason I breathe?

Your lungs are the reason you breathe.

He ran a hand over his jaw. How the hell was he going to get through this?

Talk Cat into helping you, that's how. Now get reading.

Landon tipped his wineglass in Cat's direction, his amused eyes glittering beneath the strands upon strands of soft white lights woven in and out of enormous topiary trees and along the balcony overlooking the city. "Are you feelin' less like I'm gonna dismember you, Cat?"

She felt amazing. She'd never had food quite so decadent before, literally served on silver platters and real china. "I feel a little less like I need the pepper spray, but don't you forget, my uncle Ray-Ray taught me how to shoot." Cat hitched her jaw to the can on the table next to her plate. "I'm not afraid to use it, and I'm pretty quick on the draw."

Landon laughed, wiping his mouth and dropping the napkin on the table. "So, have you had time to let my offer sink in?"

Cat fought the panic that she'd find her mother on the street tomorrow morning—evicted for her slacker daughter's nonpayment. "I'm mulling."

"Mulling, huh? Pushed it around that steel-trap brain of yours?"

If that sumptuous meal she'd spend two days running off in the park wasn't enough, the wine, rich and mellow, had calmed her nerves a bit.

He'd turned out to be the same old Landon who showed up every day at the coffee shop, sharing stories of his travels and making her laugh with his jokes.

He told her all about how he'd made his millions at a very young age with a startup internet company. He reminisced about his small hometown of Plum Orchard, Georgia, just a few hours out of Atlanta, and the people he loved there. How much he missed his friends Dixie and Caine and even the bunch of snooty gossips called the Magnolias, who ran the town like the Southern mob.

What remained for her was the same connection she'd felt to him in the nursing home. The warm joy he exuded always left her feeling good inside, feeling like they could be lifelong friends.

So Cat gave him a saucy grin similar to the ones she'd given him when male customers made unwanted advances. "Now, you don't suppose I could let somethin' like the nuttier-than-squirrel-dung offer you made me today go without at least some thought, do you, Landon Wells, you crazier-'n-a-bedbug eccentric multimillionaire? *Do you?*"

Landon grinned. "Then you'll take a stroll to the back of the penthouse with me?"

"Not without my nut-away spray." She scooped the

pepper spray and her purse up, putting her arm through his arm with a gracious smile.

His footing became unsteady for a mere second, but it alarmed her. "You okay there, fancy feet?"

If she'd learned one thing about Landon in all the time she'd known him, it was that he despised pity of any kind. He was forever waving away the nurses when they offered to plump his pillows or wipe his mouth after a particularly bad round of chemo. If he were writhing in agony, he'd tell you he was right as daffodils in spring.

"Strong as an ox. I swear on my mama's civil war-era dishes."

"They had dishes in the civil war?"

"My mama ought to know, she's at least that old."

Cat's head fell back on her shoulders as she laughed, the tension in her stomach easing.

As they made their way through the living room, past two bathrooms and a room with a pool table, Landon commented on some of the pieces decorating each area.

He stopped at two double doors, painted in black enamel with the initials *CG,* bracketed by two potted palms lush with green fronds. "Are you ready?"

Cat's stomach did that nervous-jump thing it had done when she'd first entered his apartment. "If you open those doors and there are body parts hangin' from meat hooks, I'm gonna take you out at the knees, Landon Wells. People know where I am, too, just in case you thought you'd get away with skinnin' me alive."

He laughed again, flashing his white teeth. Clearly, he was enjoying himself. "No meat hooks."

"Dead bodies?"

Landon wrinkled his nose in distaste. "I sure hope

not. Those are always a problem for Sanjeev to dispose of. And complain? You don't know complainin' until you've heard Sanjeev carry on."

Now she laughed, too. "Okay, I'm ready." She wasn't really ready. She still didn't really believe him. This job offer of his was beyond outrageous and well on its way to surreal.

Not for a second did she believe he was telling her the truth.

Then Landon popped the doors open.

And once more, her mouth gaped.

He gave a gentle tap to the underside of her chin with his index finger. "Flies. You don't want flies in there," he reminded.

Cat's eyes felt like they were going to fall out of her head and roll at her feet.

Landon crossed his arms over his chest. "It's a lot, right?"

Understatements weren't something Landon was known for, but the words *a lot* were the biggest understatement in the universe when used to describe what she was seeing.

"Do you want a minute? Maybe gather your thoughts? Put your head between your knees?"

A woman with gobs of big platinum-blond hair and nails painted a glittery purple strolled out from beyond the doors. She smiled at Landon as she passed by, her bright-hued maxi-dress trailing behind her and hugging her ample breasts. "Evenin', boss," she chirped, shooting Cat a brief if not curious smile before heading back off toward the front part of the penthouse.

He leaned into Cat. "That's LaDawn Jenkins, by the way. Best girl I've got. In case you wanted to know."

She heard Landon's words, she even wanted to acknowledge them, she just couldn't stop staring.

"Would you like to sit, Cat?"

No. Sitting wouldn't help.

Finally, Cat turned to him, taking in his expression, one she'd swear was taking great pleasure in her shock. "You really…"

His head moved up and down, his eyes reassuring. "Yep. I really do."

"You *really* own a phone sex company?" she asked, pushing the words from her lips.

He really did.

Five

Cat blinked her eyes again. When she reopened them, there were still five heads just fringing the tops of their cubicles wearing headsets and bobbing animatedly.

There were phones ringing, and lights blinking and the sound of something thwacking.

Chatter filled up the enormous room. Phrases like "Baby, that's sooo nice!" and "You dirty, dirty boy!" flew around like flies buzzing.

For a brief moment, she thought of Flynn and how uncomfortable he'd be right now. If "Spank me harder" made him blush, "Who's Mama's big hard boy?" would give him a heart attack.

Cat cocked her head in Landon's direction.

Landon smiled sheepishly at her. "Welcome to Call Girls Inc."

A woman with fingerless leather gloves and a dozen or so silver bracelets on her wrist looked up, caught sight of Landon and waved to him cheerfully, her smile broad.

"That's Sheree."

"Of course it's Sheree. Who else would it be but Sheree?" This was crazy.

"You're in shock. Why don't we sit while you absorb? Maybe in my office?" Landon pointed in the direction of the back of the room, where more double doors were located.

Disbelief finally gave her a voice. "You're really running a phone sex company you won in a poker game in Uzbekistan right here in your penthouse?"

"I am. I have all the appropriate permits and such, if that's what worries you. Everything's completely legal. Swear it on my ascot collection."

She wasn't hearing anything but phone sex. Cat waved her hand at him. "How, in all the time you've been creamin' my butt at checkers, did you manage to avoid telling me you owned a phone sex company? Who runs a phone sex company from their penthouse, Landon? *Who?*"

"Rich, crazier-'n-a-bedbug multimillionaires like me?" he asked with that teasing tone he usually reserved for the moment he yelled "Checkmate."

"You're really serious about hiring me to manage a phone sex company? A *phone sex company?*" She couldn't stop saying it. Maybe, if she said it enough, it would quit sounding so absolutely insane.

"It comes with bennies, you know."

"Ah, but the real question is, does it come with latex and nipple clamps?"

Landon let out one of his hearty laughs—the one that always reminded her it really was the best medicine. "Look, I know you're shocked, but if you'll just sit with me and hear me out, I promise you, we can mutually benefit from this. I know you're the right person for this job, Catherine Butler, and I'm not gonna stop until you say yes," he said as if he was sticking his fingers in his ears and refusing to hear her. He strolled off toward his office without another word.

That pulled her up short.

Cat Butler, you have two choices. You can look for another job, another job that pays just above minimum wage and forces you to work long hours for another sleazy boss who shortchanges his customers and makes gross passes at you, or you can finally decide to join the rest of the adults in the real world. You can have a real job, one with benefits and retirement funds—all you have to do is show up.

And then there's your mother. She needs you. In fact, if it weren't for you, she wouldn't need all this expensive therapy and around-the-clock care at Oakdale to begin with.

It was the last little push she needed.

Sold.

Cat followed him to his office, which was equally as plush as the rest of his penthouse, and dropped into a chair facing him. If she was going to consider this, she was going to be as honest as she knew how to be.

Dropping her purse in her lap with a plunk, she set out to tell Landon the truth. "So, I'm just gonna lay this on the line with you, Landon Wells. I'm a terrible employee. I'm flighty when it comes to commitment, and taken to whims of fancy, and my stick-to-itiveness is a crummy team player. I open my mouth far more often than I should, I've never, except at the coffee shop, held a job for longer than a few months and I'm not afraid to make a stink about an injustice. Just ask Arlo."

Landon grabbed a pen from his desk and flicked the

top of it with a smile. "I know all about your employment history, Cat Butler. It's as ugly as my mama's old orthopedic shoes. But I know in my gut you're right for this job. What you need is a challenge, and keeping this business, these women who work the phones, organized, is a challenge. But you won't find any injustice amongst them because all the injustice in their lives has already come and gone—it's what led them here."

"I'm not following you."

Landon leaned in, bringing that charisma he oozed with him and letting it splash all over his desk. "All of the women who work here at Call Girls have, in one way or another, been down on their luck—just like you. As long as they're employed with me, they'll never want for anything. *Ever.*"

Landon's words jarred her. Not in a bad way, though. His tone was protective, caring, but it was so fierce, and his eyes were so determined, she couldn't help but wonder what the motivation for his intensity was. Maybe Landon came from a poor background? Maybe being gay had brought such injustices to his life that he was out to fix one hard-luck story at a time?

"Why here? Why right here in your home?"

"Well, why not? Overhead's cheap, and I have the room."

"Couldn't they just do it from their own homes? Isn't that how most phone sex operators work? Self-employed?" Cat remembered seeing a documentary on the business of talking dirty once, and all of the operators were doing dishes and washing clothes while they answered calls.

They certainly weren't living in the lap of luxury. Why would Landon bring them all here to his home?

"Some of them didn't have homes," was all he said.

She looked around, her eyes widening. "They *live* here?"

Landon cupped his chin in his hand. "Yep. Most of them do. Though, Sheree has a husband who lost his job. She works a day shift and goes home to him every night. Besides, I like having the girls here. I like the prestige. It allows them to say they work in an office and have all the benefits everyone else in the corporate world has. We're a tight-knit crew, and that's how I want it to stay. The girls havin' specific hours and knowing they have to come to the office to work keeps them motivated to stay on the right path."

The right path? "I can't live here." Who'd want to live here in the lap of luxury when they had a perfectly good studio apartment they were three months behind in rent on with a bed that fell out of the wall if your footsteps were too heavy?

"Fear not, Kit-Cat. That's not a requirement."

The use of the nickname he'd given her shortly after they'd met made her smile at the familiar. But she still had questions.

No one hired a crying ex-barista for the sum of money Landon was offering without an ulterior motive. "What are the requirements? What's the catch here, Landon? There has to be one. I've been around the block a time or two, and the block always leads to ulterior-motive alley."

His wide shoulders shrugged beneath his suit. "No catches, no ulterior motives, nothing illegal. In fact, you can look Call Girls up at the Better Business Bureau online, and you'll find we have a pristine reputation. We're the single most successful phone sex company in the world, bar none. As for you, pretty Cat, I need nothing other than a good GM, and that's you."

Still, she couldn't absorb it all. "Why?" Why did he let strange women live in his private residence?

He actually looked as though he were puzzled. "Why what?"

"Why do you do this?"

"I'm missing the subtext behind your question, but if I know you, and I think I have a pretty good handle on who you are, you want to know somethin' more than why I have a phone sex company in my penthouse."

"Bingo. Why the fairy godfather act?"

Landon paused, his eyes purposely catching hers. He latched on to them and wouldn't let go. "Because I can."

Those words held significance; there was a deeper meaning to them. They had more to do with a motive that involved getting richer.

But her head was spinning. This was a way to help her mother. She had to process that properly—alone. No more whims or jobs that looked like fun.

"So how would you feel if I told you I'd like to sleep on it?"

He grinned, boyish and sweet and all Landon. "I'd tell you to sleep well, my friend." Landon pushed his office chair back and stood up.

Cat gathered her purse, dropping the pepper spray into it before rising. She took one last long look at Landon's smiling face—the one she'd seen every day for months, before muttering, "Night, Landon."

"Sweet dreams, Kit-Cat," he chirped on a cheerful wave.

As she made her way back through the offices of Call Girls, took in the relaxed poses of the women sitting in their expensive, ergonomic office chairs, eyed the empty boxes of pizza and lively, content faces, she fought the impulse to run back to Landon's office and accept.

No, she was going to think this through thoroughly. Weigh the pros and the cons of telling her mother she was the GM of a phone sex company.

No more impulsive acts, Cat.

Impulse was how you ended up making balloon animals in the mall as Coco the Clown's assistant.

Remember how that ended?

With mall security running her out on a rail because she'd called out a group of teenagers who'd made fun of a woman breast-feeding.

Mall security was no laughing matter—those zip ties they used left marks.

Six

"You stood me up."

Cat's arms broke out in goose bumps at Flynn's voice in her ear. She shut the door to her car and turned to face him. "You got me fired. You still win the fight for supremacy."

"Are we still grudging?"

"Nope. Now we're even."

Flynn smiled, all white teeth and dimples, and he made a sizzling noise with his lips. "Payback. It stings." He rubbed the spot on his chest where his heart beat.

She touched his arm before pulling her fingers away, but not before noticing how ripply and muscly he was. How nice he felt to touch. "I'm kidding. It was late when I left your building last night. I didn't want to disturb you."

A flash of something Cat couldn't define crossed his handsome features before he turned whatever it was off. "Listen, I was really serious. I'd like to talk with you about my mother. She really likes you, Cat."

Cat's insides warmed up. "I really like her, too."

"So do you mind dropping by my apartment later

today? Or maybe I could meet you somewhere so we can talk?"

Cat cupped her hand over her eyes to keep the glare of the sun from blocking her view. "What's wrong with right now? I was on my way in, anyway. Maybe we could all talk together?"

Flynn glanced at his phone, his gorgeous baby blues scanning the screen. "She'd kill me if she knew I was talking to you. She always hated anyone making a fuss over her—which could be part of the reason she's giving everyone but you such a hard time. But right now, I'm on my way to a meeting I can't miss, but if you're uncomfortable about meeting me at my place, we can meet somewhere neutral."

"Somewhere neutral? You make it sound like we'll be duelin' at dawn," she teased, twirling a strand of her hair and batting her eyelashes.

"How quickly you forget our boxing match at the coffee shop."

"Point. But I have to be in your building tonight, anyway. I have an appointment at five. So how's seven? And I'll be sure to tell Della where I'm going lest you decide to ravish me against my will."

The tips of Flynn's ears turned adorably red. He held up his hands as he began to back away across the parking lot of the rehab center. "All on the up-and-up. Promise. See you at seven."

Cat let out a ragged breath. She didn't understand this. She was comfortable with men. She liked them a lot. She was no stranger to a bit of flirting, and she was the one always in control.

But Flynn was different. She'd never had such a physical reaction to someone who'd irritated her quite the way he had in the coffee shop. He made her feel like she had no power: light-headed and breathless, and she kept baiting him because of it. To keep the control.

She fanned her face with the magazine she held in her hand and watched him stride across the parking lot. Tight blue jeans and thighs thick with muscle.

Mercy, Flynn McGrady was impossibly hard to breathe around.

"LaDawn Jenkins. Former companionator."

Cat sat at a table in the lavish break room of Call Girls that overlooked a park with a pond. Platters were piled high with fresh fruit and muffins and dainty sandwiches with the crusts cut off. "Companionator?"

The woman with a green-and-red spiked mohawk, KISS-like makeup and an innocent, sweet-as-molasses voice, who'd introduced herself as Marybell Lyman, snorted. "Hooker. LaDawn was a lady o' the evenin', weren't ya?"

LaDawn raised one penciled eyebrow in haughty fashion. "I prefer to think I gave all those lonely men companionship, not just a bosom to rest their weary heads on, Ms. MB."

Cat stuck her hand out. "Cat Butler, former balloon-animal maker, yoga instructor, tae-kwon-do assistant, file clerk, dog walker, plant sitter, bathroom attendant, nanny and, just recently, barista. Companionating was the one thing I didn't do, but I'm an almost stripper. I say *almost* because that pole and me? We'll just never get along."

LaDawn cackled, pushing her hair behind her ear. "Go on, girl. You can make balloon animals?"

Cat grinned. "Like a pro."

"I call dibs on an elephant at the next office shindig. A purple one, thank you very much."

"So, you're the new boss?" Marybell asked, her sweet voice like warm honey.

Yes. She was the new boss. After a long night, where she'd reflected on every bad career choice she'd ever made in order to feed her need for adventure and change, she was going to give this her all. That she was managing a phone sex company was the least of her concerns. Sex was sex, whether on the phone or in a bedroom.

No judgment from her.

It was the managing part of this that worried her. There'd never been a time when she'd had this much responsibility—because she'd never wanted responsibility. Responsibilities had nearly killed her mother.

Being tied down wasn't her strong suit. Giving her an office of women who talked dirty to strange men to manage was like giving the keys of a car to a ten-year-old.

But when she'd accepted the position earlier today, Landon had just laughed it off. He'd said, "Never you worry, Kit-Cat. I know what I'm doin'."

She owed this to her mother. She owed it to herself.

So, Cat bounced her head. "That's what Landon says, but how about we just call me the wrangler? Organizer, maybe? *Boss* is so strict, conformist. I'm not much for titles."

"So callin' you the High Priestess of Smut is off the table?" LaDawn asked with a chuckle.

Cat barked a laugh as she restacked the reams of paperwork she'd filled out and set it atop the manual with the company's rules. "That has a definite ring to it. Can we fit that on a plaque?" Turning to Marybell, she asked, "So, Marybell, what's your…um… What did you call it?"

"My kink?" Marybell crumpled up the wrapper from her candy bar and shot it into the wastebasket.

"Right. Your kink." *Kink.* Wow. So much to learn.

"I'm your go-to girl for all things just the other side of vanilla. A little of this and a little of that. Now, LaDawn's your dominatrix. All that thwackin' you hear from time to time is her fly swatter. She uses it as a prop for sound effects to keep her clients in line."

LaDawn's giggle was infectious. "Who knew I'd be so good at bein' bossy—with a fly swatter, no less?"

Cat couldn't get over how happy everyone appeared. All of the operators looked rested and content, and they came in at all hours of the day to begin their shifts with smiles on their faces. "So, y'all like working for Landon?"

LaDawn's thickly lashed eyes held Cat's. "Best damn thing that ever happened to me. Swear it. Came along, scooped me up off the streets after findin' me hobblin' along the sidewalk when my heel broke. Course it broke because I had to hit a john in the head with it, but neither here nor there. I've never looked back since, and it's been a year. There's nothin' I wouldn't do for that man behind that door." She pointed to Landon's office just outside the break room.

Marybell fiddled with her bracelets without looking directly at Cat, but her words were just as flattering, held just as much reverence. "Landon… I know what you probably thought when he offered you a job at a phone sex company, Cat. We all thought the same thing. None of us believed anyone as kind as Landon truly existed, but he's the best human being I know. There's no agenda here. All he asks is the kind of respect he pays us in return. There really aren't any strings."

Still, she was on the fence, a little suspicious even. Everyone had a fault, a bad trait, a defective gene.

Yet, every one of Landon's employees was as devoted to him as the next. He was like some fairy godfather. "Okay, then. I'm takin' you ladies at your word. But one wrong move, and I'll know who to come gunnin' for."

They all laughed, leaving a warm vibration in her ears. Instantly, Cat felt as though she were a part of something bigger than she was. Something that would change everything for her.

That made absolutely no sense. She didn't believe in fairy tales and happily-ever-afters, but these women had made an effort to welcome her to their fairy tale.

There'd be no spittin' that in the eye from her.

Gathering up the Call Girls manual, Cat pushed her chair back with a wink. "So, ladies, let's get this show on the road."

Flynn jumped when his doorbell rang. He'd been so immersed in one of the romance novels his mother loved that the noise jarred him.

Setting aside the knitting needles and the ball of thread, which was so hopelessly tangled it sure as hell wasn't going to turn into a scarf, he dropped the book in guilt.

A glance at the microwave's digital clock told him it was Cat. The thought of seeing her again made him smile, but then he frowned.

Cat wasn't the kind of woman he'd get involved with—she was everything he'd never date. He sensed chaos with her, a palpable force, unconstrained by rules. He liked rules.

They were what kept his world upright. Which was why, when he realized his brain didn't quite function the way it usually did when he was around her, it was a good reason not to smile about her.

No smiling about Cat.

And remember, don't be a grumpy asshole. Be charming. Be nice. Don't ogle her no matter how ogle-worthy. He'd spent far too much time wondering what she was doing here in his building.

Today, as he'd left to grab lunch, he'd watched a couple of women, one with the kind of makeup and hair you mostly only saw at heavy metal concerts, step off the penthouse elevator. And the other one—LaDawn was what the heavy metal woman had called her, with her flashy purple nails and ultrableached hair—left him wondering exactly who lived in the penthouse and what they all did up there all day.

Flynn popped the door open, forcing himself to keep his focus and not ask invasive questions. "C'mon in," he offered as casually as possible, strolling to the glass-top kitchen table and pulling out a seat for her.

As Cat pulled off her sweater, one that clung to her breasts and stopped at her waist, he yanked his eyes away to focus on her eyes. She had pretty eyes—eyes that were on fire. Eyes that expressed everything she was thinking without her ever saying a word. "Wine?"

She sighed, soft and breathy, making him wonder what it would be like to be the one responsible for making her sigh like that. "I'd love some. It's been a long, strange day."

Popping the cork on the bottle, he wondered what

was so long about it, and why did it have to be so long? Pouring two glasses, he set them down on the table and settled into a chair.

"So, what can I do for you, Flynn McGrady?" she asked, twisting a strand of her thick, chestnut-brown hair with that smile he hadn't been able to quit thinking about.

When Cat smiled, it was like she'd given you a gift. It was wide and generous and warm. *And dangerous, McGrady. She's not your type.*

Flynn cleared his throat, forcing his lusty thoughts out of his head. "Listen, I feel really guilty about the other day. I know you said to forget it, but I can't. My mother really likes you. She hasn't responded to anyone the way she has to you. Not even me, I'm ashamed to admit."

Her face, the brief distress he saw in her eyes, was a thumbs-up to his decision to ask for her help. Even if they hadn't hit it off, she liked Della enough to care about her recovery. "Your mama's strugglin' with something I don't understand, Flynn. Maybe it's something from before the accident, maybe not. I'm no doctor, and I know you'll think this is crazy, but I think it's what's hindering her progress. I can almost feel it. I don't want to pry into your private affairs, but whatever it is, it's keeping her from moving forward. I really think she's just lonely. Your father passed a couple of years ago, and I know from the nurses your sister's in Afghanistan. Maybe she just needs to know someone still gives a damn."

"Agreed."

Cat's eyes widened over the rim of her glass, her

long lashes almost touching her eyebrows. Jesus, she was sexy.

He grinned and leaned forward, unable to keep himself from her magnetic pull. "You look surprised."

"Well, I am. You agreed with me, for heaven's sake. That's cause for at least a small seismic movement beneath our feet, don't you think?" Cat gave him one of her saucy winks, stretching her arms over her head, pulling the material over her firm breasts.

Flynn swallowed hard, pushing his eyes upward. "I was a jerk the other day. Her recuperation's been frustrating, to say the least. To see her do what she did for you, well, it sorta knocked the wind out of me. It's been months since she's done much but stare out the window. Anyway, I'm here now, and I plan to stay for the long haul until she's better."

"You're a good son. But what does that have to do with me?" She cocked her head when she asked, her soft hair gleaming under the glow of the kitchen lights.

"My mother enjoys your company. She lights up when you visit with her. I've seen it. Seeing as you're unemployed, due to me and my jerkiness, I'd like to offer you a job."

"A job?"

"A job. Looking out for my mother. Reading to her, going to rehab with her, whatever it takes to get her to want to get better. I'll pay you well."

Her shoulders slumped. Not good.

"You're a day late and a dollar short."

"What?"

Cat's eyes skirted his before zooming in on her wineglass. "I just got another job. Just today, in fact. I'm sorry."

"Doing what?"

Again, her eyes avoided his. "Management."

Don't ask, Flynn. Shut up. "Managing what?" *Jackass.*

"Stuff that needs managing?"

"Whatever you're making, I'll match it—double it."

Cat began sliding her chair out, pulling her sweater back on. "Look, Flynn, I love Della. She's a terrific lady. But I'm happy to say she won't need someone to visit with her forever. She's going to get better and better, especially now that you're here. But I need something long-term. I need the security this job brings me."

Flynn rose, too, wondering exactly what managing "stuff" meant, and why there was a hint of desperation to her tone. "I can't change your mind?"

Why don't you tell her she's every breath you take? That ought to do it.

Seven

If Flynn McGrady had trouble with the words *spank me harder,* imagine the Imodium ad he'd have to keep on hand if Mr. Stuffy knew she was now the GM for a phone sex company. It was easier just to keep her flappy mouth closed.

But this was Della. She had a special place in Cat's heart. "How about I promise to drop in on your mom as often as possible? With the new job, it'll be a little less, but I'll make her my first stop after my mother."

Flynn's face went tight again, closed off. Was it because he wasn't getting his way? "I'd appreciate that."

"May I use your bathroom before I go?"

His nod was curt, probably because he didn't get his way. "Sure. Around the corner and to the left."

As she passed by the cold chrome and black end table, she stopped short, her eye catching the book on it. *"Supernaturally Yours?"*

The tops of his ears went a little red, much like they'd done in the parking lot. "You know, trying to connect and all. I thought if Mom read it, and I read it, we'd have something to talk about."

Cat scooped up the paperback with a smile. He was reading romance novels to connect with his mother. He might be conservative, but he was a conservative with a heart. So. Cute. "Look who's not such a stuffy-pants, after all."

Flynn's face hardened when he jammed his hands into the pockets of his jeans. "Don't get the wrong impression. I'm only doing this to find something relatable to my mother. Personally, I think they're ridiculous and based solely in fantasy."

Didn't all stick-in-the-muds think like that? "Of course you do, Flynn McGrady."

"What's that supposed to mean?"

"It means you're wound tighter 'n a top. It doesn't take a genius to see you're a conservative man if 'spank me harder' makes you blush like a teenage girl." *Baiting. You're baiting him, Cat. Why are you baiting him?*

His jaw, roughly sexy from five-o'clock shadow, lifted. "Would you want to know your mother reads books where spanking was involved?"

Cat traced a finger over the cover of the book with the picture of a man, naked from the waist up. A very sexy man. "I would if it meant she was on the road to recovery."

"Well, I'm here to tell you, what's contained in those pages is all a big fantasy, made up to make the rest of us men pale in comparison. Who can compete with a dark, brooding vampire with all the prowess of a sex-ninja?"

"If a man's compellin' enough, he doesn't have to," she said, winking an eye.

Flynn gave her a look of disgust. "It's unrealistic."

"I'm kind of with you on the unrealistic expectations. There are no happily-ever-afters, if you ask me. But in the meantime, what's wrong with a little fantasizin'?" She was taunting him. She knew she was, but she was enjoying how flustered he appeared. All that hot man and he was rattled—it made him hotter still.

"Have you read some of the dialogue?"

Cat propped the book open, setting her purse down on the table, letting her eyes skim his face before she looked at the words. "'I want you more than I've ever wanted anything else in centuries, Lucinda. *You're the reason I breathe,*'" she read in the sexiest voice she could muster.

Flynn came to stand behind her, his finger skimming the page. He tapped the print. "Perfect point. The guy in this is a vampire. Vampires don't breathe."

Cat rolled her eyes when she turned to face him. "There's your problem, McGrady. Not everything has to make sense if it gives you a break from real life, does it? Vampires aren't real, yet there are millions of women eatin' these up like candy." She waved the book at him. "Know what? I'm bettin' my weight in hummus you're the kind of guy who just can't let go. Who doesn't know how to just be in a moment." There was that tic in his streamlined jaw. She had an insane urge to nip at it, run her tongue over it.

"Because it's allegedly impossible for vampires to breathe, you know, technically being dead and all, means I can't let go? What kind of crazy logic is that?"

Oh, he was getting huffy again. But it was adorable. It made his nostrils flare and his wide chest rise and fall. "I mean it's symbolic of your need for rules. Sometimes, you have to allow for some artistic license. I think it's utterly romantic for a man to say something like that to a woman. It's the imagery, the idea that a man can't live without his mate? That's sexy."

"His *mate?* You make them sound like a pack of dogs."

Cat looked up at him, his eyes so serious, his delicious lips so near, and she couldn't stop herself from asking. "When was the last time you threw caution to the wind?"

His dark eyebrow rose in that haughty know-it-all way. Precise, and perfect. "Define caution."

"Did something you wanted to do just because you wanted to do it, knowing it was against your better judgment, but doing it, anyway. Live like there's no tomorrow?"

Flynn appeared to be giving that challenge some thought while his eyes flamed and his fists clenched.

Watching him get all worked up almost made her giggle, until his nostrils flared, and with a tight jaw he said, "Right now," just before he hauled her hard against him and covered her mouth with his.

Cat's heart sped up as their lips collided. Flynn's mouth was everything she imagined it would be—firm, demanding, sinful. His tongue slid against hers, hot, slick, tasting her, dueling, until she gripped his sweater in her hands and clenched from the perfection of him.

He tasted like sweet wine, he felt like a brick wall, with miles of rippled flesh, strong hands that cupped her backside until the rigid line beneath his jeans was pressed between her legs.

Cat inhaled Flynn's moan of satisfaction when they backed against the wall; clinging to him, she used his broad shoulders to hike her legs up around his waist, roll her hips in tune with his.

"Say stop, and I will," he huffed against her mouth, his breathing harsh.

Her nipples tightened, rubbing against her bra, protesting the very thought. *"Don't stop."*

It was all the incentive he needed. Flynn drove a hand up under her shirt, shoving her bra out of the way and cupping the underside of her breast.

Stars, she saw stars and flashes of white light when his thumb scraped her nipple. Now it was her moan filling his apartment, her breathing uneven and harsh. His body radiated heat, the kind of heat she hadn't felt in a long time.

Flynn's fingers found the hem of her skirt and pulled it up around her waist before he dipped into the top of her panties, skimming the soft line of her belly, then slipping between her folds in one smooth thrust.

"Ohhh," she breathed against his mouth, lifting her hips high, relishing the rough pads of his fingers pushing through her swollen flesh.

Cat gripped him tighter, fumbling for his zipper, shoving the fabric of his jeans down and away until she was able to run her hands over his rigid shaft. Thick and long, all she could think about was him inside her.

Hard and stretching her until he filled her up…made her come hard and long.

Tearing her mouth from his, she muttered, "Condoms?"

"Bedroom," he rasped back, hiking her legs around him and walking them down the short hallway to his bedroom.

Their bodies separated for only a moment when he sat on the bed, her atop his lap, and reached into his nightstand to pull out a foil packet.

Cat busied herself by yanking off her shirt, then dragging Flynn's sweater up and over his head.

The heavy curtains were closed, only allowing a small shaft of light from the day's end between them, giving her a first glimpse of his chest that stole her breath. So many planes and ridges, dusky brown from the sun and not from a fake tanning bed, and with just a sprinkling of dark hair between his pecs.

She wanted to touch his hot flesh, taste it, but not as much as she wanted him deep inside her.

He dropped his head to her breasts, pushing them together with wide hands, sipping at her nipples, nipping at them with his teeth until she thrust her fingers through his thick hair, pulling him close.

Arching her back, she let the sweet heat of his tongue carry her away while the hard flesh of his cock pressed against the space between her thighs.

When he slid her panties over, Cat gasped. Ready. So ready and wet, she lifted her hips and adjusted her trembling legs.

Poised at her entrance, Flynn let out a long breath as her fingers wrapped around his hard length and positioned him.

Flynn lifted his hips then, thrusting upward into her with a primal grunt, and again, he ripped the breath from her lungs, filled her in all the right places, stretched her until they fit.

They stilled, Cat in surprise, Flynn gripping her hips, his eyes searching hers. That moment, one of pure exhilaration for her, came and went when he pulsed inside her, the pull of their need distracting them both.

Cat pushed him back on his deep blue comforter with a flat hand against his yummy chest and closed her eyes.

All she wanted was to feel all this man, live in the very moments she'd accused him of denying himself, run her hands over his rippled flesh.

Flynn thrust upward slow and easy, rolling his hips when Cat leaned back, gripping his thighs for leverage, savoring the sweet simmer beginning in the pit of her belly.

His fingers slipped into her swollen flesh, caressing her clit until her nipples beaded tight and her desire grew slick. Her moans increased, their rhythm increased, had purpose, sought desperate release.

When she opened her eyes, the wave of heat was almost too much to bear, and combined with Flynn's gaze, dark and deep, Cat fell apart. That was her tipping point.

The moment she realized this was all too much, that it felt better than it had ever felt before, was the moment she hissed her release, falling forward against Flynn's chest, gripping the sheets on either side of his head until her teeth clenched and the sharp sting of orgasm swept her away.

Flynn's hips bucked beneath her, fusing their bodies, his hands tightening on her butt, and he groaned long and low in her ear. His muscles flexed beneath her, tensing, shifting until he came, too.

Their breath came in rapid puffs, their bodies relaxing in slow increments.

And that's when they realized what they'd done.

Cat sat upright, her eyes adjusting to the dark room. Damn, damn, damn her impulses. Usually, she was able to keep them in check—unless they had to do with an injustice, she was pretty good at keeping her clothes on until she wanted them off.

But Flynn… Something had happened tonight. Not

just incredible sex. Something she couldn't address—wouldn't look in the eye.

She'd turned down her fair share of men. She should have turned down this man. This man she'd see over and over at Oakdale until he went back to New York.

This man whose mother she'd grown so fond of. This man who'd taken only a couple of conversations to prove to her they were more than just different—they were polar opposites.

Oh, this man.

Take that, Miss Throw Caution to the Wind.

Flynn gazed up at Cat, sitting on top of him, beautiful, uninhibited and perfect. He felt as if he'd just managed to climb Mt. Everest naked. Who's Mr. Stuffy Pants now?

Cat looked down at him, her eyes shadowed for a moment before her snark took over. "So, am I the air that you breathe now?" she asked, slipping from his lap and off the bed.

Just as he was patting himself on the back for dipping his toes into spontaneity, she was slapping him down with that we-shouldn't-have-done-this look. "Is that regret I hear in your tone, Miss Live in the Moment?"

Smoothing her skirt over her gorgeous thighs, she made a face at him. "You hear nothin' of the sort."

Flynn grinned at her, pulling himself upright and sliding to a sitting position. "I dunno. I think Mr. Stuffy Pants hears remorse," he teased, walking his fingers up and over her hip.

She gave him a long glance, her eyes a fiery glow. "I have to go."

Somebody didn't like turnabout. "You don't want to

cuddle? Talk?" Because strangely, he found, he wouldn't mind. Not that he'd ever tell her that. He was enjoying her flustered state as much as she'd enjoyed his.

Cat made her way to his bedroom door. "You don't have time to cuddle. You have to join the book-of-the-month club" was her parting shot.

His laughter mingled with the tune of his front door slamming.

Eight

Leaning down, Cat gave her mother a kiss and pushed her steel-gray hair from her forehead. "How are you today, Mama?"

The lines around Tessa's eyes were deep, but her smile was always welcoming. "Plumb worn-out. This physical therapy isn't for the faint of heart."

Cat squeezed her mother's hand and tucked the blanket around her legs, scanning the room to be sure she had fresh water. This wasn't the fanciest room at Oakdale, but it was nice enough, and the care here was quality. "I know, but it'll be over soon, and then you can go home. It's only temporary."

"You look tired, sunshine. Why's that?"

"It was a really busy day at work." And a busy one-night stand last night. Phew. She didn't know if—later—she could even look Della in the eye today for all the sinnin' she'd done with her son.

Tessa's blue eyes went sympathetic. "I hate that you're workin' so hard, Cat. I told you, I don't need all this uppity therapy. I was healing okay—just takes a little longer. Just get me to the doctor once a week, and I'll be fine."

Cradling her mother's hand against her cheek, she shook her head. "No, Mama. Once a week isn't enough to help you mend that hip. I know it, and so does Medicaid. With your diabetes, you need therapy and someone who can be with you 'round-the-clock if your sugar drops. You do remember the last time that happened, don't you?"

She'd dropped by her mother's, just by chance, and found her passed out on the floor. She'd never forget that day, and it was never going to happen again if she had to use Velcro to fasten Tessa to her back and take her with her wherever she went.

But Tessa would still worry. "It's so expensive, Cat. All that money we don't have. It worries me. I don't want you in debt, workin' yourself into an early grave because of me. You're young. You should be out enjoyin' your life, maybe meeting a nice man. Don't spend your life alone like I did when you went off to college."

"I'm not alone. I have you, and I'm enjoyin' my life just fine." She'd done plenty of enjoying last night. Oh, God. Why had she slept with Flynn McGrady, and why couldn't she stop thinking about it today?

Whatever had clicked inside her when they'd finished making love, whatever that strange shift inside her was, just wouldn't quit. It was like the unreachable itch she couldn't scratch.

Tessa cupped her chin. "You're a good girl, Cat. Always takin' such good care of me."

Guilt stabbed her in the gut. "It's sort of the least I could do, don't you think?"

Tessa shifted in her chair, gazing at Cat. "Is that more

guilt I hear, Catherine? I won't stand for your guilt. It was an accident, pretty girl. Just an accident."

"Of course I feel guilty. You're here *because* of me, Mama." Her voice hitched, much the way it always did when she thought about the day she'd run her mother over.

It had all happened so fast. She'd been backing out of her mother's driveway after discovering she wasn't home.

She'd checked her rearview mirror twice because the children in her mother's subdivision were known for their disregard for the rules of the road.

"Honey, you couldn't have known I tripped and fell. You were inside the house when it happened."

Cat's smile was faint, the memory of her mother, crumpled like a rag doll in her driveway, still haunted her dreams. "Yeah, Mama. The next time you decide to fall and crack your head open like a melon, could you do it anywhere else but under my car?"

Her mother laughed, the sound tinkling and light. "It wasn't your fault, honey. How were you supposed to know I'd been out walkin'?"

Upon discovering Tessa wasn't home, Cat had climbed in her car, late as usual for work at the coffee shop. According to her mother, she'd tripped, fallen and rolled under Cat's car before she'd passed out. That's when Cat hit what she thought was anything but her mother under her car.

"I crushed your pelvis, Mom. Me. I broke you because I was late for work and rushin'."

"Like everybody isn't late sometimes?"

"I was late more than just sometimes."

Tessa's gaze narrowed. "You stop that right now. I

won't have you always hoverin' over me with that sad face. It happened. I'm doin' just fine. Now, how about you go see if they've put out that plate of doughnuts in the rec room yet?"

Cat chuckled. "You know you have to watch your sugar."

"Oh, get me one of those tough sugarless ones that taste like an old tire."

Cat tucked the blanket around her mother's knees before rising. "Don't go runnin' off on me now," she teased.

Tessa barked a laugh. "As if I could. You ruined my quest for the gold."

Cat snorted on her way out the door. "Funny, comedienne. Keep that up and we're gonna get you a special on HBO."

Thank God for her mother. She was Cat's rock. Her world. It had been just the two of them for a very long time, and she planned to keep her mother around as long as she could.

Making her way down the long hallway, she passed the nurses' station, giving one of her favorite nurse's aides a wave before poking her head in on Della, who was fast asleep with her unseemly romance novel tucked under one of her gnarled hands. Cat grinned when she thought about Della's passion for the spicy books.

Della was in one of the pricier rooms with a gorgeous view of the vast lawns outside Oakdale, while her mother's room was much smaller with only a tiny window overlooking the AC units. Clearly, Flynn didn't have the kind of financial troubles she did.

Of course he didn't. He lived in a building where the rent had a ton of zeroes tacked onto it.

Flynn. Her chest tightened and that heat he'd created in her last night resurfaced.

She'd acted impulsively again. One more rash act of her vow to rage against the rules everyone played by.

She had to stop doing that. She would stop doing that. It only led to messy entanglements she sometimes had trouble getting out of.

Flynn McGrady was definitely messy. But maybe not so stuffy.

Almost naked, he was anything but stuffy.

You will stop thinking about him right now. Right now.

As she entered the rec room, Emmet Kingsley, hair as white as snow, handsome and the ex-executive of some big company, latched on to the edge of her shirt. "Look who's here. Prettiest thing I've seen all day. You have time for a game of chess today?"

Cat grinned down at him, giving his shoulder a fond squeeze. "Not today, Emmet. I'm a workin' girl— need to get home and get my eight hours in so you can still call me pretty tomorrow. Did you drop by Mama's room? She has a new crossword puzzle book, you know," Cat said with encouragement.

Emmet had a bit of a crush on her mother, if she was reading him right, but as forward as he was with her, he was equally as shy with her mother.

He cleared his throat, two spots of red popping up on his wrinkled cheeks. "Haven't had the chance."

Cat pushed his wheelchair over to the table of doughnuts and grabbed a sugarless one for her mother—one with her favorite sugar-free chocolate frosting. She wrapped it in a napkin and handed it to Emmet. "Then would you do your favorite girl a favor and run this to her room? I've got to get a move on. Besides, wheeling this thing down the hall is good for your arm."

She'd love someone like Emmet to sweep her mother right off her feet. Her mother deserved a good sweeping after her father.

With a quick smile down at him, Cat rushed off before he could protest.

"Miss Butler?"

Her eyes flew to the man attached to the voice. Casper Reynolds, Oakdale's administrator. His suit, perfect and as black as his heart, blocked her view to the doorway to the hall outside the rec room. "We need to have a conversation."

She smiled her prettiest smile. "We do. It just can't be right now. I'm late."

His beady eyes glared down at her when he shuffled his feet. "Are you too busy to discuss your mother's stay with us? Because time's running out. I've left you several voice mails, Miss Butler. We can't house your mother for free."

The hum of the busy room dimmed, the chatter becoming hushed. A hot flush rushed to her cheeks. "If you'll just give me another couple of days, I promise you, I'll have the money."

Well, most of it, anyway. She could put off paying her rent for the moment. What was one more month? Soon enough, she'd have her first week's pay under her belt—that should appease him.

"Will you have *all* of it, Miss Butler? You're already two months behind."

"Two months? Wow. Time flying and all, huh?" She tried to joke, but Casper Reynolds wasn't having it.

"Unfortunately, this is no laughing matter."

As if she was a ball of giggles over the enormous bill for her mother's rehabilitation. "This is me not laughing," she said. "Promise, I'll have that money to you ASAP. Never you worry. We Butlers always pay our bills." She ducked and faked him out, managing to get around him and scurry out of the rec room.

Cat made a beeline for the red exit sign at the end of the hall. Her mother might not be running any marathons, but even in heels, she had to admit, she'd make a decent quarterback.

Flynn took the side exit out of Oakdale, hoping to cut off Cat at the pass.

Last night, he'd spent the rest of the evening reviewing his life after she left, going over his conservative take on things, and he had to admit, Cat's way was a whole lot sweeter.

Abandoning all the rules and living in the moment was damned hot, and now, he wanted to live in some more moments.

He'd thought of nothing else since he'd woken up but her lush lips on his, her incredible body and her passionate response to him.

That she didn't believe two people could live happily ever after had given him pause. His parents had. They'd loved each other until the day his father died. For some reason, those words—out of all their words last night—stuck and along with his lusty thoughts, he couldn't shake them.

Flynn caught sight of her, threading her way through parked cars, her long, lightly tanned legs sexy as hell in her wedge sandals. The warm breeze lifted her thick curtain of hair and swished her skirt around her thighs.

He came up on her left side and fell in step beside her. "So, how are you today, Live in the Moment?"

"Busy, vampire lover."

"Too busy to grab some dinner?"

"I don't eat."

"Wasn't that you I saw annihilating a piece of Mr. Moore's birthday cake two weekends ago when they had that big escape-from-Oakdale party for him?"

"It was my doppelganger. Or maybe my evil twin. If you're doin' your duty, and readin' those romance novels, you should know all about evil twins by now."

Flynn laughed, grabbing her hand, which she didn't yank out of his grasp but didn't exactly cling to, either. "How about I eat and you watch?"

Now she laughed, too, the sound light and breezy. "That sounds kinky."

He pulled her to a stop, keeping her hand in his, loving the way it fit his palm. "I'm buying."

She sighed and it was one of regret. Or maybe it was wistful? Whichever, it wasn't good. "We shouldn't have done what we did last night, Flynn."

"This coming from the woman who lives in the moment?" He put a hand to her forehead. "Maybe you are Cat Butler's evil twin."

She rolled her eyes, adorable and perfect. "I'm trying to be less impulsive. As you can see, it leads to nothing but trouble. We hardly know each other and yet, we bumped uglies."

He gave her a shrug of his shoulders, keeping his response casual. "I don't know, I didn't feel at all troubled by bumping our uglies—and, FYI, you're anything but ugly."

"That's because you're a man. Men never feel troubled by one-night stands. Women fret endlessly over them."

"That's not what Drusilla in *Ride the Night* says. She says she never regrets sex. Of course, she's a succubus, which is a sex demon, I think. But if she doesn't regret it, why should you? And if you have dinner with me, that'll make it a two-night stand—no fretting involved."

Her face softened in the fading sunlight. "You really are reading all those books of your mama's?"

"Kind of endearing, right?" He gave her the most charming grin he knew how to give. Then watched the wheels turn in Cat's head while she weighed the pros and cons.

"Fine. But it'll have to be quick. I have work."

"Tonight?"

She looked over his shoulder, her eyes focusing on anything other than him. "Odd shifts. All the new girls have to take them. It's in the newbie handbook."

First she was managing stuff, then she was working odd shifts all the new *girls* had to take? "We'll be in and out. Promise. My car or yours?"

As they made their way to her car, Flynn ignored the nagging questions about her employment and her lack of faith in lasting relationships, and did what she preached.

Lived in the moment.

Nine

"How did we end up here—*again?*" Cat asked, her toes properly curled.

"It was the fountain. All that splashing around you were doing was damn sexy. Wet silky shirt, plus Cat's flesh exposed beneath it, equals superhot," Flynn said, nuzzling her neck and making her purr.

After a dinner of juicy cheeseburgers at a local café, they'd taken a leisurely stroll and the temptation of the big fountain in the middle of the park they'd ended up in was more than her aching feet could bear. So she'd hopped in, taking Flynn, shoes and all, with her.

Their laughter led to one amazing kiss that led to another, until they were back at his place and in his big bed.

As he skimmed his lips along her collarbone and down over her shoulder, that wicked heat he'd just moments ago sated began to simmer between her thighs again. "Did we swap bodies?"

Flynn let his tongue flicker over her breast, making her arch upward. "Nope. Just spit. Why do you ask?"

She felt him smile against her ribs, gasped when his

mouth nipped at her waist. "I get the impression this isn't something you normally do."

Slipping his hand between her thighs, Flynn's fingers skimmed her swollen flesh. "Eat cheeseburgers?"

Cat's fingers gripped his shoulders, her nails digging into his muscles. "No. Make love to a woman when you hardly know her."

"Then let's get to know each other. Afterward, you'll be a woman I made love to and know better. I'll start," he offered, thumbing her clit until she writhed. "Are you from Georgia?"

Cat grabbed his wrist to still the white-hot heat he was evoking so she could answer. "Born and raised. You?"

He slid up the bed, kissing the side of her mouth. "Yep. Moved to New York for college, loved it, stayed. Did you go to college?"

"For about a year until I almost died of boredom and dropped out."

"What did you want to be when you grew up?" he asked, tracing her nipple.

Uncommitted to everything but the wind in her hair and the sun at her back? "Free."

His hand stilled. "Was someone holding you captive?"

Cat smiled up at him. "Not literally. I just didn't want to end up like my mother. Single parent, tied to a house she worked long hours in order to keep, bills up to her eyeballs." *Damn, Cat. This isn't psychotherapy. It's sex.* She'd said too much. So she redirected. "What did you want to be?"

"Chuck Norris."

Laughter spilled from her lips as she gazed up at

him, the dim light from the lamp enhancing his sharp cheekbones. "Like all good boys should. Did you get good grades in school?"

He gave her a guarded look. "Yeah. I did. Did you?"

"No. I didn't. I graduated by the skin of my teeth. Ever get in trouble with the law?"

"Nope."

"I did. I picketed a company once for animal testing."

Flynn grinned at her. "And let me guess, it was anything but peaceful."

Cat rolled to her side, propping herself up on an elbow. "It started out that way…and the pokey isn't such a bad place, by the way. Everyone was very nice. How many jobs have you had?"

"Counting mowing neighborhood lawns? Three. How many have you had?"

"Counting babysitting, and my esteemed time as Coco the Clown's assistant?"

"You can make balloon animals, can't you?"

"Oh, my God. I'm so good at it. I'm particularly good at a French poodle."

He laughed a deep rumble that was pleasant to her ears. "Yeah. Count Coco."

"Um, twelve. Wait, no. Counting my old job with Arlo and my new job, it's fourteen."

He whistled against her skin. "Wow. How many serious relationships have you had?"

"Counting my mother?" She was hedging.

"Sure."

"One."

His eyebrow cocked upward. "With your mother?"

"Uh-huh. I stink at relationships. I bore easily. I love to argue, as you've witnessed, and my whims drive men crazy. I've had several boyfriends, though. How many relationships have you had?"

"Two serious."

"I figured as much."

"Figured I'd only had two serious relationships? How did you figure that?"

"Because that's the kind of guy you are, McGrady. A keeper and the kind of guy who likes to keep. And that right there is exactly why this isn't a good idea."

"What isn't a good idea?"

"What we're doing right now."

He dragged her body close to his by wrapping an arm around her waist. "How can you say this isn't a good idea?"

How could she when he felt so amazing next to her? How could she when Flynn did things to her body that made her want to hang on to him forever. Because in the end, she'd freak out and run away. Just like she always did.

"I'm a huge red flag, Flynn. We're total opposites. I'm irresponsible, flighty and, in general, unreliable. You're responsible and faithful and a complete rock. You're conservative, I'm far more liberal."

He scoffed. "You make me sound like Old Yeller."

"You *are* Old Yeller."

"How about you let me decide what's good for me?"

"I'll eventually drive you out of your mind. I'm just giving you a disclaimer."

"Like a warning label?"

"Yep."

"Well, news flash. I spit on warning labels. Just ask my new mattress. I ripped the label right off the second it got here, threw it on the floor, gave it a good stomping and screamed a rebel yell. Oh, and if you can endure jail, I can, too," he joked, sliding down her body to finish what he'd started.

His lips found the space between her legs and spread her wet flesh, taking a long swipe with his tongue, slowly and leisurely.

Her thighs tensed and her hips rose to meet his mouth. Flynn's mouth was amazing, his tongue a masterpiece of carnal knowledge. For someone who'd only had two serious relationships, he certainly didn't lack expertise.

Cat wrapped her ankles around his neck, gripping his hair when he thrust two fingers inside her, rolling her hips as he ran his tongue over her clit.

When she came, it was so intense, ripping through her so unexpectedly, she had to stuff her fingers in her mouth to keep from screaming.

She balled the sheets on either side of her with her fingers when the crest rose, rocking against him until the breath left her lungs and she collapsed on the bed.

Oh, this man.

Cat's soft moans of orgasm made him harder. All he wanted to do was settle between her legs, drive into her until total oblivion took over.

But Cat had other plans. She gave his arms a tug, pulling him close to her as her breathing steadied. The soft whisper of her air releasing from her lips lingered in his ears as she clung to him.

Then she was pushing him away, rolling him to his back, slinking along his torso until her head rested on his lower abdomen.

She didn't toy with him. There was no playful foreplay involved in taking his cock in her hand and slipping her mouth around it.

He bucked beneath her, the wet heat of her tongue slithering over his length blowing his mind.

She stroked, long slow passes, mimicking his earlier ministrations until his chest tightened and he had to pull her away with a hiss.

Flynn dragged her upward, rolling her on her back, staring down at her as he settled between her legs. Christ, she was beautiful. He couldn't remember ever thinking anyone was as beautiful as she was. Long limbs, soft curves. All of it.

He may have had only two serious relationships, but he'd been with enough women to know, no one made him feel this stir in his chest, the weird tightening in his gut, like she did.

It didn't just have to do with their lovemaking, either. He'd felt it the previous night. He'd fought it all night long tonight.

Cat waited, her chest rising and falling, her lips parted, making him stiffer knowing they'd just been around his cock. He cupped her breast, keeping his gaze on hers, willing her to look at him as he thumbed her hard nipple, loving the way she stared right back at him as she took her pleasures.

Her skin glistened in the glow of the lamp, a fine sheen of sweat covering her chest. He gave the dusky tight bud of her nipple a lick, savoring the pebbled flesh on his tongue while she grabbed a condom and slid it over his shaft.

Flynn didn't waste any time when he placed his cock at her entrance and thrust upward, savoring how tight she was, how slick and hot.

That was when Cat closed her eyes, reached her arms up over her head and clung to the bars on the headboard.

It was also when Flynn thought he'd explode inside her. He loved her abandon, the way she just let go and enjoyed the physical pleasure. He hadn't experienced that with a woman, and it was like a drug.

She wasn't ashamed to lift her hips and silently ask for more, and as a result, his thrusts became more urgent and his muscles tightened.

Cat came first, unabashedly wrapping her arms around his neck and pulling him tight to her. The friction of their skin, the soft moan she made in his ear when she came, made him come, too—sharp and sweet, rattling him to his core.

She settled beneath him afterward, her harsh panting becoming soft intakes of breath, while he cradled her in his arms.

And it was then he realized he was in deep, without ever realizing he'd even jumped in the pool.

Flynn ignored Cat's words of warning, ignored the underlying note of fear in them. She was a commitment-phobe if her track record with jobs and boyfriends was any indication.

And she was right, they were complete opposites.

Still, even with all her red-flag warnings, he was wading further out into the deep end.

"You know, McGrady," she murmured, rolling out from under him and to her side, tucking his arm under hers. "Maybe you're not such a prude."

He chuckled against the back of her neck, inhaling the smell of her skin. Yeah. Maybe not.

Ten

"What is this?" Cat asked, pushing her way through the black-and-gold streamers that were hanging over the break-room door.

Marybell blew a colorful noisemaker at her and giggled. "It's phone sex Friday. One Friday every month, Landon has Sanjeev make the operator who had the most calls for the month whatever she wants for her special dinner. Naturally, LaDawn smokes us almost every time—because, well, she's LaDawn, the super ninja of phone sex. But don't think he's playing favorites because then we have tried-hard Tuesday, and the person with the least calls in a month gets her special dinner, too."

Cat shook her head with a grin. Each time she thought she'd wrapped her head around Call Girls, she was hit with yet another way Landon inspired his employees. He'd turned the drudgery of work into a celebration. The operators worked hard because they loved Landon.

And the more she showed up, the more involved she became with these women, the harder she wanted to prove not just to Landon, but to herself, she wanted this job.

The accounting class she'd taken at a local college came in handy when she'd gone over the financials just the other night. She'd marveled at how successful Call Girls really was, even with the salaried pay the operators were paid, the bonuses for exceeding the expected calls per month, the insurance plan and their 401(k)s.

"So how's your new beau, Cat?" LaDawn asked, winking an eye at her before dipping a piece of lobster into some freshly drawn butter.

Cat fought to keep her face even. She'd seen Flynn every night for two weeks without a single jittery freak-out. Something wasn't right. By now, in any other relationship, she'd have been looking for the get-out-as-fast-as-you-can door. "He's not my beau."

"Really? Funny, when I saw you two at the sandwich shop the other day sharin' a sub, you sure looked like he was your steady." LaDawn fanned herself with her napkin. "And by the by, he's hot."

And sweet, and considerate, and forcefully wicked in the bedroom. She blushed.

Even funnier than the success of Call Girls, despite Landon's lavish spending, was how they considered one another family. If one of the operators had an ill family member, they all paid them a visit. When LaDawn had been sick with a nasty stomach virus last week, they took turns nursing her back to health—literally arranged shifts so she'd never want for anything.

Because she'd been welcomed to the fold, they expected introductions to Flynn.

Marybell grabbed her by the waist from behind and

stuck her face in Cat's. "So, when do we get to meet the intended?"

Yeah. When are you going to do that, Cat? She'd avoided it so far—how did you tell someone like Flynn McGrady you worked at a phone sex company?

He'd loosened up, but she was pretty sure he hadn't loosened up that much.

For someone who's afraid of commitment, it sure sounds like you're trying to stall telling Flynn about what you're doing up here. Commitment-phobic people use that as the perfect tool to get out ASAP.

Could it be you're closing the excuse toolbox forever, Catherine Butler?

Her stomach tightened into a knot. No. This wasn't forever. Flynn had to go back to New York eventually, and she had to stay here. His mother wasn't considered long-term care.

Forever didn't work long distance.

"Kit-Cat?" Landon drawled in her ear.

She jumped in response, smiling when she realized it was Landon. He looked a little tired today. It was barely noticeable, but it was there. "Well, look what the cat dragged in." Cat gave him a tight hug, noting a slight tremor in his arms. "Have you come to check up on me and my bossin' skills?"

"I came to see what all the cacklin' was about a boyfriend. Have you left me for greener pastures?"

"Leave all this," she said, waving an arm at the elaborate meal that LaDawn and the other girls were enjoying. "Not for all the shoes in Payless."

"So is it true? Do you have a new beau and you're holdin' out on us?"

Her eyes found the first object she could focus on so

as not to look Landon directly in the eye. He had a way of seeing past her crap and into her darkest thoughts, thoughts that sometimes made her uncomfortable in her own skin. "I'm seeing someone, yes."

"And it's love," he playfully accused. "I can see it. Yippee for love, Cat. In the end, that's really all there is."

"Have you ever been in love, Landon?"

Now his eyes clouded. "I have, head over heels, in fact, but he couldn't love me out in the open. He wanted to tuck me away and keep me his dirty secret. I had too much love for that."

Suddenly, everything Landon did, the way he showed mere strangers so much kindness, the way he loved openly with words and actions, the way he expressed his feelings without pause, made sense. Because he'd once been forced to keep it all inside.

She wrapped her arm in his and leaned her head on his shoulder as they watched everyone eat and laugh. "You're the best person I know, Landon. If he couldn't love you, he didn't deserve you."

"So what about you? Is it love?"

It was something. It was anticipatory jitters, secret smiles, the race of her heart when she got a text from Flynn. "I don't know. I've never been in love."

"You know what the trouble is with you, Cat?"

Cat leaned into Landon, smiling up at him. "What's the trouble with me, boss?"

"You never stuck around long enough to find out if it could be love. You gotta stick around to see what you can see. Sometimes, you have to ride the wave, Kit-Cat, and see what beach it lands on. Could be warm and sunny there."

"Or a tsunami could be in the forecast."

"But what if there's a tropical breeze and the sun's shinin'?"

"That's my definitive sign there's going to be a tsunami," she joked, until she realized she really did expect the worst.

"Why, Cat Butler, I'da never pegged you as such a pessimist. How'd that happen?"

For all her impulsive blathering, acts of defiance in the name of right and wrong, she stunk at being left—so she left first. Left a job before she could screw up and be asked to leave. Left one boyfriend after the other so she wouldn't fall in love and end up hurt.

This way she'd never have to feel that gnawing, empty ache she'd felt when her father left both she and her mother. She'd loved him so much. She'd been his little girl, his Princess Cat.

Until she wasn't anymore.

Those long nights praying to the heavens he'd come back, finally realizing after two solid years of prayer he was never coming back, had sealed the deal for her. Her mother had been a good wife—Tessa never would have considered walking out the door and never coming back, and she'd paid the price as a single parent.

She'd struggled to make ends meet. She'd robbed Peter to pay Paul on more than one occasion to ensure Cat had everything she needed—no matter what.

The weight of that responsibility had stolen the joy from her mother's young life and bled into her middle years. Some of the best years of Tessa's life were spent working for Kahn the Wrath-maker, low pay, long hours, but she did it. She did it so Cat could go to the college she'd dropped out of.

When Tessa had finally retired from her job as a secretary, her retirement fund and Medicaid barely helped her hang on. Yet, somehow, she'd still been the best mother ever.

"I guess I am a little pessimistic."

"Or a lot."

She chuckled against his arm. "Okay, a lot."

"Why's that, do ya think?"

"Is there a lesson here, Landon?"

Landon shrugged. "Is there?"

Her breath shuddered in and out. *"I'm afraid."*

"Of?"

"Of committing. Committing to anything. I'm beginning to think it's why I never did anything worthwhile with my life. Why I'm afraid to throw myself into something all the way."

Landon pulled away from her, cupping her chin. "Do me a favor, would ya?"

"Anything."

"Don't run away this time, pretty lady. Instead, stick around and see what you can see." He gave her a squeeze and dropped a kiss on the top of her head before sauntering off to have some lobster and champagne with the girls.

Flynn dropped a kiss on his mother's cheek and smiled. She wasn't parked near a window, staring off into space today. Today, she was struggling with the knitting needles and yarn Cat had brought her.

But she was damn well trying.

"How are you today, Mom? You look pretty. Did the nurses do your hair?"

She nodded her acknowledgment, dropping the knitting needles into her lap with a disgusted grunt.

Flynn picked them up, repositioning them between her fingers and looking at the book on the table for direction. "Here, like this," he said, ignoring her surprised look.

He'd been watching YouTube videos on how to knit since his mother's doctor told him it was good hand-eye coordination for her, and he'd successfully knitted a very ugly, very skinny potholder.

"See?" he said when he placed the needles back in her hand. "So, since you won't talk to anyone but Cat, because you clearly like her better than me, how do you feel about the fact that I'm dating her?"

Della shifted in her wheelchair.

"Is that a yea or a nay?" he prodded, hoping she'd at least try to speak.

"Yeee-ah," she blurted out, the effort it took very clear.

He forced himself to be calm and not overreact to the first words she'd spoken directly to him in months. "You like her a lot, don't you?"

Della gave him a crooked bob of her head. "Good." She spat the word.

Flynn smiled, squeezing her hand. Cat was good, and the more time he spent with her, the more time he wanted to spend with her.

"Listen, Mom. I've wanted to talk to you about something for a while now. I don't know what was going on before your stroke. Probably because I worked all the time and I didn't make the time to call you to find out. I know you miss Dad and Adeline, and I live pretty far away, but I'm always here. And I'm going to make a better effort to be around more often. Okay?"

She gave his hand a firm squeeze, reaching out with

the other one to run her finger down his nose just like she had when he was a kid.

Flynn brought her hand to his cheek and kissed it. "Now, that settled, have I mentioned I've been reading a lot lately?"

Della's dark eyes grew curious.

He pulled the bag he had from under his chair at the table and grabbed a book from it. "Yep. So, here's the deal. You read it and I'll read it, and we'll discuss it. Like a book club, maybe?" He held up his copy and wiggled his eyebrows. "*Looook.* It has vampires. Cat says you like vampires. I hope they're better than sex demons. Yes. I just admitted I read a book about sex demons in front of my mother."

Della gurgled her approval, fingering the book.

Way to loosen up, McGrady.

Eleven

"You're knitting? You really are the best son ever," Cat cooed at Flynn from across his kitchen table.

Flynn took a bite of his lo mein and wiggled his eyebrows. "I suck at it."

Cat held up the green yarn in the shape of... something. "I think this is a great scarf."

"It's a pot holder."

She nodded vehemently in agreement while she chewed on the corner of a fortune cookie. "I can totally see that now. For all those long, skinny dishes. Why don't they make more pot holders long and skinny, instead of boring and square?"

Barking a laugh, Flynn shoved the containers of Chinese food out of the way. "I like supportive. It's hot on you." Taking her by the hand, he yanked her upward, pressing her soft curves against him and kissing her thoroughly.

"Are you thinking what I'm thinking?" she asked when she pulled away in that low husky voice that made his cock strain against his jeans.

Slipping his hands under her silky top, he nipped at her jaw. "Absolutely. Let's make a knit hat together."

Cat moaned into his mouth when he captured her lips—the same way she had for the past four weeks and counting. They'd fallen into a ritual of meeting for dinner at his place or somewhere out, grabbing a movie, then making love the better part of the night.

Neither of them was getting much sleep and his email response rate was probably down by fifty percent, but he didn't give a damn. Each time he saw her, he wanted to see her more. Each time he touched her, he wanted to touch her again.

"A hat?" she murmured, unbuckling his belt and unzipping his jeans. Cat never wasted time when it came to making love. Curling her fingers around his cock, she began to stroke him. "Can we do that naked?"

Driving her skirt upward, he slipped his fingers inside her silky underwear, where he found her swollen and wet, loving the small gasp she made when he circled her clit with his finger. "We can do it any way you want it."

Shoving his jeans down over his hips, she wrapped her arms around his neck. "Then I want to do it *now*— just like this."

Flynn put his hands at her waist and set her on the table, then pulled her panties off and chucked them in a corner. Seeing her lying sprawled out on his glass tabletop, half-naked, her lips swollen from his kiss, her hair rumpled in that sexy tousle of dark brown, made him want to growl and beat his chest.

There was nothing he wanted to do more than drive into her, but that would make him an insensitive ass.

Until she grabbed him by the collar of his shirt and looked him square in the eye. "I said, *now,* McGrady."

Fire shot to his cock as he parted her legs and she lifted her hips, preparing to do as the lady asked.

Flynn thrust upward hard, hissing his approval when Cat gasped, too, and in response, wrapped her legs around his waist. He slipped his hands under her ass, keeping her flush to his lower torso, creating a slow grind of heat.

Her nipples beaded through her shirt, pushing at his chest as he held her close and rocked them. Their bodies fused, Cat clung to his back, digging her nails into it, clutching his hair. *"Harder,"* she demanded, the word thick and harsh.

And he didn't deny her, pulling back, driving upward into silky wetness until his teeth clenched.

She cried out first, a long, raw sound, and he followed shortly thereafter, tensing when he came and Cat's hips writhed in a familiar rhythm.

"Wow," she panted in his ear.

Yeah. He thought the same thing every time they made love. Pulling her limp body upward, he carried her to the bathroom and set her on the edge of the sink, rinsing a cloth in some warm water and handing it to her.

"What time is it?"

Leaning down, he kissed the tip of her nose, loving how her cheeks were still flushed and her clothes mussed. This was his favorite Cat—the one after they'd made love. "I dunno. Why?"

"Because I have some work to do tonight. It was last-minute and unexpected." Again, she looked away when she said it. She always found something else to look at when she talked about work.

Rinsing his hands, he dried them and wrapped his arms around her waist. "It can't wait? How can we knit hats if you're at work."

"It can't wait," she confirmed.

What was so damn important at work that it couldn't wait? He had a million questions about Cat, and he'd tried not to pry, but Jesus, why was where she worked such a secret?

And why didn't she ever invite him back to her place for dinner? Did she have a place? She had a car, and that was the most he knew about her. Was her place her car?

"Mind telling me what you do up there in the penthouse, Cat?" He didn't mean to sound suspicious, but they'd been dating close to a month now. He knew the size of her bra, but not what she did for a living.

He was falling in love with this woman, and if she was doing what he thought she was doing, he'd find a way to talk her out of it.

He'd denied it to himself, laughed it off as crazy, berated himself for even thinking it, but all roads led to one thing. That penthouse was locked up tighter than Fort Knox. Women came and went all day long. Colorful women. Pretty women. Girl-next-door women.

Instantly, Cat's guard was up. He saw it in the way she shut down—the rigid line her spine became, the way her full mouth went flat.

That's when he knew he was in trouble.

She was lying. She didn't have to go to work. She had to go home and process. Everything was going too well, and she was neither bored nor losing interest in Flynn. In fact, he was all she ever thought about. She wanted to be with him every second of every day.

And tonight, when he'd made such incredible love to her, had tied all her fears up into one big knot... She wasn't the kind of girl Flynn dated. Opinionated, living in a studio apartment with a stove that only started if you talked dirty to it.

She hardly qualified as a career·girl. She'd only been working for Landon for a month—and to boot, the job was managing a phone sex company. Flynn had loosened up a lot—he probably wasn't that loose yet.

And he lived in New York. They didn't talk about it, but when Della was better, was he going to uproot his fancy city life to come live in Georgia? Probably not.

Add to all that, she didn't like the way Flynn had asked the question. "What's the big deal about what I do up in the penthouse?" she asked.

Flynn ran his fingers through his hair, his sigh grating. "Okay, I'm just going to ask you outright. You never look me in the eye when I ask about your work. In fact, you do what you're doing right now. Avoid. So here goes, and I'm only asking because I don't have much to go on since the coffee shop. I'm asking with absolutely no judgment. Are you an escort? Working for some drug kingpin? Doing something illegal you're afraid you can't get out of?"

Cat blinked. Had he just asked her if she was a high-priced hooker? Not that there was anything wrong with being a high-priced hooker if that's where the road led you. She just didn't happen to be one.

"Did you just ask me if I have sex for money?" she squeaked, sliding off the sink and stomping off to the kitchen to gather her things.

He followed her, the quick glimpse she caught of his eyes, hard.

"I started with, 'What do you do upstairs in the penthouse, Cat?' What I want to know is why it's such a big deal that I'm asking what your new job is. Why we don't talk about it over dinner the way we do my work? Why you're so afraid to share anything personal with me."

"No! You asked me if I had sex with men for money!"

You're not listening, Cat. You're letting him draw conclusions because you're afraid. Stop being afraid. Look at all the evidence that points to illegal activity. A penthouse where all types of women come and go from that elevator. Clearly, the person who owns it is rich. Flynn does live in a building that costs thousands of dollars for a stinking one-bedroom apartment.

He has nothing else to go on. He didn't call you a dirty slut or a drug dealer. Don't be unfair. This is something you two can laugh over someday.

"I only listed some of the illegal activities that came to mind," he said calmly. Too calmly.

Which only made her angry. "This is ridiculous. I don't have to stand here and allow you to accuse me of doing something illegal!"

"Then what do you do for a living, Cat?" he demanded. This was the Flynn from the coffee shop. Hard and angry.

Somehow, this had become some weird bone of contention for her. As though holding back the information was her secret trump card.

So she threw up another hurdle. "It's none of your business what I do for a living, Flynn! You know, not all of us are rich enough to be able to afford Oakdale. My mother's in there on a wing and a prayer right now, and it's up to me to be sure she stays there until she's healthy enough to leave. If I'm doing something illegal, it's none of your damn business. I'll do whatever it takes to take care of my mother!"

"This isn't about my money, and you know it."

"No. You're right. This is about us being two totally different people."

Flynn held up a finger, so arrogant, so sure. "No, this is about running away, because it's easier. If what you're doing isn't illegal, then it shouldn't be a big deal to tell me what it is. You're running away, Cat. You're avoiding the question because you want to find any excuse you can to call this over because *you're afraid*."

As she stuffed her sunglasses in her purse Cat shook her head. "I'm not afraid of you, Flynn McGrady!" Yes, she was. She was so afraid she wouldn't measure up, right now, in her mind she was in a tight panicked ball of fear.

He took two long strides before he was in front of her, his nostrils flaring. "Yes, you are. You're afraid you're falling in love with me, and you'll use any excuse to run away from it. It all leads back to that conversation we had that night. Your endless jobs, your failed relationships, the way you consider yourself irresponsible. You're running away because you're afraid to stick around and do the hard stuff. That's what you've always been afraid of."

Oh, the truth. Hearing it out loud really was as painful as she'd heard it was. She backed toward the door, keeping her tears in check. "Well, you have it all figured out, don't you, Doc McGrady? You don't even need me here to fill in the blanks, do you? I'll leave you to that, because it's obvious you've got it covered," she yelled.

Cat yanked open the door and slammed it shut behind her.

Walking away from her fears. Walking away from taking the chance Flynn would walk away first.

Walking away from seeing what she could see.

Twelve

"Kit-Cat?"

Landon pushed his way through her office door. Dusk had fallen outside, making his face appear gaunter than it had a week ago. Fear swept over her. She dropped the papers she'd been reviewing. "Boss?"

"Why are you here so late?"

Because I just broke up with the most amazing man for calling me a hooker.

He didn't call you a hooker, he asked a question all people who date ask. He didn't ask what your bank balance was. He asked you what you did for a living.

You blew it all out of proportion because you wanted to find a way out before he found one for you.

Her chest felt as if it had an elephant on it. "Just some stuff I wanted to look over before tomorrow. Everything okay?"

Landon crossed his arms over his chest, his eyes grim. "Bad news, sunshine."

"Did Sheree call another wife of a client a dried-up prude? I told her the other night, if a spouse calls upset with their phone bill, direct the call to me."

Landon held out his hand to her, his eyes, usually so bright, rather dull today. "Walk outside to the terrace with me?"

Worry began its slow simmer. "Landon, you're scarin' me," she said, her feet dragging.

Pulling open the French doors, he motioned her forward, out into the humid night air.

Her heart began a painful beat. *God, please don't let it be what I think it is.* "What's wrong?"

"It's back."

"What's back?"

"The cancer, Kit-Cat."

No. No, no, no. She had to grip the edge of the iron balcony to hold herself upright. "No," she whispered.

"I'm afraid so, pretty lady."

"More chemo?"

Landon looked her right in the eye—dead on, and there was no fear in his gaze. "Not this time, I'm afraid. I'm end-stage now. Nothin' to do but tie up loose ends."

"But you said you were better when you left Oakdale. You said no more chemo," she whispered.

"That's what the doctors said, too, Kit-Cat. But I know my body. I knew what my gut was sayin' despite what the medical profession was telling me. If I told you I was nearin' the end, would you have come here because you wanted to finally stop hopping from job to job or because you wanted to help me? You're always helpin' everyone else, Cat. But what you needed to do was help yourself."

"I…" It all made sense now. He'd brought her to Call Girls for a reason—to show her she could stick something out for the long haul when it really counted.

Her vision blurred with hot tears. "You did this for a reason."

"Aw, Cat. All those talks we had all those months while I was in and out of Oakdale, you made me happy. You never forgot to stop and talk. I'm not the only one who's a good listener, Cat. You are, too. Do you know how important that is to some of the people at Oakdale? It might be a mighty expensive private facility, but all the money those people have comes with a price. Sometimes, it means your family members are just waitin' on your exit stage left. Do you have any idea what it means to have someone like you come along and stick a silly blue candle on a cupcake for your birthday when you can buy and sell the cupcake factory? Do you know how much it means when you pick up romance novels for Della or make sure Emmet Kingsley gets a good game of chess in to keep his mind sharp? Do you even know who Emmet Kingsley is?"

Cat shook her head, the rush of her anguish pushing at her temples. "No…"

"He's the retired CEO of one of the biggest oil companies in the world, pretty girl. You know why you don't know what he does? Because you don't care about his money. You care about his emotional state. You care about hearts, feelings. He was lonely, Cat. So lonely, but you came in, and you treated him like he mattered, and that's who I want running my company when I'm gone."

Gone. She couldn't bear the word. When she didn't respond, when the tears splashed to her feet, Landon pulled her in for a hug, resting his chin on top of her head.

"You make people happy. You're good with them. You're good at organizing things. You're good at knowin' when someone needs a hug. The girls—some of 'em have had it real rough in life. I needed someone who'd care enough to give 'em a hug. I knew you were flounderin' at Arlo's. I also knew I couldn't run Call Girls anymore, but the person I left in charge had to be someone who'd give a damn. The girls are my family. I wasn't gonna just leave anyone to look after them. Some cold, impersonal jackass who could run this like a well-oiled machine, but didn't give a damn about the cogs in those wheels? The cogs are important, Cat. Just as important as the machine. I won't let the girls ever think they don't matter again. So, as they say, timing is everything. I always believed I met you for a reason, Kit-Cat. The reason is this."

Cat wanted to scream her outrage, yell out her indignation at the unfairness of it all. Instead, she couldn't get her tongue to move, couldn't get past the thick knot in her throat.

That he trusted her enough to keep this legacy of love he'd created was almost more than she could bear. Irresponsible, ex-assistant to Coco the Clown wasn't so irresponsible, after all.

"When?"

"Months, maybe. Can't say for sure. Those doctors have been wrong before, you know. But this time, Kit-Cat, I feel it. Right here." He pointed to his gut.

"The girls. Do you want me to…" How could she even begin to say those words out loud?

"I'll talk to the girls tomorrow, Cat. Spend some time with them."

Suddenly, her words were back, with a vengeance. "I'll help. I'll do whatever you need. And I'll be there with you, for as long as you need…." She couldn't see that far ahead. She couldn't see a day without Landon in it, but she'd do whatever he needed because he'd given her a place to belong.

Cat felt him shake his head as she pressed her face into his chest to thwart the tears she couldn't stop. "No, Cat. I don't want that. As much as I love y'all, I don't want anyone cryin' over me. You hear? I'm goin' off somewhere peaceful to wait it out. I'll know when the time comes to leave Atlanta. Now, I know you don't think that's fair, but it's how I wanna depart this earth."

"Where?"

"Somewhere quiet where I can talk to my maker and hear *Him* talk back."

Cat sucked in a breath. God, he was so brave.

"Now, there is one last thing I want you to promise me. Well, maybe two."

She couldn't stop her shoulders from shaking, but she sucked in gulps of air and found a way to speak. "If you said three things, I was so out."

"That's my favorite girl. I need you to go find this boyfriend, honey. Don't miss the shot to have something great because of fear. He's a tropical beach. Swear it. Promise me, you'll see what you can see."

"How do you always know?"

"You were in here cryin', honey. It sure wasn't over some phone sex."

Gripping the lapels of his suit, she laughed. "Number two?"

"You smile whenever you think of me, would you? Please. Please smile."

"Always."

Always.

* * *

Flynn followed Nella, one of the nurse's aides, and backed away from his mother's wheelchair after positioning her in a patch of sunlight.

"Thanks, Nella," he said on a smile he didn't feel.

He pulled a chair out and sat down, grabbing his mom's hand. "Hey, Mom. How goes it today?"

The corner of Della's mouth lifted and she squeezed his hand. There was warmth in it. Every day, she warmed up a little more.

"Did you finish *The Sheik's Baby Mama?*" he teased.

Her tongue slipped out from between her lips and she tweaked the skin on the back of his hand, sharing her displeasure at his joke.

Flynn laughed. "Okay, fine. So I finished *Supernaturally Yours....*" he said with a leading tone.

Her eyes flashed her approval as she waited.

"You want my opinion?"

Della nodded.

"Say the word *yes,* and it's all yours. I know you can. Cat told me you can. So no holdin' out on me now." He grinned at her

Della's lips screwed up as Flynn watched her try to make her lips and her brain connect. "Ye...sh..."

"Good job, Mom. Okay, so here's my two cents. That Dimitri was a total player. Telling Lucinda he had to have sex to live? How did I miss trying that line out?"

Della swatted his hand with her ever more fluid fingers. "Sto...op, sill...ee," she chastised, but her eyes were glowing.

Flynn grinned again. "Oh, c'mon, Mom. How many women do you think would fall for that in this day and age? Okay, I'll give you this, he's a vampire, and they have all sorts of special needs. They drink blood, blah, blah, blah. But did he try *not* having sex to find out if he'd live? He didn't have to because Lucinda all but fell at his feet. And the soul-mate thing? I can't remember the last time I talked a woman into believing she was my soul mate because I was a vampire from 1822."

"Rowwmantic." Della shot the word at him, sitting back in the chair, pleased with herself.

Flynn made a face at her. "You women and your romance. Whatever happened to pizza and a movie?" he teased. "You know what my favorite part of the whole book was? The showdown between Gor and Dimitri. Now that was my kind of romantic."

"Bah," Della murmured, then cocked her head. "Cat?"

Yeah. Cat. "What about her?"

"You li…ke her!" she said triumphantly.

"She's very nice, Mom."

Della lifted a crooked finger and shook it. *"Girlfriend."*

Well, look who could talk now. Cat was like the magical answer to everything. "No. She won't be my girlfriend, Mom."

"Whyyy?"

Because it was over. Because he lived in New York and she lived here in Georgia. Because she didn't believe anyone stuck around. Because she was chaos and he was organization.

Because the bridge he'd tried to build had crumbled. Because she didn't want it as much as he did. Because he'd sort of called her a hooker.

"Because we're not right for each other, Mom. Cat

doesn't want the things I want. She's everything I'm not. I need someone who's…"

His mother waited patiently, tucking her chin to her chest.

"Never mind. How about we just leave it at, Cat's not the right girl for me?"

Damn. That hurt.

Thirteen

"Landon? Landon Wells?"

The man dressed in an expensive suit with a lemon-colored ascot turned around. "That's me." He held out his hand, his eyes greeting Flynn with warmth.

Flynn grasped the hand, unable to shake the strange feeling he'd like this man if they met under any other circumstances.

But today, he was pretty sure he wasn't going to like Landon Wells. Somehow, he'd gotten lucky when he'd caught the postman delivering the mail, and managed to catch sight of the name attached to the penthouse address.

To say Flynn was shocked he knew him not only as an internet business icon, but also as someone from his father's hometown, was understating it. It left him with the perfect opening to get some answers.

Measuring his words, he said, "You probably don't remember me, but I'm Flynn McGrady. My cousin Emmaline Amos is from your old hometown. I'm sure on my visits there, we must've crossed paths as kids."

Landon's smile grew as though he'd just put the

pieces of a puzzle together. "Of course! How could I forget the last name McGrady? Emmaline, such a great soul. What brings you to Atlanta? Business?"

"My mother, Della. She's over in Oakdale, recuperating from a stroke."

The surprise on his face was evident. "How did I miss that connection? If I had known Emmaline's aunt was holed up over there, I'd have paid her my propers. How is your mama? Better now, I hope?"

"She's doing much better, thanks. So you really are the guy who owns the penthouse?" Was this man really the legendary millionaire who came from his father's childhood home in Plum Orchard? He ran an escort service?

"That's me."

"Does a Cat Butler work for you?"

Landon's expression changed. It was a quick-fire moment that passed before his eyes went right back to being cheerful, but Flynn saw suspicion written all over his face. He did own an escort service. Cat really was an escort. Jesus.

"Why do you ask?"

Because he had to know. No way was he going to let her do something illegal to pay for her mother's care. He'd help. He'd protect her. "Forget it. It was rude of me to put you on the spot."

Landon put his hands on his hips. "Whoa. Whoa, whoa, doggie. *You're* her boyfriend, aren't you? Holy heck! Can't believe I didn't put the two together. Chalk it up to my forgetfulness these days."

"So she does work for you?"

"You bet she does."

Why would he so freely admit Cat worked for him

as an escort when her boyfriend didn't even know she was an escort? Was he just okay with spilling the beans on Cat? What wasn't fitting here?

The elevator doors from the penthouse shot open and the two women he'd seen a few weeks ago spilled out. The one with the bleached-blond hair and the other with the KISS makeup. His stomach sank—sank hard.

Landon watched Flynn for a moment before his eyes popped open. "Oh, naw," he sputtered. "You think…" He didn't finish the sentence before the lobby filled with his laughter, the echo of it taunting Flynn until the tips of his ears turned red.

Landon laughed so hard, Flynn thought he'd pass out. When he finally caught his breath, he sputtered, "Oh, this is beautiful. B-E-A-U-tiful! I don't own an escort service, and I'm not some drug kingpin. Call Girls is a phone sex operation. Cat's not having sex for money, you fool! She's working an honest nine-to-five as my general manager."

The color drained from his face. *Oh, McGrady, you've fucked up. Big. So, so big.*

"I can see by the way you're as pale as those vampires you're readin' about, you had yourself one big dilemma, didn't you?"

"I…" Flynn looked down at the book in his hands.

Landon clapped a hand on his shoulder and captured Flynn's gaze. "Would you have loved her any less if she was a hooker or sellin' drugs, buddy?"

"Who said anything about love?"

Landon gave his shoulder a shove. "Bah! Don't play games with me. I'm not some heartsick fool who can't see past his own nose. You love her. She loves you. But that's not what I asked you. I asked you if you'd love her even if she was an escort?"

He damn well would. "Yes."

"Were you makin' all sorts of plans in your mind about how to get her out of the lifestyle and into your arms?"

He damn well was. "Maybe."

Landon barked another laugh. "You are priceless, but you also just passed the test. So one more question and then a bit of advice."

"What's the question?"

"How do you feel about Plum Orchard?"

None of this made any sense. What did that have to do with Cat? "I liked it when I visited as a kid."

"Would you follow Cat there if she was goin'?"

"I can go anywhere. My company is internet-based."

"Not what I asked, and remember, I've seen all your cards."

"Okay. Yes. I'd follow her anywhere."

"Because?"

"Because I'm madly in love with her."

"So soon?"

"Don't get your meaning."

"Y'all have only been datin' a few weeks...."

"But I've waited thirty-six years for her."

"Ha! Good answer! So, come in close now." He pulled Flynn in for a huddle. "'Cus here's my advice if you wanna get your girl back...."

Cat skidded to a stop just outside of Della's door when she caught sight of Casper Reynolds and began to run the other way. Damn him. She had something important to do.

Tell Flynn she was a fool. A total moron for even considering running away. After her talk with Landon last night, where she saw, up close and personal, what it was like to leave this world with no regrets. Landon had shown her what pure love was. What a pure heart looked like. He'd shown her that time truly was always of the essence, and she didn't want to waste any more time.

Huffing out a breath, she headed for the exit by the rec room.

Who knew Casper had it in him to keep up?

He cut her off at the exit door by the rec room, putting his hand on the wide bar.

Damn. She held up her hands, her eyes grainy and sore from last night. "Look, I know I'm late with Mama's payment, but I promise, I'll be all caught up by the end of the month. Please, please, please, don't boot her out, Mr. Reynolds! She needs care around the clock till she heals. You wouldn't kick someone out and leave them to their own devices when they're so down on their luck, would you? You're not that kind of man, are you? Mama—"

"Save it, Miss Butler. The bill's been paid with an open tab until your mother leaves."

Cat's eyes flew open. "What?"

"You heard correctly. Your mother's bill is handled."

How? Who? "Who paid it?"

"A benevolent donor who wishes to remain anonymous."

Landon. Somehow, he'd found out about her predicament. He was like God. Everywhere. Of course, it was Landon. He knew everything. "But…"

Casper stuck his hands in his trousers and rocked back on his heels. "Figured I'd better tell you before you had to start training for marathons just to get away from me. Have a good day, Miss Butler." He gave her a tip of an imaginary hat before strolling off to the rec room.

Before she did anything, before she went and found Flynn to tell him what a complete fool she was, before she begged him to give this another shot, she was going to call Landon and give him some good old-fashioned hellfire and brimstone.

He was dying and while he was doing it, he was still saving everyone. How he had the wherewithal to manage to think of everyone else but himself made her love him even more. But she was standing on her own two feet now, thanks to him.

That was more than enough.

Pulling her phone from her purse, she unlocked it and scrolled until she pressed Landon's private number.

"Kit-Cat?"

"Landon, sit down—because I'm about to give you some hell!"

Fourteen

"Cat?"

"Flynn?" She whirled around, so glad to see his handsome face—so afraid she'd screwed up the one thing that was finally right. As he walked toward her down the long hall to her mother's room, gorgeous and tall and strong, with what looked like a hat in his hand, she began to speak. But he caught her up in his embrace and put his finger to her mouth, pulling her tight to him.

"Just so you know, you're the air that I breathe. And you know that's true because I'm not a vampire and I really have lungs."

Her head tipped back and she laughed, before she popped upright and began to recite what she'd practiced in her head. "I'm sorry," she blurted out, all her thoughts, all her fears, colliding into one big thought. "It was all too good. Too much. I was convinced it couldn't last. We come from very different places, and I did everything I could to use our differences against you. Against us."

He pulled her in for a kiss. "So now, you have to tell me, because I'm not letting up until you do—why, why are you so afraid everything will fall apart when it was going pretty great?"

Her worst fears. She was going to share her worst fears with the man she was falling in love with. "It was the same way it was with my mom and dad. One day we were all on a picnic, eating fried chicken and potato salad on a blanket, laughing, being a family, and the next day, he was gone, and he never came back. No warning, no goodbye—just gone. Every time I thought I might be getting close to that with anyone, I ran away, because I was convinced if I left first, it would hurt less. This time, it didn't hurt less. It hurt more."

Cupping her cheeks, Flynn gazed down at her. "I'll never do that to you, Cat. But you have to give me the chance to show you I'll never do that to you. I can't promise we won't have problems. I can't promise there won't be times when we disagree—because we're different, we're really different. There's no denying that, but if you ask me, that just means we can see both sides of the fence better. Don't run away, Cat. Don't run away because you think I will first."

She buried her face in his strong chest, inhaling his scent. Flynn's scent. "You paid Mama's bill. Why would you do that?"

"How did you find out it was me?"

"Because it wasn't Landon. It had to be you."

"You promise not to get mad."

"I promise," she murmured against his chest.

"You're going to laugh."

"Probably, but it'll be with you, not at you."

He rested his chin on the top of her head with a sigh. "In my mind, I was saving you from either selling your body to strange men for a fee or ending up in federal prison for being a drug mule. I know, I know. Crazy, right? But do you see why I thought you were doing something illegal? I was just connecting dots, and I wanted to help. The thought of you... Well, you know what I mean. I just wanted you not to have to worry about your mother."

Cat laughed harder, loving the idea that Flynn wanted to help her.

"I think that's laughing at me," Flynn teased.

"I think you're right, but I swear, I'm not doing anything illegal."

"I know all about the phone sex job, honey."

She leaned back in his embrace, confused. "Who told you?"

"Landon. After he was done busting a gut. I ran into him in the lobby of the apartment building. And I know you probably thought conservative me wouldn't like it, but I'm okay with it. Not that what I think matters. It's your career. Your job."

She didn't know what to say, but Flynn apparently did.

"Did you know, my father's from his old hometown? Plum Orchard? He knows my cousin Emmaline."

"What a crazy small world, huh?" The mention of Landon made her tear up. "I have so much to tell you."

Tipping her chin up, he swiped at a tear rolling down her cheek. "I know about Landon, Cat. He told me. From now on, talk to me. Always talk to me. When you're afraid, when you're overwhelmed, when one of your friends is dying. Just talk to me, and we'll figure it out. I promise."

"Okay, then, right now, I'm afraid. I'm afraid I won't be able to pull off what Landon needs me to do. I'm afraid of the day he won't be here anymore. I'm afraid of losing him."

"You have every right to those fears. But I'll be here to help you. I'll always help."

Standing on tiptoe, she gave him a soft kiss. "Now about that hospital bill…"

"Don't get mad, now."

Cat shook her head. "No. I'm not mad," she whispered. "Thank you…"

Flynn planted another kiss on her lips before grabbing her hand and pulling her toward Della's room with a grin. "So I made you something."

"You did? For me?" she asked as they strolled hand in hand.

"I worked on it for two solid weeks. It was torture. Tedious. Intricate work. I spent hours picking out the right color, all in an effort to win your heart." He pulled that something out of his pocket and held it up with a grin.

The hat. A purple-and-white hat, totally crooked on one side, and sort of loosely threaded on the other with what she thought was an attempt at a pom-pom. "For me?" She squealed her happiness. "Does this mean we're goin' together, Flynn McGrady? Anyone who knits a hat as fine as that beauty right there must mean business."

He stopped her just outside of Della's doorway and put the hat on her head, kissing the tip of her nose with a chuckle. "I learned how to purl stitch for you, you bet I mean business."

Cat giggled, the empty well of her fear filled up with one Flynn McGrady. "How could I ever consider turning down a man with a purl stitch as fine as yours?"

"Just you wait until I show you the afghan I started. You'll be crazy about me in no time."

She pulled Flynn to her, cupping his jaw, running her thumb over his lips, smiling up at him. "I think the crazy-about-you part is taken care of, McGrady."

Yeah, the crazy-about-him part was good.

So good.

Fifteen

One year later...

"What are you doing here, Kit-Cat? It's five in the morning."

"I know... I know where you're going, Landon," she whispered, a rasp of hushed words in the purple glow of early morning.

She'd awakened beside Flynn, warm, happy—feeling the incredible joy she felt since they'd moved in together a couple of months ago. The completeness that burrowed deep in her heart when she realized she was in his bed, wrapped in his arms. Then a strange sense of urgency had driven her from the safe confines of the blankets, and she knew she had to go upstairs to the penthouse.

To see Landon. One last time.

Flynn had thrown the covers off and rushed to make her a cup of coffee while she dressed, sending her off with a kiss and the words, "I'll be right here when you get back."

She and Flynn had spent a great deal of time with

Landon over the past months, and he'd become as good a friend to Flynn as he was to her. They were always talking business strategies and football, making bets on the game and sharing the occasional scotch on the terrace.

She loved the way Flynn laughed with Landon and the girls at the office. It was easy, rich and full. She loved the way the tips of Flynn's ears turned red when he heard LaDawn or Marybell talk dirty.

She loved all the good things that had happened since Flynn, Call Girls and Landon had become a part of her life. So many good things. So many things she was trying so hard to be grateful for instead of crying over the sting of inevitable loss.

Just like Landon.

He'd surprised them all by rallying for quite a while, far longer since he'd initially told her the cancer had come back, and much longer than the time frame the doctors had given him. But when his decline came, it was rapid.

Sometimes, when she cried, Flynn would hold her, rocking her quietly as she prepared for the inevitable— privately. So Landon wouldn't see.

Seeing him now at early dawn, she saw the toll this horrible disease was taking, and she knew she had to let go.

Cat kept her voice low so as not to wake the girls, but she understood why he was leaving this way, and she was trying like hell to respect his choice. Landon could make a fuss over you, but you couldn't ever return the favor.

He wanted to go quietly. He didn't want to see their tears. He wanted to savor the good like he savored the steam rising from his coffee each morning. With a smile and a sigh of appreciation.

Yet, tears rushed to her eyes, falling hot and heavy down her cheeks. "I…I had to." Cat fought a wail, a primal scream at the injustice, by biting the inside of her cheek.

"Don't cry, pretty Kit-Cat. Please don't. When I get on this elevator, I wanna see you smilin' at me. Just like you used to when you brought me coffee every morning at Oakdale. That's what I want my last memory of you to be."

"How?" Cat fought a ragged sob. "How do I let you go?" *How do I say goodbye forever?*

That's what this was. A forever goodbye.

Landon's eyes were warm, so warm you could wrap yourself up in them. "You just do. You do it because I need that right now. I've had everything I've ever wanted in this lifetime. Plenty o' money to do almost anything, see all corners of the world. But in the end, right now, I just want this one thing. I want to see your smile."

"Then I want just this one last thing." She didn't wait for him to answer. Instead, Cat lunged at him, wrapping her arms around his waist and hugging him tight. "Thank you, Landon. Thank you for giving me this— *all* of this. For showing me how to stick around just to see what I could see. *Thank you.*"

Landon squeezed her shoulders with his fingers, his shortness of breath falling upon the ear she pressed to his chest. "You've proven to me month after month that finding you was like finding an angel. You're so dang good at this job. You inspire the girls to take business classes, to learn, to grow in case they don't always want to work for Call Girls. You nurture them. You encourage them. I believe you've even come to love them. So you go see what you can see, Kit-Cat. And remember, you're the best GM I've ever had. Remember, you make my heart glad. So damn glad."

He pulled away then, stepping into the elevator and lifting a finger to his lips to remind her of his last wish.

And Cat smiled even with the warmth of his arms gone. She smiled. Bright, wide, full of every moment of laughter they'd shared, for every second of their friendship, for every kind word, for helping her to finally find her way.

The elevator doors slid closed with a hush, and then Landon was gone.

It was forever goodbye.

She slipped to the cushioned chair by the elevator doors, pulled her knees up to her chin and wept. Not in anger that they wouldn't be able to be together, but in gratitude for a friendship that had touched her very soul.

She let the tears come, didn't bother to hold them back. She wanted to get it all out so she'd be strong when the rest of the girls woke up—because Landon was counting on her to keep everything together.

Now it was time for Cat to do what she'd promised— keep team Call Girls strong.

Cat stood on tiptoe, planting a kiss on Flynn's lips, sighing with happiness. Each night when she came through the door it was like a homecoming for her. Each day since she'd taken Landon's advice and decided to see what she could see, better than the last.

No one but Sanjeev knew where Landon had gone to spend his final days. He would only tell them Landon was safe and loved, sat where he could see the sky every night and sip sweet tea by the light of a buttery moon. Emmaline Amos, Flynn's cousin, was with him in his last month, handling legalities he needed taken care of, tending to his every need. And one of his old friends from Plum Orchard managed to come and say goodbye, too.

As much as she and Flynn and the girls had all wanted to be with him, hold him, maybe even pray, instead they did their best to keep Team Call Girls upwardly mobile while sometimes as a group, and sometimes separately, they tried to work through their grief.

The word had come just yesterday he was gone—really gone, and she and the girls had a small party to celebrate his life. They'd made all his favorite foods, put pictures of him smiling all around, laughed and told funny stories about him.

And they'd planned for this thing Landon wanted Cat and the girls to do. They'd all put their hands in one big circle and vowed to make right their promise to him—as a team.

And it had been full of the love Landon wanted left in his wake.

Cat took a deep, shaky breath, and snuggled against Flynn. "So did you get that couch delivery all squared away for your mama?" Della now resided right next door to her own mother at Sunshine Falls Senior Living.

Thanks to Landon's generosity and influence, Della and Tessa hadn't been put on the long waiting list for entry. Della had taken recuperation to a whole new level and though she still occasionally struggled with her speech, she was taking on the world with a renewed sense of joy. Making matters even better, Tessa would never have to worry about her healthcare again, and neither would Cat.

When she'd told Emmet Kingsley where her mother was, he'd gotten his real estate agent on the phone and sent him off to find an apartment for him, too.

Flynn rubbed circles against her back with the flat of his palm, pulling her close. "I did, and have I mentioned she's been turning some heads? Not sure how I feel about that, but it's time she let go of my Dad and move on."

"See?" Cat teased, pulling him with her to the couch. "It's all those romance novels. They taught her all those smooth moves."

Flynn pulled her into his lap and peered at her, his gaze full of concern. "So, how are you? Are you okay?"

He was referring to the DVD Sanjeev delivered earlier. The one Landon had left for her to watch only upon his passing.

He'd left Call Girls three months ago, but in Cat's heart, he left the day the elevator doors closed on his beautiful face, and since then, she'd spent all her time organizing his last wish. "I haven't watched it yet. I wanted you to be here with me."

"I'll always be here with you, Cat. But if you're not ready…"

Cat shook her head, her heart aching. "It's time-sensitive. According to Sanjeev, Landon asked that I watch it as soon as…as soon as we had word he was gone. The minute I agreed to organize the move to Plum Orchard just after he told me his prognosis, he also told me he had a specific reason he wanted Call Girls back in his hometown. I need to know what that is so I can do it exactly as he wanted."

Flynn pulled her into his embrace, wrapping his strong arms around her. "Then let's do this for Landon," he said, taking the remote and pressing Play.

Landon flashed onto the screen, propped up by pillows on a bed and surrounded by the flowers he loved. He looked fragile, but his smile, the purest part of him, still managed to find its way across his lips.

"Lovely Catherine. Did I tell you how much I'm gonna miss your fire? That feisty way you have of takin' up for the underdog, lookin' out for those who can't look out for themselves?"

Cat fought to catch her breath. Everything about him outwardly had changed. He'd lost even more weight than the last day she'd seen him before he left. His eyes were glassy and sunken, and his skin gray and waxy.

"I sure will. Remember I told you how good you were at makin' people so happy? I need you to help me make two people very happy. I have another special girl who needs me now more than ever. I'm hopin' she's not too blind to see she needs lookin' out for, and I'm hopin' what I'm going to ask you to do for me isn't askin' for too much."

Cat paused the DVD, her chest so tight, it almost choked her. Flynn tightened his hold around her when she buried her face in the warmth of his chest. "I can't... I can't. That's not my Landon."

Flynn kissed the top of her head. "And that's why he chose to leave, honey. He didn't want anyone crying about the end of his life. He wanted you all to celebrate the insane amount of life he managed to pack in while he was here—celebrate living. Right now. Right this minute. You know what he said to me that day when he told me about your job at Call Girls? He said,

'Flynn, if you really love Cat, you'll tell her right now. Right this second. Doesn't matter that y'all are as different as night and day. Just matters that you love her. Go love her and figure the rest out later. But right this second, love her, and then love her some more till you both figure it out. Don't miss forever.' And he was right. That's how Landon lived. Every second of every day was always about living. And that's how I intend to follow in his footsteps."

Love swelled in her chest. So much love in the midst of so much sadness. More tears fell from her eyes, but she forced herself to press Play again. Whatever Landon wanted, whatever it was, she'd do it. She started the DVD again.

"So here's where you come in, and I know it's puttin' a lot on you. If you decide to stay with Call Girls in Plum Orchard, where you and the girls will always have the best life has to offer as long as you work for me, swear, you're gonna learn to love livin' there. It's a bit of a ways from your mama and Miss Della, so if you don't want to plant your feet there for good, I'd understand. I just need you to get everybody there safe and sound and set up shop. I've taken care of the legalities and Sanjeev has the rest. He'll explain it all if you decide to do this for me. All you have to do is keep right on doin' what you've been doin'. Carin' about the people I care about.

"Now, about Plum Orchard. It's a small town, Cat. Minds there are probably even smaller, but if we don't do this, two of the people I love most in the world are gonna ruin their lives for good. Seein' as I can't be there to help 'em fix it, I gotta count on you and all my crazy afterlife machinations to do it for me. And Kit-Cat? Never you worry about the buncha old biddies you're gonna encounter. They're crawlin' out from the woodwork, but you can bet, my Dixie'll have your back."

Dixie. That was Landon's best friend. Dixie and Caine were his two childhood friends. He talked about the two of them all the time.

"And that's what this favor comes down to. Dixie and Caine. What I'm gonna ask you to do with those two nitwits is probably gonna shock you, even coming from me, but someone's gotta get their heads screwed on straight. Now, mind you, you're gonna run into some steep hills you'll have to climb. But I promise you, when you crest the top o' that hill, you'll see forever.

"I grew to love you in our short time together, Kit-Cat. I hope you'll always remember that. I hope you know how much you bein' my friend meant to me. You be good to yourself. No more runnin' away from what's right there in front of you now. You really can have a happily ever after. Swear it's true. And, Flynn? You take care o' my girl, you hear? And hold on tight. You're in for a wild ride." Landon smiled again, his eyes so warm, it filled Cat back up. "Love to you both—*always love.*"

The DVD shut off with a snap, leaving them in silence. Tears fell from Cat's eyes. There'd been so many tears lately between her and the girls, they could fill an ocean.

She didn't want to cry anymore. She wanted to do what Landon said. She wanted to live—every single second.

Flynn cupped her chin, kissing the tip of her nose. "You okay?"

"Did you know?"

"About?"

"What Landon wanted—about Plum Orchard?"

"I didn't know what it meant till now, but when he told me not to give up on you, he asked me if I'd ever been to Plum Orchard."

"Have you?"

Flynn's smile was fond. "Only a couple of times when my father visited Em's mother, his sister, my aunt Clora. What I remember most about it was the ladies there—always dressed up with those big hats and fanning themselves. It was a nice place."

"So how do you feel about going there—relocating? About doing this with me, for Landon?"

Flynn pressed his lips to hers. "The same way I felt about it when he asked me if I'd consider it."

"He asked you if you'd move to Plum Orchard?" She should have known Landon had figured this all out long before he left this earth.

"He did."

"And what did you say?"

Flynn pressed his nose against hers. "I said I'd follow you anywhere you wanted to go because I was madly in love with you. You know, after only knowing you for a few weeks and in the interest of throwing all that caution you talked about to the wind."

Cat smiled through her tears, letting Flynn wipe them from her cheeks—mad about this man who'd shown her not everyone left. She didn't have to cut and run the second her fears began to eat her up.

This time, she was going to ride them out. This time, she was staying until the end.

"I love you, too, Flynn McGrady. So let's go to

Plum Orchard, and see what we can see," she whispered against his lips.

With Flynn by her side, she always wanted to see what she could see.

* * * * *

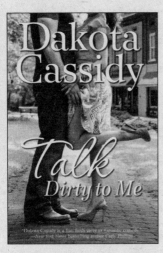

National Bestselling Author
Dakota Cassidy

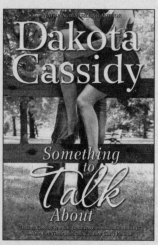

Emmeline Amos is sick of her ex saying she's boring and prissy. After all, she works for a phone-sex company! (As general manager, but still.) Fueled by blender drinks and bravado, she accepts a shocking dare—to handle a call herself. But it's tipsy Em who gets an earful from an irate single father on the other end of the line.

Worse still—he's the gorgeous new programmer for Call Girls. Jax Hawthorne is upset that his daughter called the "girlfriend store" on his behalf, but he can't deny he'd choose a hot-librarian type like Em if he were looking for love. Which he's not.

So Em makes a bawdy bargain with Jax. They'll keep it strictly physical. Except as soon as they settle on no strings attached, things start to get tangled....

Available now, wherever books are sold!

Be sure to connect with us at:
Harlequin.com/Newsletters
Facebook.com/HarlequinBooks
Twitter.com/HarlequinBooks

#1 *New York Times* Bestselling Author

DEBBIE MACOMBER

It was the year that changed everything...

When Susannah Nelson turned eighteen, she said goodbye to her boyfriend, Jake—and never saw him again. Her brother Doug died in a car accident that same year.

Now, at fifty, she finds herself regretting the paths not taken. Long married, a mother and a teacher, she *should* be happy. But she feels there's something missing.

Her aging mother, Vivian, a recent widow, is having difficulty adjusting to life alone, so Susannah goes home to Colville, Washington. Returning to her parents' house and the garden she's always loved, she also returns to the past—and the choices she made back then.

What Susannah discovers is that things are not as they once seemed. Some paths are dead ends. But some gardens remain beautiful....

Available now, wherever books are sold!

Be sure to connect with us at:
Harlequin.com/Newsletters
Facebook.com/HarlequinBooks
Twitter.com/HarlequinBooks

HARLEQUIN® MIRA®
www.Harlequin.com

MDM1632

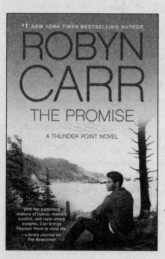

REQUEST YOUR FREE BOOKS!

2 FREE NOVELS
FROM THE ROMANCE COLLECTION
PLUS 2 FREE GIFTS!

YES! Please send me 2 FREE novels from the Romance Collection and my 2 FREE gifts (gifts are worth about $10). After receiving them, if I don't wish to receive any more books, I can return the shipping statement marked "cancel." If I don't cancel, I will receive 4 brand-new novels every month and be billed just $6.24 per book in the U.S. or $6.74 per book in Canada. That's a savings of at least 22% off the cover price. It's quite a bargain! Shipping and handling is just 50¢ per book in the U.S. and 75¢ per book in Canada.* I understand that accepting the 2 free books and gifts places me under no obligation to buy anything. I can always return a shipment and cancel at any time. Even if I never buy another book, the two free books and gifts are mine to keep forever.

194/394 MDN F4XY

Name   (PLEASE PRINT)

Address   Apt. #

City   State/Prov.   Zip/Postal Code

Signature (if under 18, a parent or guardian must sign)

Mail to the Harlequin® Reader Service:
IN U.S.A.: P.O. Box 1867, Buffalo, NY 14240-1867
IN CANADA: P.O. Box 609, Fort Erie, Ontario L2A 5X3

**Want to try two free books from another line?
Call 1-800-873-8635 or visit www.ReaderService.com.**

* Terms and prices subject to change without notice. Prices do not include applicable taxes. Sales tax applicable in N.Y. Canadian residents will be charged applicable taxes. Offer not valid in Quebec. This offer is limited to one order per household. Not valid for current subscribers to the Romance Collection or the Romance/Suspense Collection. All orders subject to credit approval. Credit or debit balances in a customer's account(s) may be offset by any other outstanding balance owed by or to the customer. Please allow 4 to 6 weeks for delivery. Offer available while quantities last.

Your Privacy—The Harlequin® Reader Service is committed to protecting your privacy. Our Privacy Policy is available online at www.ReaderService.com or upon request from the Harlequin Reader Service.

We make a portion of our mailing list available to reputable third parties that offer products we believe may interest you. If you prefer that we not exchange your name with third parties, or if you wish to clarify or modify your communication preferences, please visit us at www.ReaderService.com/consumerschoice or write to us at Harlequin Reader Service Preference Service, P.O. Box 9062, Buffalo, NY 14269. Include your complete name and address.

Dakota Cassidy

31627 SOMETHING TO TALK ABOUT   ___ $7.99 U.S.   ___ $8.99 CAN.
31619 TALK DIRTY TO ME   ___ $7.99 U.S.   ___ $8.99 CAN.

(limited quantities available)

TOTAL AMOUNT $ _____
POSTAGE & HANDLING $ _____
($1.00 for 1 book, 50¢ for each additional)
APPLICABLE TAXES* $ _____
TOTAL PAYABLE $ _____

(check or money order—please do not send cash)

To order, complete this form and send it, along with a check or money
order for the total amount, payable to Harlequin MIRA, to: **In the U.S.:**
3010 Walden Avenue, P.O. Box 9077, Buffalo, NY 14269-9077;
In Canada: P.O. Box 636, Fort Erie, Ontario, L2A 5X3.

Name: _____
Address: _____ City: _____
State/Prov.: _____ Zip/Postal Code: _____
Account Number (if applicable): _____
075 CSAS

*New York residents remit applicable sales taxes.
*Canadian residents remit applicable GST and provincial taxes.

HARLEQUIN® MIRA®
™ www.Harlequin.com

MDC0714BL